STORM IN THE DARKNESS

BOOK 8

THE TALES OF THE TERRITORIES

PETER WACHT

Storm in the Darkness
By Peter Wacht

Book 8 of The Tales of the Territories

This book is a work of fiction. Names, characters, places, and incidents are the product of the author's imagination or are used fictitiously. Any resemblance to actual events, locales, or persons, living or dead, is coincidental.

Copyright 2025 © by Peter Wacht

Cover design by Ebooklaunch.com

All rights reserved. In accordance with the U.S. Copyright Act of 1976, the scanning, uploading, and electronic sharing of any part of this book without the permission of the publisher constitute unlawful piracy and theft of the author's intellectual property.

Published in the United States by Kestrel Media Group LLC.

ISBN: 978-1-950236-49-7

eBook ISBN: 978-1-950236-52-7

Library of Congress Control Number: 2024912750

❀ Created with Vellum

ALSO BY PETER WACHT

THE REALMS OF THE TALENT AND THE CURSE

LEGEND OF THE DRAGON LORD

The Painful Truth (short story)*

Stealing the Light (Forthcoming 2025)

Sacrificing the Queen (Forthcoming 2025)

Roar of the Broken Bear (Forthcoming 2025)

Rise of the Dragon Lord (Forthcoming 2026)

THE TALES OF CALEDONIA

(Complete 7-Book Series)

Blood on the White Sand (short story)*

The Diamond Thief (short story)*

The Protector

The Protector's Quest

The Protector's Vengeance

The Protector's Sacrifice

The Protector's Reckoning

The Protector's Resolve

The Protector's Victory

THE TALES OF THE TERRITORIES

(Complete 8-Book Series)

Stalking the Blood Ruby (short story)*

A Fate Worse Than Death (short story)*

Death on the Burnt Ocean

Monsters in the Mist

The Dance of the Daggers

Bloody Hunt for Freedom

A Spark of Rebellion

Shadows Made Real

Shadow's Reach

Storm in the Darkness

THE SYLVAN CHRONICLES

(Complete 9-Book Series)

The Legend of the Kestrel

The Call of the Sylvana

The Raptor of the Highlands

The Makings of a Warrior

The Lord of the Highlands

The Lost Kestrel Found

The Claiming of the Highlands

The Fight Against the Dark

The Defender of the Light

THE RISE OF THE SYLVAN WARRIORS

*Through the Knife's Edge (short story)**

THE FALLEN KNIGHT SERIES

*The Death of the Dragon (short story)**

The Dragon Awakens

Duel With a Dragon (Forthcoming 2025)

Beware the Dragon (Forthcoming 2025)

The Dragon Returns (Forthcoming 2025)

* Free stories can be downloaded from my author website at PeterWachtBooks.com. My books are also available on Amazon and other online retailers.

This eBook is a prelude to the events in my series *The Tales of Caledonia* and is free to readers who receive my newsletter.

Join Peter's newsletter and get your FREE eBook.
PeterWachtBooks.com

SETTING THE STAGE

The Tales of the Territories continue the adventures of Bryen Keldragan and Aislinn Winborne as they travel across the Burnt Ocean to the Territories, what will eventually become the Kingdoms of *The Sylvan Chronicles*.

The events occur more than one thousand years before the happenings in *The Sylvan Chronicles* and take place in the lands far to the west of Caledonia that have been opened for colonization thanks to territorial grants sold by the deceased King Corinthus Beleron.

There Bryen and Aislinn will take on new challenges, make new friends and enemies, and continue to battle those who have turned to the Curse.

In the Territories, sometimes called New Caledonia, as in the other realms, the ability to use the Talent sets apart the person gifted with this unique skill. But being able to use the Talent is only part of the dynamic. For if a Magus chooses to follow a darker path, the Talent becomes the Curse.

The Sylvan Chronicles, The Tales of Caledonia, and *The Tales of the Territories* are a part of the larger world of *The Realms of the Talent and the Curse.*

1

TIME TO ADVANCE

"It is as we thought it would be, Lord." The fog masked the Wraith Hunter's features but for the pure black of his eyes and the sense of tangible menace that radiated from his thin, emaciated frame.

The Wraith Lord stood silent in the Murk, the wispy tendrils of grey swirling around him. At first, he didn't bother to acknowledge his second in command. Lost in thought. Finally, he nodded.

The arrangement his Hunter had made with the Dark Magus had little chance of success to begin with. To learn that it had failed to bear any fruit didn't surprise him.

No matter.

That poor though expected result simply meant that the time had finally come.

That conclusion sent a spark of pleasure through him.

There would be no more poking and prodding. He would grasp with clawed hands what belonged to him and his Horde. He would remake the world into what it needed to be for his Wraiths to reign supreme.

"Where do our preparations stand?"

"Our Scouts are returning from the mountains of the Dragon Spine. They have finished their work there, ensuring that we have nothing to worry about to the north of the Wyld."

"How soon?"

"They will be here in a matter of days, Lord." The Wraith Hunter smiled, the flesh on his skeleton-like face drawn even more tightly across his skull, his sharp, fanglike teeth briefly revealed. "They are hungry, Lord. They are ready for the Hunt."

"They should be," rasped the Wraith Lord. "We have waited a long time for this. Centuries. So many centuries." He was silent for a time, considering his next steps. "We cannot allow anything to prevent us from achieving what we have dreamed of doing for so long. What we must do."

"Yes, Lord. We are excited, Lord. We are ready. The Scouts understand. The Hunt will allow us to make the world our own. We will make our history what it should be."

The Wraith Lord shifted his dead-eyed stare to his Hunter. They looked much the same in appearance. Yet there was a clear distinction with respect to the Wraith Lord.

All of the Wraiths were creatures of the Murk.

Born to it.

Bred in it.

Because of that, all of the Wraiths had been touched by the Curse, a residue of that ancient evil flowing through their veins.

However, the true source of the Curse in the Murk, the source of the Curse for all the Wraiths, resonated within the Wraith Lord. The reservoir of corrupt power that only the leader of the Wraith Horde could tap into was unimaginable. Almost uncontainable. And it was that tainted energy that the Wraith Lord would unleash on the vermin to the south.

An energy that contaminated everything and everyone it touched.

An energy that twisted all that it kissed into a tool for its own use.

With his first step, so it would begin.

The end result?

The world of man would die, the Wraiths building right on top of it.

"I selected you as my Hunter for a reason. You know that. There were many candidates, but of them all I believed that you were the most driven. The most capable. The most willing to do whatever is necessary to achieve our ends."

"Yes, Lord." A trace of nervousness touched the back of the Wraith Hunter's throat. He didn't translate what his Master was telling him into a compliment. Instead, he perceived it as something else entirely. A warning. "I am grateful for that, Lord."

"You should be." With a flick of the Wraith Lord's clawed hand, the wispy grey tendrils that separated him from his lieutenant spread apart, clearing a space between them. A reminder of the power at the Wraith Lord's beck and call. "You should also be wary. Even frightened. You are cognizant of the cost of failure?"

The Wraith Hunter quietly cleared his throat, understanding that he needed to answer in a strong voice. "I do, Lord. You have nothing to worry about."

"I don't?" mused the Wraith Lord. "Despite the stories that I've heard?"

A flush of shame rushed through the Wraith Hunter. He had hoped that those stories would not reach the ears of his Master. Not until he had dealt with the one obstacle that threatened to slow their advance.

He really shouldn't have been surprised. He should have assumed that his encounter with the Wraith who is not a Wraith would come back to bite him.

There were a select few in the Horde jockeying for his position as the Hunter. Sowing the seeds of worry in the mind of their Lord was an expected and time-tested tactic. If he was in their position, seeking his place, he would have done the same.

"Yes, Lord. You have nothing to fear. I promise you that. All will go as planned. Nothing and no one will be able to stand against us." He made sure that he said the last with as much confidence as he could muster. Yet, as he did so, a hint of doubt took root in the back of his mind, growing slowly as he thought more about the cause of his Lord's discomfort and the source of his own angst.

Once again silence descended between them, the Wraith Lord deep in thought. The master of the Wraith Horde stared off into the swirling grey. Seeing all that was happening in the Murk. Seeing what was beyond as well, his gaze turning toward the southwest and the Bloody Steppe. Beyond that was their first target. The Northern Peaks and the city that was nestled within.

Shadow's Reach.

"We should not have trusted the woman to find the one we seek," the Wraith Lord finally said.

"We didn't, Lord. We gave the Dark Magus time to prove her worth. Nothing more than that." The Wraith Hunter shrugged. He was pleased to see that his Lord seemed to agree with his assessment, though he could sense his increasing impatience.

The Hunter understood from where that impatience came. It had taken the Wraith Lord an enervatingly long time to reach this point, and he wanted to make the most of what could be his brethren's only opportunity. The future success and survival of the Wraiths depended upon it.

"We did not believe that she would succeed, yet there was nothing lost in letting her try," the Hunter explained. "The one we seek is too elusive. Too much like a Wraith for her to do what we required of her."

The Wraith Lord remained quiet for a while longer, not even offering a grunt of acknowledgment. The Wraith Hunter continued, feeling the need to fill the silence. "It matters not, Lord. We were not ready then. With the trouble to the north, we could do nothing more than probe. We needed more time to prepare. With the trouble to the north no longer trouble, now we can do what is required of us."

"You are certain that we are ready?" The Wraith Lord wasn't nervous. He just wanted to be sure. "We cannot fail. You cannot fail. A chance like this will not come again."

"We are, Lord. I promise you. We can release the Horde on your command."

The Wraith Lord waited several heartbeats before replying, his eyes locked onto those of his Hunter. He had selected this Wraith for this task because he knew his qualities. What he could do. What he had done. What he would do to achieve what was demanded of him.

Yet for some reason that he did not quite understand, the Wraith Lord experienced a touch of unease. A wisp of uncertainty flowing through him.

An unfamiliar feeling.

Was it because the time had finally come after such a long, almost unbearable wait? Or was there more to it?

His eyes flashed when he realized what was needling him.

It was the boy. No more than vermin and having no place in the Murk, yet still he entered it with impunity. He hunted in it just like his Wraiths did.

The fact that he was concerned about a creature that should be beneath the notice of the Wraiths gave him pause. It also unsettled him, although he made sure that he did not reveal that to his second in command.

"You know our history?"

"I do, Lord," the Wraith Hunter replied quietly, respectfully. "We all do. Our history is who we are, Lord. We understand that. We revere it. We build upon it."

The Wraith Hunter didn't need to remind the Wraith Lord that every Wraith learned the history of their kind, imbued it, became one with it, because their history was more than just a history. It was a way of life. A way of moving through the world.

A map for gaining revenge on those who had wronged them.

A map for making the world their own.

The Wraiths had been oppressed long ago, forced down a path that was not of their choosing. Consumed by the Curse. Made into the image of the Curse against their will.

Yet that subjugation had proven to be a blessing as well.

Because having been touched by the Curse, the Wraiths became something different. Stronger. More dangerous. Deadlier. Something more rapacious.

Thanks to the Curse, the Wraiths became a threat, their maker no longer able to control them. No longer able to compel them.

With the power that only they could call upon, the Wraiths broke their bonds, accepting both the gifts and the limitations that the Murk granted them. Mastering them. Making them their own. Allowing those gifts and limitations to make them stronger. More resilient. More determined.

When they were ready, when they were certain that their maker could no longer stand against them, the Wraiths used the Murk to conquer Frisia. They made the ancient kingdom into their home.

Most essential to their success, they sent their maker – the Dread -- fleeing beyond the Murk. And those who tried to stand against them were sent to the other side. Painfully. Without a hint of remorse, and with a great deal of pleasure.

Since then, the Murk had remained in place for a thousand years and more, staked over that land of yore. A birthplace of heroes becoming a home to monsters.

From time to time, the Wraith Lord grew restless, using his power to push the Murk beyond what had been old Frisia. Testing what could be done with the thick blanket of grey.

Learning. Mastering. Planning. Yet each time he did so, he always had to relent, the Murk settling back into place within its original boundaries.

But no more.

As the centuries passed the Wraith Lord became one with the Murk. So much so that he learned how to move the Murk where he wanted it to be. That meant that his Wraiths, inextricably linked to the Murk, could go with it.

And now it was time for the Murk and the Wraiths to travel beyond the boundaries of the ancient kingdom that they had claimed as their own.

For good.

Because now was the time to expand their lands. Their power.

It was time to make the world as the Wraiths believed that it should be. As they needed it to be.

"Then write our history as we know that it should be written. Let the world discover what happens to those who seek to oppose us."

"Yes, Lord," replied the Wraith Hunter, breathing a silent sigh of relief. For a few heartbeats, he feared that he wouldn't be going with his Scouts. That his service had come to an end and that his Master was prepared to select a new Hunter as payment for his failures. So few though they were. Yet still so important. Therefore, best to make the most of his reprieve. "I will do as you command."

The Wraith Hunter turned and faded into the Murk, not wanting to give his master the chance to rethink his decision.

The Wraith Lord had pulled back the Murk closer to the borders of their homeland to ensure that the problem in the north could be put to rest with little difficulty. That challenge resolved, now the Wraith Hunter could push his skirmishers farther to the south in preparation for the coming of the Horde.

He and his Scouts had a long way to travel, and they needed

to move swiftly if they were to get into position in time. Never-theless, he was certain that they would do what was required of them because the Wraith Lord already had begun to push the Murk toward their first target.

The grasping grey flowing beyond the Wyld and Old Frisia.

Toward the Bloody Steppe and beyond.

The Wraith Hunter would advance with the vanguard. The Wraith Lord would follow a few days behind.

Yet as he headed off to set the Wraith Horde in motion, the Hunter couldn't escape the gnawing feeling that ate at him.

The man he had fought on the street in Shadow's Reach. The one who had sliced across his thigh. He had been a challenge.

Yet the Wraith Hunter had little concern about that master of the blade. If he still lived, the Wraith Hunter had little doubt that he would kill him if they encountered one another again. The human had gotten lucky.

The Wraith Hunter had slipped on the cobblestones. It had been no more than a quirk of fate.

Not so the boy he had fought in the Murk what seemed ages ago yet was no more than a year.

The boy who had given the Hunter a permanent limp thanks to his driving a dagger through the top of his foot.

The Wraith Hunter knew that the boy was still alive. That the boy still moved within the Murk with a confidence that grated.

The Wraith who is not a Wraith.

His only true rival among the vermin he was charged with exterminating.

The one who had almost cost him his place beside the Wraith Lord.

For the Wraith Hunter to continue to lead, to continue to live, the Wraith who is not a Wraith needed to die.

It was as simple as that.

One for the other.

Because no matter how hard the Wraith Hunter tried to ignore the feeling that had settled into the base of his spine, he couldn't. That feeling refusing to leave him be.

In fact, the more he thought about the Wraith who is not a Wraith, the more that feeling festered. Expanded. Burrowed deeper within him. Distracted him.

The Wraith Hunter struggled to manage that feeling, because it was so unfamiliar to him.

It was a feeling that he thought he had conquered long before.

A feeling of fear.

Fear that not only would he fail to kill the Wraith who is not a Wraith, but also that this boy, who he should have killed so many times before, would prevent the Wraiths from achieving their primary objective.

Blanketing the Territories with the Murk.

Slaughtering the humans.

Claiming the lands of the vermin as their own.

Then moving on to the next Realm and then the next.

Until there was nothing but the Murk.

Nothing but the Wraiths.

The Wraith Hunter feared that this Wraith who is not a Wraith would be the reason that the Wraiths' thousand-year dream would be extinguishcd for good.

That the Wraith who is not a Wraith would write the history rather than the Wraiths themselves.

He couldn't allow that.

Death would be much preferred to the shame of that failure.

Yet to avoid that and to make his ilk's dream a reality, the Wraith Hunter needed to conquer his fear.

And he needed to kill the Wraith who is not a Wraith.

2

A FORMER ACQUAINTANCE

"How far away?" asked Lycia. She pushed the edge of her shovel deeper into the hole that she was digging, twisting the handle to break apart the packed soil.

"Less than a mile," Jakob replied. He took a moment to wipe the sweat from his brow, pickaxe in hand and at the ready to cut through any more roots that might get in Lycia's way, just as he had been doing for the last few minutes. "They're not in a rush. They don't seem to be all that concerned about us."

"The scouts they sent ahead?"

"Yes, I guess they saw what they wanted to see and not what they should have seen."

Lycia smiled as she dug a little deeper, judging that it wouldn't be long before she hit the required depth. She didn't say anything else.

In more ways than she cared to acknowledge, the Lord of the Highlands reminded her of Bryen Keldragan. The good things, she corrected quickly in her own mind. Not the irritating ones.

Jakob had plenty of his own characteristics that she found irritating.

And she had little trouble dealing with those. She had managed worse.

Davin was her brother after all.

Thinking of Bryen brought to mind the conversation that she had with him the night before last. Jakob and the other Highlanders had bedded down. It was the early morning, Lycia standing guard with three others, each one focused on a cardinal point of the compass. More habit than anything else since Jakob used the Talent to search around them frequently to ensure that all was as it should be.

Bryen had reached out to her with the Talent, providing a brief update on what was happening in Shadow's Reach as well as his suspicions, Lycia sharing with him what was happening in the Highlands. And that, inevitably, led their conversation to the topic of Jakob Kestrel.

"What do you think of the Lord of the Highlands?"

"You're asking my opinion?"

"Of course I'm asking your opinion," Bryen had replied with a hint of amusement in his voice. *"That's one of the primary reasons that I asked you to join him. So that we could get a better read on him and coordinate our efforts if doing so made sense."*

"You sure you want to do that?" Lycia had asked.

"Why wouldn't I?"

She hesitated for a few heartbeats before responding, a smile audible in her voice. *"Why would you?"*

"Why are you making this difficult, Lycia?"

She had heard Bryen's sigh of exasperation in her mind. *"Because it's fun."*

"You really can be a pain sometimes."

"Strange hearing you say that," Lycia had replied. *"Ironic, in fact."*

"Yet true, nonetheless. Wouldn't you agree?"

She ignored his question. If she had been standing next to him, she would have expected to see that grin of his that was both endearing and aggravating. Instead she had given Bryen a mental nudge. *"Even so, you still love me."*

"I do."

"What's Aislinn up to?" Lycia sought to avoid Bryen's primary reason for linking to her for a little while longer.

"Trying to keep me out of trouble."

"Trying?"

"You know how it is," Bryen had answered with a mental shrug. *"I'm not always patient, and I might be pushing a little harder than I should."*

"That I do." With her tone, Lycia had communicated her sense of commiseration with the Lady of the Southern Marches. *"Poking and prodding to see what happens."*

"It almost sounds like you want to be here with me and Aislinn."

"I don't," Lycia had clarified quickly. *"Have no fear of that. Aislinn can manage you just fine. I did enough of that when we were in the Colosseum."*

"I'm not a horse."

"I didn't say you were a horse."

"You implied it," Bryen had said, although he sounded more amused than anything else.

"No, you inferred it."

Rather than continuing down a road from which Bryen doubted that he would have an easy time coming back from, he had returned to the reason he wanted to converse with Lycia over such a great distance.

"Tell me what you think of Jakob Kestrel."

"He's a good man," Lycia had replied, thinking for a few seconds about what she wanted to say and how she wanted to say it. *"He believes in what he's doing. He believes it needs to be done for the people living in the Highlands. Perhaps even more important, the Highlanders believe in him. They believe they can gain their freedom so long as he's with them."*

"*Jakob Kestrel doesn't expect to get anything for himself out of all this?*"

Lycia had understood why Bryen felt the need to ask that question. If she were in his position, she would have as well. "*He doesn't want anything for himself. He doesn't even want to be the Lord of the Highlands. He just wants to do what's required of him so that the people he's responsible for get what they deserve. No more than that. No less.*"

"*You're sure about that?*"

"*Completely and unequivocally sure. He's exactly as you said he would be.*"

Bryen had caught the hitch in what she had just offered him. "*What's the matter, Lycia?*"

"*If I told him how I felt, how do you think he would react?*"

Bryen had hesitated before responding, not believing that was a question that he should answer. It was too personal. Especially with the history between them. "*How do you think he would react?*"

Almost a minute passed before Lycia answered. "*I think he would be open to it. But that doesn't necessarily mean I should take the risk.*"

"*Do you want to talk to Aislinn about this?*" Lycia had sensed that Bryen didn't feel completely comfortable speaking with her about her dilemma.

But that hadn't bothered her. Bryen had always been honest with her. And he never failed to speak his mind. Something that she needed from him then.

"*She'd probably be more helpful since you try to avoid awkward matters whenever possible.*" Lycia had hoped that Bryen understood the subtle dig that she had just given him. "*Nevertheless, I'd prefer to talk with someone I can trust who never fails to give good advice.*"

"*You don't believe that I'm giving good advice?*" Lycia had sensed the amusement in his tone again. Only he would be in a good mood after he and Aislinn had walked directly into a lion's den.

No, she corrected. Lions were too easy to read. More like a viper pit in Shadow's Reach, because the Volkun didn't quite yet know who was going to try to bite him.

"How am I supposed to know?" she had replied with a hint of frustration. *"You're not offering any advice. You answered my question with a question."*

"That's because you already know the answer to your question," Bryen had said with a certainty that she couldn't ignore.

"You really are a pain in my ass."

"I do what I can," Bryen had replied, a chuckle sounding in the back of Lycia's mind. *"Are you going to do what you want to do?"*

"I'm not sure if I should do what I want to do. What if he says ..."

"Lycia, you gave me good advice with respect to Aislinn," Bryen had said, cutting her off.

"What was that?"

"You don't recall? You were quite insistent. Painfully so, in fact."

"Now who's being difficult?" Lycia had challenged.

"Don't wait." Bryen had shrugged mentally again. *"Simple advice, but as Declan likes to say, the best advice is the simplest advice."*

"Actually, if I remember correctly, that was Rafia's advice. Not mine."

"Now you're just trying to avoid the issue."

"I'm just stating the truth," Lycia had replied with a false innocence. *"I simply repeated it when the time was right."*

"Do you always need to be a pain in my ass?"

"Yes," Lycia had replied instantly, a large dose of humor in her tone, enjoying her interaction with Bryen.

"I disagree."

Bryen had known what she had been trying to do. Deflect. Duck. Dodge. Just as she had done so effectively on the white sand with her steel. Yet she couldn't turn a blind eye to the truth. She had raised the issue, but she was afraid of the answer he might offer. *"Now you're just being a pain in my ass."*

Ignoring her attempt to get a rise out of him, Bryen had offered another bit of sage advice. *"Just as in the Pit, you don't know what the next day will hold."*

Rather than continuing to get under his skin, she had left off, tiring of the game she had begun. Lycia had nodded mentally. *"That was good advice, if I do say so myself."*

"Then perhaps you should follow your own advice."

"I'll think about it." Lycia had refused to commit to a course of action even though a part of her was desperate to do so.

She had fought on the white sand for five years, hating the experience. Yet in a strange way she had relished it as well. Because in the Colosseum there was a certainty involved that appealed to her.

Lycia had learned that if she listened to Declan, if she trained hard, if she put into practice what Declan, Bryen, and the other gladiators taught her, that she would likely win her next combat. And the one after that. And after that.

Having left the Pit, she had learned that gaining the certainty that she preferred, that she craved, was proving to be a much more elusive task in the real world.

Letting go of that memory, Lycia scraped a bit more at the packed earth at the bottom of the hole, then pulled back the shovel and slammed the sharp edge into the loose dirt, adding to the pile that had grown larger by her feet.

Seeing that Jakob was lost for a moment, once again using the Talent to search around them, Lycia took a few seconds to wonder at how the fortunes of the Highlanders had changed so drastically in just a matter of days.

All thanks to Jakob demonstrating an aggressiveness that both impressed and worried her.

The Highlanders had seized the largest mine that Governor Sharperson operated in the snowcapped peaks.

It had proven to be a hard fight. A surprising one as well.

Duff had gained the revenge that he had sought for more than a decade against the man responsible for murdering his wife and children. And along with that personal victory, the Highlanders had freed more than a hundred prisoners. They also had killed or captured three times as many soldiers loyal to the Governor.

Within a day of news of that victory spreading, Torstan Sharperson had pulled his soldiers back even closer to the Stone and the few mines that remained under the control of his Guard, ceding all of the Highlands to the Lord Kestrel except for the few leagues surrounding his incomplete citadel.

Just as important to the Highlanders' overall success, they had slaughtered several dozen Stalkers, primarily because of Jakob's use of the Talent. Although the risk that he had taken to achieve that victory remained a heated topic between them. Rightfully so in Lycia's opinion.

She certainly valued Jakob's bravery. That was one of the reasons that she felt so drawn to him. Nevertheless, she questioned his constant need to put himself in danger when so many others relied upon him.

They had yet to finish that argument. She didn't doubt that Jakob hoped that with the passage of several days, Lycia would let it go.

She hadn't. And she would teach him that she was just as tenacious with a sword in her hand as without.

"You sound quite proud of that." Lycia gave him a wink.

Jakob ignored her smirk, keeping his expression neutral. "I'm just saying that it seems like our friends have fallen for our deception."

"Right. That's all it is." Lycia kept her eyes on him. Waiting.

Wanting to learn if what she regularly did to her brother would work on him. Probably not, but it was worth a shot.

It didn't help her cause that Jakob understood what Lycia was doing. Trying to get him to crack.

Senna had attempted much the same, remaining quiet but insistent, calm but demanding, demonstrating an aggravating level of patience until she gained what she wanted. Although he had only allowed her efforts to work when he wanted them to, never revealing that to her.

He smiled sadly as he thought of the woman he had lost on the other side of the Burnt Ocean.

Senna and Lycia were similar in many ways. Tough. Driven. Focused. A good sense of humor. And in other ways quite different.

Senna had been uniquely empathetic, feeling the world more than moving through it as Lycia did. And, of course, there was a clear difference with respect to their skills with a blade.

Not wanting to give Lycia the satisfaction of knowing that she was affecting him, Jakob avoided her gaze. He took another quick look around the farmstead to ensure that all was as it should be.

He and Lycia were working at the western end of the property, which was centered on a two-story farmhouse made of stout stone and a thick wooden door. On the eastern side, because of the dangers stalking across the land, the older couple who owned the spread had transformed what had started out as a root cellar accessed through a narrow crevice in the ridge not too far behind their home into a small stronghold, the steel door they had set in place several inches thick.

When the Murk covered the peaks or the Stalkers emerged with the darkness, that's where the family and their workers hid. Just as they were doing now. Because Jakob had told them who was coming their way.

"You can think what you want, Lycia," Jakob said with a

mischievous smile, finally looking her way. "That doesn't mean that you're correct."

"What am I thinking, Jakob?" She crossed her arms and lifted an eyebrow. "You know, I'd really like you to tell me what I'm thinking."

Jakob didn't reply right away, recognizing how Lycia's expression was actually a mask. Seemingly welcoming at first glance, yet really just a trap. He needed to tread carefully, because he had learned quickly that just like Senna, Lycia had quite a temper.

"That I shouldn't be the one out here in the open. That another Highlander could have just as easily taken my place. That I'm taking too much of a risk because I'm stubborn and don't listen to reason even when that reason is presented multiple times by someone as sagacious as yourself."

"You did read my mind," Lycia said with a nod. She chose to ignore his obvious sarcasm, not wanting to give him the pleasure of knowing that he had achieved his objective of irritating her. "You shouldn't be out in the open. Another Highlander should have taken your place."

"Yet here I am," Jakob replied with a shrug.

"Just because you are doesn't mean that you made the right decision, Jakob. As we've discussed a nauseating number of times in the last few days, you can't constantly put yourself at risk."

"I'm not putting myself at risk."

"You are putting yourself at risk," Lycia replied, a bit more heat in her voice, trying once again to make her point. Her arms remained crossed, but she tilted her head slightly and leaned more on her back left leg.

Another habit that reminded Jakob of Senna. He knew what that stance meant. He would have to tread even more carefully now.

"I appreciate your concern, Lycia." He raised his hands in a placating gesture. "I do. But I need to be out here. I can't hide behind Duff or any other Highlander."

"I didn't say that you needed to hide."

"You implied as much," Jakob shrugged, although he made sure that his voice was even, not wanting Lycia to think that he was trying to antagonize her into another argument.

"You're too important to what is happening in the Highlands for you to risk it all just so that you can …"

Lycia's eyes widened and her voice trailed off when she saw how Jakob's expression hardened, his voice just as much, though it was no more than a whisper. "You can finish what you were going to say."

She sighed. "I'm sorry, Jakob. It would have been wrong of me to do so. It's just that you have a unique way of getting under my skin. When I beat anyone else about the ears, eventually they give in. Even my brother. And his head is almost as hard as yours. But you? You're more stubborn than a pig that's found a hidden stash of truffles." Her arms dropped to her side and she shuffled her feet. "I'm sorry. It's just that I worry about you."

After thinking about her analogy for a few seconds, Jakob smiled and nodded, accepting her apology. Although it really didn't sound like an apology to him. Rather, he took it to be another play on her part to get him to change his mind. That guiding his perspective, he stared hard at Lycia, wanting to end this seemingly never-ending conversation that had been taking place between them for the last few days.

"I understand the risks I take, Lycia. But if I'm going to do what I promised to do, then I need to take those risks."

"Yes, but Jakob …"

"Lycia, please." His voice was soft but insistent. To Lycia's ears commanding. "This needs to stop if only for my own sanity. I like you, but you're really getting on my nerves. Once you bite into something you never let go."

She ignored most of what Jakob had just told her, giving him a soft smile and focusing on one particular part of what he said. "You like me."

Jakob stared at the gladiator for a few heartbeats, caught by her impish smile, realizing what he had just let slip. He wasn't sure what to say to get himself out of what had become an uncomfortable situation. "I should have assumed that you would focus on that part."

"You know me quite well," Lycia replied, her smile only getting bigger, "and we haven't even been together that long."

"Better than you think," Jakob grumbled just beneath his breath. He tried again. "What I was trying to say is that I need to take certain risks. In that respect I am no different than any other Highlander. The burden needs to be shared equally. I can't ask a Highlander to do something that I'm not willing to do myself."

She was still smiling, but her eyes were just as flinty as Jakob's. "Jakob, you are truly a difficult ..."

"Lycia, you're like a dog with a bone. You just ..."

"You're not going to tell me again that you like me?" Lycia countered, trying to throw him off balance ... and nearly succeeding.

Jakob closed his eyes and took a deep breath. He had to work hard to not lose his temper. He didn't understand why she affected him in this way. Getting a rise out of him so easily. The only other person who could have done this to him, essentially tie him in knots with just a few words, was Senna.

"Definitely not," he replied finally. "Not with you throwing it right back at me." He shook his head as he took another quick look around them. It wouldn't be long now.

"What I was going to say was that I am no more and no less than any other Highlander," Jakob continued. "I am what I am because the Highlanders believe that I am what I am. And for me to continue to be what they need me to be, I need to be with them. That means I need to fight with them from the front. Every time. Because that's who I am. I don't like being the Lord of the Highlands. But I can be the Lord of the Highlands so long as I can also be myself."

"That's a unique way of looking at it," Lycia acknowledged, not having a good counter to his argument. Never having considered his perspective. "A little convoluted as well."

"It's the only way I can look at it and still remain sane," Jakob clarified. "I've seen what happens when someone gives you power that you don't deserve and you begin to define yourself by that power rather than by what's truly important."

Lycia nodded, never having experienced this side of Jakob before. She liked it. "And what is truly important, Jakob?"

"Being true to yourself and true to the people you are responsible to and for."

For several heartbeats, Lycia could do nothing more than stare at the man who wasn't much younger than she was who had been pushed into the role of Lord of the Highlands. She needed to remind herself to breathe.

Initially Lycia had thought that the Highlanders selected Jakob as their leader because of his courage and skill in arms. His willingness without a second thought to challenge Stalkers and Sharperson's soldiers turned slavers. His willingness to enter the Murk and hunt the hunters within. His ability to use the Talent.

Yet she realized that although those were all important factors in the success he had achieved since being named the Lord of the Highlands and beginning the rebellion against Torstan Sharperson, that really wasn't why the Highlanders selected him. They chose him because of who he was and how he looked at the world. How he looked at himself.

"It's really hard to stay angry at you," Lycia grumbled. "You know that?"

"I do."

"Even now, after what you just said, I should be angry with you. Your explanation should have sounded slightly obnoxious. Perhaps even a bit arrogant. But it didn't."

"I'm sorry that I disappointed you."

"There it is," Lycia said with a smile. "I knew you couldn't hold it in for long. A touch of obnoxiousness hidden within your sarcasm."

Jakob smiled, giving her the small victory that the gladiator needed. "So can we move on from this now? I'm really tired of having this argument with you."

"Only if you make me a promise."

"What promise would that be?" Jakob believed that his slightly worried expression was justified, because Lycia was not someone that he cared to bargain with.

"That if you feel the need to take a risk ..." Lycia stopped herself. "Who am I kidding? When you decide to take a risk, you make sure that I'm at your side. Always. Do we have an agreement?"

Jakob stared hard at Lycia, understanding the seriousness of what she was proposing. What it truly meant. Struck by the language that she had used.

She was seeking a contract of sorts. A binding one. Nevertheless, he didn't hesitate for long.

"We do."

Lycia smiled, pleased by the small victory that she had just earned, in large part because she anticipated more of a fight from Jakob. "I really hope that I don't regret this."

"Why would you say that?" wondered Jakob.

"Because even though I haven't been with you for very long, it's quite easy to see that you like to live dangerously."

"That's only because I trust the people around me."

"All of them?"

"What do you mean by that?" Jakob asked, slightly surprised by her question.

"Nothing," she backtracked, cursing herself under her breath for not thinking before speaking.

She wasn't ready to have this conversation with him, not sure yet if she should voice her concerns. Rather than taking her seriously, Jakob might perceive what she had to say as jealousy, or perhaps just nerves. Besides, they had to deal with the approaching threat first.

Jakob stared at the gladiator for a little while longer, not saying a word, trying the same tactic on her that she had tried on him just a few minutes before. He doubted that she would crack, but nothing risked, nothing gained.

The entire time she stared right back at him. All the while he wondered why she would raise such a concern. Then, he realized that he was wondering about the wrong thing.

Lycia wouldn't put a concern like that out there unless she believed that she had good cause to do so.

Even so, he would have to wait to pursue it with her. Their visitors were almost upon them.

After searching the mountains around them Jakob selected this farmhouse because the two dozen slavers coming up the trail had to pass by it in order to continue on their way to the mine that was a few leagues to the west.

Or rather the mine that had been there as of yesterday morning. As of yesterday afternoon, Jakob and his Highlanders had seized the mine, freed the hundreds of prisoners forced to work within its depths, and eliminated the two score soldiers stationed there.

Jakob doubted that the slavers coming his way were aware that the mine they were hiking toward was no longer in their possession. They were likely just using the mine as a starting point for another raid in among the peaks, seeking to kidnap more poor souls and put them to work for the benefit of the Governor.

And he understood why this group included twenty-four

slavers, double the number of most raiding parties. It suggested to him a growing desperation on the part of Torstan Sharperson.

That thought pleased Jakob. He and his Highlanders had claimed most of the Highlands from the Governor and his Guard, placing a noose around the Stone and its environs and slowly pulling it tighter. And he hoped that what was going to happen in the next few minutes only intensified that pressure.

Because desperate people made mistakes, and that's what Jakob's Highlanders were waiting for.

Once the Governor made that mistake, and Jakob had no doubt that he would, they would be ready.

"You want to hand me that post?" Jakob asked. He had tried to pierce Lycia's defenses, but no luck. His failure didn't surprise him in the least. And he didn't mind. Where was the fun in life without a challenge?

"Now? Are you serious?" Lycia glimpsed the first of the slavers walking up the trail that cut through the forest a quarter mile below them. The two dozen men would be joining her and Jakob in just a matter of minutes.

"We might as well finish what we started. No point in doing a good deed if you don't actually do it."

Lycia stared at Jakob, a look of bewilderment crossing her face. Then she bit her lip as she tried to hide her smile. She should have assumed as much.

Shaking her head, Lycia reached down and handed him the post. She then held it steady once he set it in the hole that she had dug and began to shovel the dirt back in place. When he was done, they both packed down the earth. Lycia with the flat of her shovel, Jakob with the head of his pickaxe.

All the while hearing the men approach from behind, the sound of metal clinking against metal, even the snap of a whip. Still they ignored the slavers until they completed their task.

They had spoken to the husband and wife who owned the

land. Slavers had marched through dozens of times in the past, always failing to break through the small but solid bastion they had built. The opportunity presented to the slavers now …

Jakob doubted that they would be able to resist.

When Jakob and Lycia turned around, the encounter began exactly as they anticipated.

"Looks like we've got at least one tasty morsel, boys," said a stocky fellow whose dirty beard was split into two roughly twisted strands. He carried a battle axe in one hand, his other scratching at the back of his head. He smiled when his men laughed and then licked his lips when Lycia shifted her hard eyes toward him. "I can't wait to take a bite."

The slavers, all of whom moved like the soldiers they were, formed a semicircle, effectively pinning their prey against the fence.

"I'd certainly like to have a go, Maksin," said a tall fellow with bad teeth who leered at Lycia with an undisguised hunger.

The leader, his belly hanging over his belt, nodded. "We'll all get a chance, Lars." He gave Lycia a wink as he played with the two twisted strands of whiskers with his free hand.

Lycia stared daggers at the two men. Then her right eyebrow rose. She offered them a smirk. A promise that sent a clear message about what would happen if they cared to take their chances with her. Seeing that, several of the slavers took a step back, including Lars.

"I doubt you'd enjoy the taste." Jakob tried not to smile, recognizing how Lycia relished the challenge before them. Two dozen slavers in all. Based on her expression, she seemed to think that she could work her way through all of them on her own with relative ease. "Quite bitter as you might have guessed."

Jakob's comment earned a scowl from Lycia then a grudging shake of her head at his humor, as well as a long round of laughter from the slavers.

"Funny, lad," Maksin said, giving Jakob an appreciative nod. "For that, if you come quietly, we won't beat you too badly along the way. A fair trade, don't you think?"

Jakob studied Maksin closely. The slaver obviously liked to hear the sound of his own voice. Yet Jakob saw something else behind the man's beard that curled his lips into a knowing grin. Something that he intended to make use of.

"I think not."

"You sure about that, lad?" the portly leader asked. "You think you and your woman can take us on? All by yourselves?" He motioned to the men around him. "We don't look like much, I know, but appearances can be deceiving."

"You're quite right about that," Jakob agreed. He reached behind him and pulled free one of the double-bladed, bone-white daggers he kept in a specially designed sheath on his back. At the same time, Lycia picked up the pair of swords that lay in the grass at her feet.

"Is that one of those Wraith blades?" Maksin asked, intrigued by the weapon.

"It is."

"You find it after the Murk lifted?"

"Something like that," Jakob replied.

"You haven't cut yourself with it yet?" Maksin wondered, laughing heartily at his joke. Several of his men chuckled with him. "Farmers like you should probably just stick to pitchforks and hoes."

"Steel is steel," Jakob replied with a shrug. "The only thing that matters is that you know how to use it."

"And you believe that you know how to use that weapon?" asked Maksin. "That blade takes a skill that I doubt you have."

Maksin was trying to demonstrate a confidence that he wasn't really feeling even with the large number of men at his back. He had only agreed to lead this hunt because the Governor promised him twice his usual cut. With the threat presented by the Highlanders only a few leagues from the Stone, the promise of so many golds was the only way to get him out of the barracks.

His decision, based on greed, still bothered him. And now, facing off against a couple caught out and cut off who based on their appearance couldn't have much experience with a blade, he was beginning to feel uncomfortable. He didn't quite understand why when he had so many handpicked men standing at his back. All of them veterans. None of them put off by the dirty work that was often required of them.

Maybe it was because the young man standing before him looked strangely familiar.

Maybe it was because the young man had begun spinning the dagger across his fingers, demonstrating a remarkable, almost frightening dexterity with the blade.

Maybe it was because he was beginning to think that the young man might not actually be a farmer.

But it was too late now. The engagement had begun, and Maksin needed to finish it. He couldn't afford to lose the respect of his men before they had even begun their sweep through the peaks.

"All right, lad. If that's the way you want it, then that's the way it will be." Maksin turned away from Jakob, catching the eyes of all of his men. "If the lad is too much trouble, kill him. Regardless, don't harm the lass. We'll need her healthy and whole if we're going to have a little fun with her as we make our way to the mine."

Before Maksin turned back around toward his two victims, his men were advancing on Jakob and Lycia. Some chose to use their swords and axes, others selected the whips with which they were so familiar and skilled.

When Maksin followed a few steps behind his men, his eyes were drawn to the young woman with the short red hair. She was smiling now and shaking her head. Her expression made him even more nervous. She seemed to be hinting that he was making a terrible mistake.

He shifted his focus to the young man. Again trying to place him. Not understanding why he seemed so familiar. Also not understanding why he felt as if he and his men weren't moving toward an easy capture but rather toward their own deaths.

Just a second later, he got his answer.

A massive blast blew apart the earth right in front of the slavers, the flash so bright that for several seconds the men not caught in the explosion were blind. Those who bore the full brunt of the bolt of energy that slammed into the ground were thrown backward thirty feet or more, many to never rise again, while those lucky to survive were stunned and disoriented.

Before the slavers could recover, Marchers erupted from the hide holes they had dug along both sides of the trail, their shallow depressions covered with mats woven of long grass, Jakob and Aislinn completing the deception with a thin layer of dirt.

With Duff leading the way, his oversized blacksmith's hammer in hand, the clash was brief and not even sharp, which perfectly suited the Highlander's taste. The handful of slavers not killed in the explosion who were able to get back to their feet were wobbly at best, falling back to the ground and puking out their guts at worst.

The Highlanders made quick work of the slavers who flailed about with their swords, axes, or whips. Those few who couldn't get back to their feet were disarmed even faster, tied up, and then added to the pile of groaning or unconscious men.

Maksin watched it all with a mixture of shock and awe, focusing most of his attention on not releasing his bowels as a frigid chill crept down his spine. He was beginning to understand the mistake that he made.

He had been so sure of the picture that the two young farmers were presenting that he had never considered that they might not be farmers. More like not wanting to acknowledge the truth of what he was seeing.

Finding a Wraith's dagger in the grass?

He had been a fool to suggest such a thing. There was only one way to obtain a Wraith's dagger, and that was virtually impossible. And then that blast of lightning coming down out of a cloudless sky. That was completely impossible.

Unless you ...

"Maybe instead of you having your fun with me, I'll have my fun with you."

Maksin tensed when he heard the soft whisper of the red-haired woman's voice in his ear, whimpering and shaking when she pressed the cold steel blade against his throat.

Having the blade just a hair away from digging into his flesh was bad enough. What really frightened Maksin was that the woman didn't sound angry.

Rather, she sounded quite calm. Cold even. And, worse, expectant. As if she couldn't wait to draw his blood with her steel.

"Tell me again what you wanted to do to me," Lycia hissed.

She took a half-step back then, catching the scent of urine and then seeing the stain work its way down the front of the slaver's breeches. "Really? That's the best you can do? How very disappointing."

"Don't kill him, Lycia. At least not yet."

"Spoilsport," she grumbled. "You take the fun out of everything."

Jakob stepped around Lycia and came to a stop a few feet in front of the slaver. Although not so close as to stand in the puddle of piss that had turned the dirt around the slaver's boots to mud.

"How long have you worked for Governor Sharperson?"

Jakob gave Lycia a look. She took another step back.

He could tell just how much she frightened the man, and

he wanted to conduct the interrogation quickly and with a minimum of fuss. Unless Maksin made a little fuss a required part of the proceeding.

That wouldn't bother Jakob. It just meant that any resistance on the slaver's part would require a bit more effort and time.

The effort that might be required he was more than willing to give. But time was short. He preferred to stay on the move when he and his Highlanders were so close to the Stone.

"I don't work for the Governor," the slaver replied, beads of sweat beginning to trickle down his brow.

Jakob frowned and nodded sadly, giving Lycia another look. She shrugged.

Neither of them understood why the initial response from so many of the slavers who were placed in a position such as this one was to lie. An ingrained quality because they had been lying to themselves for so long? Some residue of fear knowing what the Governor would do to them if he learned that they had collaborated with his enemy?

Jakob sighed sadly. If that's the way Maksin wanted it, so be it.

Jakob knew what he had to do. It was quite simple, really.

It all came down to fear. The slaver needed to fear him more than he feared the Governor.

Jakob had some experience in making that happen.

"That's the answer you're going to stick with?"

"I am. I have no reason to lie."

That response curled Jakob's lips into a wider smile. "I see. So you're an honest man at heart."

"I am, yes."

"Did you hear that, Duff?" asked Jakob. The Highlander had walked up behind him, his blacksmith's hammer resting on his shoulder.

"I did."

"Should we believe him?"

Duff snorted. He gave the slaver a menacing look. The scar circling his bald head only helped to increase Maksin's fear, the man gulping nervously.

"The only thing that we can believe from this one is that he's going to lie to us."

"I won't," the slaver protested, his eyes widening in alarm. "Truly. I don't work for the Governor."

Duff snorted again then spit a glob of phlegm into the mud. "That's a load of horse muck. I still don't get why these fools are seeking to protect a man who will leave them to their fate as soon as they're no longer of use. Like now."

"And you're not a soldier?" Lycia asked from behind the slaver, resting one of her blades on his shoulder.

Maksin jumped at the touch of steel, having forgotten while caught by the gaze of the fearsome Highlander that there was just as dangerous a threat at his back.

"I'm not a soldier," the slaver replied. He tried and failed to stop himself from gulping again.

"You look like a soldier."

The coldness in her voice sent a shiver of fear down Maksin's spine. "I'm not. I promise you that."

"So you say," Duff said.

"I do, truly." Maksin tried to get a handle on his rising panic, understanding just how difficult a situation he was in. With all of his men dead or captured, he really only had one more card to play. Admittedly, it was a longshot at best. But what did he have to lose? He gulped as he thought about it a bit more, already knowing the answer. His life.

"You understand how hard that is to believe?" asked Jakob. He spoke in a clipped tone. Clearly he was losing patience, a fact that the slaver couldn't miss.

"Truth be told," continued Maksin, understanding that he

had entered the critical part of the conversation, "I don't want to be doing this. But I have no choice."

Duff laughed softly, amused in an angry sort of way. Jakob simply stared at the man, his flashing green eyes flinty.

Neither believed what they were hearing. However, both were interested to see how Maksin was going to try to worm his way free.

"Why is that?" Lycia asked. She rolled her eyes and shook her head. They knew that the slaver was lying. The slaver knew that they knew that he was lying. Yet still he persisted. Did he take them for fools?

"I had no prospects in Caledonia," Maksin began. "Thus my decision to come to the Territories. I was to meet my brother in the Northern Territory." Maksin shrugged, as if to say that what happened next was beyond his control. "Sailing into Ballinasloe, I made my way with my family into the Highlands. We didn't get far, though. My wife and I, our young ones with us, were waylaid not too far north of the Stone. I was given a choice. Help snare the men and women needed to work the mines or become a miner myself."

"So you chose the easy way out?" prodded Lycia.

She was less than impressed with the slaver's effort, but he had started his tale, so she might as well hear all of it. Although she did hope to speed him along. The Highlanders had a great deal more to do on what already had proven to be a very successful day.

"It was the only way out," Maksin clarified. "Two children, neither one older than five. And my wife has arthritis in her hands that's so bad that she can't do many things for herself. I need to be with her as much as I can to help her. I know what happens in the mines. I do. I truly do. I know that what I'm doing is wrong. But I needed to think of my family first. I needed to embrace a bad choice."

Maksin looked away for a moment, almost as if he was

trying to prevent tears from running down his cheeks. Jakob was impressed. When Maksin looked at him again his eyes were red. "I hate myself for it, but if I needed to do it again, I would. Because I need to do what's best for my wife and my family. You understand that? Don't you?"

He nodded toward Jakob, hoping to see some sympathy in his hard gaze. Because the Highlander with the hammer leaning against his shoulder wasn't having any of what Maksin was trying to sell him. Nor the woman resting her blade on his shoulder. "You'd do the same, wouldn't you? You'd put your family first?"

"I would put my family first," Jakob replied, giving the slaver a nod. "I couldn't fault you for that. An almost impossible situation such as the one you depict, boxed in like that, my family would come first."

"Thank you," Maksin sighed. "I knew that you would understand."

"The only problem is that you don't have a family, Maksin. You don't have a wife. You don't have two children."

Maksin's eyes widened until they were as big as saucers. The lad had sniffed out the lie. That was bad. But how could he ...

"How could you possibly know that?" he croaked, his throat dry.

"You've forgotten me already?" Jakob asked. "I haven't forgotten you, Maksin. You were a liar before you ever took ship to New Caledonia. You never had a wife and children. And I promise you that you never will."

"I don't understand," Maksin sputtered. "How could you ..."

Jakob lost his desire to continue with the game that Maksin had thrust upon him. It was time for him and his Highlanders to get back to work.

Searching around them with the Talent during Maksin's tall tale, he identified the long column of soldiers that had left the

Stone and was working its way in his direction. He had no desire to be here when they arrived in a few hours. Not without a good many more Highlanders with him and a few surprises lying in wait.

Making use of a thin stream of the Talent, a ball of energy appeared just above Jakob's palm.

Maksin gasped and tried to jump back, terrified of the power that was playing across Jakob's fingers. But the slaver couldn't. Because Lycia was there, the tip of her sword now pressed into his back.

"I grow tired of you, Maksin," Jakob said quietly. "Just as I did in Roo's Nest. All bluster. All promises. All lies."

Maksin stared at the young man standing before him, barely able to breathe, his mind working frantically as he dug through his memories.

Not just a young man, he corrected. Also a Magus. But who?

For several more heartbeats, he wracked his brain for an answer. The lad had looked familiar when he first caught sight of him. Why?

Maksin's mystified voice revealed his shock. "You're Dougal's boy. Jakob Bl ..."

Jakob cut the slaver off. "Enough about me, Maksin. Let's talk about you. Tell me how things work around the Stone." Jakob added two more fiery balls to the palm of his hand. Then he began to juggle the spheres. "And don't waste my time. A blast of lightning isn't the worst way that I can kill you."

"You know that we're just cleaning out the weeds doing this," Lycia said.

She sat across the fire from Jakob, the flames mesmerizing as she poked at the logs with a long stick.

Almost mesmerizing.

They would have been if she could have relaxed.

She was edgy.

She wanted to move.

They had enjoyed some success against the slavers. But she didn't feel as if the work was complete.

More important, she didn't believe that their current strategy would get them where they needed to go fast enough.

"You really can't help yourself," Saraa tsked, shaking her head and offering a soft, scornful snort.

"How so?" Lycia didn't care for Saraa's tone.

"An opinion about everything," Saraa said in a whisper that sounded more like a hiss.

It was clear that the Highlander's temper was beginning to boil, just as it always did when she spent too much time around Lycia, which occurred more often than she would have liked.

Saraa had been sitting with Jakob for a few minutes of quiet. Happy to be close to him. Until the gladiator stalked out of the darkness and ruined it for her.

And Saraa believed that stalked was a good way to describe how the woman moved. It was like she was still on the white sand of the Pit. Just another reason she disliked her so viscerally.

"I only offer my opinion when it's welcome," Lycia replied, keeping her voice even, unemotional, not having the desire or the energy to get into another argument with the prickly Highlander.

"You offer your opinion ..."

"What do you mean?" Jakob asked, interrupting Saraa, reaching out a hand and resting it gently on the Highlander's arm for a few seconds, wanting to make sure that she didn't lose her temper. He had no desire to deal with one of Saraa's outbursts that evening.

"Eliminating these squads of slavers is necessary, but it's only a temporary solution."

"We just took more than twenty of those bastards off the table," protested Saraa. "The more we kill now, the fewer we'll have to kill later."

"That's true, but we can't kill them all and expect to achieve our primary objective."

"Why do you say that?" Saraa felt the need to remain difficult. Even so, she reluctantly heard the truth in the gladiator's words.

"Because it's a matter of numbers. The Governor has how many soldiers under his command?"

"Four thousand," Jakob replied quietly.

"And we have how many?"

"Roughly two thousand. A few hundred more will join us, but not much more than that."

"And that's my point," prodded Lycia. "We can't kill all the soldiers. We can't kill all the slavers. No matter how much we might want to. We're just cutting at the edges by doing that."

"You're right." Jakob sighed and leaned back on the log upon which he was sitting, stretching out his legs. "Killing soldiers and slavers – there's really no difference between the two – certainly helps us. But Sharperson will just fill his empty ranks with others who can't resist his gold, no matter the risk we might present to them. Better to be a slaver ..."

"Than a slave," finished Lycia. "Besides, if I learned nothing else during the overthrow of Marden Beleron, better a brief rebellion when the odds and the numbers are against you. Less time for you to make a mistake. Less time for your adversary to turn their many advantages against you."

"What advantages besides his soldiers?" demanded Saraa, her voice containing the hint of a challenge, just as it always did when she spoke with the gladiator.

"Other than his allies, the Stone for one. A supposedly impregnable fortress. If we don't dig the good Governor out of his citadel, we can say whatever we want here in the mountains. Jakob can claim to be the Lord of the Highlands. But he really won't be the Lord of the Highlands until Sharperson is gone. Better to make that a reality as soon as possible. We don't want to give the Governor the belief that he can wait us out. We need to take a more aggressive approach. Remove the Governor and we can get rid of his Guard that much more easily."

"A more aggressive approach? Are you serious? Now?" Saraa shook her head contemptuously, as if Lycia had no idea what she was talking about. "Is it a risk that we need to take? Yes. But is now really the time?" Saraa turned her blazing eyes toward Jakob. "Are you certain that you should trust the advice of a woman who has been with us for less than a year?"

"I have every reason to trust her, Saraa." Jakob spoke calmly, reasonably, disappointed that his friend was working herself into a lather again, although he knew why.

Jakob was spending more time with Lycia than Saraa would have liked. In fact, Saraa would have preferred that Jakob spend no time at all with Lycia, shunting her off to the side instead. Sending her on some assignment that would take her into the wilds of the Highlands.

But he wasn't going to do that.

He had learned quickly that he needed Lycia close.

Because Lycia offered certain skills that he required that no else could provide.

And, after their experience together during the attack at the mine and then their escape through the depths of the mountain, he trusted Lycia with his life.

"I just don't understand why ..."

"Saraa, please. We need to do this."

Saraa grumbled under her breath, yet at the same time she nodded reluctantly. "Fine. But this is going to be extremely difficult to pull off."

"Perhaps," Jakob agreed. "Then again, no more than any other challenge we've taken on."

That comment made Lycia smile. It brought to mind one of her first conversations with Jakob, when they were both feeling each other out and trying to get a sense of the other. Both needing to determine if this partnership between them was going to work.

"How did you get that scar?" she had asked, nodding toward the pale line that split his cheek and ran from jaw to brow.

"A Wraith. One of my first encounters with one of the monsters in the Murk."

Having just entered the Highlands, Lycia had yet to see the Murk or come up against the Wraiths herself, so he had taken the time to tell her more about those lethal creatures.

Even more importantly, how to fight them. Because he had been certain that the time would come when she would stand across from them. And he had been right.

"I'm assuming that you killed the Wraith who scarred you."

"I did," he had replied quietly. Clearly he didn't take any particular pleasure or pride from that statement. He simply offered it as a fact. She had liked that.

"Was the Wraith hard to kill?"

Jakob had thought about her question for several seconds before replying, shrugging, as if to say he really wasn't in a position to judge. "No more than anything else."

Lycia had studied Jakob for quite some time upon hearing that. She had liked that answer as well. She had decided then that she and Jakob could work together. And they had, quite well in fact, ever since.

"Would you mind checking the sentries, Saraa? We can catch up later once we're in a better position to discuss strategy."

Saraa grumbled some more under her breath, recognizing the request as the gentle dismissal that it was. Still, she heeded it.

Having to spend too much time near the gladiator did more

than just make her edgy. It made her skin crawl. It made her want to do things that went against her very nature.

Watching Saraa head off beyond the light of the fire, Jakob searched around them with the Talent once more. Just as it had been the hour before and the hour before that.

The column of soldiers that had left the Stone hadn't gotten very far. No more than a league before they set up camp for the night.

So no concerns regarding them. Or Stalkers for that matter. None of those monsters were within thirty leagues.

The Murk and the Wraiths remained far to the north. That terrible grey hadn't moved from the borders of old Frisia for several weeks now. But he didn't expect that insidious fog to remain there for much longer.

It wasn't just a feeling that told him that. His assumption was based on past experience.

The Murk came into the Highlands on a regular basis. One or two times a week since he arrived in the Territory. So it would drift down to the south once again, bringing with it the Wraiths.

He didn't mind the break. However, he certainly was curious as to its cause.

"She really doesn't like me," murmured Lycia, watching the Highlander stomp off into the darkness, moving away from what little light was provided by the small fire.

"That's an understatement," Jakob replied, giving her a wry grin.

His humor made Lycia smile. "I don't get the feeling that I'll ever be able to change that."

"No, unfortunately her dislike for you is ingrained within her. So there's really no point. Better just to coexist if you can."

"I have never done anything intentionally to make it this way."

"I know that." Jakob shrugged. "Saraa knows that too."

"But ..."

"But that doesn't matter. She doesn't like ..."

"She doesn't like me because of you."

"Yes."

"You really are a pain in the ass, you know that, Lord Kestrel?"

Jakob smiled. "I think you've told me that a time or two before."

"It's deserved."

Not wanting to continue with a conversation that he knew that he couldn't win, Jakob shifted to the topic that had begun their dialogue in the first place. "What did you have in mind, Lycia?"

"If you want to kill a snake the best way to do that is to cut off the head."

Jakob nodded, giving Lycia a cunning look. He had expected this from her. In part because he had been thinking much the same. He just hadn't figured out how to do it. "You want to go after the Governor."

"I do." She gave Jakob a discerning look. "You don't seem all that surprised."

"I'm not."

"Why not?"

"Because even though you describe me as a pain in your ass, you and I tend to reach the same conclusions at the same time."

"I can't argue that."

"Good, because I'm tired of arguments." He patted the seat next to him on the log that he pulled up closer to the fire. "What did you have in mind, Lycia?"

3

BLOOD ON THE STONE

"Now this is something that I can use," Davin murmured appreciatively, eyeing what lay at his feet.

After his latest fall, he pushed himself back up with a slight groan, his scraped knees and palms the least of his concerns, the insistent urge to keep moving sounding like an alarm bell in the back of his skull. Even so, he needed to take a brief rest first, enjoying the touch of the cool stone on his back as he leaned against the wall.

The gladiator took several deep breaths, calming himself, his eyes turned back toward the direction from which he had come, searching for any hint of movement.

Nothing.

At least not yet.

Then he smiled. He wasn't out of danger. Not by a long shot. Nevertheless, he felt good about what he had accomplished.

He had gotten farther than he ever thought possible. Just a half hour before, his captor was about to do her worst. Strapped down to a stone slab, Hakea Roosarian taunting him, promising him a future that was worse than death. Stalkers staring hungrily at him from the cages lining both sides of the torture chamber.

Funny how events could change so quickly and drastically. And all because he had gotten lucky with a few drops of blood.

He really wasn't surprised, however. It had been much the same way on the white sand. An unexpected slip. A lucky strike. The sun hitting his opponent's eyes at exactly the wrong time.

There was no point in thinking about why it happened. Better just to be pleased and thankful that it did.

And Davin was.

He would never forget Roosarian's malicious, almost seductive, grin as she held that vial of horrific black liquid just above his mouth, a single drop of that putrid concoction just a breath away from dripping down his throat. By the skin of his teeth, he had escaped from Roosarian before she could transform him into one of the monsters hunting him.

Declan had taught him and all the other gladiators sentenced to the Pit that in order for them to succeed, in order for them to survive, they needed to control as many variables as they possibly could despite the precariousness of their circumstances. And, inevitably, when they couldn't, they needed to be ready to act when fate smiled down upon them.

Davin had been ready, even though he never expected a Stalker to break free. He never anticipated that all the monsters would escape their cages in the ensuing chaos. He never believed that he would unstrap himself and get out of the killing ground before he joined the unlucky Captain Oselnik, who was gutted by a Stalker at the start of the clash.

Since then, Davin had stumbled down the darkened corridors beneath the Rock, turning left or right based on a whim rather than any real knowledge of where he was going.

All he wanted to do was put some distance between himself

and the monsters that were hunting him. He would worry about where he was once he found a place safe from his pursuers. Assuming that he could.

Lost within the warren of corridors running beneath the citadel, he had yet to find a door that wasn't locked or, in fact, any location that would allow him to better defend himself. The only option that he had found so far was where he stood now. One corridor running into another at a right angle. Limiting the direction from which a Stalker could come at him.

Adding insult to injury, Davin couldn't remember how many times he had fallen. In part because of the darkness. He could barely see in the pitch black that only so often shifted to a dull grey when he walked beneath one of the few slit windows positioned far above him.

Primarily because he was having such a hard time staying on his feet. The injuries he had suffered before and then during his imprisonment slowed him down and forced him to nothing more than an awkward hobble and shuffle.

As he stumbled along, he had done his best to ignore the Stalkers' shrieks and screams that echoed down the narrow hallways. The sound, similar to steel scraping across stone, made his teeth hurt.

He had been hoping for more time, maybe even the chance to evade his hunters entirely, but it hadn't taken the monsters long to take up the chase. They had his scent, and one of them already had a taste of his blood.

Pushing his fears to the side, he concentrated on the monsters coming his way. He was moving more slowly than he would have preferred, but he was moving.

Now, with the Stalkers drawing closer, he needed to avoid another fall. Because he feared that if he went down hard again, he wouldn't be getting back up. Then he'd just be easy meat.

Rather than allow his fears to drive him, he decided that he would worry about his hunters when he saw their blood-red eyes in the darkness. Until then, he would look for the one feature in the tangle of corridors beneath the Rock that might help him stay alive.

And at least now he was in a slightly improved position to stand against the beasts when they appeared. He had found a new tool that should prove more effective against his hunters than the one that he never would have escaped without.

Sliding between his ragged breeches and the small of his back the bloody spade that had helped him get past the Stalkers in the torture chamber, he reached down, picking up two of the sharpened steel rods, each about three feet long, that he had tripped over just a moment before. He had only succeeded in keeping himself on his feet because he had come to another turn in the corridor, the unyielding wall to his front preventing another tumble, the price he had to pay for that kindness a bruised shoulder.

He didn't know who had left the steel spikes there or why. He really didn't care. He was grateful to his anonymous donor.

Fate was smiling down upon him, and Davin wanted to make the most of it while he could.

He held the two steel spikes up to the dim light that battled the darkness above him.

He nodded in satisfaction. Things were looking up.

He had a better chance of seeing his pursuers in the greyish gloom. And, although the spikes were a little rusty, they still held a keen edge. These would do nicely indeed.

Davin was about to continue on his way, hoping to find what he was looking for before the Stalkers found him. But it was too late.

He pushed himself off the wall and turned to face the darkness from which he had emerged just minutes before. Even though he knew what was coming, the shriek that blasted down the hallway sent a shiver through his entire body.

He didn't have to wait long. The twilight shifted, a massive figure disturbing it.

He couldn't make out much of the monster except for its dim, towering shape, the creature blending too well into the darkness, and those blood-red eyes that blazed with an insatiable hunger.

He was really getting tired of this.

The smart play was for Davin to run. There was more light in the direction that he was going, and there might be some space just a little farther down where he could better defend himself.

Davin shook his head slowly from side to side, biting his lip, as he considered that strategy for a few seconds then threw it away.

He really didn't care about making the smart decision now.

He was done running.

He refused to give the Stalker the satisfaction of chasing him down from behind.

If this Stalker was going to kill him, then Davin was going to make the monster do it looking him in the eyes.

Jumping over the pile of steel spikes that had almost taken him to the floor, Davin raced down the corridor in a stumbling gallop, screaming at the top of his lungs.

The Stalker's shriek died in the monster's throat, shocked to see its prey charging right at it.

That heartbeat of hesitation worked in the gladiator's favor.

Davin didn't even bother to swing. He knew how hard it would be to get in a good strike with the darkness hiding the Stalker so well. Instead, he focused solely on the monster's eyes. Where the eyes were, so was the Stalker.

He barreled right into the beast, at the very last second

ducking and turning, his shoulder slamming into the Stalker's gut and sending the beast stumbling backward.

Using his momentum to his advantage, Davin went with the monster. Staggering for a few steps and then falling right atop the Stalker's broad chest and forcing it to the floor.

Davin smiled maliciously, hearing the air escaping from the Stalker's lungs when the beast's back hit the unyielding stone of the hallway.

Grunting, struggling to breathe, the Stalker was slow to raise its arms to defend itself.

Davin didn't hesitate, swinging his makeshift spears with a wild abandon. Arm, chest, neck, groin, gut. It didn't matter what he hit so long as he hit some part of the Stalker's body.

Davin allowed his rage to take over. To drive him. His only concern was keeping the monster on the ground. Giving into a desperate need to hurt the beast as badly as he had been hurt himself.

When he began his assault, savoring the beating that he was administering to his hunter, Davin thought that he might succeed. In fact, he thought he detected a whimper as the Stalker thrashed about, struggling to evade his powerful blows.

Davin realized that he had misjudged the situation when he felt himself soaring backward through the air.

The Stalker, ignoring its injuries, surged up off the ground and howled in triumph.

Davin landed heavily on his back, lying there for just a moment, seeking to reclaim the air knocked from his lungs.

When he finally took a breath again, he realized that it might be his last one.

Those blood-red eyes were coming directly toward him. The monster soaring through the air, claws reaching for him.

Understanding that he had no chance of getting out of the way in time, Davin reacted instinctively. He lifted the steel spike in his right hand and angled it toward his target as best as he could in the hindering darkness.

Davin grunted in pain, the breath knocked from him again, several ribs cracking, as he was crushed against the rough stone. The seconds that followed passed slowly.

He expected to feel one of the Stalker's razor-sharp claws digging into his gut or his throat or his chest, and when he didn't that fear was overwhelmed by his fight to fill his lungs with air.

Finally, black spots at the edge of his vision, he gasped, taking a much-needed breath.

Rather than the excruciating pain of his body being ripped open, he felt the heavy weight of the monster lying atop him. Then the touch of wetness as a liquid that was invisible in the dark trickled down over his forehead and face.

Turning to the side, he spit it out, wiping his eyes with the back of his free hand.

Blood.

He spat a few more times, attempting to get the metallic taste out of his mouth even though he knew that it was a lost cause.

Despite his new predicament, he smiled then sighed with relief.

Through a quirk of luck, the second touch of luck that he had experienced since sneaking into the Rock, the steel tip of the spike that he held out before him had hit its mark. Puncturing the Stalker's eye, punching all the way into its brain and killing the monster instantly.

For just a few seconds more, Davin lay there, the crushing weight of the dead Stalker pressing down on him. He was struggling for breath. Bruised and battered. Every part of his body hurt in some fashion. Covered in blood. But most of it wasn't his blood, so what did he care?

He did care that there were more Stalkers hunting for him

in the warren of hallways beneath the Rock. That reality made clear as several more shrieks echoed down the corridor.

Davin judged these hunters to be no more than a few hundred yards away.

Understanding just how poor his chances of survival were, he thought about simply staying where he was. He could be done with it all. He could escape the pain. The terror.

Davin snorted softly in disbelief, disappointed that he had allowed that self-defeating concept to pop into his brain.

Giving in, no matter the poor odds, simply wasn't in him.

Taking as deep a breath as he could manage with the dead Stalker lying atop him, Davin tried to push the monster off him. The body wouldn't budge. The beast must have weighed four hundred pounds if not more.

Hearing more shrieks drifting down the corridor, the shrill noise once more setting his teeth on edge and filling him with a desperate urgency, Davin pushed with all the strength that he could muster. Which, to his regret, wasn't all that much after all that he had suffered through during the last few days.

No success.

He barely shifted the corpse lying atop him.

Worse, now the Stalker was pressing down even more on his chest, making it harder for him to take a breath.

Davin tried again, not only pushing against the monster's chest, but also trying at the same time to turn his hip so that he could roll the beast off him.

Grunting and groaning, after several seconds of strenuous effort, he was able to shift the Stalker an inch. Maybe two. But no more than that.

Davin cursed, not quite believing how his luck had changed for the worse so quickly. Then again, he should have expected as much.

It was no different than fighting in the Pit. And now, his exhaustion almost complete, his muscles were shaking from what had proven to be an almost useless attempt to escape the dead weight pressing down upon him.

Two more shrieks echoed down the corridor. Davin guessed that the Stalkers couldn't be more than a hundred yards away.

And he was trapped beneath the body of one of their dead brethren. How remarkably appropriate.

The thought that he could be done with it all again flickered through the back of his mind.

He could do it.

He could give in.

He could accept his fate.

He had fought the good fight.

And in the end, just as he had learned on the white sand, he could only fight so hard. He could only give so much.

Because no matter what he did, no matter how much he gave of himself, no matter how hard he tried, fate would come calling for him.

Eventually, like it or not, he would go to the other side.

No!

Davin refused to give in.

If he was to go to the other side, then it would be on his terms.

He would never give in.

He would not leave this world until he could no longer draw breath. Until every drop of blood had been drained from his body. Until he could no longer fight.

That's how Declan had trained him.

That's who he was.

That sense of urgency mixed with desperation allowed Davin to connect with a hidden reserve of strength within him. With a last gasp of effort, every muscle in his body straining, he heaved the dead Stalker far enough to the side so that he was able to scoot the rest of the way out and finally take a deep breath again.

Pushing himself back to his feet, wobbling a bit because of his shaky legs, with a steel spike in each hand, he began to hobble down the hallway, taking some comfort from the dim light of the early morning that streamed through the narrow windows thirty feet above his head.

If the Stalkers were going to kill him, he was going to make them work for it.

4

BOILING BLACK

"Are they close?"

Aislinn had been searching around them with the Talent as they moved deeper beneath the Shadow Keep. Despite her best efforts, she found it exceedingly difficult to catch a whiff of the Fiends that had attacked them in their guest quarters just minutes before.

The magical scent of the monsters called forth from the Spirit World played at the edge of her senses. Teasing her. Prodding her. Yet refusing to give her a clear direction to follow. The challenge made more difficult because the stench permeated the fortress. The stomach-churning miasma everywhere and nowhere.

As she and Bryen hunted for the Fiends, she was having a hard time coming to grips with what they had just fought off.

The noxious mist streaming through the gap between the bottom of their door and the floor.

That cloud of menace frothing until it consumed the foyer.

Then, much to her shock, the wisps of black splitting apart into four strands.

In just seconds, four hideous creatures born of that swirling black standing in front of them.

Misshapen skulls that were too large for their tall, thin bodies, the weight of their oversized heads pushing their shoulders toward the ground and giving the creatures a stooped appearance. Their grotesque teeth, sharpened to a fine point and matching their needlelike, three-digit claws. And finally their black eyes, which burned with an unquenchable hatred.

Monsters that had no place in their world.

Monsters that inhabited the realm of the Ancient One.

Aislinn still hadn't wrapped her mind around that last part. She was familiar with the Spirit World and the evil overlord said to rule it. Thanks to her training with Sirius, she knew of the legends surrounding the domain of the dead and how it was juxtaposed to the Natural World.

The former, a cold, soul-crushing place. Home to the spirits, menacing shades, and creatures of the dark that sought to reclaim the world that they had lost.

The latter a world for the living. A place of warmth and hope, dreams and desires.

Aislinn understood there was no point in trying to ignore this new discovery. Ever since she and Bryen had joined their futures together, it seemed that legends became truths and myths were made real with a terrifying frequency.

So rather than question, better to accept, to adapt, and then move forward.

As Sirius had liked to say, in every myth there was a nugget of truth. And based on her experience, the old Magus had the right of it.

"They're just ahead of us," Bryen replied.

Leaving her Protector with the responsibility of tracking the fleeing Fiends, Aislinn used the Talent to light their way, small spheres of energy drifting all around them, eliminating the shadows of the dry and dusty passageways. Even better, the energy keeping pace with them burned through the tangle of cobwebs that hindered their advance.

They had chased the Fiends through the upper levels of the Shadow Keep, following one deserted hallway after another, until they had been forced to stop right in front of a stone wall. Just a little farther down the corridor was the locked door that led to Kendric Winborne's private office.

Aislinn had found the location of their quarry's disappearance strange, although not necessarily surprising with all that Bryen had revealed to her after his excursion into the city and then his confrontation with Ursina, her uncle's wife.

Their dilemma hadn't stymied Bryen for long. She had a difficult time tracking the creatures. Bryen less so thanks to the Seventh Stone that resided within him.

Using the power of the artifact, he latched onto the Fiends who raced away down the hidden passageway behind the wall. He had watched as the virulent black mist transformed once again, splitting into two strands that assumed corporeal form, the creatures, several heads taller than a man, loping with a surprising grace toward the lower levels of the citadel.

Knowing what was behind the wall, it hadn't taken Bryen long to identify the small latch hidden near the bottom of the stone wall. A few more seconds of effort to release the catch and they were through.

They had kept to the secret tunnels for several minutes, all the while moving deeper beneath the citadel. Not closing the distance to the fleeing Fiends but not losing them either.

It wasn't long after entering the corridors catacombing behind the walls that they had been forced to stop once again. Only for a few seconds, however, Aislinn using the Talent to identify the hidden lever that once again was close to the floor, a slab of the roughly hewn stone wall swinging open when she pressed down with her boot.

From there, Bryen leading the way, they entered a section of the Shadow Keep that was still under construction. Or rather it had been.

It didn't look like work had taken place in this section of the fortress for several months. They found that curious since Kendric was so intent on completing the Shadow Keep as quickly as possible.

The Fiends may have escaped them, but they couldn't evade the power of the Seventh Stone. Keeping up the chase, it wasn't long before Bryen and Aislinn advanced into the first of what would be many caves that were situated below the fortress and were linked to the tunnel they were walking through.

"How much farther?" Aislinn asked.

"We're here."

"What do you mean we're here?" The corridor came to an end in another cave. A small stream trickled out of the wall in the back and flowed into a hole that led away through a fissure in the stone. Other than that, there was nothing about the chamber that suggested that there was another path to take. They had reached a dead end.

"We're here."

"The Fiends are here?"

"No, they went even deeper beneath the citadel."

Bryen stepped up to the stone wall on the left side, Aislinn joining him, the spheres of light hanging just above their heads illuminating the way.

"An illusion? Like Rafia used so frequently when we were seeking to escape the Ghoules while we made our way to Haven?"

"Of a sort," Bryen said, staring at the rock blocking his way.

He reached out with a hand, touching the stone wall.

He nodded to himself. Just as he suspected.

The stone wall that was impeding them was really just an image of what they assumed should be there, the magic used playing off their expectations.

Aislinn reached out and touched the stone as well. "Impressive. But there's more than just the Talent here." She could sense the corrosive taint mixed in with the energy used to create the deception.

"The Curse, yes. A unique strain of it as well."

"Unique strain? How do you mean?"

Bryen shrugged, not really sure how to explain what he had discovered. "An older strain. Ancient." He ran his fingers over the illusion one more time. "The Curse is the Curse. There is only one Curse."

"You do realize that you're talking in riddles right now?" Aislinn asked, giving Bryen a small smile and a raised eyebrow.

"It's just difficult to explain," he grimaced. "It's something that Sirius used to tell me. The Curse is the Curse. There is only one Curse."

"All right," Aislinn said. "Try me. The Curse is the Curse. There is only one Curse."

"Simple but difficult both at the same time," Bryen said, picking up where he left off. "The Curse consumes the user. It makes their power its own, essentially a merger of the two. So when sensing the Curse in the Ghoule Overlord, it's distinct in many ways when compared to the Curse employed here. Just as was the case with Tetric. He had accepted the gift of the Curse. The power he exercised was much the same as that of the Ghoule Overlord, but then again slightly different because Tetric was Tetric and the Ghoule Overlord was the Ghoule Overlord."

"Because the user of the Curse, or rather the individual being used by the Curse, is unique," offered Aislinn, nodding as she thought about what Bryen was telling her. "The Curse is the Curse. There is only one Curse. But there are unique strains within it because of how it interacts with whomever is foolish enough to make use of it."

"Exactly," Bryen said with a smile, glad that Aislinn had

been able to stay with him because he didn't think that he could explain it in any other way. "The Curse used to craft this illusion has the same foundation as that employed by the Ghoule Overlord and his Elders, Tetric as well. Yet, from there, it takes a new direction. A new strain."

"And this strain is older you said."

"I did."

"Could that result from Ursina's use of the Curse? The dark taint changing her? Merging with her?"

"In part, perhaps. But there's more to it than that. There's a hint of Ursina in it, but it's overwhelmed by another presence."

"You'll need to be more specific."

"I don't know that I can be."

"Try," Aislinn urged.

"The feel of the taint in the Curse ..." Bryen began, thinking about it. "It feels almost primordial. As if it's the original strain. As if all the others we've come into contact with come from it."

Aislinn took a few seconds to think about that. An interesting proposal. A frightening one as well. "Are you talking about the power of the Ancient One?"

She didn't really want to consider that possibility. But she had to after they had come up against the Fiends.

The Ancient One was the source of many a nightmare. Supposedly no more than an evil presence that had become a part of the mythology of the Realms.

Yet clearly there was much more to the myth than that if what Bryen was suggesting was correct.

"Unfortunately, yes. This strain of the Curse ..." Bryen hesitated for a moment, gathering his thoughts. "This might sound foolish, but if what little we know of the Ancient One is correct -- not the scary tales for children but the actual history as kept by the Order of the Magii -- then this strain of the Curse confirms the Ancient One's existence. I felt much the same as I do now with Tetric, the Ghoule Overlord, even the Kraken

King. Faint hints unlike the stronger touch here, but there, nonetheless. A foundational strain to the Curse."

Aislinn studied Bryen for several heartbeats. This was an astounding finding. A terrifying one as well.

Because the Ancient One, if the histories were to be believed, was the greatest threat ever faced by the Order of the Magii and, in fact, by all the Realms.

The ruler of the Spirit World had but one objective. Merging his domain with the Natural World and thereby ruling both.

"Have you talked to Rafia about this?"

"About what?"

"About your ability to identify strains within the Curse?"

"Briefly," Bryen replied. "While we were crossing the Burnt Ocean."

"What did she have to say?" Aislinn wondered. "Because for me, just as Sirius told you, the Curse is the Curse. Whether I was fighting Tetric or the Ghoule Overlord, I didn't sense anything that suggested there was a difference between the two."

"Rafia believed that it might have something to do with the Seventh Stone becoming a part of me." Bryen shrugged. "We didn't really have time to go much deeper than that. It wasn't long after I raised the topic that the Bakunawa were sighted. Our priorities shifted then."

Aislinn certainly couldn't argue that point. Their voyage across the Burnt Ocean had been fairly uneventful until those sea dragons appeared, the Bakunawa seeking to take them to the bottom.

"There's something else that you haven't told me," Aislinn pushed.

Bryen snorted at Aislinn's comment. He should have assumed that she would pick up on that. She knew him much too well.

"I've only encountered the Ghoule Overlord, Tetric, the Kraken King, and now Ursina, but in all four I've identified the same strain running through them." He shrugged again, not really sure that Aislinn was going to want to hear what he was thinking. "This strain of the Curse, which I believe can be tracked to the Ancient One ..."

Aislinn's eyes widened, already knowing what he had concluded. "Are you suggesting that the Ancient One is the source of the Curse? That the Dark Magic of the world that stands in opposition to the Talent comes from him?"

Bryen finally pulled his gaze away from the illusion blocking their way, smiling sadly as he looked at Aislinn, always taken by her beauty. "I'm not not suggesting it."

Aislinn stared at Bryen, her eyes narrowing. "That's not very helpful."

Bryen gave her a grin. "Sorry, but that's the best I can do right now. It's a theory, nothing more."

"You seem to think that it's more than just a theory," challenged Aislinn. "You wouldn't have raised it otherwise."

Bryen nodded. "I do, you're right. But I'd like to talk with Rafia first. Get more of her input. From what she told me when I was training with her and Sirius at Haven, she spent a good bit of time when she was younger studying the Ancient One and the power that he wielded. If anyone is in a position to mold my suspicions into more than just a theory, it's her."

"Fair enough," Aislinn said. "We can talk more about this later."

"Sounds good."

"Now can you get us past this barrier? I'm worried about trying because of the Curse running through it. And we still have some Fiends to kill."

"You're right. We do." Bryen turned and stared at the image of the stone wall for quite some time. Finally, he nodded. "I can. But you need to be aware of something."

"What's that? You're worried about the Curse that was used to create this deception?"

"No, I think I can manage that," Bryen replied honestly, not a hint of arrogance in his voice. "As I said, your uncle's wife is the source of the Curse in the Shadow Keep and the city."

"I understand, and I don't disagree with you." Aislinn scrunched up her face as she thought about the implications of what Bryen had just said, and then she nodded knowingly. "Do you think Kendric knows?"

Bryen shrugged. "I couldn't say. Although I think based on what you told me with respect to his health that she's been using the Curse on him."

"Why would she do that?" Aislinn demanded. She didn't want to believe it. She couldn't refute it, however. Not after spending time with Kendric and watching him struggle through several strange and concerning episodes that hinted that Bryen had the right of it. "I understand there's more to Ursina than meets the eye, but she seems to really love him."

"I don't know," Bryen replied. "That's one question we still need to answer. And she might be the only one who can tell us."

Aislinn nodded, promising herself that she would get that answer. "So what do I need to be aware of?"

"That when I do this, it will probably alert your aunt. This is her work. I'm certain of that. It has the same signature as the power she attempted to use on me when we were talking."

"She'll know that we're here," Aislinn murmured quietly. She wasn't surprised and it didn't bother her if Ursina became aware of what they were doing. It simply meant that she could get the answers that she wanted sooner rather than later. A confrontation was inevitable. Why delay?

"She'll know that we're here," Bryen confirmed.

"You think she might try to take more direct action against us?"

"I think she already has," Bryen replied.

"The Fiends." If what Bryen was insinuating was correct, then it only made sense.

"The Fiends," Bryen agreed. "Simply more confirmation when added to the strain of power within the barrier in front of us that points directly toward the creature that's really seeking to exercise power in Shadow's Reach and then beyond."

"She's not only a Dark Magus," mused Aislinn, "but also a servant of the Ancient One."

"That would stand to reason," Bryen agreed, "and that changes the equation somewhat."

"You're worried that I won't do what's necessary if we need to fight her?" Aislinn's tone came across as a challenge, as if she couldn't quite believe that Bryen was making such a suggestion.

"No, not in the least," Bryen replied. "My worry is that if we engage in a combat with her, and we defeat her ..."

"How do I deal with my uncle?"

"Right. She's touched him with the Curse. You know what that means."

"I do," she replied sadly. Once touched by the Curse, nothing could be done. The Curse would work its way through Kendric. Consume him. Ensure that he served the Curse rather than the other way around. "A worry for another time. What we face now is more important."

Bryen expected just such a reply. "I thought that you would say that."

Placing his hand against the stone wall, Bryen called upon the power contained within the Seventh Stone. The ancient artifact was already awake within him, sensing the energy that was within Bryen's grasp, interested in exploring it.

Bryen had never asked to join with the Seventh Stone. It had happened once when he was a child by mistake and then again when Aislinn passed the test to become a Magus. He had remained outside the Aeyrie, trying to prevent the Ghoules and Elders that were hunting them from interfering.

He would have died if Sirius hadn't called upon the power of the Seventh Stone. And, for quite a while after the artifact had joined with him, he thought that perhaps it would have been better if he had died.

Because though the Seventh Stone did, indeed, offer access to a great deal of power, that power came with an immense amount of risk and responsibility.

A fate worse than death if he didn't master the energy available to him fast enough.

The Seventh Stone functioned as an amplifier. The artifact strengthened a thousandfold the power that an individual could employ, whether the Talent or the Curse. It was also a reliquary, having the capacity to hold an immense amount of energy, again either the Talent or the Curse, or both.

Two distinct capacities, yet linked, which meant that when the Seventh Stone joined with Bryen, it had not only saved his life but also transferred its properties to him.

"Do I have to kill you now?"

That phrase passed quickly through his mind as he prepared to remove the illusion. It had been Rafia's favorite question for quite some time. A private joke between them, as they were both concerned about the same threat. Yet a promise as well, the Magus standing ready to kill him if he ever made a mistake and allowed the Curse to touch him.

Since Bryen had become the Seventh Stone and assumed its qualities, he had taken in a great deal of the Curse. Unavoidably while fighting the Ghoule Overlord and his Elders.

Thankfully, with the assistance of the Ten Magii, he had learned how to ensure that tainted power never touched him, and in the end he had mastered the skill required to rebuild the Weir, knitting together both the Talent and the Curse into an unbreakable bond.

Now, having learned how to function as the Seventh Stone, he had little to fear from the Curse, even the original strain that had been woven throughout the image of the stone wall that he needed to break through.

Comfortable and confident in his own abilities, Bryen sent a thin stream of energy into the illusion. For several seconds, nothing happened. The Talent pressing without any real effect against what appeared to be a stone wall.

Slowly a small bulge appeared exactly where Bryen was applying the Talent. Then deeper still, the image warping because of the consistent pressure.

There was a moment of resistance, no more than a few heartbeats, the Curse mixed in with the deception pushing back. Defending itself.

Yet once the Curse realized that it could not stand against the pressure Bryen was applying, the tainted power shifted its strategy, seeking to use the Talent that Bryen was employing as a pathway to connect to him. To corrupt him.

Having more experience with the Curse than he cared to admit, Bryen anticipated just such a play.

And he was ready for it, because that was the sign that he was looking for. That one moment of weakness on the part of the Curse.

Just a few breaths after that, it was done. The Seventh Stone latched onto the energy used to create the deception, both the Talent and the Curse. Refusing to let go, Bryen drained the energy from the illusion, pulling it into the artifact, into him, until the image faded away.

His work revealed a long passageway lit by a thick layer of luminescent green moss that led away from the cavern.

"Are you all right?" asked Aislinn, reaching out a hand and placing it on Bryen's forearm, worried about her Protector. Remembering some of the struggles he faced when first coming up against the Curse.

"I'm fine," he replied, patting her hand with his own. "You have nothing to worry about."

And she didn't. The Seventh Stone within him had taken in the Talent and the Curse without issue, without complaint, relishing the brief infusion of power while ensuring the Curse didn't touch him. Having done it so many times before, he had mastered the skill.

"With you I always have something to worry about," she murmured, giving him a mischievous smile and a wink.

"Why do I put up with you?" Bryen asked quietly, almost to himself, although loud enough for Aislinn to hear.

"Because you couldn't survive without me," Aislinn replied as she allowed the spheres of light to wink out, no longer needing the additional illumination. "Come on."

She started walking down the tunnel, Bryen following just a few steps behind her.

He didn't bother to respond to her comment, not wanting to give her the satisfaction of knowing that she spoke the truth. Instead, he extended his senses with the Talent.

"I'm having a hard time locating the Fiends."

"You lost them?" Aislinn didn't believe that was possible.

Bryen shook his head. "No, I know they're just up ahead. But they're shielded."

"Shielded how?" They only had ten more yards before they reached the end of the tunnel, an even brighter glow of green emanating through the roughly cut doorway that was just up ahead.

"Not so much shielded as hidden."

"You're the Seventh Stone. How could Fiends hide from you?"

"I don't know that they're hiding so much as they're in a space where there is so much of the Curse that they simply blend in with it."

Aislinn stopped upon hearing that, the entrance now just a few feet to their front. "That doesn't sound promising."

"It wasn't meant to be."

"So be ready for anything," Aislinn grumbled.

"Just as always," Bryen replied.

With a nod to one another, they stepped through the doorway, the blades on the Spear of the Magii and Aislinn's sword glowing brightly at the touch of the Talent.

They only advanced a few feet beyond the entrance before they stopped, fearing a trap.

The large chamber was roughly cut, the stone along the wall jagged and sharp. As if a monstrous claw had reached beneath the mountain upon which the Shadow Keep had been built and torn out a large handful of rock.

There didn't appear to be anything in the hall except at the far end. What looked to be a large cauldron chiseled out of the stone that was supported by three legs.

They couldn't get a good look from where they were standing, although the bubbles of black popping just above the rim were visible.

"Were you expecting this?" asked Aislinn.

Her eyes swept back and forth over what was in front of her, taking Bryen's warning to heart. The Fiends were here. She didn't doubt that. It was just a matter of where they might be hiding.

"Actually, I didn't know what to expect."

They both took a few steps farther into the chamber. "Could that be the reason why you can't locate the Fiends?" Aislinn nodded in the direction of the cauldron.

"It likely is, yes," Bryen confirmed.

Before they could end their speculation and get a closer look at the bubbling black, a shadow emerged from between the legs supporting the cauldron, that shadow revealing itself to be a Fiend as the monster shifted swiftly to its corporeal form.

The creature shrieked in rage then sprinted across the chamber with a surprising speed, needing only a half-dozen steps to close with Bryen and Aislinn, claws seeking to rip into their flesh.

The gleam in the Fiend's black eyes suggested that the monster believed that it had two easy kills. Aislinn dissuaded her attacker of that assumption in an instant.

Ready for the assault, she stepped forward to meet the Fiend's advance, swinging her blazing sword in a two-handed slice from her left shoulder to her right knee.

If she had connected with the Fiend, she would have sliced the beast open from chest to groin. But no such luck.

The Fiend demonstrated a unique agility, turning its body so that its chest was parallel to the floor as it leapt over her blade. At the same time, the Fiend stuck out one clawed foot as it hurtled through the air, targeting Aislinn's face.

Aislinn pivoted at the very last moment, avoiding the talon that missed her throat by a hair. She continued her lightning-fast motion, keeping her elbows tight to her body to increase the speed of her slash, cutting across the back of the Fiend's other leg.

The Fiend hissed in agony as the blazing steel cut into its body, the use of the Talent preventing the monster from turning into the mist that would have allowed it to avoid the painful slice.

Caught by surprise and thrown off balance, the Fiend crashed into the back wall, smacking into the stone with its shoulder and head. Screeching in fury, the Fiend was back on its feet in a flash, hungry to kill the human who had harmed it. Yet worried as well. Struggling to stay erect because of the wound inflicted upon it.

Aislinn stood just a few yards away from the Fiend, her eyes blazing just as brightly as her sword. Ready for the combat.

Looking forward to it. Having no doubt that she could destroy this monster.

It was just a matter of having the patience to find another opening.

This monster from the Spirit World clearly had underestimated her, and that didn't bother her in the least. In fact, she planned on making it pay the ultimate price for that mistake.

Instead of going to Aislinn's aid when the Fiend launched itself at her, trusting in her abilities Bryen turned to his left, the blades of the Spear of the Magii flaring to life as he sliced through the space right in front of him.

The other Fiend thought that it could hide in the chamber because of the tremendous amount of the Curse that pervaded the space. The monster misjudged, however, not knowing that Bryen's senses and instincts had been honed to a razor's edge thanks to the decade he spent fighting on the white sand.

Catching the hint of movement to his side, Bryen slashed, his steel a streak of light, wanting to get in the first strike. And he did.

The Fiend hoped to take him unawares while its partner attacked. It didn't work out as the monster planned.

Caught out, the Fiend hissed in pain as it tried and failed to dodge out of the way of Bryen's attack, the blazing steel cutting across its midsection.

When the Fiend looked up again after studying the wound that it had taken, it saw standing before it a sight that it had never expected to see. The human appeared confident and completely unafraid, that blasted double-bladed spear of his twirling slowly in front of him, almost mesmerizingly so as the human shifted the haft from one hand to the other. Waiting for the Fiend to make the next move. Unconcerned by whatever it might attempt.

The Fiend had invaded the Natural World several times before. Although the last incursion had been long, long ago.

Then, the kills had been easy, its adversaries never getting in a strike, most just running when they saw it. If they saw it. What was supposed to be a fight quickly devolving into a chase, which appealed to the Fiend.

A kill was a kill.

And the easier the better.

Now, for the first time, the Fiend faced a real challenge, never expecting a human to have the courage or the capacity to stand against it.

Before the Fiend could launch its next attack, Bryen glided toward the beast, his spear slashing through the air with such speed that his assault appeared to be no more than streaks of light cutting through the green luminescence.

The Fiend lunged at Bryen several times, then realized that doing so was futile. The monster had no chance of forcing its way past the blazing steel much less escaping it.

Wounded, its flesh still burning because of the touch of the Talent, the Fiend sought to stay clear of those deadly blades, scrambling away from the human as best as it could, having no choice but to retreat toward the cauldron.

On the other side of the chamber, Aislinn demonstrated her mastery of her blade, slashing and slicing, ensuring that the Fiend that had charged at her, hobbling badly on its wounded leg, could only focus on her. The Fiend desperate to avoid another touch of her blazing steel.

The Fiends were fast. Incredibly fast.

In Aislinn's opinion, faster even than a Slayer. Nevertheless, she was calm and confident. She had gained the upper hand in her combat, and she refused to relinquish it.

That required that she maintain a consistent attack so that the Fiend couldn't slip past her. And she did that with a grim determination, slowly but surely maneuvering the Fiend exactly where she wanted the monster.

Pushed up against the wall, its gleaming black eyes revealed a rising concern, the Fiend not liking how the lack of space limited its movement. Hating that reality when Aislinn's cuts began to slice into its substance with greater regularity.

Nothing as debilitating as the initial wound across the back of the monster's leg. Even so, certainly enough to irritate the beast. To anger it. To drive the reason from its brain. Which was exactly what Aislinn wanted.

Enraged to be put in such a position by a human, the Fiend shrieked in fury. No longer able to contain itself, the monster lunged.

The Fiend's claws missed her cheek by no more than a knuckle.

A close call.

But she needed to take the risk.

Because now the Fiend was open to her counterattack.

With a quick flick of her wrist, she slid her blade through the creature's arm pit, the point sticking out beneath the other shoulder, spitting the monster like a pig.

The Fiend, stuck on the blazing steel, could do nothing more than shriek in agony, its strength disappearing, dying slowly, its flesh flaking off until there was nothing more than a pile of ash at Aislinn's feet.

Having won her combat, she turned to aid Bryen, ready to join the fight. Instead, she held back.

Her clash against the Fiend was fairly straightforward. His was anything but.

Just as she had done, Bryen had forced the Fiend where he wanted the creature to go, backing the monster deeper within the chamber. Even so, this last Fiend played a smarter game than its dead brethren.

The Fiend kept its physical form some of the time, attacking with its claws. Even trying to bite Bryen's flesh. And then in just a breath the Fiend transformed back into a cloud of black, swirling through the air, attempting to break free from the combat.

A good ploy against some other opponent perhaps.

But not against her Protector.

Bryen refused to allow the Fiend to slip away, his Talent-infused blades ensuring that his adversary couldn't get past him regardless of the form it took.

Just as Aislinn had done, Bryen maintained a steady attack. Cutting away at the Fiend, whether flesh or mist, wounding the monster more than a dozen times. Striving for that killing blow.

When Aislinn approached from behind, she took up a position to ensure that the Fiend in its ethereal form couldn't escape the snare Bryen set for the monster.

Recognizing the trap, the Fiend howled in rage, backing up against the rim of the cauldron.

The Fiend scraped at the air a few times with its claws to demonstrate its rage and to keep its attackers away from it, but both Bryen and Aislinn knew that was more for show than anything else.

The monster didn't stand a chance against them both, and the Fiend knew it.

Bryen could see it in the Fiend's eyes. The resignation and anger mixing together and revealing its shock at not achieving the kills required of it. Its disbelief that a human was getting the best of the combat.

With a final shriek of anger, the Fiend leapt above the cauldron. While still in the air, the monster transformed into a cloud of mist, those streaks of whispery black not trying to get past Bryen and Aislinn, but rather shooting down into the roiling black liquid contained within the stone cauldron.

A silence settled within the chamber then, the only noise coming from the frothing black.

Despite the calm and the quiet, they waited for several

minutes. They wanted to ensure that there weren't any more Fiends waiting for them, hidden within the essence of evil that smothered the chamber.

Bryen searched around them several times with the Seventh Stone, finding nothing that gave him any cause for concern.

Yet even after Bryen confirmed that, still they waited. Sensing that the conflict in this secret chamber had not yet concluded. That it had only just begun.

Bryen had no doubt that Ursina was aware of where they were and what they had done.

Would she come for them here or did she have some other play in mind?

Increasingly confident that Ursina wasn't going to challenge them, the silence deepening, Bryen stepped closer to the cauldron, Aislinn staying with him.

"Do you remember what Rafia was telling us day before last?" Bryen asked.

"You think this is it? What was used in Ballinasloe by Roosarian?"

"It stands to reason, don't you think?"

Aislinn nodded. The intense essence of the Curse swirling in the cauldron put her on edge, her stomach feeling as if she had drunk curdled milk.

The Magus had received a vial of black liquid from Talia Carlomin. After Rafia's analysis, she had reached out to Bryen and Aislinn, explaining that the vile fluid had been used to create the Stalkers. Based on what she had told them, it was likely the same liquid they were staring at.

Aislinn and Bryen gave each other the same, knowing look. Simply additional confirmation that Ursina was the cause of many of the problems in the Territories.

The most obvious her being the maker of the Stalkers. And,

based on what Bryen had learned with respect to the Curse, and then confirmed with the appearance of the Fiends, most likely done at the urging of her master.

The Ancient One.

5

EVERYONE DIES

Davin swung the steel spike in his left hand with all the strength he had left. It wasn't much based on his usual standards, though it proved to be enough. At least this time. The sharp edge sliced across the forearm of the Stalker that reached for him, a splatter of blood splashing across him and the wall at his back.

The monster stumbled back a few feet, roaring more in anger and surprise than in pain.

Davin was happy with his strike even as he struggled to stay on his feet. He couldn't enjoy his small victory for long, however, because he couldn't press the beast like he wanted to.

The Stalker just to the right of the one he had struck decided to make use of the space that appeared, lunging for him, razor-sharp claw shooting through the gloom.

The Stalker should have ripped out Davin's throat with that swipe.

Davin was slower than he ever had been before, his many wounds sapping his vigor and his agility. Nevertheless, he still could rely on the anticipation that had proven so important to him during his time fighting on the white sand, calling upon his preternatural sense of what his opponents were going to do to save himself.

Relying on his instincts, Davin pivoted to the side.

The Stalker's claw shot past him by no more than a hair, a sharp nail catching on his ragged, bloody shirt and ripping off a long strand of the stained fabric.

Davin grinned, hearing the satisfying crunch when the bones in the Stalker's claw broke against the wall. He didn't take the time to savor the monster's shriek of pain and surprise.

Instead, he cut it off.

With the Stalker leaning in so close to him that he could smell its rancid breath, Davin didn't even have to adjust his positioning. He simply punched up with the steel spike in his right hand, driving the sharp tip up and through the monster's bottom jaw and into its brain.

The Stalker became a dead weight in a heartbeat. Not wanting to be burdened by the corpse, Davin ripped the spike free and nudged the falling body with his hip, at the same time turning to face the Stalker he had wounded just seconds before.

The injured Stalker growled, then lifted its forearm to its fang-filled maw. Its long, pink tongue sliding out from between its jaws, the Stalker slurped greedily at its own blood.

"Really," grunted Davin, his stomach souring in an instant. "You had to do that?" The Stalker grinned, revealing its fangs. Roaring in anticipation of the kill, the monster leapt forward, right claw reaching for Davin's throat.

Understanding his current limitations, Davin sidestepped the attack. Bringing the steel spike in his left hand up vertically to the floor, he deflected the Stalker's claw.

Davin's blow wasn't very strong, but it took the monster completely by surprise, sending the creature stumbling toward the wall behind him.

It was Davin's turn to smile as the beast slid past him on his knees. He certainly was glad that he had found this small alcove. Knowing that he'd never be able to escape his pursuers, he had only one real option left. And it was the option that he preferred.

He couldn't flee.

But he could fight.

As soon as he'd found this more protected position, he'd turned to face his hunters. The alcove protected him from both sides and, because of its narrow width, only one of the beasts could come at him at a time.

Just as important, a narrow stream of light from a slit in the stone far above him turned the night to dusk, allowing him to better track the movements of his attackers.

Davin watched with an almost barbarous pleasure as the Stalker, unable to stop as it skidded across the floor on its knees, slammed face first into the stone wall, shattering several of its fangs and likely breaking many of the bones in its face. Although dazed, the monster already was tensing its shoulders to take another swing at Davin's midsection.

Before the beast could complete its motion, Davin stabbed the spike in his left hand through the back of the Stalker's neck.

After that, Davin heard nothing more than a sad whimper that slowly faded away. When silence once again descended around him, he pulled the steel spike free.

He stood there for a time. The Stalker crumpled at his feet, Davin took several deep breaths, trying to gather himself and calm his nerves. His entire body was trembling, the last of his energy slowly draining away.

If he was ever going to escape the Rock, now was the time. While the other hunters scurried about trying to locate him. Besides, he didn't have much left in him, having little doubt that his next combat would be his last.

Once he felt more under control, Davin lifted his head. Finally, he had a sense of where he was beneath the Rock.

If he turned to his left, he should be able to follow that corridor all the way back to the chamber where he and Talia watched the cowled woman create the Stalkers what seemed like years ago but was only days.

From there he could slip through the crevice in the wall that they had used to gain entry into the fortress and make it out to the beach.

He didn't want to think ahead any farther than that. If there wasn't a longboat waiting for him there on the shore or at the dock a few hundred yards farther down, he'd probably die on the sand.

That possibility really didn't bother him, however.

Better to die on the sand than in the dark.

Satisfied with his plan, Davin was about to step out of the alcove and turn to the left. He stopped with his foot still above the ground.

Only twenty yards down the corridor, breaking up the gloom, two sets of blood-red eyes fixed on him.

The pair of Stalkers had come upon him quietly. Apparently not feeling the need to shriek and scream like so many of their brethren did.

Clever.

Maybe they understood after following so many of their dead ilk to find him here that there was little that they could do to frighten him.

When the pair of monsters took a few steps closer before stopping again, Davin reluctantly allowed his plan to fade into the gloom like ash drifting away from a dying fire.

He could allow his disappointment over his attempted escape coming to an end bother him.

But what was the point?

Declan had taught him that hope was a fleeting thing. Besides, the Master of the Gladiators had always been ready and willing to remind him, more often than Davin cared to remember, that it was better not to trust in hope.

Better instead to trust in himself.

That memory brought a smile to Davin's bloody, cracked lips. Even now, he couldn't escape the person who had played such a pivotal role in his life, helping to mold him into the man that he had become.

While Davin fought in the Colosseum, he had fought for himself. That was true. He had to. Because if he hadn't, he would have died. Violently and swiftly.

He had taken as his own the objective that Declan had given him when he first set foot in the Pit.

To focus solely on his current combat.

To stay alive.

That was it.

He had also fought to make Declan proud. The Master of the Gladiators had invested so much in him because he cared about him, and Davin wanted to show Declan just how much he appreciated his efforts.

Davin smiled as he thought about that. Declan would never admit to the last part. But he wouldn't deny it either.

That conclusion widened Davin's smile even more.

He was in pain.

He was exhausted.

He struggled to lift his arms above his head.

His legs didn't want to listen to him anymore. As a result, he could barely run without falling flat on his face after taking only a few steps.

Yet none of that mattered.

The only thing that mattered in that moment as the two Stalkers prepared to advance toward him was another of Declan's sayings that chose that moment to run through Davin's mind on a continual loop.

"Everyone dies. Not everyone dies with honor."

Davin sighed. If there were truer words, he had yet to hear them.

He had wanted an adventure. He had been desperate to feel that rush of adrenaline through his veins that he craved after spending five years in the Pit.

And he had gotten it.

More than he bargained for actually. So if he was about to go to the other side, at least he had that.

Davin closed his eyes for a few seconds, the two Stalkers still not having rushed him. Instead just watching him. Curious. Waiting to see what he was going to do.

Making use of the extra time his adversaries gifted to him, Davin remembered his many combats on the white sand. The many times that he felt as he did now. And those many times when even though he felt as he did now, still he had walked off the sand rather than being dragged from it.

Opening his eyes again, his expression hardened. There was no emotion there. No feeling. Only purpose as he stared down the corridor at his next two opponents.

He realized then that there were more than a pair of Stalkers glaring at him. At least four of the monsters now.

No, he was wrong. Turning the corner fifty yards back. Another Stalker. So five in all and probably more on their way to join the fun.

So be it.

The odds were stacked against him, just the way he assumed that they would be.

And just the way that he preferred it.

The challenge Davin faced now might have terrified someone else. Who was he kidding? Pretty much anyone else who had not fought in the Pit.

But the five Stalkers crowding the corridor, flexing their claws, obviously looking forward to killing the prey that had eluded them for much too long, didn't bother him in the least.

Actually, his adversaries helped him as he sought to narrow his focus just as Bryen had taught him to do.

Blocking out everything else around him.

Ignoring what wasn't important.

What was only a distraction.

Honing his perspective.

Honing his mind.

With that effort came the welcome and necessary surge of adrenaline that he had savored so much while fighting in the Colosseum.

The power that came from his very core.

A strength of will that energized him in a way that nothing else could.

It pushed his pain to the side until it was no more than barely a whisper in the back of his brain.

That potency gave him a clarity that he could enjoy at no other time but then.

Everything around him appearing keener, even the dim figures of the Stalkers gaining substance and breaking away from the gloom.

Davin chuckled then, the raspy sound reverberating down the corridor. The Stalkers not understanding what he was doing and why.

They didn't comprehend that in just seconds Davin had become someone else.

He was no longer the hunted.

He was the hunter.

Because he was no longer Davin Noname.

He had become what he needed to be to walk off the white sand every single time he entered the Pit.

He remembered who he was now.

He remembered what he had done in the Colosseum.

He remembered that while fighting on the white sand, he would do anything that was required of him to survive.

Here, now, in the dark beneath the Rock, facing off against a fist of Stalkers, he was once again the Crimson Giant.

If he was going to lose this combat, he could accept that bitter truth. But he would gut as many of these beasts as he could before they gutted him.

One of Declan's favorite mantras played through his mind once again. Whispering into every facet of his consciousness.

Charging the potency already surging through his blood.

That he coveted.

That gave him a chance of success, no matter how slim.

"Everyone dies. Not everyone dies with honor."

Davin had no doubt that he was going to die in this dark corridor. But he would do so with honor. He would make Declan proud.

Flexing his fingers before gripping his steel spikes tightly, a low growl emanating from deep within his chest, the Crimson Giant began walking slowly down the darkened hallway toward the Stalkers.

After just five steps he was up to a trot, the monsters just twenty yards away. Still not having moved. Still not comprehending why their prey was coming toward them rather than running away.

In five more steps, the Crimson Giant was screaming in rage, sprinting through the gloom, steel spikes at the ready, already stained by Stalker blood and eager for even more.

6

SOURCE OF THE CURSE

R afia had been quite adamant while speaking with Bryen and Aislinn. If they located the source of the pernicious liquid, then at all costs they had to destroy it. There was no other way to ensure the demise of the Stalkers.

"Do you think that you cleanse it?"

"Cleanse it?" asked Bryen, giving Aislinn a brief look of confusion.

"Yes, cleanse it."

"You mean like what I did with the help of the Ten Magii to build the Weir?"

"Yes, exactly that."

"That's a good question." Bryen took a few seconds to think about Aislinn's suggestion.

"I thought so," Aislinn said with a bright smile and a nudge of her shoulder against his. "Although I'm not suggesting you try it if the risk is too great. I don't know how what we're looking at now compares to what you had to work with in the Sanctuary."

She knew how hard it was for him to maintain control over

the Curse when it resided within him as part of the Seventh Stone. He had mastered the skill only after almost being consumed by that evil power and turned toward its malignant purposes. So she really didn't want Bryen to test himself again if doing so put him at risk.

"From what I've learned it comes down to intention."

Aislinn nodded, remembering that they had engaged in a similar conversation not so long ago. "Intention is a key part of the application of power. You would need to shift the intention of that power. Correct?"

"Yes, I would. You're right." Bryen stared at the swirling black, trying to discern a rhythm to the liquid's motion, after just a few seconds giving up. The roil within the cauldron was nothing more than chaos. There was no way to identify a pattern because there wasn't one. Of course, upon thinking about it some more, that only made sense when it came to the Curse.

"Can you?"

"I don't know. And I'm not sure that I want to try."

"Adopting a cautious approach," Aislinn replied. "I'm impressed. Finally a display of common sense rather than charging toward every challenge and trying to find the solution on the fly."

"I don't know if I should take that as a compliment or as an insult." Bryen's eyes were still locked onto the boiling liquid.

"As a compliment," Aislinn confirmed. "Clearly."

"Funny." Bryen barked out a brief laugh, finally tearing his gaze away from the roiling black. "Humor at a time like this doesn't become you."

"Now who's being funny?" Aislinn replied, nudging him with her shoulder again. This time hard enough to force him to reset himself in front of the cauldron.

"You're complaining about me acting more like Davin yet

now you're acting more like Lycia, trying to get a rise out of me."

"I don't know whether I should take that as a compliment or an insult."

"I'm sure you'll figure it out," Bryen assured her, working hard to keep a straight face.

"Point taken," Aislinn said. "If cleansing what's in front of us is a dangerous proposition, how would we go about trying to destroy it? The Seventh Stone?"

"Perhaps," Bryen murmured, "although I'm not entirely sure. I never had a chance to discuss that with Rafia. Not enough time." Then he nodded, his brow furrowing as an idea came to him. "However, I know someone who might be able to help."

"Is that wise? As you said, Ursina likely knows that we're here. We might not have much time."

"True. Nevertheless, having a little help wouldn't hurt if we come up against her." Bryen shrugged, once again looking at the boiling black, finding it hard to take his eyes away from the churning liquid. "And I don't think we need to worry about your aunt. She hasn't made a move in our direction yet. She's still in her suite with your uncle."

Aislinn nodded at that, thinking about Bryen's argument, unable to poke any holes in his logic. "If that's the case, then let's get to it. I feel like a sitting duck down here."

Bryen went to work immediately, because he agreed with Aislinn's assessment. They were vulnerable until they destroyed the source of the Curse.

Using the Talent, he called forth Viktor Keldragan from the Seventh Stone. The spirit that took shape next to him looked much like Bryen. The only real distinction being the Magus' lack of scars and not a hint of white in his hair.

Bryen's uncle was the Magus most responsible for ensuring that the first Weir was constructed before the Ghoule Legions could invade Caledonia a thousand years before. Of course that had required a sacrifice that most others wouldn't have been willing to make.

Viktor and the Ten Magii had given their lives without a second thought, refusing to allow the Curse to turn them into monsters more terrible than the Ghoule Overlord.

The spirit didn't say a word once he appeared, his gaze immediately drawn to the pool of boiling black.

"The Curse made tangible," the Magus whispered after more than a minute passed.

"Yes, unfortunately so," Bryen confirmed. "There's more to it than just that, however."

The spirit of the Magii stared a bit longer at the fluid, his forehead crinkling, mirroring Bryen's expression. He reached for the Talent so that he could gain a better sense of the churning pitch. His eyes widened in shock.

"It seems, nephew, that you simply move from one fairy tale to the next."

"But this isn't a fairy tale."

"No, it's not, I'm sorry to say. It's all too real."

"The Ancient One is real," Bryen said quietly.

"He is," Viktor confirmed. "The Order had hoped that he would never touch the Natural World again. Foolish thinking on our part." He shook his head sadly. "It seems that we put too much faith in hope rather than thinking about how the Ancient One would seek to get around the limitations placed upon him by the Spirit World."

"This is how the Ancient One touches the Natural World?" asked Aislinn.

Viktor nodded. "It seems so. These repositories of the Curse. There was one in the Lost Land, but we don't need to go into all that. You know it. You lived it. I assume you've figured out the rest?"

"That the Ancient One used the Curse to mold the people

once living in the Lost Land into the Ghoules?" asked Bryen, although the question wasn't really a question. "Yes, we assumed as much."

"And it seems much the same is happening here," Viktor said, "although it appears to be in its emergent stages."

"So we can do something about it?" asked Aislinn. "Prevent the Ancient One from gaining a grip on the Northern Territory?"

"We can try, yes."

"You don't seem all that confident," prodded Aislinn.

"I just feel the need to be wary," explained Viktor. "The Ghoule Overlord was a dangerous creature. The Kraken King that you two faced in the Jagged Islands just as dangerous, if not more so. But the Ancient One ..." Viktor took a moment to decide how he wanted to say what he needed to say. "There is nothing that compares to the Ancient One. The evil contained within him. The evil that he can employ. What he is willing to do to achieve his ends. He is a monster in the truest sense of the word. A rapacious creature interested only in feeding his own needs and desires."

"That sounds much like some of the other servants of the Curse that we've come up against."

"True," Viktor admitted. "However, Bryen, when it comes to the Ancient One, you need to think about scale. The goals are always the same, but the capacity differs."

"Meaning, for example, if we compared the Ancient One to the Ghoule Overlord ..."

Viktor turned away from the roiling black, locking eyes with Aislinn. "The Ancient One controls a corrosive power that's a thousandfold more potent than that manipulated by the Ghoule Overlord. The Ghoule Overlord and Kraken King and whatever other creatures there are in the Realms that we have yet to come across who have tied themselves to the Ancient One are no more than his vassals. Children. Novices in the application of the Curse. Tools for his use. No more than that."

"That doesn't give me a good feeling about what we need to do," Bryen murmured softly.

"It shouldn't," Viktor confirmed.

"Then how did you succeed in trapping him in the Spirit World?" Aislinn asked.

"We didn't," admitted Viktor, Aislinn and Bryen knowing that he was referring to the Order of the Magii. "His brother did."

"His brother?" Aislinn had never heard this part of the story.

"Yes, his brother."

"How do you know so much about him?" Aislinn pulled her eyes away from the corrosive liquid, not an easy thing to do, fixing her sharp gaze on the Magus instead. "Did you study the Ancient One while you were at Haven?"

"In part," admitted Viktor, the hazy figure of the Magus flickering a bit, Aislinn assuming that it was because of the emotions that were passing across his face. Disappointment primarily. In himself perhaps. "Also because I knew him. We were friends once. Before he chose a path that corrupted him completely."

"You were friends?" Aislinn was shocked, not quite believing what she was hearing.

"We were. You need to keep in mind that the Ancient One wasn't always the Ancient One. He became the Ancient One because he couldn't help himself. He couldn't stop himself from pursuing knowledge that was better left alone."

"What else can you tell us about him?" asked Aislinn.

Viktor smiled fondly, caught in a memory. Then his expression hardened, all the other memories relating to the Magus who had become the Ancient One taking its place.

"Marcus Blackgard became the Ancient One. He was skilled

in the Talent. In fact, he was the most powerful Magus of his time. My time. Likely of all time. I was newer to the Order, but we became friends. I didn't realize upon meeting him that he had already started down a path from which there was no return. Had been on that path for quite a long time, in fact, hiding his true self."

"Blackgard?" asked Aislinn. "He was a Lord of Skaffa Falls?"

"He was," Viktor confirmed. "We don't need to or have the time to go into what happened to that Kingdom, how the Valley of the Dead came to be and the role that was forced upon the Blackgards and their Sentinels that they continue to perform to this very day – all because of Marcus -- but it is worth mentioning that when he began his quest, he did so with the highest of purposes."

"How do you mean?" asked Bryen.

"Marcus didn't seek the Curse. He didn't desire the power offered by the Curse. He simply traveled down a path that he shouldn't have, looking for new ways to employ the Talent. In fact, in my conversations with him, he was seeking a way to eliminate the Curse entirely."

"The Curse existed before the Ancient One?" asked Bryen. "I was under the impression that the Ancient One is the source of the Curse."

"He is," Viktor confirmed. "But the Curse existed before him. It was always there. Always a counterpart to the Talent. Just not as strong then as it is today."

"Then how could he be the source?"

"At that time, none of the Magii had made the mistake of seeking to tame the Curse. They knew what it was. That it existed. But they stayed away from it. That meant the Curse had very few tools to work with."

"Marcus didn't," nodded Bryen, beginning to understand.

"He didn't. Because he believed that he could do what he wanted to do. Because he was the strongest Magus to ever live, he believed that he could eliminate the Curse entirely. Playing right into the desires of the Curse."

"Arrogant and foolish," nodded Bryen.

"His heart was in the right place," Viktor sighed, "but you're right. Arrogant and foolish."

"What went wrong?" prodded Aislinn.

"Exactly what you would expect to go wrong."

"He believed that because he was the strongest of the Magii that he could manipulate the Curse without fear," Bryen murmured quietly. "His arrogance did him in. He made a mistake."

"Exactly so, lad. Marcus was a good person, but he didn't believe that he could make a mistake. He had an undying conviction in his own abilities. And it was for that reason that he failed."

"Combining the greatest Magus to ever live with the Curse was a bad combination," offered Bryen.

"Indeed it was," agreed Viktor. "Marcus realized what was happening to him while he was experimenting. He tried to help himself, believing he could solve this challenge on his own." The spirit sighed heavily. "He couldn't. When I tried to help him, it was already too late."

"Just one touch," murmured Aislinn.

"Correct, lass. That one touch was all it took. With that one touch the Curse had him."

"Did he try to fight it?" wondered Bryen.

"He did," Viktor replied, a trace of sadness in his voice.

"He didn't succeed."

"He didn't, lad. Nothing he tried worked. At that first touch of the Curse, Marcus was lost. He began to change almost immediately. The Curse taking him. Hungry for the victim that was so necessary to its success. Making him its own. Marcus didn't realize it, but it was obvious to me and several others. What he began doing with the power he controlled, he began doing because of the Curse. That evil essence was changing him. As you know, power and intention are inextricably linked. Marcus gained more power than anyone could imagine, yet he lost the ability to determine how that power would be employed."

"We just spoke about power and intention," confirmed Aislinn.

"It's a worthwhile conversation to have," Viktor agreed. "But I think in this story, the lesson is clear."

"Be satisfied with what you have," Aislinn replied quietly. "Don't allow your desire for more to rule you."

"I couldn't have said it better myself," replied Viktor. "Regardless of Marcus' original intention, no matter how high-minded it was, the simple fact is that Marcus' desire to do good, to destroy the Curse, was irrelevant. What he did, he did for himself. Despite having the best of intentions, Marcus couldn't help himself. Once he got a taste of the Curse and what it could do for him, he thirsted for it. As more of that tainted power became a part of him, he changed. Drastically and irrevocably."

"He became the Ancient One."

"He did, Aislinn. He became a tool of the Curse. A conduit. And, in a very real sense, the merger between the power that he controlled and that of the Curse, it's fair to say that he indeed is the source of the Curse, because all of the threats against the Realms that have come from the Curse since Marcus became the Ancient One begin with him. It's because of him that the Curse has been able to pick and probe, identifying weaknesses and opportunities within the Realms and then seeking to exploit them."

"An overarching enemy, in a sense," suggested Bryen.

"Just so," agreed Viktor. "I won't bore you with all that happened at Skaffa Falls, the sacrifice that Henry Blackgard made to trap his brother in the Spirit World before Marcus could conquer the Natural World. But it was because of Henry that the Natural World has been free of the Ancient One's touch for more than a millennium. Or at least as free as it can be, since so long as there is the Talent there will always be the Curse."

"How did Henry do it?" asked Bryen, curious, wondering if what Viktor might be able to tell him would prove useful with respect to his current dilemma.

"A little subterfuge and a weapon the Order of the Magii commissioned from the Giants of the Rime."

"The Blood Dagger and the Blood Ruby," Aislinn offered, confident in her reply, recalling one of her lessons with Sirius.

"Correct. Henry tricked his brother, getting him where he could best use those weapons to imprison the Ancient One in the Spirit World."

"But apparently for only so long," prodded Aislinn.

"Nothing lasts forever," Viktor confirmed.

"No, it doesn't," Aislinn agreed.

"Before I helped to craft the first Weir in response to the threat presented by the Ghoules," Viktor continued, "I was speaking with many of my colleagues in the Order of the Magii. It was obvious that Marcus, even though he was confined to the Spirit World, still had the capacity to touch the Natural World, although it was limited. He could not free himself from the Spirit World, but he could rely on intermediaries in the Natural World to do his work for him. Some of his servants able to travel through the Rip in the Veil."

"What did the Order do about that?" asked Aislinn.

"Not what we should have," Viktor replied. "They were so distracted by the Ghoules that they failed to see the larger picture. They didn't realize that the Ghoules were the symptom of a more virulent disease."

Bryen nodded then, understanding. "The Temple of the Ghoules was a repository for the power of the Ancient One just as this cauldron is."

"Well done, lad," Viktor said proudly. "Somehow, Marcus succeeded in placing these repositories of evil throughout the Realms. He believed that doing so would aid his efforts to destabilize the Realms and prepare the way for his return from the Spirit World."

"He would need the Blood Ruby and the Blood Dagger to do that, though, wouldn't he? His servants couldn't do that for him?"

"To rip the Veil entirely so that he could pass through? Yes, he would need to be the one to do it and he would need those specific artifacts," Viktor confirmed, pleased that Aislinn was already well ahead of him in the discussion. "Only Marcus has the power required to perform that act, in combination with the weapons crafted by the Giants of the Rime. But those two artifacts are missing. He's been waiting for his servants to find them. And when they do, he'll make use of the discord he's been sowing within the Realms. The weaker the Natural World is when he returns, the easier it will be for him to conquer it."

"He was succeeding in the Lost Land," said Aislinn. "He had taken the people who became the Ghoules for his own."

"Yes, and he's begun the same process to do that here," Viktor stated with a sharp nod. "It's just the start admittedly. But once the Curse takes hold in this land, it will be difficult to stop."

"Ursina is doing this," said Aislinn. "She's his servant here in New Caledonia."

"Who is Ursina?" asked Viktor.

"A Dark Magus. Do you know her?"

"No, but that's not all that surprising. She must have joined the Order after the First Ghoule War and I became a part of the Seventh Stone. Better to ask Rafia about that. She will know the more current history of the Order."

"We will," Aislinn promised.

"We can't allow the Curse to take hold here," Bryen said with an absolute finality.

"You can't," agreed Viktor.

"What needs to be done?"

"You know the first part already, nephew."

"Kill Ursina."

"A grim reality, but your reality nonetheless," Viktor nodded. "As you know, once touched by the Curse, you are the Curse. You obey the Curse. There is no way to escape the taint or what the Curse demands of you. And here, now, clearly when we are speaking of the Curse, we are speaking of the power of the Ancient One."

"And the second part?"

"Destroy this vile concoction," Viktor replied. "Ensure that no one else can make use of it. But you already knew that. Otherwise, you wouldn't have asked for my assistance."

"Any thoughts on how to do that?"

Viktor offered a suggestion. "Do you remember what you did while fighting the Golem in the Sanctuary?"

Bryen nodded. He would never forget that. The Ghoule Overlord had formed the Golem out of the Curse, giving his Dark Magic substance and life. The monster proved to be indestructible, until Bryen used the Seventh Stone against it.

"If he does as you suggest, does he have to worry about becoming corrupted himself?" Aislinn's worry was written all over her face. She knew that Bryen was quite skilled now in making use of the Seventh Stone, but she was concerned after listening to how the power of the Ancient One was a thousand times stronger than that of the Ghoule Overlord.

"That's a question for Bryen," Viktor replied. "Only he can answer it."

Bryen took his time before doing so, staring at the bubbling and roiling black. Finally, he nodded. "I can do it."

"Then I suggest you begin," Viktor urged. "The sooner this is done, the better."

Bryen didn't need to be told twice. Stepping up to the rim of the cauldron, ignoring the thin wisps of black that rose up from the pool because of his presence, the Curse reacting to the artifact that had joined with him, he called on the power contained within the Seventh Stone.

He welcomed the surge of warmth that flowed through him. However, before he could even think about attempting to draw the Curse now swirling around the cauldron into the Seventh Stone, the bubbling black became even more violent, swishing and swirling in a nauseating rhythm, drops of the Curse splashing over the rim.

Bryen stepped back a few feet, Aislinn moving behind him, neither understanding why the mixture was acting as it was.

Viktor remained in place, however, studying the pitch-black liquid that resembled the beginnings of a volcanic eruption. He turned quickly, some aspect of the churn worrying him.

"Bryen, you need to ..."

Viktor never got the rest of his words out, the spirit disappearing in a blast of black mist that exploded out of the cauldron and smothered the chamber.

Although Bryen wasn't quite ready to try his hand at destroying the Curse with the Seventh Stone, he was prepared to use the artifact for a more immediate and necessary purpose. Taking in the power gifted to him by the ancient artifact, a shimmering shield of white blinked into existence, protecting both him and Aislinn.

And just in time.

The powerful blast of the Curse sent Bryen and Aislinn flying backward, though the shield saved them from the worst of it. They landed heavily on the stone floor a dozen feet away from the cauldron, suffering only a few bruises.

Bryen pushed himself up a heartbeat after he hit the floor,

offering a hand to Aislinn and helping her to her feet. He released his hold on the power shared with him by the Seventh Stone when the diaphanous folds of the Curse that were all around him grudgingly retreated to the cauldron.

Taking a quick look around, Bryen and Aislinn confirmed that they were not under any immediate threat after the blast. Nevertheless, a key variable in the scene that had been playing out was gone.

Viktor Keldragan.

Bryen's connection to the Magus severed by the explosion of Dark Magic.

And, shockingly, in his place a new spirit had joined them in the chamber.

The figure was wrapped in a multicolored cloak, his hands hidden within the folds of his sleeves. That, in itself, wasn't remarkable. What was remarkable was that the spirit floated directly above the cauldron, the wisps of energy rising up from the boiling black and nourishing the phantom.

He wasn't as tall as Bryen. And his features appeared almost youthful in comparison, the whiskers on his cheeks a light brown. Yet the power that radiated from the spirit was unmistakable.

A Magus.

There was more to the spirit than just the fact that he was a Magus, however. Because there was one critical distinction with respect to the man who, after surveying the chamber, smiled down upon them warmly.

The intensity of his countenance.

His grin would have seemed welcoming, if not for the spirit's midnight black eyes that flashed like a lurking cobra's.

Clearly not just a Magus, they both realized.

More than a Magus.

A potentially unimaginable threat.

They would need to tread carefully.

"You are the one who I have been seeking," the spirit said, his gaze fixed on Bryen. His voice was melodic, almost as if he had trained as a singer when he was younger.

"Me?"

"Of course you. You are the Seventh Stone, are you not?"

"How can you tell?"

The spirit floating above the now still liquid that had solidified into a black ice laughed heartily at Bryen's question. "How can I not? The power you have at your beck and call truly is astounding. I can feel it surging within you, wanting to be set free."

"You seem quite sure of that," replied Bryen, a hint of a challenge in his tone.

"What I say is, young man. Best that you remember it."

Before Bryen could ask what the Magus was talking about, the spirit turned his gaze toward Aislinn. "And you, young lady, are not too far behind the young man in terms of the power you can manage with the Talent. Truly impressive."

"Are you ..." While Bryen had engaged with the spirit, Aislinn had been trying to determine who the figure floating above them was.

She thought she knew. Only one possibility really made sense. But she was having a difficult time fitting together the image that she had created in her own mind with the handsome young man standing before her.

"Marcus Blackgard?" asked the spirit. He smiled again, offering her a slight nod. "I am, yes."

"If you're Marcus, that means that you're ..."

Marcus nodded again, his furrowed brow revealing his embarrassment. "You know your history, young lady. Now I am truly impressed. So many have forgotten." Marcus pulled his hands free from his sleeves, held his arms out to the side, and offered Bryen and Aislinn a slight bow. "Yes, I am also known as the Ancient One. Although you should be aware that I did not pick that name for myself. Rather, those who sought to challenge me, who did not understand what I was doing for them, how I was making their lives better, did. From my perspective, an unfortunate and undeserved gift."

The Ancient One.

Neither Bryen nor Aislinn could quite believe that they were in the presence of such a notorious being. A creature purportedly able to freeze a man's heart with just a thought.

Yet based on where they were and why they were there, it all made sense in a horrifying kind of way. The spirit could be no one else.

Perhaps that's why Bryen and Aislinn were so astounded. Worried as well.

Instead of a ghoulish appearance, flashes of black energy sparking off his cloak, fangs instead of teeth, and a sinister glare, the Lord of the Spirit World resembled anyone who might have once been a member of the Order of the Magii.

Most jarring, their gazes kept getting drawn back to Marcus' pitch-black eyes.

More than just jarring upon second thought.

Threatening.

A promise of ill intent rested there. Only serving to make the image before them so dissonant and that much more difficult to accept.

Catching Aislinn's eye with a light touch on her arm, Bryen nodded toward the wall behind the Ancient One. She frowned.

A thin layer of ice covered the glowing green moss growing on the rough-cut stone. It was thickening by the second and spreading along the walls and the ceiling. That ice helped to lower the already chilly temperature in the chamber even more, Bryen and Aislinn's breaths now puffs of white moisture.

At the same time, behind the Ancient One threads of wispy grey tinged with black seeped out from his cloak, highlighting him in an almost ethereal light.

Perhaps Bryen and Aislinn were correct. Perhaps there was more to Marcus Blackgard than met the eye.

"You are not the only one I seek," the Ancient One continued, returning his focus to Bryen. Frowning. Disappointed for just a heartbeat. "You are not the Bearer. But you have a use to me still. As I said, I sense the power within you. You as well, young lady. You would both be assets in the work that I must do."

"You're getting ahead of yourself," Bryen replied. "Neither of us will be used by you. If you can sense the power in us, then you should be able to sense that as well."

"You both would challenge me?" The floating figure nodded as if he were amused. "That's very brave of you. Foolish as well."

"We will if we must," Bryen replied. "We do not shirk from what might be required of us."

"You know who I am, Protector. Do you not know what I can do?" asked the Ancient One. He smiled when he saw the brief flash of surprise in the back of Bryen's eyes that vanished just as quickly as it appeared. "Yes, I recognize the circlet. I know its meaning. I know what you are. And I know that you are more than just a Magus, just as I am."

He fixed his gaze on Aislinn. "And if you chose to work with me, my dear, I would ensure that you became more than a Magus as well. As I said, your strength in the Talent can only be exceeded by your Protector. If you both allowed me to help you, you could both become so much more than you already are. The restrictions of the Natural World would no longer apply to you. Think of all that you could do knowing that."

"You seem to think that we are much like you."

"No one else in this world, past or present, even in the future, can or ever will be like me. Don't flatter yourself, Protector." The Ancient One said it with a smile on his face, although his gritted teeth revealed his dislike at being challenged.

"Have no fear. I have no desire to be like you."

The Ancient One chuckled at that. "You say that now. Allow me to show you what it is that I can give you. How it will change you. Then you will desire nothing more than to be just like me. You will relish the power that I gift you. You will thank me for it. You need only show some courage. You need only decide to take the road that most others don't have the fortitude to take."

"Tempting, but I think not," replied Bryen. "I do not crave power. I crave peace."

"With power you can create peace for yourself, Protector. Think on that for a time."

"You were once a Magus," interrupted Aislinn. She saw how Bryen was flexing his fingers, a sign that he was losing interest in talking. Yet she was not yet ready to end the dialogue, hoping that she could extract more information that could be of use from the surprisingly voluble Ancient One before the conversation became a confrontation. "And now you're not?"

"Now I am not. But only because I find terms such as Magus limiting. So you are correct, Lady of the Southern Marches." The Ancient One smiled again, pleased that his knowledge surprised her. In fact, he knew more about her than she could possibly imagine. Yet he doubted that he would need to make use of that information in order to turn her, because he had yet to find anyone able to deny for long the gift he offered. "Now I am much more than a Magus. I am power made flesh."

"Actually, you mean spirit rather than flesh. Don't you?"

The Ancient One's black eyes flashed dangerously at the Protector's comment. Still, he succeeded in controlling his reaction.

"How is it that you made that happen?" prompted Aislinn, giving Bryen a look that told him not to push. She believed that for a little while longer she could play off the Ancient One's arrogance by stroking his ego. "It couldn't have been easy."

"I was chosen," the Ancient One replied simply, shifting his attention away from the Protector. "You see, I was quite different from the other Magii of my time. They were afraid. Bound by rules that had been in place for centuries. Rules that might have made sense at one time, but no longer did."

"You were willing to take risks that they were not," Bryen murmured.

"Indeed, Protector. How else are you supposed to learn, to grow, to become more than you ever thought you could be, if not by taking a risk from time to time." The Ancient One's eyes locked onto Bryen's. "But you already knew that, Protector." Bryen didn't reply. Even so, the Ancient One could see from the Protector's expression that he had struck a chord, and he chose to play it with the goal of bringing him under his sway.

"No matter what anyone else might believe, no matter what the histories say about me, the truth is that I had an insatiable desire to learn the truth of the world. Because of that, I was chosen. Because of that, I did learn the truth. I learned more than I could have ever possibly imagined. Wouldn't the both of you care to learn more about those truths rather than being trapped by ignorance?"

Aislinn and Bryen took a few steps away from one another, the blades of their weapons coming to life with the Talent in response to the sparks of black that had begun to dance across the Ancient One's robes as his excitement grew. They didn't know what to make of it, although both assumed it couldn't be good. Therefore, they wanted to be ready.

The Ancient One had yet to do anything threatening. However, that didn't mean he wouldn't. Therefore, Bryen stood ready to put another shield in place with scarcely a thought. Because he knew that this wasn't just a conversation with the Ancient One. It was a test.

"Come now," chided the Ancient One, not realizing or not caring that the black sparks jumped off his cloak with an even greater frequency. "There's no need for that. We are all friends here." He motioned with one of his hands toward the blazing steel. "Can we not just have a civilized discussion?"

"You don't seem the type who would want to talk," said Bryen. "You seem the type who will do whatever is necessary to gain what you want."

"You're basing that perspective on what?" huffed the Ancient One, his midnight black eyes flashing with amusement. "What others have told you? Those who don't really understand the world and how it works? Who don't understand me and what I can do for the world? What I can do for the both of you?"

"And how does the world work?" asked Aislinn.

"Now that is a good question," the Ancient One replied, nodding his head in respect toward the Lady of the Southern Marches. "The answer is a simple one and one worth remembering. The world works as I want it to work."

"So let me get this straight. At first you wanted to have a conversation," interrupted Bryen, "but now you're going to tell us how the world works? The two don't really fit together."

Taking his measure once again, for several seconds the Ancient One stared at the gladiator.

His pulsing black eyes had little effect on the Protector, who didn't wilt under his scrutiny as so many others had. As everyone else had, in fact.

That realization only confirmed for the Ancient One that the Protector was someone he wanted at his side. Obeying him. Doing whatever was required to make his vision a reality.

Bryen didn't flinch under the Ancient One's gaze. He didn't turn away. Actually, his own expression, hard to begin with, became even flintier.

He didn't mind conversing with the Ancient One. Aislinn was right. Any discussion could prove useful, providing them with information that they wouldn't have obtained otherwise.

Yet he had no illusion whatsoever as to how this test was

going to conclude. The Ancient One was going to find both him and Aislinn lacking, because neither of them would ever deign to bow the knee to the Lord of the Spirit World.

"Better to know than not, don't you think?" suggested the Ancient One, his amiable tone not matching his flashing black eyes.

"And how do you want the world to work?" prodded Bryen. His tone implied that he was less than convinced by the Ancient One's proclamation. "And which world? The Spirit World where you've resided for how many centuries? Or the Natural World that you seek to make your own?"

"Bryen, do you think that this is wise?" whispered Aislinn. Bryen's questions were annoying the Ancient One, who clearly had little patience for being questioned in such a way.

"Probably not," Bryen replied just as quietly. "But we both know how this is going to end. If we can get him to function based on emotion, we might have a slim chance of getting out of here alive?"

"You don't think we're going to get out of here alive?"

Bryen gave her a smile and a wink. "Of course we are." He tried to infuse as much confidence in his reply as he could, because he had his doubts. With the Seventh Stone he sensed the power emanating from the Ancient One. He wasn't entirely certain that even with the artifact he'd be able to stand against the source of the Curse.

"The worlds will work as I want them to, Protector," the Ancient One explained. "Because the two worlds -- the Natural World and the Spirit World -- will become one. Exactly as I want them to be."

Bryen nodded, expecting just such a response. His lack of emotion seemed to throw off the Ancient One, almost as if the former Magus expected to see a hint of fear or perhaps even excitement because of his declaration.

Yet Bryen revealed nothing at all. He simply stared at the

Ancient One. Taking on the countenance that had served him so well when fighting on the white sand.

"You seem quite confident about that."

"Do you doubt me, Protector?"

"I don't doubt your desire. But wanting and doing are two different things."

Rather than the angry response that Bryen was hoping for, the Ancient One stared at Bryen, then smiled before breaking out into a low chuckle.

"Excellent advice, Protector. It sounds much like what my father told me when I was growing up."

"I thought it might." Bryen had learned the saying from Declan, the Master of the Gladiators also a Blackgard. It seemed that some of Declan's maxims had traveled down from one generation to the next uninterrupted. "Now what is it that you truly want from us? I can poke and prod for as long as necessary, but that gets tiresome after a while. Better just to get to the heart of the matter."

"Well said, Protector," murmured the Ancient One appreciatively. "Put simply, I want both of you."

"You want both of us?" asked Aislinn, not quite understanding.

"Yes, my lady. I want you and your Protector. No other Magus can stand against either of you. The power you wield would prove incredibly beneficial to my efforts."

Aislinn nodded knowingly, her lips twisting into a less than pleasant smile as she considered the implications, not expecting the Ancient One to make such a request. "That would require accepting the touch of the Curse."

"It would," the Ancient One replied with a broad smile, "and I understand your hesitation. I do. Truly. But as I said, the power you two can exercise is unmatched by any other Magii I have ever come across. With the additional potency that I can gift you, that the Curse can gift you, think of what you could do."

Aislinn looked at Bryen, who in turn glanced at her. She nodded, giving him permission to reply.

"We think not."

"You think not?" asked the Ancient One, his tone slightly incredulous.

Bryen nodded. "Correct. We think not. We have no desire to accept any gift that you might have to offer."

Silence descended in the chamber for several seconds, the ice spreading even faster across the walls, now at least a foot thick, the grey wisps forming a dense cloud behind the Ancient One, both actions clearly tied to the spirit's darkening emotions.

In a flash Marcus disappeared. Dark black robes replaced the multicolored cloak. The welcoming grin of the Magus transformed into a scowl, the brown hair fading to a scraggly white, the pockmarked skin on the Magus' face tightening across his bones and giving him a skeletal appearance. The only feature that remained of the young Marcus was the pitch-black eyes.

"You think not!" raged the Ancient One, the ruler of the Spirit World revealing his true self. "What you think is of no concern to me! The only thing that need concern you is obeying me!"

Bryen had fought too many times on the white sand not to know what their adversary was about to do. A split-second before the stream of black energy shot from the Ancient One's bony fingers, Bryen fixed his shield back in place.

The violent concussion caused by the two distinct ener-gies meeting was deafening, the backlash knocking loose massive boulders from the ceiling that crashed down around them.

Neither was greatly concerned, Bryen relying on the power

of the Seventh Stone to protect them from the Curse and the falling stones.

It wasn't long before the roar subsided. Soon replaced by the Ancient One's high-pitched cackle, the spirit sending one powerful blast of the Curse after another toward them. The tainted energy smacking against the shield with the repetitiveness of a monstrous battering ram being used to break through a castle's gates.

"Are you ready?"

Aislinn gave Bryen a shrewd look. "Are you sure that you want to do this?"

"What choice do we have?" grunted Bryen, the burden of maintaining the shield becoming more difficult with every breath. The Ancient One increasing the intensity of his assault with every strike. "We can't stand against him forever."

"You make a good point," agreed Aislinn. "Now!"

Bryen and Aislinn rolled away from one another. At the same time Bryen released the shield.

The stream of the Curse that was already streaking toward them shot past and slammed against the back wall, shattering the stone. The entire chamber shook, the ceiling threatening to collapse.

Bryen and Aislinn sought to use their adversary's momentary surprise at the ease of their escape to their advantage, initiating a series of attacks from two different directions. They sent streams, bolts, spikes, and other forms of the Talent streaking toward the Ancient One, forcing the spirit to defend himself. Not wanting to give the Ancient One the chance to attack again. Knowing the likely result if that happened.

For the next several minutes, the battle raged throughout the chamber.

The Talent and the Curse surging through the air.

The Ancient One floating above the cauldron, unable to move away from the spot where he had joined them from the

Spirit World. Requiring the anchor provided by the Curse in physical form. In the Natural World, not powerful enough to break free entirely.

At least not yet.

Bryen and Aislinn were grateful for that limitation. Never staying in one position for more than a few breaths, they continued their attacks. Doing all that they could to occupy the former Lord of Skaffa Falls. Understanding what would happen if the Ancient One caught them flatfooted.

Yet despite all that they tried, they never got a clean strike at the Ancient One.

Worse, the Ancient One seemed to be enjoying the contest, the creature who had once been Marcus Blackgard cackling with glee, seemingly unconcerned by anything that the Protector and the Lady of the Southern Marches threw at him.

"Enough!" roared the Ancient One, finally having grown tired of the exercise, signaling his impatience by sending a bolt of the Curse directly into the stone in front of the cauldron.

The blast was so powerful that Bryen and Aislinn were forced to abandon their attacks and dive behind a large boulder that had fallen from the ceiling, Bryen forming another shield around them right before the aftershock struck, saving them from being flung like rag dolls against the unforgiving back wall.

Once again the ceiling threatened to collapse, the chamber swaying dangerously. Yet somehow the underground hollow remained intact.

"This has been quite enjoyable," rasped the Ancient One once the dust and debris cleared. "But you are not ready. Not yet. Both of you require a little more curing." The Ancient One nodded to himself as if he were considering his options. "Remember, children. This was just a test. You do not have the power to stand against me. I will take you both when the time is right. Because even in death, you will be mine."

Then with another cackle of delight, the Ancient One fired a bolt of the Curse directly at Bryen and Aislinn.

Bryen's shield held, though the strength of the Ancient One's attack was so strong that it blew apart the boulder that had protected them and knocked them backward several yards.

And right through a portal of spinning black that neither Bryen nor Aislinn had been aware was even there.

In a heartbeat, the Ancient One was gone, replaced by a greyish white mist that was so thick that neither of them could see the other despite the fact that they stood shoulder to shoulder.

7

HUNT IN THE HALLWAY

"Are you certain this is the way?"

"Not entirely, no." Declan gave Talia a shrug of apology, unable to prevent his concern from leaking into his words. He didn't look at her, instead keeping his eyes focused to their front, searching for any hint of movement. "But it's the only option we have. So we see where this leads."

Talia nodded. She couldn't argue with the Sergeant of the Blood Company's logic. What he said made sense. She realized then that she needed to concentrate on what she was doing. Not on what she wanted. It was the only way to maintain a tight grip on the anxiety roiling within her.

"Magus Rafia was certain that he was down this way?"

She tried to keep her voice even and under control. Just as if she were standing on the helm of the *Swift*. It was more of a struggle than she would have liked, her angst and guilt seeping into her voice.

Davin was here somewhere beneath the Rock in who knew what kind of condition.

Because of her.

He had sacrificed himself for her.

He had given her the chance to escape, deciding to face all on his own the Stalkers coming for them both.

She hated him for it.

And she also lo ....

Talia shook her head, misery and confusion clouding her thoughts. She usually knew what to do in most any situation.

But now?

Now she felt lost.

Whether because she exercised so little control over how the events of the next few hours might play out or because Davin wasn't standing at her shoulder as he usually was, she couldn't say.

Worse, she didn't know if Davin was still alive.

She hoped that he was.

Desperately.

Talia hadn't known Davin for long, yet in the months they had been together, he had made an indelible impression upon her. One that she hadn't anticipated. One that she valued in a way that she never imagined possible.

She had seen him as she wanted to see him, only slowly beginning to realize that her initial impression of him was off the mark. Because she had allowed her perception to guide her rather than taking the time to recognize Davin for who he truly was.

She was a fool for doing that.

And now Talia didn't know if she could bear the burden of his death. For more reasons than she was willing to admit to herself.

Trying to shake herself free from the anxiety that had draped itself over her like a wet cloak, she turned her attention to the gloom she advanced through, trying to peek around Majdi's large frame as they moved farther along the darkened passageway. The gladiator held one torch at the front of the small group, Jenus doing the same at the back, the flicker of light piercing the darkness only a few dozen feet in each direction.

Her disquiet was aggravated in large part because their search for Davin was taking so long. That grated on her even though she understood that caution was necessary.

No matter how much she wanted to, moving faster could lead to a fatal mistake. They needed to ensure that none of the monsters that blended so easily into the gloom were waiting for them, hidden within a crevice or, as they had discovered, hanging from the ceiling.

If not for Declan's preternatural sense of danger, one of the monsters would have dropped down right in their midst. Instead, thanks to Declan's cry of warning, Majdi and Jenus pinned the monster clinging to the stone above with their spears, not allowing the Stalker to fall to the ground until it was dead.

So definitely the need to be wary.

Still, she was having a difficult time focusing on anything else other than the red-haired gladiator with the easy smile and the unique ability to get under her skin with no more than a look.

Ever since she had arrived in Ballinasloe and begun building the Carlomin Trading Company with her mother -- and from that taken on the challenge of sweeping the pirates from the Sea of Mist and then removing Hakea Roosarian from the seat of power in Fal Carrach -- she had lost more people who were important to her than she ever thought possible.

It was inevitable, she knew, when assuming such responsibilities and taking on such challenges. Those she had lost all understood the risk involved. Yet they had been there at her side despite that.

Because they believed in her.

Because they believed in what they were doing.

Every loss affected her deeply, the face of every person who had died in her service passing before her eyes before she fell asleep at night. However, she did not feel as heavy a guilt when thinking of those friends and comrades as she did now for the gladiator she had no interest in working with when he was first thrust upon her.

She had wanted to refuse his assistance, but she couldn't. Not if she wanted an ally in Bryen Keldragan. She had accepted him aboard her ship reluctantly, only doing so because he was the means for her to gain the assistance she needed to achieve her goals in the waters around New Caledonia.

She had told the gladiator as much. He had shrugged and given her that sly smile of his that always put her on guard.

He didn't care. He understood how the world worked. He just wanted to see more of it.

Talia had believed that the Crimson Giant would only be a nuisance. A constant distraction specializing in getting in her way. His perspective on the world often clashing with her own.

Yet somehow during the time that they spent together -- and for the life of her she couldn't quite explain even to herself how it happened -- Davin had become more than just a gladiator from the Pit. More than just another spear who could fight for her when there was need.

He had become a friend.

Perhaps even a ...

Talia quashed that thought before it could take root. Now was not the time to focus on what she wanted. Now was the time to focus on what needed to be done.

She needed to refocus, to stay sharp, and to help her do that she welcomed the anger that was rising within her.

Anger at herself for allowing Hakea Roosarian to escape.

Anger at Davin for deciding to play the hero and not believing that they could have evaded the Stalkers together.

"As certain as she could be," Declan replied quietly. "As Rafia explained it to me, there's a reek of evil within this fortress, drifting up from the lower levels, that prevents her from seeing all that she could usually see with the Talent. Still, she was as sure as she could be that he was down this way. In part because she couldn't sense Davin anywhere else within the citadel."

"Alive?" Talia asked.

Her anxiety threatening to break through, she could say no more than that, worried that her voice would crack and then the façade she had built around herself would as well. Not realizing that her decision to leave the fight in front of the gates to her family's compound in order to help the Blood Company free Davin said more than anything else ever could about her feelings regarding the gladiator.

"He better be alive," rumbled Majdi, the gladiator who filled the tunnel almost all by himself gliding right in front of Talia. "If he's not, he'll have some explaining to do on the other side, and he won't like that conversation. I promise you that."

"You've got that right," added Jenus. He walked behind Declan and Talia, guarding their backs. "He can't get away from the Blood Company that easily. Once a gladiator ..."

"Always a gladiator," Majdi finished in his deep rumble.

"Before she sent us this way, Rafia believed that he was still alive." Declan smiled at the gladiators' comments, taking heart from them.

When you fought together in the Pit, a bond inevitably formed that linked the men and women sentenced to such a brutal fate in a way that someone who had never experienced the horrors and challenges of the white sand could ever understand. A bond that could never be broken. Even in death.

"Hold on a moment," Declan ordered quietly.

Talia, Majdi, and Jenus stopped. They had reached a junction in the tunnel, another corridor meeting theirs at a right angle. Coming toward them from that corridor were two torches, the darkness preventing them from getting a good look at who it was.

"Trouble?" asked Majdi, his eyes glittering with anticipation.

It sounded like the gladiator was raring for a fight. Perhaps even hoping that the soldiers of the Roosarian Guard who were failing so miserably against the Blood Company several floors above them were attempting to escape the citadel.

Declan waited a few second more before replying. "Yes, but not the kind that we're worried about."

Asaia appeared out of the darkness, Dorlan and Kollea with her.

"Still haven't found the little one?" asked Asaia.

The gladiators standing around her laughed quietly. Davin was taller than all of them, except for Majdi and Jenus.

"Not yet," Declan replied. "No sign of him the way you came?"

Asaia shook her head. "Nothing back down that way other than a few dead Stalkers," she replied casually, the challenge of killing the beasts clearly not an issue for the gladiators.

"Good to hear. That also means we only have one direction to go now."

"And if we don't find him down this way?" asked Dorlan.

"Let's worry about that when we have to," Declan suggested.

Declan didn't want to consider the possibility that Davin might be gone. He had raised that young man since he had arrived in the Colosseum with his sister. If Davin remembered everything that Declan had taught him, then he just might still be alive.

Yet for how much longer?

Declan feared that he already knew the answer. Time was short. They needed to find Davin swiftly or they wouldn't find anything more than a corpse.

The gladiators began their hunt again, walking down the

corridor that began to slope deeper beneath the citadel. All of them feeling a sense of urgency that increased in intensity with every step they took.

Nevertheless, they controlled their impulses to push ahead faster. They understood the risk of advancing without taking care. Of the danger that could be lurking just beyond the light of their torches.

In the last hour, the gladiators had fought and killed more than a dozen Stalkers. They had to assume that more waited for them up ahead.

The deeper they went below the citadel, the more suffocating the quiet became, an eerie silence descending around them. It was so quiet, in fact, that they could hear nothing except for their own breathing.

Until they stopped a quarter hour later. Catching a very familiar sound at the very edge of their hearing.

"Wedge," Declan ordered in a whisper. The gladiators immediately assumed the appropriate formation. "We advance at a trot. It seems that the Crimson Giant could use our help."

As one, the gladiators advanced down the corridor at the prescribed pace, the sounds of a combat drawing them on. The curses streaming from Davin's mouth that grew louder by the second making more than one of the gladiators grin viciously.

It was just as they thought.

No one had been able to kill the Crimson Giant in the Pit.

They doubted anything or anyone could kill him here a few hundred feet beneath the Rock.

EVER SINCE HE had left the Pit, Davin had craved adventure. His fervid desire to experience a new thrill knew almost no bounds. So much so that he felt more dead than alive when he didn't get a chance to fight for his life every week.

He understood why he felt this way, that sense of exhilaration burying itself within him and never letting go. So deeply, in fact, that he didn't have a clue as to how to eliminate the urge.

Though he understood as well that it wasn't healthy, he had become used to it. The feeling ingrained within him.

The need to test himself in ways that others believed foolish.

The need to challenge himself.

The need to push himself to his very limits.

Because that's how he had survived the Pit. And he had yet to learn any other way to function.

Davin struggled constantly against the need to experience again and again the rush that proved to be so addictive while fighting as a gladiator. That he yearned for. That he found so hard to ignore.

He had hoped that joining Talia Carlomin on her endeavors would allow him to find a new means to experience that surge of adrenaline through his veins once again, although without having to worry about a sea dragon gobbling him up in one bite.

Davin had learned quickly that his decision had been a good one. Taking on the pirates in Smuggler's Cove and then escaping the Rock the first time had certainly aided his quest.

Although he could have done without his swimming with great whites on both occasions. That had taken some of the luster off those experiences.

But now, fighting in a darkened passageway illuminated only by an inconsistent scattering of torches running along the wall, he was beginning to think that maybe it was time to stop trying to attain that rush that had been so critical to his success in the Colosseum.

After killing the pair of Stalkers, Davin had only gotten a few hundred yards farther down the corridor before the monsters who had arrived late to that combat caught up to him. And this time there was no nook close by that he could use to defend himself.

The only bit of luck he enjoyed was that these Stalkers were coming at him from one direction. None were attacking him from behind. Not yet anyway.

If he could keep all the Stalkers to his front, he stood a chance of surviving this combat. Thanks to the width of the corridor, only two of the monsters could come at him at a time, and even when they did more often than not the beasts simply got in each other's way because of their size and aggressiveness.

Yet even though Davin knew exactly what to do to protect himself -- having faced similar circumstances more times than he could count -- and he was conducting his defense in a way that would have made Declan proud, he realized that there was a weakness in his strategy that he wasn't sure that he could get around.

Himself.

That was a difficult fact to acknowledge, because Davin had never viewed himself as the weak link. He had never had to. Until now.

The wounds and other stresses inflicted upon him were taking their toll. He was exhausted. And he could tell that even though he was doing a passable job of holding off the two Stalkers attacking him, he was slower than he needed to be. Even worse, he couldn't ignore the fact that he was only going to get slower.

That conclusion led him to a hard truth.

Eventually, he would make a mistake. The Stalkers would break through the web of steel that he wove around himself.

And then he would be done.

It was inevitable.

It was just a matter of how long Davin could delay meeting his fate.

Davin crossed the steel spikes right in front of his face, catching one of the Stalker's claws before it ripped into his chest. He couldn't afford to stay in that position for long, however, anticipating that the other Stalker was going to reach around his brethren's shoulder in order to take advantage of Davin's dilemma.

Gagging at the stench of the Stalker breathing in his face, Davin allowed the beast to push him back against the wall. Using the stability provided by the stone, he kicked forward with his left leg, smashing his boot against the Stalker's right knee.

The Stalker grunted in pain. Yet still the beast remained right in front of Davin, pressing down on his steel spikes, grinning maniacally as it tried to use Davin's own weapons against him.

Davin should have assumed the combat would move in this direction. Nothing was ever easy when it came to these beasts. They were almost as difficult to kill as the Slayers he and the Blood Company had fought on the Breakwater Plateau.

Davin lashed out again with his boot. Then again. And one more time as the Stalker's groans of pain became louder with each kick. Finally, on the fourth strike, the Stalker's grunts turned into a shriek that was a mix of agony and fury.

The Stalker's knee couldn't withstand the punishment that Davin meted out, the joint bending backward at a terrible angle on the last kick, the kneecap and fibula shattering.

No longer able to stand on its right leg, the Stalker pulled back one claw from Davin's steel, hoping to catch him with a quick swipe before it lost its balance.

Davin was ready, expecting just such a play. When the Stalker reached back, the monster unavoidably tilted toward the right side, the leg that Davin had injured so severely giving out.

Davin simply accelerated the Stalker's momentum, ducking

down in that direction and taking the Stalker, who still gripped the steel spikes with its other claw, with him.

The monster collapsed on the stone floor. Off balance. Its swipe at Davin missing by a wide margin and making the beast go down that much faster.

Davin ignored the floundering monster for just a few heartbeats, turning his attention toward the Stalker that tried to come at him while he was engaged with its now wounded brethren.

Slashing down with the steel spike in his left hand, Davin broke the Stalker's left arm, preventing the monster from driving its claw between his ribs. That Stalker now bent at the waist and screaming in pain, Davin didn't hesitate.

With the three-foot spike in his right hand, he drove the steel through the Stalker's ear and into its brain. The monster died instantly, Davin ripping the bloody spike free before the body hit the ground.

Pivoting as fast as he could, which really wasn't very fast at all by Davin's standards, his movement feeling heavier and more awkward than it ever had in the past, he gripped a steel spike in each hand and punched down.

The Stalker with the bad leg tried to shriek but couldn't, Davin driving one piece of steel through the beast's right eye and the other into its throat, whatever protest the dying monster wanted to offer drowned out by the blood pouring from its mouth.

Davin had no time to enjoy his success. Pushing himself back to his feet, he turned just in time to knock away another Stalker's claw.

The monster leapt forward as soon as the corridor cleared, desperate to claim the kill as its own. Yet despite its ferocity, the Stalker wasn't fast enough. Davin catching the movement out of the corner of his eye just in time.

Not knowing how much longer he could keep fighting, the

muscles in his arms and legs turning to jelly, his loss of blood making it hard for him to focus, his vision tightening at the edges, Davin took a step back, leaning his shoulders against the wall.

Instinctively, Davin moved his head to the side. The Stalker's claw passed right by his ear and punched into the wall instead of his face.

Davin smiled when he heard the bones in the Stalker's claw break, taking some pleasure in the monster's hiss of pain. He did no more than that, however, recognizing the opportunity his adversary had given him.

Leaning down, Davin pushed his shoulder into the Stalker's chest then punched up with his body. Gaining the few more feet of space he desired, Davin stabbed the monster in the groin and the gut. And then again. And one more time just to make certain.

Before the dying Stalker could fall on him, Davin shouldered the monster away, the beast falling backward over the two Stalkers Davin had killed just moments before.

Usually, Davin would be quite pleased with himself after killing a trio of Stalkers in just as many minutes. Especially in his condition.

Sadly, he wasn't. Because although only two of the Stalkers from the original fist remained, four more of the creatures were sprinting down the hallway to join the fight.

Davin sighed wearily, closing his eyes in resignation. It seemed that he was getting more than he bargained for or wanted.

He had craved the chance to experience the rush that he had relished on the white sand. But here, now, beneath the Rock, he just wanted it to stop.

He wanted to rest.

He wanted to see Talia ...

Davin forced that stray thought from his mind.

He didn't have time for it.

Pushing himself off the wall, he turned to face the Stalkers racing toward him.

He was the Crimson Giant.

No one had defeated him in the Pit.

And if he was to go to the other side on this day, then he would take as many of the Stalkers with him as he could.

Six Stalkers blocked Talia and the gladiators as they approached at a trot, but that didn't faze them. None of the Stalkers were paying attention to what was coming at them from behind, instead fixated on the combat playing out before them.

The monsters yearned to join the fight, but they couldn't get past their brethren who crowded the corridor. The two Stalkers at the front were having a difficult time achieving the desired killing blow, the narrowness of the walls and the skills of their prey impeding their efforts.

Talia followed right behind Majdi, who was at the point of the wedge. Declan was on her shoulder. When she tilted her head in just the right way, she could see Davin around Majdi's hip if the Stalkers blocking their path were accommodating.

Talia was impressed. Three Stalkers lay dead at his feet.

She appreciated how the corridor aided Davin's efforts. The constricting space prevented the Stalkers at the back of the scrum from getting into the fight.

And she was grateful for that.

But she was worried as well.

She could tell that Davin was flagging. She didn't find that surprising upon spying all the bruises, blood, and wounds that covered his body.

The sense of urgency that plagued her became that much more consuming.

Talia was desperate to get to Davin.

To help him.

To get him out from beneath the Rock.

To save him as he had saved her.

First, though, they needed to get to him. And that was going to take time that they might not have.

Majdi and Declan killed two of the beasts before the Stalkers even realized they were under attack. Majdi punched his spear through one of the beast's shoulder blades, the steel tip piercing the monster's chest. He then pushed the dying beast into the creatures in front of him, sending several tumbling into their brethren and then to the stone floor.

Declan slashed across the back of another Stalker's legs. When the monster reared back in shock and pain, Declan pierced the back of the creature's neck with the tip of his sword.

A good start to the attack, Talia believed, her hope that they could get past these monsters surging. Unfortunately, her confidence was short-lived, the remaining Stalkers recovering quickly.

The Stalkers turned and lunged at the gladiators with a terrifying speed. However, the attack was no different than what they had faced before. The gladiators kept their shields in place, the Stalkers' claws scraping against the steel rather than ripping through their flesh.

Talia had little doubt that the gladiators would kill these beasts. They were too skilled in their work not to, the monsters' shrieks, snarls, and frenetic stabs and swipes scarcely resonating with them.

The key issue, however, was when. Because on the far side of the corridor, behind Davin, whose attention was firmly focused on the pair of Stalkers seeking to gut him, she caught a hint of movement.

There was a shadow moving out of the gloom toward her gladiator.

She couldn't glimpse a face from where she was, too many large bodies blocking her view, but she did catch the brief flash of steel as the shadow slunk past a torch.

"Declan, I need to get to Davin now!"

Declan didn't reply. He had seen the threat approaching Davin from behind as well.

There was no chance that he and the other gladiators were going to reach Davin before the shadow struck. Still, that didn't mean that they shouldn't at least make the effort.

"Twenty steps back lass. Then come forward as fast as you can."

Talia didn't bother to ask Declan what he had in mind. Time was running out for Davin. She would do whatever was necessary to get to him.

Trotting backward, Talia then did as Declan ordered, sprinting toward him as fast as she could.

"Dorlan!" Declan called.

The gladiator, spear in one hand, shield in the other, who stood right behind Majdi and Jenus, knew exactly what Declan had in mind. They had practiced this maneuver multiple times on the training ground.

Already in motion, he stabbed quickly over Majdi's shoulder, breaking the Stalker's collarbone with an audible snap. Ripping the steel tip of his spear free with a vicious tug, he knelt and angled the shield over his back.

Talia realized at the very last moment, no more than ten feet from the gladiator, what Declan expected her to do. Despite her doubts, it was too late to stop.

As soon as her front foot hit the gladiator's shield, Dorlan shot up from the ground, combining his strength with Talia's momentum to hurl her through the air.

Talia soared over Majdi and Jenus, and thankfully over the

Stalkers as well, who, so intent on tearing down the steel wall in front of them, noticed too late what was happening above them.

Talia kept her arms out in front of her, as if she were diving into the ocean off the deck of the *Swift*. She avoided scraping along the ceiling by less than a finger's breadth, the ground coming up on her fast. Rather than smashing face first into the stone floor, she bent her knees, leaned forward, and rolled.

Back on her feet in an instant, she didn't worry about whether the Stalkers fighting the gladiators might come after her. She doubted that they would.

Her flying above them had distracted the monsters, if only for a second, yet that was long enough for Declan and the others to make use of that brief moment of confusion.

One of the Stalkers died with a spear punched through its mouth, the tip piercing the back of its head. Another was mortally wounded, its guts spilling out, Declan swiping his sword across its belly.

The last two monsters now were less interested in her and more in trying to stay alive, the gladiators pushing hard to finish the job they had started.

Majdi forced his way between the two Stalkers, knocking one to the floor. The other had no chance to attack him from behind, Jenus advancing toward the monster, and he wasn't in a good mood.

Knowing how events were going to play out behind her, Talia raced down the passageway. The shadow was drawing closer to Davin. No more than a dozen paces away now. The steel gleaming brightly in the torchlight.

Needing to get past the monsters keeping Davin in place to have any chance at stopping the shadow so intent on striking him down from behind, she targeted the Stalker right to her front. Pleased that the beast had no idea that she was racing up from behind.

The Stalker was about to lunge at Davin. The other Stalker had forced him to turn to the side to avoid the slash of the beast's claw across his belly, leaving him vulnerable.

If Talia was going to have any chance of success, if she was going to keep Davin alive, she would need to time what she had in mind perfectly.

DAVIN GRUNTED both in pain and effort.

Pain because the Stalker right in front of him was faster than he anticipated. Or rather Davin was slower than he should have been.

Regardless, the Stalker succeeded in raking its claw across Davin's shoulder.

Effort because at the same time the Stalker dug its dagger-like fingers into his flesh, Davin brought his knee up hard into the Stalker's thigh. And then one more time faster than the sting of a wasp.

He didn't break the Stalker's leg. He did knock the monster off balance, sending the Stalker head first against the wall.

Ignoring the fiery agony in his shoulder as best as he could, Davin slammed his other shoulder into the Stalker's lower back when the beast tried to push off the wall.

Hitting the stone face first again, the Stalker's snarls of rage ended with a whimper when Davin punched one of his steel spikes into the monster's side, shredding a kidney. Then one more time right between the two lower ribs, giving the steel several violent twists before pulling the spike free.

The dying Stalker sliding down the wall, its life draining away quickly, Davin didn't have the time to enjoy his success. He turned to face his next attacker, sensing the movement to his side, the Stalker's razor-sharp claw slashing toward his throat.

Not wanting to get stuck against the wall and become an even easier target than he already was, Davin swung the steel spike in his left hand in a wide arc. For just a heartbeat, he feared that he was too slow, his exhaustion finally getting the better of him.

He smiled thinly when he caught the Stalker's arm.

Confident that he was about to kill its prey, the Stalker had thrown everything it had into the slash.

That proved to be a mistake.

The beast pulling itself off balance for just a heartbeat, Davin acted based more on instinct than thought, turning his hip, bending at the waist, and then shooting up.

The Stalker tried to turn back around, but the monster's timing was off, allowing the top of Davin's head to crunch against the bottom of the Stalker's jaw, the sound of the sickening crack music to Davin's ears.

Davin's unorthodox blow caught the monster by surprise, the Stalker tumbling backward over one of the bodies of its dead brethren.

Before Davin could finish the beast, the Stalker struggling to get free from the corpse, he turned again, catching another hint of movement off to his side. Another Stalker had emerged out of the gloom, intent on gutting him.

Davin dodged to the side just in time, the Stalker's claw missing his hip by less than a hair. He then dodged again, this time to the other side. Really no more than a drunken wobble but enough to avoid another swipe.

Not wanting to cede the momentum to the Stalker, Davin kicked forward with his right foot. He caught the monster in the chest and knocked the Stalker back several feet.

Before the Stalker could recover, Davin swung with the steel in his right hand. The spike cut across the Stalker's face, ripping off the monster's nose.

The Stalker screamed in fury, ignoring the wound and the

blood pouring down its face. Enraged, the Stalker rushed toward Davin, claws swiping down toward him.

Davin raised his two steel spikes just in time, crossing them above his head. His quick thinking prevented the Stalker from slicing him open from chest to groin.

Yet as if fighting off more than a fist of Stalkers wasn't bad enough, now he faced a new dilemma. He couldn't break free from the Stalker, the monster grasping the spikes with its claws, eyes blazing with a manic intensity as the beast pushed down, its sharp teeth gnashing the air right in front of Davin's face.

Now he was stuck in a contest that he was certain he couldn't win.

Having no other options, Davin put all that was left of his strength into keeping the Stalker's claws from getting too close to him.

It wasn't enough.

He was asking too much of himself.

The Stalker was too strong and too determined. The daggerlike claws inching closer and closer to Davin's cheeks, now no more than a few knuckles away.

Even worse, Davin caught another flash of movement out of the corner of his eye.

He didn't know what it was, but he could guess. And he realized that he stood no chance of taking on whatever was coming to kill him from behind while locked in a battle of strength with his current adversary.

8

THE LITTLE PIT

Lycia stood just outside the rough-hewn gate that would grant her access to the bloody sand just beyond.

She frowned, disappointed, although she couldn't say that she was surprised after sneaking past Sharperson's Guard, making her way to the Stone, and then spending a few days getting her bearings at the Governor's citadel.

Torstan Sharperson had grand designs. Yet he didn't seem to have the capacity to bring those designs to life.

A few pieces of timber hastily nailed and lashed together. She was used to a great deal more extravagance and gravitas after fighting on the white sand. The gates leading to the Colosseum in Tintagel were crafted of finely wrought steel, flecks of gold sparkling brightly. And the stadium itself was constructed of a white stone that shone blindingly bright in the sun, visible no matter where you were in the city.

Yet here, built on a plateau that could only be reached by a crosswalk from the citadel that bridged a gap of several hundred feet, the stone of what Torstan Sharperson liked to call the Colosseum in the Peaks was a blackish grey, matching the jagged spires that surrounded the much smaller construction.

Of course, the stone covered only a small portion of the arena. The rest of it was wood.

More telling, the sand was brown. Not white.

It didn't gleam as did the surface of the Pit she had stalked across for five years. Instead, the clumpy grit, which reminded her of the beaches that ran along the eastern coast of the Highlands, appeared to drink in the light. That, along with the drab stone, gave what most everyone called the Little Pit a dark and dreary appearance.

She could only imagine how these differences must bother the Governor of the Highlands. He had spared no expense to recreate a smaller version of the Tintagel Palace and the Colosseum. Yet, he had failed in almost every respect.

This pale reflection was at best a quarter of its size, having space for ten thousand people. Maybe twelve thousand if you risked packing in the rest along the battlements at the very top of the arena that appeared to be anything but sturdy.

Yet she doubted anyone would make such a foolish mistake and brave the shoddy construction again.

The evidence on the far side was undeniable, visible through the holes in the gate. Scaffolding covered more than a quarter of the stadium, the outer wall having collapsed and taking with it several dozen rows of seats. And from what she had learned, several hundred people as well.

The Governor had opened the stadium before time, refusing to listen to his foreman's warnings.

It only made sense.

Jakob Kestrel and his Highlanders had done an excellent job of eliminating Sharperson's primary source of revenue.

Sharperson had been desperate to begin the New Caledonian Games as he was calling them. Desperate to gain the golds he earned for every combat, taking a cut of the winner's purse. Desperate for the fee each free gladiator paid to compete. Desperate for the coins that every attendee paid to gain admittance.

That desperation and inability to make a dream real explaining in part why the arena was sparsely filled that early afternoon. And, after watching a few of the combats, Lycia confirming that another likely reason was the lack of quality within the ranks of the gladiators.

High expense and high risk to watch what she had judged to be a low-quality exhibition.

Not a good combination.

Still, she was here. And for two good reasons.

Greed and that same desperation.

Two qualities that rankled Lycia to no end. However, she was more than happy to make use of them if they helped her to achieve her purpose for being there.

Distract Sharperson for a few days so that the Kestrel could streak down out of the clouds with his claws outstretched and seize the Stone.

The strategy that Lycia was putting into play was hers. Jakob had agreed to it. Reluctantly.

His hesitation came not because he didn't believe that it was a good plan. Rather, he was worried about her.

What she proposed put her in a great deal of danger. She would be in a position where Jakob couldn't get to her in time if something went wrong.

Jakob didn't like that. A discovery on her part that she found both unsettling and comforting.

He hadn't put it into words. No matter how much he may have wanted to, he kept his mouth shut. Yet she had recognized his concern for her in what he said and how he said it. His almost pained expression giving him away.

While she stared at him expectantly, finally he nodded, convinced by her own confidence in what she proposed.

She could tell that it had been difficult for him to do so. And she had been grateful that he had treated her with such respect, believing in what she could do.

Believing in her.

To avoid any awkwardness between them, they immediately moved on to doing what needed to be done so that she could get to where she needed to be.

Standing in front of the gates that led into the Little Pit.

Her strategy was a simple one, and it certainly made sense considering their target.

Torstan Sharperson dreamed of being a king. He believed that his first step in that process was the completion of the Stone. A monumental fortress that would serve as a symbol of his power, wealth, and stature.

Not a very original approach in Lycia's opinion, but she didn't think that Sharperson was all that original to begin with. He was following what he believed was a tried-and-true blueprint for consolidating his gains.

There was a problem buried within his approach, however.

Building a fortress and growing and maintaining a Guard many thousand strong cost money. A lot of money.

And his treasury was dwindling thanks to the Highlanders seizing control of Sharperson's mines.

Therefore, to build revenue until he came up with some solution for reclaiming those mines along with the Territory that he was supposed to be ruling, he put much of his energy into hosting this bloody spectacle.

While giving him the chance to add to his coffers, the contests of skill also allowed Sharperson to play the lord in front of a very large audience. Or what would be a large audience if the quality of the competition was worth the spectators' time and money.

That would be the hook that she would use to find her place here.

This was where she would begin the groundwork. By showing Sharperson what was possible when he had a real gladiator fighting in his Colosseum in the Peaks. Giving him a glimpse of the value that she could provide. Capturing his attention so that he ignored for a time what might be occurring beyond the walls of the Stone.

The combats were fought to the death just as in Tintagel. But there was one key difference.

Unlike in the larger Colosseum, any man or woman could compete as a gladiator. They simply had to pay the entry fee, recouping that and more if they won. And if they lost ... well, then the lost golds really wouldn't matter. They had little value on the other side.

And, in an attempt to make these games more appealing and pull in more spectators, since the tremendous interest in the competition that Sharperson imagined had yet to materialize, he threw into the mix criminals waiting for judgment on various offenses.

Some of those crimes were real. Most were imagined.

Sharperson's definition of what was and wasn't against the law depending on his own needs first.

Therefore, in addition to his greed and desperation, from what Lycia had learned about the Governor, she believed that she could use his vanity and his desires against him as well.

That last part was what had sold Jakob on her proposal.

He couldn't disagree with her in good conscience. Not based on the reports that Duff's spies within the Stone provided that bolstered Lycia's argument for how to dig him out.

The Governor was hunkering down in the Stone, only pushing out his Guard a few leagues from the fortress. For the time being, he was ceding almost all of the Highlands to the rebels.

In truth, based on the success of the Highlanders, it wasn't a bad decision. Jakob and his rebels had seized all the mines.

Sharperson's Guard couldn't travel beyond their defensive perimeter unless they went in force. Even then, they rarely did, because the Highlanders were always ready and willing to have a go at them.

And if the Highlanders bit off more than they could chew, they simply slid back into the wilderness, taking refuge in the many hidden mountain valleys that allowed them to bite at any soldiers foolish enough to follow them. They could also wait out Sharperson's troops in their brochs, knowing that the Lord of the Highlands would come to their aid in force. The Kestrel seeing all that occurred within the mountain peaks. Never shy about reminding Sharperson of the precariousness of his position.

As a result, there was little else that Sharperson could do to change his circumstances.

Not until he earned more golds or got lucky.

In truth, however, there was little that Sharperson had to do. Although weakened, he remained in a strong position. Because the Highlanders didn't have the numbers to engage in a pitched battle.

And unfortunately for the Highlanders, they didn't have the luxury of waiting him out with the other challenges they faced.

The Stalkers remained a problem. As did the Wraiths, the Murk drifting in more and more frequently and bringing with it the monsters in the mist.

Therefore, the order of battle remained the same. Before Jakob could turn the Highlanders' attention toward eliminating the Wraiths, he needed to expel the Governor and his soldiers, thereby clearing the board of the Stalkers.

Far from easy.

Yet what in life that was worthwhile was ever easy?

That had been the last point she had made to Jakob to earn his agreement and set her on the road that had taken her to the entryway to the Little Pit, the lukewarm cheers sneaking through the gaps in the gate making her frown deepen.

Disappointing, yes. But definitely an opportunity.

Thinking about that discussion and her efforts to convince Jakob only made her smile and chuckle softly.

Although not softly enough. Her opponent for her first combat, a man almost as large as Majdi, although lacking much of the gladiator's muscle, stepped a few feet farther away from her. She assumed that he thought that she wasn't quite right in the head.

That was fine with her. To help convince him, she laughed a little louder, adding a cackle at the end that hinted of a cracked mind.

She snorted, the man now standing as far away from her as he could, enjoying how the spark of concern grew bigger in the back of his eyes. That should make her combat against him even easier than she already anticipated it would be.

Shifting her focus back to the gate, she listened to the sounds of the combat that was taking place on the other side. The grunts and groans, screams and roars, the clang of steel on steel … undeniably they were music to her ears.

Yes, she was definitely where she was supposed to be.

Jakob had known that she was right even though he didn't want her to be. Sharperson didn't have a clue as to how to reclaim the Territory that he had lost, likely hoping a Stalker sent to kill Jakob got lucky.

With no other options in sight, he had turned inward. Having an obsessive personality, Sharperson had become consumed by the bloody sport that had claimed his attention since his older brother first took him to the Colosseum.

From what Lycia had learned, Sharperson wasn't a great fighter, no more than adequate with a sword. However, he was quite taken with great fighters.

And she was a great fighter.

She could say that in complete honesty and without a hint of arrogance.

Lycia loosened her neck and flexed her shoulders, the gates to her front finally opening. The last fight concluded.

The winner, bloody from several wounds across her torso, two of them quite deep, staggered across the sand in Lycia's direction, one hand trying to keep her guts from slipping out, her determined gaze suggesting that she wanted to claim her earnings quickly so that she could pay for the physick who would be instrumental in determining whether she lived or died, assuming she even gained assistance in time.

The man she defeated was coughing up blood, his chest ripped open, not yet dead but soon to be. The attendants were dragging him out through a door on the other side of the arena where he would be left to die alone before being buried in a potter's field.

The gruesome reality of life as a gladiator.

Yet she had seen worse. Much, much worse.

Ignoring the two fighters who preceded her, she savored the rush of sensations that struck her as she prepared to walk out onto the brown sand. All the images, the sounds, the smells that she had tried to forget slamming into her all at once.

Her vision sharpened.

Her muscles tensed.

Her thinking sped up and gained greater clarity.

A charge swept through her body, prickling across her skin.

She was a gladiator again.

She was doing what she was trained to do.

She was fighting for her life.

She was where she had never wanted to be again.

Yet, in some strange way, she felt like she was home.

Good for her.

Bad for her opponent.

"Come on, big man," Lycia said as she strode through the gate and out onto the sand. "Time to die."

She didn't bother to watch how her adversary reacted. She kept her shoulders back, her confidence radiating from her, as she ignored the tepid cheers of the half-filled stadium.

She had eyes only for Torstan Sharperson.

The Governor of the Highlands.

The ruler of the Stone.

And the man whose eye she needed to catch if her plan was to have any chance of success.

"My friends!" shouted the master of ceremonies, the man's small frame seemingly out of place compared to his stentorian voice, which traveled easily to every seat in the Little Pit. "For our next combat, we give you the beauty versus the beast. You can decide which is which."

The announcer's clever quip earned a round of laughter from the sparse, slightly disinterested crowd.

Lycia ignored the man who stood right up against the railing at her back. She needed to stay on task. With that in mind, she stared at Sharperson. She refused to release him with her eyes until she was done with him.

Her efforts were made that much more difficult because she really couldn't say that she was all that impressed with her target. He reigned over a large box that was empty except for him.

It reminded her of the royal suite in the Colosseum in Tintagel. Just not stuffed with hangers-on and lackeys seeking to advance in Caledonian society.

She couldn't say that she was surprised.

His desire to emulate the Belerons and gain the power and wealth that they had acquired certainly fit with what she had learned about him. But it seemed that the charisma necessary for that task was lacking.

"Fight!" the little man shouted.

Lycia barely heard him despite the buzz of anticipation that swept through the crowd. Of course, she didn't really need to.

She had done this more times than she cared to remember. So many times, in fact, that she didn't even need to think about what to do when the hulking presence to her front stampeded toward her.

Letting her instincts take over, she twisted to the side as the fighter named the Butcher swung the overlarge cleaver he held in his right hand, trying to cut her in half with a single swipe as if she were a steer's carcass.

A good move, Lycia acknowledged. He had recognized that she was faster than he was, so why not try to end the fight before he got himself into trouble?

And such a strategy might have worked against another opponent.

Not against her, however.

Not only was she too fast, but she was too experienced and too skilled.

The Butcher would find that out soon enough.

Instead of taking Lycia's head from her neck, the Butcher stumbled for a few steps and then fell to his knees, the sharp tip of his cleaver digging deep into the sand. The hulking fighter unable to halt his momentum in time.

Hoping that his adversary had just gotten lucky, although not wanting to take the risk that he was wrong, the Butcher pushed himself up as quickly as he could, which really wasn't very fast because of his bulk. Grasping the handle of his weapon and pulling it free from where it stuck up out of the sand, he spun around.

Not luck, he realized much to his regret as he stared across the ten yards that separated him from his opponent.

This woman was different from all the other gladiators he had fought in the Little Pit. She radiated a menace that made him think that rather than walking from the sand as he had done after every one of his previous combats that he might be dragged out of the ring instead.

Not a conclusion that he really wanted to consider as he searched frantically for a weakness in the woman who stared at him with a cold disregard that made him gulp.

Lycia stood there calmly, a sword in each hand. She shook her head slowly from side to side, a hint of disappointment in her expression.

The innocuous movement sent a shiver of fear down the Butcher's spine. A sensation he had never experienced before on the brown sand.

Trying to kill the red-headed woman before she was ready. That was a smart move. The mistake that he made was that he had failed.

And now he was going to pay for that mistake.

He was certain of that.

Coming to that realization, the Butcher hesitated. He understood now that he wasn't just up against a woman who carried two swords. He was up against a woman who knew how to use those two swords. She was more skilled than he was with a blade. And she was faster than he was. A lot faster.

That left him with few options.

"Come on, Butcher! Kill the girl!"

"She's making you look the fool, Butcher! Kill her!"

Many more similar shouts erupted from the crowd, the moment of silence before the combat replaced by a lukewarm cacophony of noise that combined cheers and jeers.

"Kill her, Butcher!"

"Kill her like all the others!"

"Give us the blood, Butcher!"

"Carve her up like you did the others!"

The demands from the crowd, becoming more and more insistent, pushed the Butcher into motion. The large man charged across the brown sand, screaming at the top of his lungs, cleaver held poised above his shoulder.

He was hoping that he might startle her. Catch her by surprise. Maybe force her into a mistake.

No such luck for the Butcher, unfortunately.

Lycia didn't bother to stand in his way. At the very last second, right before his cleaver sliced into her shoulder, she pivoted out of the way. And, as a final gift, she kicked out to the side with her left foot, knocking the Butcher's left foot into his right.

The large man, unable to arrest his progress, crashed face first into the sand, plowing a small wake through the gritty surface.

She could have killed him then. Easily. He was struggling to push himself up off the ground. She saw the reason why when he groaned in pain.

The Butcher of the Little Pit was cradling his wrist against his chest. Based on the angle of his hand and the white splinters poking through his skin, a very bad break. Lucky for him it was his left hand. He could still fight.

When he turned to face her, she saw it in his somber eyes. He knew.

She had yet to even raise her sword to defend herself. She had yet to even attack him. Nevertheless, he understood that he had no chance of winning this combat.

While she had every chance of killing him.

"Who are you?" the Butcher demanded through clenched teeth, the gruesome injury to his wrist making him feel light-headed.

Lycia shrugged. "Does it matter?"

Before he could offer his reply, she was on him, her swords singing through the air.

The crowd, having gone silent at the shocking turn of events, was entranced by the sound, on the edge of their seats, captivated by the speed and elegance put on display.

The Butcher did his best to defend himself, understanding as he did so that his effort was for naught. Even if he hadn't broken his wrist, he couldn't stand against her.

After Lycia scored him several times -- two across the chest, another on his arm, one on his leg, all in just as many seconds -- the Butcher gave up trying to protect himself. Instead, he heeded his more animalistic instincts, swinging wildly with his massive cleaver. Understanding that all he could hope for now was a lucky strike.

But his luck had run out the second he stepped onto the brown sand.

The end came quickly, the Butcher dropping to his knees, the slash across his throat drenching his chest and staining the ground beneath him.

The dying fighter gurgled a few times, seeking the air that wouldn't come, before he collapsed into the sand.

Lycia stood just to the side of him. Unemotional. Under control. Knowing from the start that this was how the combat was going to end.

She didn't bother to look at the crowd as she turned for the gate. Although she did see out of the corner of her eye that the Governor was nowhere to be seen.

"Reeki, come here."

Torstan Sharperson stood close to seven feet tall, yet the large bulky robes he preferred hid his true size. He stood leaning against the railing of his private box, just twenty feet below him the brown sand of the Little Pit soaking in the bright sunlight. A large awning rose above his head, protecting his bald pate from the sun.

He had been rubbing his scalp in frustration, just as he did every time he studied the surface upon which his gladiators fought. He still couldn't understand why it was so hard to import the white sand that was used in Tintagel.

If he could do just that, then he would elevate his gladiatorial games to new heights. Then again, perhaps the woman gliding out into the ring could do that for him.

"Yes, Governor Sharperson."

"Who is that woman?" He nodded toward the red-haired fighter with the serious countenance and the eyes of a caged beast just raring to be let loose.

He couldn't take his gaze from her. In part because those terrible, frightening, alluring eyes of hers were locked onto his and refused to let him go.

He realized in an instant that he had no control over the encounter with this enticing woman, and he didn't mind in the least. She was in charge, and she wouldn't release him until she was done with him. Just the way he liked it.

There was an unmistakable fire within her. He liked that as well. Because he had a weakness for fiery women.

"The gladiator, Governor?"

"Yes, the gladiator. Of course the gladiator." His tone revealed a key aspect of his personality. Petulance. "Who else do you think I'm talking about?"

Reeki ignored Sharperson's sarcasm that was laced with a heavy dose of scorn, in large part because it went right over his head.

Not unexpectedly, these outbursts were becoming more common now that events had turned against Sharperson in his

Territory. Thus Reeki's desire to stay in his master's good graces. A task that was becoming harder and harder to do.

If Sharperson lost his grip on the Highlands for good, Reeki wanted to be well away from him, which was a new and strange desire. Reeki had been tied to Sharperson's hip since the Governor was a boy. He worried about the Governor because of his vindictive streak, having seen it applied, in fact being the one to apply it on more than one occasion, more times than he could recall. Knowing that even he wasn't immune from his ward's wrath.

But he feared more the upstart Highland Lord, having heard too much about him from the other soldiers, and because of that understanding the justice that the Kestrel would mete out to those responsible for seeking to subjugate the Highlanders.

A charge that Reeki had relished and at which he thrived.

Yet a charge that placed him in a tenuous position.

"The woman?" It was taking Reeki some time to catch up, having just received another update from one of the sergeants.

Two companies of Sharperson's Guard, two hundred men in all, had gone missing. They had been sent into the Highlands, ordered to make contact with the mine closest to the Stone. But not a word, and they should have been back days ago.

That didn't bode well. Yet he really couldn't say that news was an anomaly. Soldiers disappearing, likely at the hands of the Highlanders, was becoming all too common.

Reeki decided to keep that information to himself. With the Governor already in a dour mood there was no reason to rile him up.

The usurper had been tightening his grip on the Highlands mile by mile until only the few leagues around the Stone remained under the Governor's control. If not for the fact that the Guard outnumbered the Highlanders by at least three to one, Reeki would have expected this Lord Kestrel to be knocking at the gates of the Stone by now.

Besides, it appeared that Governor Sharperson had a new diversion.

Looking down at the gladiator, he had to admit that she was quite fetching with her bright-red hair. Even the many scars crisscrossing her arms and legs made her oddly appealing.

"Do you really think I'd be curious about the Butcher?" scoffed Sharperson. "The man carries a large cleaver. What can be so interesting about him?" He motioned toward the large, pudgy fellow who was circling around the woman, never getting too close. "The man has no creativity. He simply uses his size to his advantage, absorbing any blow thrown at him, waiting to deliver the one strike that will send his adversary to the ground where he can finish him. Why would I possibly be interested in the Butcher?"

"No, of course not, Governor Sharperson. My apologies. I was distracted for a moment."

Sharperson shook his head in frustration. Things had started well in the Territory, yet they had soured just as quickly in the last few months.

Once he figured out how to deal with the Kestrel, then it was likely time for him to make a change. Reeki had served him faithfully since he was a child, but here, now, his limited skill set was proving to be a hindrance. That was a thought for another time, however, his eyes still locked onto those of the gladiator.

"What can you tell me about her?"

"Not very much, I'm afraid, Governor Sharperson. She didn't offer a name when she paid her fee to fight today."

Sharperson thought about that, all the while unable to tear his gaze away from the woman. She appeared dangerous. Very dangerous. And the sharpness in her eyes sent a shiver down his spine that he found to be absolutely delightful.

"Does she look familiar to you Reeki?"

"From the games in Tintagel? Yes."

Sharperson nodded to himself. Could it even be possible?

LYCIA GLIDED THROUGH THE GATE. Eyes forward.

She was intent on the compound beyond until a large presence stepped up to block her way.

Torstan Sharperson.

She kept the smile that threatened to break free under control. It seemed that much of what Tommie had told her was accurate.

"I know you."

"I know you too," she replied. "Do you mind?" She nodded in the direction that she had been going, telling him with her eyes that she wanted to get by.

He ignored her, holding his place.

Lycia took that to be a good sign. He believed that by doing as he was he was demonstrating his dominance. Not realizing that his need to crowd her was actually a sign of weakness.

"You're the Crimson Devil." He was certain that he had seen her fight in the Colosseum.

"I was," Lycia replicd. "Now I'm just a fighter trying to collect her winnings. And you're in my way."

Sharperson smiled at that. He was both intimidated and smitten with her at the same time, and he savored the strange, uncomfortable, slightly arousing feeling that flowed through him as a result.

"That's why you're here?"

"Why else would I be here?" Lycia challenged. "I have a debt to pay. Kill a few more of these fighters and I'll clear the books. Then I can move on."

"What if I told you that I'd happily pay your debts if you were willing to do something for me?"

Lycia squared up to him. "I'd tell you to get out of my way. I'm not that kind of woman. Besides, I don't have time for games."

The sharp glint in her eyes made Sharperson step to the side.

Lycia waited just a second, nodding toward Sharperson, much as she would to a dog who had brought her a stick, before striding by. She watched in amusement as his eyes widened in delight and then again with another more libidinous emotion that she didn't want to think about when she brushed by him.

"You should listen to what I have to say," he called after her.

"I know of you, but I don't know you," Lycia replied without bothering to stop. "I don't have cause to trust you."

"How can I remedy that?" Sharperson asked quickly, almost pleadingly.

"You'll figure it out."

9

DEBTS PAID

Talia slid right between the legs of the Stalker to her right. Davin had knocked the monster to the ground, but the beast was back on its clawed feet in a flash. It didn't stay there for long.

The Stalker collapsed again as soon as she passed. Pulling the dagger from the sheath on her hip, she sliced across the back of its right hamstring, severing the muscle while she skidded across the rough floor.

The badly wounded Stalker shrieked. One of the monster's limbs useless, it floundered about, trying to untangle itself from its dead brethren.

Talia ignored the wounded Stalker, certain that the beast was no longer a threat to her or Davin. She had eyes only for the danger lurking at the gladiator's back.

Covering the last few feet in a heartbeat, she raised the sword she pulled from the scabbard across her back and crossed it with her dagger, using the smaller blade to buttress the steel.

Just in time. The clang of metal on metal was almost deafening in her ears, yet it sounded oddly sweet as well.

Talia prevented the blade that was aimed for Davin's back from striking true.

The steel didn't stay on her blade for long, however. The shadow pulled the sword back quickly and swept it down at her just as fast as before, the steel singing through the air.

Talia blocked the powerful blow once again, but only just barely. Almost losing her grip on her dagger because of the force behind the strike.

"You!" snarled the shadow.

Grunting with effort as he pressed down on Talia's blades with his own, the cloaked figure leaned closer. The hood had slipped from his head because of the ferocity of his last swing, revealing his scarred visage. What was most unsettling, however, were his eyes, which burned brightly with a terrifying hostility.

"Me," Talia replied through gritted teeth, keeping her gaze fixed on the steel above her.

She did her best to control her shock, that flash of surprise in the back of her eyes burned away in an instant by her spark of determination. She refused to give the man who towered above her what he wanted.

A look of fear.

Of terror.

All she gave him was a grim resolve.

Scowling, Ronild Magnison pushed down even harder with his sword, refusing to allow her to disengage. His anger driving him, he forced the sharp edge of his steel closer and closer to Talia's face as she struggled to match his strength.

"I've been waiting for this chance for quite a long time, my love."

"You're going to have to wait a while longer," Talia replied, her teeth grinding, the effort to keep his sword clear of her flesh becoming more and more difficult with each passing second.

"I doubt that," grunted Ronild, his eyes flashing with a

twisted pleasure. "You escaped me once. You won't escape me again. I promise you that."

Her arms beginning to shake with the effort of grappling with the man she was supposed to marry, the man who should have been dead and evaded her once before, Talia ducked to her left and slid to the side. His steel scraping off hers. Ronild growling in fury.

She hoped to catch Ronild off guard with her swift play so that she could put a few feet of space between them.

But it wasn't to be.

Ronild moved with her, his sword screaming through the air.

If Talia hadn't gotten her sword and dagger back in place in the blink of an eye, he would have split her head open like a melon.

Even so, she was barely able to prevent his blade from slicing across her face, Ronild pressing down even harder now, groaning with the effort, his sweat dripping down onto her forehead as he used his overwhelming leverage against her.

"You won't be getting away from me so easily this time, my love," grunted Ronild. "You thought you had left me for dead, didn't you?" He chuckled harshly at the thought. "No such luck. The question is, should I kill you now or make you marry me first?"

"You think you can kill me, Ronild?" hissed Talia. "You failed the first time. What makes you think that you can do it now?"

Ronild snorted at Talia's bravado, never having seen this side of his fiancée before. He had to admit that it enticed him in a way that he hadn't anticipated. Still, he was there to complete a task in the bowels of the Rock. And he couldn't do that until he got past his betrothed.

"What makes you think that I can't?" demanded Ronild, his

face turning red from the effort of applying even more pressure. His sword drifting closer to Talia's nose.

"Because you're a coward at heart, Ronild," Talia replied softly, gasping for breath while she called upon a hidden reserve of strength to keep his blade from slicing into her. She realized that she needed to change the game quickly, because that essential reserve was already beginning to drain out of her.

"You know it just as well as I do. Why else would you go running to Hakea Roosarian as soon as you arrived here? You weren't man enough to take me on by yourself. You were afraid of what I might do to you. The little girl getting the better of the big, strong man."

Talia laced as much scorn into her voice as she could. "You needed someone to hold your hand, didn't you, Ronild? A lost little boy afraid to challenge me directly. How sad. How very ... very ... sad."

Seeing how Ronild's eyes flashed dangerously each time she offered him a new insult, she hoped that his rising rage would give her what she wanted.

A brief moment of lost concentration.

Trying to catch him while he was momentarily distracted, she kicked out with her foot. She hoped to strike Ronild's injured knee and force him back against the wall, giving her more space to maneuver.

A good strategy.

Much to her chagrin, it didn't work. Her fiancé turned his hip at just the right time to absorb the blow.

"Clever, Talia," chuckled Ronild. His face twisted into a cruel smile, the scar stretching from his brow to just below his chin giving him a gruesome appearance. "But not clever enough, my love."

Ronild returned the favor, kicking out with his boot. Thinking that she wouldn't expect him to attempt the very same maneuver that had failed on him.

Talia shifted her hip to the left at the last instant, Ronild's foot smashing against the wall instead with what sounded like a very painful crunch. She smiled when he yelped and then grimaced. That grimace becoming a snarl when he tried to put his injured foot back on the ground but found that he couldn't without a searing pain racing up his leg.

She hoped that his injury would slow him down and allow her to step back and regroup. Yet despite the agony of his injury and the fact that he was finding it harder to keep his balance with only one foot fully on the ground, Ronild still had the presence of mind to keep Talia trapped against the stone.

"Not very creative on your part, Ronild," teased Talia. She didn't want him to be annoyed. That was his usual state. She wanted him beside himself. In a rage. If she could rile him up, then he wouldn't be able to think clearly, and she believed that she could use his damaged foot to do that. "But then again, you were never the creative sort. Just the greedy sort. Always wanting more than you deserved. Always wanting whatever it was that someone else had."

"I'll get what I deserve, Talia," grunted Ronild. "Have no fear of that. And I promise you that you'll get what you deserve as well."

He continued to apply a steady pressure to her blades, still intent on pushing Talia's own steel into her flesh. But he was having a harder time doing that now.

Ronild couldn't put any weight on his injured foot. Every time he tried to set it on the ground, he had to bring it right back up because of the spike of agony that shot through his leg.

That made it that much harder to keep Talia in place. He realized that he needed to finish this combat in the next few seconds. Otherwise more likely than not she would slip free from him. Once she did, Talia could use her freedom of movement against him. Then he would be vulnerable.

"What would that be, Ronild? There's so much that you believe that you deserve."

Talia wanted to keep him talking. Nudge him into a mistake.

Ronild kept shuffling his feet, trying to maintain his position. But what just moments before had been a simple task was now much more demanding. The pain in his foot, now a hot fire, becoming too much for him.

She just needed to keep a sharp eye, because she was certain that she would get her chance. And if she didn't make the most of it … then she was dead. Davin as well, and that she refused to allow.

"You, Talia. I will get you," promised Ronild, a thin line of spittle dripping from his lips as he pushed her blade to within a hair of her throat. "Whether you like it or not, Talia, you will be mine. Maybe not in heart and soul, but in body you will be mine. And that's all I need for what I have planned."

Even with his debilitating injury, he believed that he could still best his betrothed. But he needed to be careful.

If he didn't keep his feet, he feared that she would scamper away from him. Having no choice but to acknowledge that reality, he shifted his strategy.

He didn't have to kill Talia to get what he wanted. All he needed to do was wound her.

It was her body that mattered. If he had her body, then he had her. He could do what he wanted with her.

Once he sliced his blade across her flesh, he was certain that she would capitulate. Having spent so much time with her in Roo's Nest, grooming her to be his wife, he doubted that she had the backbone to resist him if his blade dripped with her blood.

"You will never have me, Ronild. Ever. Count on that."

"Promises, promises, Talia," Ronild tsked. "We had such a bright future, or at least I did, until you decided to do this to me." He nodded his head to the right, the light of the torch in front of him drawing her eyes to the terrible scar that extended down his brow. The terrible scar that she had given him when she decided to take him to task for a privilege that he believed she had no right to refuse him.

"And I still do have a bright future now that I am here," he continued. "Because just as I planned to do when we were in Roo's Nest, I will take your company from you. That will give me what I need to make the Duchy mine."

"You will never take my company from me, Ronild," hissed Talia. "Never."

She tried to control her building rage, knowing that it would only impede her efforts to stay clear of Ronild's sword and divert her from her primary objective.

Finding that weakness within him that would allow her to escape his trap.

But it was exceedingly difficult to do.

Ronild had struck a chord within her.

And he knew it, because he tried to play it again.

"But I will, Talia. I will cut you here beneath the Rock and then I will take your company after I take you." Ronild snorted with disdain. "Then, once I have you in a cage, you think your mother would risk trying to stop me?" He chuckled at the thought. "She couldn't stand against me on her own. She won't even try once she knows that I have you by my side, my blade at your back, my lips just a breath away from yours. A different kind of death for you, but death all the same."

"You wouldn't dare, you son of a ..."

"What's the matter, Talia?" prodded Ronild, seeking to strike that chord one more time, relishing how easily he was getting under her skin. "Do you want to go running to your father?" Ronild's eyes widened with feigned shock. "Oh, wait. You can't. Because your father is dead. How sad. How so very ... very ... sad."

Screaming in rage, Talia no longer able to control the emotions surging through her, no longer wanting to, she gave into her fury and pushed with all the strength that she could bring to bear.

She was desperate to throw Ronild off balance. To knock that smug grin from his face.

It was wasted effort, the towering figure in front of her barely budging even with his injured foot and knee. Worse, it appeared as if he had used her ploy against her.

"You never did have the good sense to die as you should have," Ronild Magnison laughed, enjoying how he had so easily broken through the armor she had built around herself. "And now you're going to pay for that arrogance. You're going to pay for believing that you're better than you truly are."

Ronild leaned forward, pressing even harder against Talia's dagger and sword. Pressing against her with his chest. Bending her backward at the waist. "You're a harbor rat, Talia. That's all you've ever been. That's all you'll ever be."

Talia strained to hold him back, her grip on the hilts of her weapons beginning to slip. He was too strong for her. Too determined.

She had been a fool. She had allowed him to crack the resolve that she had been using to defend herself.

As a result of her weakness, the keen edge of his blade was about to slice across her face.

Talia's eyes widened in worry as she let out a gasp. What he intended to do to her striking her like a slap across the cheek.

She had thought that Ronild was trying to kill her. That end she could deal with. If that happened, so be it. So long as Declan and the other gladiators rescued Davin.

But she refused to permit Ronild to achieve his real objective. To scar her just as she had scarred him. To put her in a cage for him to play with as he destroyed everything that she had built in Ballinasloe and turned it toward his own purposes.

That she would never allow.

Better death than that.

Calling on the last vestiges of her strength and will, she smiled at Ronild, hoping that it might throw him off.

"I had the good sense to get away from you," she hissed. "A man who can barely wipe his ass without Hakea Roosarian there to help."

"You think you know me, but you don't ..."

Talia cut him off. "I do know you, Ronild. I didn't know you then, but I know you now. You're a coward. You always have been. That will never change. No matter what you do now, you will always be a coward. And how couldn't you be? You didn't even have the courage to kill me when you had the chance."

Ronild Magnison stared down at Talia with hatred in his eyes. This was the look that he had given her when she was fighting for her life in his private study. After she had cut him. After he realized that she wouldn't be the complacent wife that he had wanted.

But now, Talia worried that she might have pushed too hard, a sharp stab of fear burying itself in her chest and working its way out to her extremities.

For just a second, memories of that terrible night in his family's manor house flashed through her mind. What Ronild had wanted from her. How he planned to use her and her family. How he had attacked her, the man who she thought she loved becoming a monster in just a heartbeat. How she had escaped him when she refused him.

She had barely gotten away. She had barely escaped his guards, almost falling to her death from the battlements.

When she had reached her mother and the ship waiting for her, Talia believed that she had killed him.

But she hadn't. Somehow he had survived her driving her dagger right between his ribs.

She was still having a hard time grasping the fact that he was alive.

The last time she fought him off she was too afraid. Only wanting to get away. Unable to take the time to confirm that she killed him.

Now she really wished that she had killed him then.

As she stared into his eyes, she studied the anger residing there. She had learned much too late that Ronild was the vengeful type. In fact, he was probably less angry that she had marked him with the dagger he had gifted her than with the fact that she had embarrassed him by wounding him.

She had made him appear weak and unable to manage his bride to be as he thought he should.

And to think that she was foolish enough to be taken in by the façade he presented to the world, almost finding out too late what kind of person he truly was.

"Say what you want, Talia, but your words have no meaning now, and they will have no meaning in the future," Ronild promised. "They will be nothing more than a few discordant notes on the wind. No one will hear you. No one will care. Because you will never get away from me. I will keep you alive if for no other reason than the knowledge that it will only increase your suffering. You having to watch as I make mine everything that your family built is a punishment worse than death."

Ronild's eyes glimmered with desire. He tilted his shoulder. He was no longer trying to cut across Talia's nose. Instead, he was fixated on cutting across her cheek with his steel.

He wanted to give her a taste of what it felt like to have a blade slice into her flesh.

He wanted to make sure that every time she looked in the mirror she shivered in fear at the memory of what he did to her.

He wanted to make sure that every time her damaged flesh pinched and burned she thought of him.

In fact, Ronild was so fixated on achieving that one goal that he forgot how she had slipped away from him when he tried to kill her back in Roo's Nest.

His eyes almost popped out of his skull, the air punched from his lungs, when Talia brought her knee up into his groin.

Not once.

Not twice.

Rather three times in rapid-fire succession driven by an unquenchable rage that she no longer had any desire to control.

Gulping for air like a fish out of water, Ronild sagged against Talia, thoughts of scarring her driven from his mind.

Talia acted swiftly, using his lack of balance to her advantage. Ducking her shoulder, she twisted away from him, finally clear of his steel.

Talia stared across the few feet between them. Her betrothed was bent at the waist, clutching his groin with his free hand, struggling to suck in air, the sword that he still gripped in his other hand an afterthought.

For just a heartbeat, she castigated herself. She couldn't quite understand why she had fallen for him in the first place.

He was vain. Arrogant. Full of himself.

He had tricked her into seeing something in him that had never been there to begin with.

No, that wasn't right. Better to be honest with herself.

She had seen what she had wanted to see and not what was actually there because she was lonely and uncomfortable in her own skin.

Because he was the first person who had ever shown more than just a fleeting interest in her as a woman.

She wanted to believe in the fairy tale, and she had been so desperate to do so that she ignored the truth of what he really wanted from her.

Her name. Her family's business. The assets that she and her family were creating.

Now, she knew the truth. She knew who he truly was. She acknowledged what he had always been.

A predator.

Nothing more. Nothing less.

And she had only herself to blame for falling under his spell.

Pushing himself up to his full height, wheezing as he tried and failed to take a deep breath, spittle dripping from his lips, Ronild glared at Talia with pure loathing in his eyes.

"You bit ..."

Ronild never had the chance to finish his expletive.

Talia leapt forward, sword to her front, intent on completing the task that she had failed to accomplish atop the plateau in Roo's Nest.

She had thought that she had killed her betrothed when she escaped Caledonia.

She had failed the first time.

She wouldn't the second.

~

Davin could barely catch his breath, the last few seconds of activity draining what was left of that hidden reserve of strength upon which he had been relying for far too long.

As he swung his steel spikes, slower and slower each time, his muscles quivering from the effort, he wracked his brain for some solution to break away from the Stalker so intent on tearing out his guts.

All that Declan had taught him, all that Bryen had taught him, all that he had learned from the many other gladiators and friends who had fought with him in the Pit, passed through his mind and disappeared just as swiftly. He was too tired, too preoccupied, to latch onto anything that might be of use.

It was taking almost all of his concentration just to stay on his feet.

He was desperate, a feeling that he had rarely experienced before.

As he faced off against the Stalker, all he wanted was just one more second of life.

That's what he had been reduced to. Taking as many seconds as he could get before he was dragged to the other side.

Hoping that every second he earned was another second that might allow him to find some way to make his escape.

But he knew how much hope was worth.

Better to focus on surviving for as long as he could since that seemed to be all that he was capable of doing in that moment.

Davin moved his head to the left, and just in time. The Stalker feinting a stab with its left claw.

Clever.

The beast was trying to get Davin to commit so that it could swipe its other claw across his face.

No such luck. Despite his weariness, Davin saw the move coming in the back of the Stalker's blood-red eyes, having defended against much the same tactic more times than he could count.

The Stalker roared in anger at its failure, pulling back its damaged claw, three of its daggerlike digits bent the wrong way thanks to the unyielding stone propping up its prey.

Davin didn't have the energy left to laugh at his attacker's misfortune, although the Stalker's anger did bring a slight smile to his lips. It also gave him a short burst of confidence, a characteristic that had been lacking within him, and strangely so, ever since he started his flight from the torture chamber beneath the Rock.

What Davin had first viewed as his escape had quickly denigrated into nothing more than a series of combats, much as if he were still fighting for his life in the Colosseum.

That memory brought back a sharpness to his gaze that, along with his energy, had been fading with every slash he attempted with his steel spikes.

He could do this.

He needed to believe that.

If he didn't, then he was dead.

He just needed to fight for a little while longer.

One second.

Then one more.

And then another after that.

Every breath that he took was a victory.

That's what he needed to believe.

He would find a way out of this mess.

He knew it.

He had done it so many times before.

What was a fist of Stalkers compared to a Bakunawa biting at the back of his board?

Davin tried to imagine that he was back on the white sand. Thousands upon thousands of spectators screaming and cursing, the noise deafening, the Colosseum shaking with excitement and bloodlust, filling him with a cold resolve, a desire to fight, a desire to win, a desire to live.

He was no longer Davin Noname

He was the Crimson Giant once more.

The Crimson Giant had never been defeated in the Pit.

He was second only to the Volkun in the Colosseum.

He was one of the deadliest fighters to ever stalk that bloody arena.

No one could stand against him.

No one wanted to stand against him.

No one dared to stand against him.

Davin grunted, wavering briefly as he blocked another of the Stalker's swipes then pivoted as the beast lowered its shoulder and attempted to crush him against the wall.

Even with what he perceived as a much too slow sidestep, Davin still got the better of the beast. Moving out of the way by a whisker, the Stalker growled in pain, the unyielding stone greeting the beast.

Identifying what could be his best and only opportunity, Davin stabbed with the spike in his right hand.

He let out a stream of curses under his weakening breath.

He had missed.

Davin couldn't believe it.

He never missed.

Ever.

That had been his chance. With a quick jab between the monster's ribs he could have ended this contest.

But he hadn't.

He had failed.

Davin knew then what his fate would be as he set his back against the wall and prepared to meet the Stalker's next and most likely last attack.

The monster growled deeply as it pushed itself away from Davin and flexed its claws. Believing that the combat was at an end.

The cold reality of what was coming was like a slap across Davin's face, and he couldn't argue the truth of it.

He had suffered too much in the last few days.

He had taken too many wounds and injuries at the hands of Hakea Roosarian, her torturers, and her monsters.

He had given all that he could. More than could be expected of most.

He had tried to meet the standards that Declan had set for

him when he first walked out into the Pit. The standards that he had tried to live up to every day since.

Even so, he was disappointed.

In what fate held in store for him.

Even more so in himself.

That was a feeling that he hated, in large part because it was so unfamiliar.

Yet there was little that he could do about it now.

He had been given a chance, a better chance than he could have asked for, and he had failed to make the most of it.

Just minutes before, he had thought that he was about to die, the shadow coming at his back preparing to run him through while he was engaged with the same Stalker that was about to kill him now.

But he had been wrong.

Gratefully so.

Davin was both surprised and energized when he saw Talia sprint past him.

Not quite believing that she was there for him.

Not really understanding how she had found him.

And, honestly, not really wanting her there despite his dire circumstances, not after all that he had done to get her out from beneath the Rock in one piece.

Yet, much to his shame, the spark of anger that he expected to feel at Talia's arrival was instead a spark of relief.

He felt guilty about that now, that she was sacrificing herself for him, because he was about to squander the gift that she had given him.

He was going to lose this combat.

He knew it.

The Stalker did as well.

The beast wasn't rushing to attack now, not after suffering for its impetuousness during its last few assaults.

Now the Stalker was taking its time. Looking for the right

moment. Understanding that Davin had nowhere to run. Nowhere to hide.

No!

Davin refused to give in.

Not after all that he had been through.

Not after all that he had given to survive.

Not after the risks that Talia had taken by coming back for him.

Talia was dealing with the threat at his back. And he could see just over the Stalker's shoulder that Declan and his friends were almost through the last of the monsters blocking the corridor.

In that direction just one more Stalker remained a threat. Fighting savagely but uselessly against a well-coordinated attack, Majdi and Jenus holding off the beast with their shields. Dorlan punching over their shoulders with his spear as Asaia waited for a clean strike with her whip. It was only a matter of time before the beast died at the hands of the Blood Company.

Just a little while longer.

One more second.

One more after that.

Then one more.

The longer that he could stay on his feet, the longer he could stay alive.

Then, even if he didn't kill the Stalker, maybe one of the other gladiators would.

He still had a chance. Slim. But a chance, nonetheless.

Ignoring the voice in the back of his head that was telling him to be cautious, Davin surged forward. He slashed with his steel spikes, relying on the last of his fury and forcing the Stalker back against the far wall of the corridor.

The monster screeched in rage, raising its arms in a desperate attempt to block Davin's quick succession of blows.

Failing. Not fast enough. Several of the painful strikes sneaking past.

Davin smashing his spikes against the Stalker's nose. Its cheek. Its forehead. One crack right after another, steel against flesh.

Again and again.

Blood and pulp flying in the air.

Staining him.

And then, even though Davin missed with his last swipe at the monster's throat, when he pulled back the steel tip caught the Stalker's three fingers that were bent the wrong way, slicing off one and earning the gladiator a welcome shriek of pain from his severely wounded opponent.

The Stalker, wanting to shield its injured claw, tried to step back even farther, seeking to put some space between them before figuring out its next move. But there was nowhere else to go. In its rush to get away from Davin, the beast only succeeded in slamming the back of its head against the stone.

That proved to be the least of the Stalker's worries.

Davin used what little momentum he could build up in just a few steps to fall into the Stalker and drive the sharp tip of one steel spike through the monster's gut.

Then, when the Stalker inevitably bent at the waist when the spike punched through its back, Davin thrust up with the spike in his left hand, driving the steel through the monster's mouth, out the back of its neck, and into the rock wall.

The Stalker's shriek swiftly faded into a sad sigh, the beast dying slowly, held in place by the spike that Davin had sunk into the wall.

Davin took a deep breath as he stared into the Stalker's eyes, the life slowly leaving them, the blood-red fire fading to nothing more than a few smoldering embers before finally winking out for good.

He pushed himself off the beast and then turned around,

placing his back against the stone right next to his dying adversary.

He needed the support.

His strength was gone.

He had given everything he had to win the combat and now he had nothing left.

And, thankfully, he hadn't wasted the chance that Talia had given him.

Sagging back against the wall, his legs wobbly, fearing that he might slide to the floor, he looked up, searching for Talia, hoping with all his heart that she had survived her encounter with the shadow that sought to stab him in the back.

A hot bile rose in the back of his throat.

He didn't see her, the Huntress blocked from his view.

He did see the Stalker that he thought he had dispatched earlier staggering toward him on one good leg, reaching for him, claw about to swipe across his throat.

TALIA'S SWORD slid off Ronild's blade with an ear-piercing screech. She didn't hear it. Her sole focus on the assignment she had to complete.

She had succeeded in forcing her betrothed away from Davin. A small victory, true. But she had missed the chance she had been seeking.

She hadn't finished the job, Ronild recovering faster than she thought possible.

"Did you really think you could escape me, Talia?" Ronild attempted to chuckle, wanting to demonstrate his disdain for her. It didn't work as he wanted, the dying wheeze coming out more as a rasp thanks to the pulsing ache in his groin that she had gifted him. "You should have known me better than that after all the time that we spent together."

His raised eyebrow was meant to make her uncomfortable, to get her thinking about their past rather than their present, but realizing that his hint had little impact, he continued to push. "When I want something, I will do whatever is necessary to make it mine. I wanted you then. I want you now. And I will have you."

"You should be dead," Talia muttered, still angry at herself for not killing him back in Roo's Nest and then in Smuggler's Cove. Even more angry now since she had just failed again. "The world would be a much better place if you were."

"You can't kill me, Talia," snickered Ronild through gritted teeth, the pulse of pain between his legs threatening to disable him. He refused to allow that to happen, however. He was here because Talia was here. He was here because he could finally gain his revenge upon her if the next few minutes played out as he wanted. "But I can kill you. And I can do so much worse before that."

Ronild leapt at her, swinging his sword in a vicious downward arc. If he accomplished what he intended, he would have slashed across her right arm and taken her sword from her.

No such luck.

She glided away from him with ease, reading what he intended before he had taken more than two steps.

His failure didn't stop Ronild from continuing his attack, slashing and slicing, grunting and groaning, soon thereafter growling because of his lack of success.

Despite putting all his knowledge of swordplay to work, despite trying every trick that he had learned, every means to catch an adversary by surprise, Talia danced away from him with a skillful and irritating grace as she put into practice much of what she had learned from Davin while they trained in the practice circle.

After more than a minute of frenetic and useless activity, Ronild had no choice but to step back. He was exhausted, sweating through his clothes, and he still wasn't able to extend to his full height because of his aching groin. To say nothing of his throbbing knee, a gift from the gladiator fighting for his life just a few yards away from him, and what he assumed was a broken foot. With all that, he needed a few seconds to recover before he had another go at his bride to be.

More wary of her now, Ronild ran an appraising glance over Talia. He was impressed, although he refused to show it. She had changed a great deal since he had last seen her.

"You've gotten better with a blade," he muttered, breathing deeply, trying to push past the discomfort that continued to haunt him and, he believed, hinder his efforts, not wanting to give Talia too much credit for his delayed victory.

"I have a very good instructor."

Ronild tried to laugh. Unfortunately, it came out as a snort mixed with a gasp, the pain in his crotch almost getting the better of him. "The gladiator? Really? He used to be a slave." Ronild shook his head in bewilderment, trying to recapture some of his bravado as the pain between his legs eased slightly, the pulsing now dull rather than sharp. "What could he possibly have taught you?"

Talia smiled as she thought about his question. "Other than how to beat a Lord of Roo's Nest in a combat, he taught me to judge a person by his actions. Not his words. A lesson that would have served me well when I was with you. Perhaps I wouldn't have been such a fool."

"Perhaps," Ronild replied with an ingrained smugness. He nodded ever so slightly as he studied her, not really knowing what to expect from her since that fateful night between them. "At first, upon seeing you, my only desire was to kill you. To repay you for the terrible harm you did me." He flicked his hand toward the scar marring his features to remind her yet again.

"This was bad enough," Ronild continued, "but when word

spread in Roo's Nest that you had done this and that you had escaped me as well ..." Ronild shrugged then shook his head.

"I'm in line for the throne of the Duchy. It's only a matter of time. This wound was a shock. Your ungratefulness even more so. But much worse were the looks of disdain I received because of you. How people began to look down upon me. The loss of standing that I and my family had to endure because of you was almost too much to bear."

"Then kill me if you can ... *my love*," Talia taunted, biting off the last of her words with a sarcasm that was reflected in her eyes.

She wanted to push Ronild into a drastic action. He had the advantage over her in size and strength, although not speed, and she hoped that if she could nudge him over the edge, she could catch him in a mistake.

"I think not," Ronild replied, refusing to be baited. "No, that would be too easy for you, wouldn't it?" He stepped toward her then, pushing himself off the wall, sword at the ready.

"You don't deserve an easy death for what you did, Talia. You deserve to suffer. So I'm going to stick to my original plan. I'm going to knock some sense into you now and then put you in a gilded cage. Once that's done, I'm going to take your company and take you back to Roo's Nest. And once there I'm going to put you on display after you marry me. No longer a person, just a prize. A death of sorts, just not the physical kind."

He chuckled then, warming to his decision. "I will show you off to those who need reminding of what happens if they dare to cross a Magnison."

For several heartbeats, Talia didn't reply, simply glaring at Ronild. His threats were becoming repetitive. It was as if he were reading from a script.

Then she smiled and snorted in disgust. She knew who he was now. She understood that his words were more for himself than for her.

Ronild lacked something critical in a leader. Spine.

"Come and try, Ronild. You failed the last time. And the time before that. What makes you think you will succeed now?"

That last taunt did the trick, Talia watching as the spark of pleasure behind Ronild's eyes after his speech shifted in just a flash to rage. That same rage that had almost killed her before she escaped to New Caledonia.

"You will do what I tell you to do, *my love*. Always! Forever!"

Ronild rushed toward her, sword slashing through the air, although this time targeting her thigh rather than her throat.

Despite his anger, his thoughts remained fixed on wounding her, disarming her, and taking his betrothed out of the fight.

Ronild knew exactly what he wanted, and he was going to get it. At all costs. Just as he always did.

It wasn't to be, however, his desire getting in the way of his reason.

Talia slid to the side. At the same time, she kicked out with her right foot.

Her timing was perfect, striking his injured knee a hard blow that almost sent Ronild tumbling to the ground.

The wall saved him, the space so tight that after he stumbled a few steps trying to keep his feet, he crashed into the stone with his shoulder, grimacing as a bolt of pain shot down his arm, his fingers on his right hand tingling and then losing feeling.

Thankfully for just a few seconds, no more, Ronild getting his sword in place just in time to block Talia's slash.

If she had connected, she would have slit his throat and been done with this drama.

But just as with Ronild's last attack, it wasn't to be.

They were back where their combat had begun. Blade pressed against blade. Body pressed against body. Glare matching glare.

Although this time, Talia was in a better position, having taken away several of Ronild's advantages. His groin ached as did his shoulder, Ronild now struggling to keep his sword in place as Talia sought to use her steel to press her former fiancé's own blade into his flesh.

And by the look he was giving her now, one of shock and almost despair, he had realized that he could do little to stop her, not with him down to one good leg and the stone at his back a necessary aid for keeping him on his feet.

He couldn't quite believe how quickly she had changed the dynamic on him. And by the glint in her eyes, Ronild knew that he needed to regain the momentum. Quickly. Before she finished him.

Recognizing his limitations, he was about to push off the wall, hoping to use his greater weight to take Talia down to the floor with him where his lack of mobility would be less of an issue. Before he could do that, however, he felt a searing pain between his ribs.

Ronild stared down in shock at the blood seeping out from his side, his mind having a hard time coming to grips with this latest wound as an enfeebling coldness spread through him, washing away the pain that had been wracking his body.

Talia kept her sword in place, held against Ronild's. Not willing to take a risk. Wanting to make sure. Even though by his sharp gasp and the distant look in his eyes, she knew that she had won. She had caught her betrothed just as she had intended.

Not with her sword. Instead with the jewel-encrusted dagger Ronild had given to her as an engagement present. Driving the steel between his ribs and then twisting the razor-sharp blade a few times before yanking it free.

"You bi ..." Ronild found his words difficult to come by. It was as if all of his energy was flowing out of the wound along with his blood. "You can't ..."

Talia kept her eyes locked on Ronild's. She had finally completed the task she had set for herself in Roo's Nest.

She had killed him.

Ronild just hadn't realized it yet.

Instead of watching him die, instead of offering some smart reply that would confirm her victory, Talia shook her head in disappointment. At herself mostly for allowing herself to be taken in by her betrothed. Then she spun around. Letting Ronild sag against the stone, she sprinted back down the hallway.

At the same time that she had struck her killing blow, Talia had heard the shriek behind her and then the sound of a clawed foot being dragged across the stone floor. She knew what that meant, and she cursed herself for not making certain the beast was dead.

A small voice in the back of her head reminded her that she hadn't had time to finish the job. If she had, then Ronild would have killed Davin.

That didn't matter, however. The Stalker that she had wounded before she challenged Ronild had gotten back to its feet and still was intent on killing Davin. She hadn't injured the beast as badly as she thought she had, the Stalker having found the will and the desire to push up off the floor and stagger down the corridor toward its prey.

The monster's daggerlike claws were reaching for Davin, just an arm's length away from ripping into his flesh, the gladiator spent, caught off guard, having no way to defend himself.

Talia was still too far away to put herself in front of Davin, so she did the only thing that she could. She threw the bloody dagger that she had used to kill Ronild, hoping that Tennyson was guiding her aim from the other side.

She sighed with relief when she realized that the crusty old sailor was.

Talia's dagger streaked through the gloom, and just as had

happened so many times on the deck of a ship, her aim was true.

The blade lodged itself in the Stalker's neck, the beast rearing up more in surprise than pain. Its claws, just a hair away from slicing across Davin's throat, instead scrabbling against its own throat, seeking to grasp the hilt of the dagger.

Talia was there an instant later, knowing that this was her best chance to finish the beast.

When the Stalker, mewing feebly, dropped to its knees, its effort to free the dagger only speeding up the loss of blood, she slid her sword through the Stalker's armpit and into its heart.

The Stalker collapsing face first to the ground, issuing a final sigh before it died, Talia rushed up to Davin, reaching out and cupping his sagging head in her hands.

"Davin! Davin!"

She was about to slap him across the face, terrified that she had lost him, when he looked at her through exhausted eyes. "What's the matter? I'm just resting."

"Resting?"

Talia stared at the gladiator in disbelief, taking in his many wounds, the blood and gore covering him, his inability to do anything more than lean back against the stone wall. "You look more like death warmed over."

Davin smiled at that, even as he struggled to keep his eyes open. He was tired. So very, very tired. "Thank you."

"We're going to get you out of here, lad." Declan trotted over. The gladiators had killed the last of the Stalkers. Now it was just a matter of taking Davin to Rafia so that she could heal him.

Davin nodded, although just barely, finding the movement almost too much for him, as Declan kneeled down and began ministering to the worst of his wounds.

"Asaia, I need some clean bandages!"

The gladiator, handle of her whip still in her grip, the spike streaked with blood, was already on the way over with a satchel draped over her shoulder.

"You're going to be fine, lad," Declan said, assuming that they could get him to the Magus quickly, several of Davin's wounds worrying. And he had no doubt that they would. The gladiators would see to that. They looked after their own.

"Thanks for coming back for me," Davin whispered to Talia. "You didn't have to. You really shouldn't have. I'm mad at you for that, by the way. Really mad. You should have left me. That was the smart thing to do."

For just a second, Talia didn't know what to say, tears beginning to stream down her cheeks.

"I did have to come back for you, Davin," she was finally able to say, her emotions threatening to overcome her. "I really did."

Then she kissed him, pressing her lips gently against his.

Talia's action brought a brief spark of energy to Davin. He hadn't been expecting her to do that. Although he couldn't say that he didn't welcome her affection.

With the very last of his strength, he kissed her as well, although it was much too fleeting, because Asaia arrived at his side then.

"Enough of that, young ones," she said, kneeling down next to Declan. "Leave it for when the Crimson Giant is feeling better."

10

GREY BLANKET

"I wasn't expecting that," Aislinn breathed. Nerves raw, her heartbeat pounding in her ears, adrenaline flowing through her veins, she was still on edge from the combat.

Aislinn knew where she was, but that didn't make the rapid shift any more palatable. The transition from being beneath the Shadow Keep, the cauldron of boiling black with the misty figure floating above it demanding all of her attention, to this world of muted color and silence disorienting.

She stood in the thick grey of the Murk, Bryen right next to her. Although she didn't see him so much as sense his presence, the blanket of swirling and folding mist so dense that she was blind to everything around her.

She understood why the Wraiths reigned supreme in the Murk, having experienced this same isolation once before. Yet she couldn't quite turn her mind toward the monsters in the mist.

Not yet.

She was still thinking about the creature that had once been a Magus. The creature that was more than a Magus. The creature that had blasted them back through a portal of spinning black with little difficulty to send them where they were now.

A world in which they didn't belong.

A world in which they were the prey.

"Another myth made real?" wondered Bryen. "Why not? That seems to be standard practice for us."

"Now's not the time for your dry wit." Aislinn allowed a hint of testiness to creep into her voice. With her senses constrained by the fog, she felt distinctly out of place. She didn't like it.

"I disagree. Dry wit is perfect for a time like this."

"Because we just met a monster of legend against which the Ghoule Overlord couldn't hold a candle?"

"Among other reasons," Bryen admitted.

Aislinn couldn't see the shrug of his shoulders despite his proximity, the wispy grey hiding the motion, but she could feel him doing it. Rather than allowing her testiness to reign, she focused on the issue that had consumed them both as soon as the first bolt of black energy shot toward them.

"What are we going to do about the Ancient One? If he achieves his objective, then ..." Aislinn didn't need to complete her thought.

"Nothing yet," Bryen sighed, not happy with the answer he gave, though he believed that it was the right one. Even so, he couldn't keep a touch of concern from drifting into his voice. Her worry matched his with respect to their new foe. "The Ancient One is still locked away in the Spirit World."

"But for how much longer?"

"Your guess is as good as mine."

"That's not helpful," Aislinn chided.

"It wasn't meant to be," he replied in a placating tone. He understood why Aislinn was agitated, because he was as well.

They had just faced off against a creature that wasn't supposed to be able to touch the Natural World, but clearly he had and he was.

A creature that had the power to destroy every living thing within the Realms.

A creature against which they could barely defend themselves, and they were two of the strongest Magii ever to walk the earth.

"The Ten Magii?" suggested Aislinn.

"Yes, that's where we start," Bryen agreed. "First, though, we've got a more pressing concern."

Aislinn didn't bother to reply. Bryen was correct.

Reaching for the Talent, she searched around them. They were to the northeast of Shadow's Reach. Close to the southern border of the Wyld.

Just another reason to fear the Ancient One. That monster had sent them several hundred leagues to the north and neither she nor Bryen had been able to prevent it.

"Why would the Ancient One send us here?"

"Maybe he thought that the monsters in the mist could do his work for him," suggested Bryen.

Aislinn nodded in understanding. "The Ancient One is testing us."

"I think he is," Byren confirmed.

"He seemed to think that if you died, he would be able to take the Seventh Stone from you more easily."

"He said as much," Bryen agreed.

"And if not, he would come after you at his leisure."

"A comforting thought, yes, and by doing this he has nothing to lose." Bryen tried to fill his voice with a confidence that he didn't feel. Confronting the Ancient One had unsettled him in a way that nothing else had in quite some time. The only other instance in his life when he had felt like this was when he walked out onto the white sand for the first time.

He wasn't afraid of dying. He had spent too long in the Pit to allow that fear to rule him.

But he was afraid of not being able to stand against the

Ancient One when that confrontation came. When the consequence of his losing meant more than the loss of his life.

"Bryen ..." warned Aislinn. She didn't believe that he was taking her concerns seriously enough.

"Sorry, you're right."

"That's why he didn't kill us beneath the Rock," Aislinn said softly, fitting the pieces together.

The Ancient One was a great deal stronger than they were in natural magic. Moreover, they didn't have access to the only weapon that gave them any chance of harming him. Yet still he had banished them here instead of seeking to finish the fight in the chamber beneath the Shadow Keep. That could only mean ...

"He's not strong enough here," Bryen said, finishing her thought for her. "He can touch the Natural World, but he can't step into it completely. Not yet. So he can't bring his full power to bear."

"That's why we're still alive."

"Right, assuming that we can get away from the threat coming toward us now."

Aislinn turned toward Bryen then. By using the Talent as Jakob had suggested, they could see all that was hidden within the Murk; most important, the hunters coming toward them at a fast clip. "Well, you did say that you wanted to learn more about the Wraiths. What better way than this?"

"Now you with the dry wit?" Bryen sounded disappointed, trying to keep his amusement hidden.

Aislinn arched an eyebrow. "I can have a little fun as well. I don't have to be the serious one all the time."

"You don't think I'm the serious one?" Bryen asked. After fighting in the Pit for ten years, dry wit was about the limit of the humor he was willing to offer to the world.

"Point taken," Aislinn replied. "Should we start this?"

Bryen waited a few heartbeats before responding. "Let's see what they have to say first."

They didn't have long to wait. Two fists of Wraiths materialized out of the grey. If not for the clarity granted to them by the Talent, Bryen and Aislinn never would have known they were there. Not until the Wraiths ran their bone-white blades across their throats.

The creatures looked exactly as Jakob described them. A consequence of the Curse that had been used to make these men and women what they were now.

"Soldiers of the Ten Thousand," Bryen called out. "Preparing to hunt beyond the borders of Frisia once again?"

His words stopped the Wraiths in their tracks. Double-bladed daggers already in their clawed hands, they had been ready to kill these two interlopers with a few fast swipes of their blades.

It was plain, however, that this man and woman were more than they appeared to be. If only briefly that gave the Wraiths pause.

Because in the last few months all had not been as it should be in the Murk. A series of surprises and setbacks had slowed the Wraiths. Complicating their plans. Putting their primary goal at risk.

"Who are you to speak of the Ten Thousand?" hissed the Wraith who stepped out in front of his hunters. "Who are you to challenge us?"

The Wraiths shifted ever so slightly, forming a semicircle around their prey. The two Wraiths at each end pinched in closer, now no more than ten feet away on either side. Within striking distance with just a lunge. A fact that didn't go unnoticed by Aislinn or Bryen.

"I am who I am."

Bryen and Aislinn used the silence that greeted his reply to study the Wraiths. The monsters in the mist seemed at their ease, unconcerned that they had been identified before they could attack.

However, there were a few signs, barely there though still noticeable, that suggested otherwise. A slight shift in weight from the right foot to the left by the Wraith to their far left. One of the Wraiths flexing his clawed digits, clearly impatient to make use of his dagger. And the leader of this squad, eyes narrowing, tilting his head to the side, curious. Also slightly concerned, although trying not to show it.

"Do not play with me human," the Wraith Hunter warned in a soft voice that pierced the gloom like a bolt of light. "Who are you?"

"No one of consequence," Bryen replied quietly.

The Wraith Hunter took his time before responding. His finely tuned senses could detect nothing within the Murk that would be of interest to him except for this man and woman. Nothing that should give him any cause for concern.

The Murk was his domain and that of his brethren. Yet at this very moment, he felt uneasy. An uncommon experience for him.

That realization suggested the need for caution. At least until he could learn more about this pair of humans caught in the Murk who didn't appear to comprehend the peril they were in.

"Why do you speak of the Ten Thousand?" the Wraith Hunter rasped. "The Ten Thousand are gone."

"The Ten Thousand are gone," Bryen agreed. "Yet some of the Ten Thousand stand before me."

"You have no right to speak of us," the Wraith Hunter said, fixing his gaze on Bryen. "You are insolent."

"Among other things," he replied.

The Wraith Hunter didn't say anything else for several

seconds, taking in the man standing before him. Based on his posturing and positioning, he appeared more than competent, the double-bladed spear that he gripped casually helping to confirm it.

Yet there was more to the man than just the steel he carried. What that could be, though, he wasn't quite sure yet.

That fact troubling him, the Wraith Hunter turned his gaze to the woman next. She stood calmly by her companion's side, holding a sword, tip pointed toward the grass.

Clearly competent with that blade. And just as was the case with the young man, there was more to this young woman as well. A power radiated from her, telling him that she was a great deal more than she appeared to be.

"You trespass on our lands."

"We are not in Frisia," Aislinn replied calmly. "It seems that you are the ones who are trespassing."

The Wraith Hunter smiled at that. Yes, he was right. There was a steel within both these humans that he had found lacking in so many of the others he had hunted in the Murk. Lacking in all but one other, in fact.

"We are not in Frisia," the Wraith Hunter agreed. "But Frisia is only a name from history. Here, now, where the Murk goes so go the Wraiths. Boundaries and beliefs mean nothing to us. We take what we need. We take what we deserve."

"Apparently you believe that you deserve quite a lot," Bryen offered.

"Your insolence will be your downfall, human. I promise you that."

"Not you?" asked Bryen.

"I am the Wraith Hunter, human. Second only to our master. You would dare to challenge me?"

"Hunting us?" Aislinn cut in. There was a value in Bryen antagonizing the Wraith Hunter. And she knew that this confrontation only was going to end one way. Before it did, however, she wanted to dig out a little more information if she could. "That's your purpose for being here?"

"Hunting whatever chooses to enter the Murk," the Wraith Hunter replied. "That is what we do. That is how we become more than what we already are."

"And you are one of the Ten Thousand?" Aislinn asked. She knew the truth after Oraan Kvo had revealed as much to them during their last conversation. Still, she wanted to hear it from their adversary.

The Wraith Hunter turned his gaze back toward her, his eyes having been drawn to the young man. The coldness of his expression suggesting that he knew what was coming next. "I was."

"But no more?" she prodded.

"No more," the Wraith Hunter confirmed. "We are what remains of the Ten Thousand, but the Ten Thousand are gone. We are something more now."

"You are slaves to the Curse," interrupted Bryen.

"We are slaves to no one," hissed the Wraith Hunter, the creature's preternatural calm shattered by that single comment. "We are the Curse and the Curse is us."

"Anyone who is of the Curse is a slave to it."

The Wraith Hunter stared at Bryen, growling softly. "Brave words while trapped in the Murk."

"True words."

"Last words," the Wraith Hunter stated with a lethal finality. "You've made a mistake by coming here. This is our land."

"And you seek to expand your land?" asked Aislinn.

"We do." The Wraith Hunter laughed softly, the sound a scratchy growl. "We are growing in power. We must use it. We must take what belongs to us."

"And what belongs to you?"

"Whatever we want belongs to us," the Wraith Hunter replied. "And we will take it. We deserve no less."

"Others have tried," Aislinn challenged, "and they have failed."

"Perhaps," the Wraith Hunter allowed, the creature actually offering a barely perceptible shrug of his narrow shoulders. "But those others are not us." The Wraith Hunter's eyes blazed brightly then, the black visible within the gloom. "We are no longer the Ten Thousand, but we still hold to the strictures of our corps. What we say will be, will be. We always make it so."

"I've got a friend who has a thing for maxims," Bryen said. "I'll pass that one on to him. I have no doubt that he'll like it."

"You're taunting me, human," the Wraith Hunter hissed.

"No more than you deserve," Bryen replied calmly.

For a moment, Aislinn and Bryen both believed that their adversary was going to order the Wraiths to attack. To their surprise, he laughed instead.

"You are not afraid of us."

"We aren't," Aislinn confirmed.

The Wraith Hunter nodded again. "There is another human like you. One who is not afraid of the Murk, who is not afraid of us. One who I plan to kill when next we meet."

"Good luck with that," Bryen replied with a twist of his lips that earned another soft growl from the Wraith Hunter. "He's not an easy kill."

"No, he's not," the Wraith Hunter agreed. "But you two are a different matter entirely."

The Wraith Hunter barked sharply. The Wraiths, unmoving during the conversation, glided forward at their leader's command.

Bryen and Aislinn knew that the Wraiths could move fast. Just not this fast, covering the ground between them in two steps. Even so, they were ready for the monsters in the mist.

Taking hold of the Talent, Aislinn sent several thin threads of energy pinwheeling with such speed through the Murk that they resembled blazing wheels.

The Wraiths demonstrated their remarkable agility, dodging or diving out of the way just in time. Except for one.

The unlucky Wraith was so focused on Bryen that he didn't see the fiery circle streaking toward him until it was too late. The creature collapsed to the ground, eyes wide with shock as the light faded from within, the energy burning through his chest and leaving a hole the size of a giant's fist.

After that initial strike, the caution that the Wraiths exercised aided Aislinn and Bryen. None of the creatures wanted to meet the same fate as their comrade, whose body continued to burn just off to the side of the battlefield.

Aislinn, her sword blazing with the Talent, sought to maintain the initiative despite being outnumbered. She stepped forward, surprising the Wraith who was closest to her.

The creature, who had been sneaking up on her from the side, hesitated, losing his footing, slipping in the wet grass.

Aislinn didn't hesitate. With a quick slice across the Wraith's belly, she left the creature crumpled on the ground.

Certain that the Wraith wouldn't be getting back up, she pivoted to her right, sword leading the way. Her movement was so quick and so precise, her glowing steel sweeping through the Murk in deadly arcs, that the pair of Wraiths who thought to come at her from two different directions at once instead were forced to step back in order to avoid a fatal slash.

In seconds, what the Wraiths viewed as an easy kill became a fight for their lives. Neither of the creatures anticipated such an outcome. Neither yet to face a real challenge even after entering the Territories to the south more than a handful of times already.

Aislinn made use of her opponents' indecision, smiling wickedly as she continued her assault. Refusing to break away. Keeping the two Wraiths to her front.

These Wraiths weren't used to a fair fight. They were used to always having the advantage. To using the Murk against their prey.

Yet here, now, they had a real combat on their hands. And she had every intention of giving these former soldiers of the Ten Thousand exactly what they deserved.

Bryen used the distraction that Aislinn provided with her initial attack to create one of his own.

Energy dancing across his fingertips, he whipped his arms down toward the long grass.

Two bolts of lightning blasted into the ground right in front of a pair of Wraiths. The force of the blow so powerful that it sent one of the creatures flying backward.

The monster crashed heavily in a heap well beyond the Wraith Hunter. Not moving. Not getting back up.

The other Wraith caught in the blast disappeared entirely, obliterated by the bolt of lightning that shot down from the unseen sky.

Just like Aislinn, Bryen employed the same strategy, taking the fight to the Wraiths who shifted their positioning to block his path to the Wraith Hunter.

Bryen leaned back just enough to avoid the wickedly sharp steel that sliced through the air right in front of him, missing his throat by no more than a knuckle. The power of the Wraith's swing pulling the beast slightly off balance, Bryen's kick to the creature's hip sent his attacker tumbling to the grass.

The other Wraith saw his chance. Believing that he could come at Bryen while he was engaged with his now fallen brethren, the creature slashed with the double-bladed dagger in his right claw.

The dagger proved to be no match for Bryen's double-bladed spear. Not even bothering to look, his eyes still on the fallen Wraith, Bryen swung his glowing weapon behind him.

The gurgle he heard just a heartbeat later told him all that he needed to know. That and the sound of the Wraith who had been about to cut across the back of his neck collapsing to the ground, sighing softly, his throat cut.

The Wraith Bryen kicked away was already pushing himself back to his feet. However, the remarkably fast creature wasn't fast enough.

Bryen pivoted, his blade scything through the air and coming back around, separating the Wraith's head from his neck along the way.

His two adversaries no longer threats, Bryen extended his senses. He was under no immediate threat.

Bryen took a step toward Aislinn to offer his help, but he realized that doing so wasn't necessary. Aislinn had eliminated one of her adversaries, the body of the Wraith crumpled in the grass off to her right. The other Wraith wasn't faring much better.

Her current opponent was struggling, blood dripping down from several long and bloody stripes on various parts of his body, a larger sheet of blood pouring down the monster's chest from Aislinn's latest slash, which cut deeply through flesh and muscle, revealing the ribs beneath.

Even though the creature's death was imminent, the remaining Wraiths made no move to help their wounded brethren.

In fact, the Wraiths moved behind the Wraith Hunter, not joining the fight after Aislinn and Bryen killed so many of their comrades in what seemed to be no more than a few blinks of the eye.

The gasp to Bryen's left pulled his eyes briefly away from the Wraith Hunter. Aislinn finished her combat with a lightning-fast slash, slicing open the Wraith's neck, the creature falling not too far away from his dead companion.

That done, Aislinn turned slowly, ready for the next

combat, fixing her gaze on the leader of the monsters in the mist.

"Impressive," the Wraith Hunter growled.

And the Wraith Hunter was impressed. He had lost more than half of his Wraiths to these humans in less than a minute. Although he wasn't surprised considering what they were.

Before the clash had begun, the Wraith Hunter had sensed something off about the pair. They had been kind enough to provide him with the missing piece, his initial caution when he first came upon them justified.

"Then perhaps you'd like to test us yourself instead of sending your Wraiths to do your dirty work for you," Bryen suggested. "What kind of leader would you be if you didn't have the courage to challenge us?"

"A leader who continues to draw breath," the Wraith Hunter explained in a scratchy laugh, obviously unconcerned by the number of bodies that littered the ground. "The Wraiths you killed were weak. They deserved their fate. And if I were so foolish as to jump into the ring with either of you, I would be found wanting as well."

"Afraid to test what fate might hold for you?" Aislinn wondered if another barb could push the Wraith to draw his blades.

The Wraith Hunter laughed again. Clever on the woman's part. But not clever enough. "Not afraid, Magus. Simply realistic."

"Too bad," Aislinn replied in a disappointed tone. "We were hoping for more of a challenge."

"Next time, Magus, have no fear. I promise you that you will have the challenge that you want. A challenge that you will not survive." The Wraith and his hunters started to glide away from them, heading deeper into the Murk and back toward the north. "Next time we meet, Magus, your power won't save you. Because my Master will be with us. And with him will be the Horde. You may kill some of us, but you cannot kill us all."

"Don't be so sure of that," Aislinn called after him.

"Your courage does you credit, Magii," the Wraith Hunter said, his words fading quickly as he moved away from them. "But it will do you little good in the end. When the Murk comes, we come. Your land will become ours. You can't stop the Murk. You can't stop us."

Bryen and Aislinn remained where they were for several minutes more, watching with the Talent until the Wraith Hunter and the last of his fighters were well and truly away.

"We could have gone after them and finished this," Aislinn said. She had yet to wipe the Wraith blood from her blade. Her eyes still burned brightly, the tension that she always felt, that she always welcomed, when she drew her steel racing through her.

"We could have, you're right," Bryen agreed. "But now we've given the Wraiths something else to think about."

"You believe that we might have bought some time before they come in force?"

Bryen shrugged. "Maybe. I hope so. But if we did, we didn't buy much. Hopefully enough to be ready for them."

"Happy that you finally got the chance to meet the Wraiths face to face?" sighed Aislinn, the energy within her beginning to fade. She knelt down, wiping the blood from her blade in the long grass before sheathing the Blademaster's gift in the scabbard across her back.

"More dry wit? You're really outdoing yourself today."

Aislinn smiled. "We need to figure out some way to prevent the Wraiths from coming south."

"Agreed. Even with the Talent, we won't be able to stand against them for long."

"Stop the Murk and we stop the Wraiths."

"Right again," Bryen murmured.

"But we need to do something else first." Aislinn already knew what was on Bryen's mind.

"Deal with your aunt. After what we've just learned about her …"

"I know. She's not just a Dark Magus. She's also a servant of the Ancient One. If we're to have any chance of dealing with the Wraiths, we need to deal with her first."

11

A PROPOSAL

Having just won her latest gladiatorial combat, Lycia cleaned herself up as fast as she could. Her hair still wet, she put on her best clothes, which meant the one pair of breeches and shirt that weren't covered in dirt, sand, and blood, none of it her own, of course.

She had been required to leave her weapons behind, which was why she felt naked as she walked through the Stone.

To settle her unease, she reviewed in her mind the combat she concluded just an hour before.

She couldn't help it. Declan trained her to function this way.

To learn from what she did right.

To learn from what she did wrong.

Then move on, but not until her analysis was complete.

This last combat had been the first time that she faced a real challenge on the brown sand of the Little Pit. The previous four contests including her first had taken no more than a minute. Two at the most.

But that only made sense. Sharperson knew who she was

after her first fight, and he had used that knowledge right from the start.

The Governor of the Highlands believed that her name would pull more people to the Little Pit despite the now higher cost of attending.

The Crimson Devil, an undefeated gladiator from the Colosseum who helped to overthrow the Beleron dynasty, gracing the brown sand of the Little Pit. Who wouldn't want to watch such a warrior doing what she did best?

His strategy worked. Probably better than he anticipated.

Today, for the first time since Lycia arrived, the stadium had been completely full. Except for the stands on the far side that had collapsed last year. Yet even there a few brave people climbed through the debris and broken boards to find an unsafe perch.

She had fought against three criminals. Men accused of murdering a family that had just arrived at the Stone.

The parents were going to open a bakery.

At least that's what the master of ceremonies explained to the crowd, weaving a story that captured their attention and their favor before Lycia even stepped out onto the sand.

Was the story true? Lycia didn't know.

She did know that the men, whether criminals or just a trio unlucky enough to be swept up off the street for the combat, were all veteran soldiers. They weren't particularly skilled with their blades, at least not in her own estimation. Nevertheless, they were better than any of the other combatants she had faced since she assumed the mantle of gladiator once more.

In large part because they understood tactics. They knew what to do when they enjoyed the advantage in numbers and they were fighting one person.

Yet even with that knowledge, the combat only lasted a few minutes more than the others.

Lycia knew what Sharperson wanted from her on the brown sand. That was fine with her.

Because she believed that if she gave it to him, then he would give her what she wanted.

An opportunity.

As soon as the combat began, the three soldiers stayed away from her.

They moved as quickly as they could in the wet sand that sucked at their feet -- a rainstorm drenching the crowd right before the bout began, forming a triangle around her.

Lycia had expected just such a maneuver. She also had expected what came next.

The soldiers began to circle around her, always keeping their distance, waiting to see what she would do. Hoping that she would make a play for one of them, thereby giving the other two the chance to finish her.

Much to their surprise, she didn't do anything. She simply stood there, not even bothering to move her head to track the movement behind her, holding the hilt of a sword in each hand, sharp end pointed down toward the sand.

Calm. Composed. Seemingly unconcerned by three experienced fighters no more than ten feet away who were intent on killing her.

Not sure what to do, the soldiers continued to circle around her. Although it wasn't long before their impatience got the better of them.

The soldiers moved closer to Lycia, closing the distance between them.

She didn't move.

Not even a twitch.

Not even a glance.

Standing stock still.

Waiting.

Heedless to the danger they presented.

That confidence, what some might call arrogance, drove the spectators into a frenzy. They couldn't quite understand how the Crimson Devil could maintain her composure as the sense of impending doom grew thick in the arena.

Her three combatants took her composure as an affront. An insult. The Crimson Devil not believing that they were worthy to stand against her.

At least that's what they told themselves, Lycia assumed, just as she believed that they would. Because the trio of soldiers continued to tighten the circle.

Every so often one of the men stabbed at her with his short sword, then quickly scrambled back.

Lycia didn't bother to move. She didn't feel the need to defend herself.

Her opponents were just testing her. Wanting to see what she would do. Never getting close enough to cut into her flesh. Still wary. Worried about what she would do if they gave her an opening.

Her refusing to engage only served to drive the crowd into an even greater tumult. That didn't please the soldiers at all, perceiving Lycia's disdain as her mocking them. And though they might not have reputations that matched that of the Crimson Devil, still they were proud.

That's what Lycia was counting on.

The first soldier to give in to his anger paid for that mistake with his life.

The man circling behind Lycia stepped forward on fast feet, stabbing with his short sword for the spot right between her shoulder blades.

Lycia barely moved. Not trusting the wet sand, she pivoted to her right.

The soldier tried to arrest his progress in time.

He was desperate to do so.

But he couldn't.

The wet sand caused him to slide farther forward than he wanted.

Before he could pull back, with a backhanded grip Lycia ran the sword in her right hand across his throat. Although it was more a situation where she held her steel in place and allowed the soldier to do the bloody deed himself.

She then took a few steps away from the dying soldier, his blood puddling in the already soaked sand.

As the crowd's screams for more blood increased in intensity, Lycia focused on the two remaining soldiers.

The veterans had a hard time believing just how quickly she had dispatched their friend, causing the uncertainty that had plagued them since the combat began to worsen.

They knew who the Crimson Devil was. They knew what she could do. But they never believed that she could do it to the three of them with such proficiency.

Two they corrected.

Lycia fought the urge to kill the pair immediately. It's what she would have done if she had been fighting in the Colosseum. But here, now, she couldn't. Not if she wanted to achieve her objective.

So she allowed the two soldiers to live a little longer.

And the men obliged by doing exactly as she thought they would. They took up positions on the compass that were directly opposite from one another.

There they waited. A minute passed. And then another. Finally one more.

The pair expected her to respond in some way. Make a play for one of them, which would give the other a chance to get in a strike. Hopefully before the soldier she attacked didn't fall victim to one of her swords.

Yet she didn't do as they hoped she would. She made no move toward either of them. Simply turning sideways, a blade held loosely in each hand, pointing toward each man.

Most galling, however, was the fact that she hadn't yet deigned to look at either one. They couldn't quite see from where she was standing, but it appeared as if she had closed her eyes.

Their rage building – at how the Crimson Devil was insulting them, at the loss of their friend -- they charged at her at the same time. Roaring at the top of their lungs. Swords held above their heads and already swinging through the air. Certain that one of them would earn the kill.

Their blades never connected with their target.

At the very last second, Lycia spun around, a blur of motion, her swords singing through the air at shoulder level.

When Lycia completed her motion, she glanced to the left and then to the right, seeing exactly what she expected to see.

For just a heartbeat, the two soldiers remained standing, swords held loosely by their sides. Then their free hands went to their throats. Tentatively at first. Not quite comprehending what had occurred.

Not realizing that it was too late for them to change their fate.

Their blood poured down the front of their leather armor, Lycia having cut through their necks all the way to the vertebrae.

A second later, both men dropped as if they were puppets on strings, their master having let go of their guides.

The eruption of the crowd's approval after her victory had set the Little Pit shaking.

Dangerously so.

So much so that she feared that the entire structure might collapse.

Completing her review, Lycia decided that the only mistake that she had made was to allow the combat to continue for so long. As Declan had taught her, the more time that she spent on the white sand, the greater the chance that something that she couldn't control would happen.

She agreed wholeheartedly with that maxim. But how she had managed the combat was necessary. Therefore, she didn't fault her approach. If she had killed the soldiers too quickly, she wouldn't be where she was now.

She certainly didn't relish her success, the role she had been forced to play. She did understand its importance, however.

Besides, Jakob had not asked her to do this. She had asked him to allow her to do this for him.

"Hello, my dear." Torstan Sharperson stood in the foyer that led into his private quarters. He motioned for her to come in. "A pleasure to have you here."

Lycia nodded, her expression wary just as she thought it should be. Then she walked by him.

As she did so, Sharperson blocked her way partially, forcing her to scrape past him, just as he had done the last time she had spoken with him.

She ignored the game he was trying to play, instead allowing her eyes to slide swiftly over the room and then the ones beyond. With the opulence on display it was hard to miss how Sharperson was trying to impress all those who might enter his chambers.

Finely woven rugs. Antique couches and chairs set in front of the three fireplaces just in this chamber alone. Brass sconces lining the walls, lamps burning brightly, the light reflecting off long pieces of carved gold set along the walls that displayed scenes from Caledonian history.

The obvious demonstration of wealth put her slightly off balance. She tried to ignore the display as best as she could, although she realized that demonstrating a little nervousness might aid her with respect to the Governor.

And try as she might, she couldn't ignore the eight soldiers who were arrayed around the dining room into which he ushered her. She took a seat across from him, forcing herself not to acknowledge the two soldiers at her back. The same two soldiers who had required her to lift her arms and allow for a quick but thorough search to ensure that she didn't carry any hidden weapons before they allowed her to approach Sharperson.

Lycia hadn't challenged them when they made that demand of her, even though she considered their effort a waste.

She didn't need a blade to kill Torstan Sharperson. She could eliminate him just as easily without. And she could do it with eight soldiers standing in the room with her.

"Please, sit." He pulled a chair out for her.

Lycia didn't say anything. She didn't even nod.

Staying in character, maintaining the persona of an uncomfortable visitor with a chip on her shoulder, she sat down, placing her back against the hard wood of the uncomfortable chair.

Sharperson gave Lycia an ingratiating smile. Then he maneuvered his bulk into a chair larger than all the others placed around the table. Although not without a good bit of effort, the chair creaking loudly as he struggled to find the most comfortable position.

While he did that, Lycia examined the meal already laid out for them. Pheasant. Boar. Venison. A variety of vegetables. Enough food, in fact, to feed all the gladiators who fought in the Colosseum before Bryen freed them.

"So tell me, my lovely, what should I call you? The Crimson Devil just doesn't seem right in this delightfully intimate setting of ours. Especially if we are to get to know one another better."

"Why do you need a different name?" Lycia asked tartly.

Sharperson stared at her for a time, his expression sharpening.

Lycia stared right back at him. He was measuring her. She viewed that as a good sign.

They were going to be partners of a sort, and she needed to be perceived as a reluctant partner.

Then he smiled. "That same keenness I've had the pleasure to watch these last few days follows you everywhere, doesn't it?"

"It's why I'm still alive," Lycia replied, lightening her tone, giving him a small smile that made it seem as if she were bestowing a great favor upon him.

She didn't want to drive him away. Rather, she wanted to reel him in.

Sharperson studied her a few seconds more, then laughed softly. "I can understand that." He leaned forward then, placing some of his bulk on the table, his belly threatening to cover his plate. "But here you have nothing to fear, my lovely. Here, with me, you are safe." He leaned back then, hoping that doing so would make her feel more at ease. "So please, relax. Enjoy yourself. You sit at no finer a table than any in all of the Highlands."

Lycia actually preferred the campfire meals that she enjoyed so much with Jakob and his Highlanders. She kept that to herself, of course.

When she pulled her eyes away from the spread before her, the bile rose in her throat. The look in Sharperson's eyes was the same one that her uncle had given her just moments before she stabbed him.

"Lycia," she finally told him, having to work to keep the contents of her stomach where they belonged.

"Lycia," Sharperson repeated. "That's a lovely name. And your surname?"

Lycia didn't reply for several heartbeats, turning her eyes away, trying to make the Governor think that she was ashamed by what she was going to tell him next. "I don't have one."

Sharperson nodded. "That's nothing to be embarrassed

about, my lovely. Many face the same circumstances as you have. It just so happens that you've found a way to rise above the hand that fate dealt you while others haven't." He picked up a fork and stabbed a large piece of venison, the gravy dripping across the table before the slice of meat was safely on his plate. "Eat. Please. You must be famished after today's combat. We can talk business when we're done."

Lycia ate only a little of the food, picking at the pheasant, concentrating on the vegetables. While she chewed slowly, her eyes slid over the room, never staying in one place for very long, keeping to character, a fighter slightly out of her depth. Although doing enough to keep an eye on the soldiers standing around the table, their backs up against the wall.

Not because she had any real concern about most of the men, although she needed to make Sharperson believe that she did. Only one soldier, a brute of a man with a gruesome scar running down his neck and a large portion of one ear missing, who stood directly behind Sharperson gave her pause.

Her eyes never stayed on him for long, but she knew that he was doing the same thing that she was doing. He was studying her and trying to do so without her knowing it.

Although that wasn't what was making her so uncomfortable every time she glanced in his direction.

It was because of the scent he gave off.

Not a smell. Rather a feeling.

Much like she had experienced on the streets of Tintagel and then in the Colosseum. The feeling that life and death held little meaning to the man, except when he had the chance to take a life.

The soldier guarding Sharperson's back was a predator. He enjoyed killing. Of that she was certain.

"You barely touched your food, my lovely," Sharperson said when he was finally done, his plate wiped clean, more than half the food that had been set on the table devoured.

During the meal, he had regaled her with stories of his youth. Once done with that, Sharperson spoke of his plans for the Stone and the Highlands.

She listened intently, searching for any useful piece of information and finding for the most part only chaff.

"I'm not very hungry," she murmured softly.

"After a combat like yours, I find that surprising."

"The combat isn't over," Lycia explained.

"Isn't over?" he asked, somewhat perplexed. "What do you mean?"

"I'm still working through it in my head."

He raised an eyebrow as he stared at her again, understanding slowly dawning. Then he nodded his head in appreciation. "I should have expected as much. Always on the white sand."

"Always."

"Then let us talk about why I asked you to come here. I hope you understand that it's rare for someone of your stature to be invited into my presence."

Lycia fought hard not to snort out a laugh. Able to maintain her grim expression, she nodded ever so slightly, afraid of what would come out if she opened her mouth.

He motioned to the man standing behind Lycia who had been leaning against a table covered by a large cloth. Moving with a surprising dexterity, the soldier stepped to the side and took the cloth with him.

Lycia's eyes widened. On the table lay brand-new leather armor, a pure black, that she was certain would fit her perfectly, along with metal braces for her arms and two swords, currently sheathed. She could only assume the blades were of the highest quality and likely worth a great deal more than the ones she had taken with her from the Colosseum.

"I don't want all this," Lycia mumbled when she could

speak again. She wasn't just playing a role now. She had never been the beneficiary of such largesse before.

"But I do."

Lycia turned toward Sharperson, her gaze sharp again. She noted how he had reacted to her surprise, relishing it, just as he was meant to.

"What do you want in return?" She was afraid of how Sharperson was going to reply, because although there were certain requirements she was willing to agree to, there were quite a few others that she was not. And what he said next would determine whether her efforts to ingratiate herself with him were worth her time, effort, and the bile rising in the back of her throat.

"I want to pay your debts."

That response only surprised her a tiny bit. She expected more directness from him, but then again, that really wasn't his way, was it?

From what she had learned, Sharperson preferred to come in a roundabout way to the matters that were most important to him.

"You'll pay my debts?"

"This very second."

"That's very generous."

"It's the very least that I could do since you've helped to fill the seats of the Colosseum in the Peaks."

Lycia nodded as if his thanks was of little matter to her. "I hope you understand the amount is not a small one."

"How much?"

"Three hundred golds."

Sharperson's eyes widened. That was quite a sum. "How did you manage that?"

"Bad decisions."

Sharperson nodded. Upon hearing that, he was even better positioned than he thought he would be when he first put this scheme together in his mind. "I'll have the golds to your new room by tomorrow morning."

"My new room?" That last comment surprised Lycia.

"Yes, your new room. Not too far from mine here in the Stone." He didn't explain further, just giving her a wink.

"Why?"

"Because if I'm paying off your debts, then I'm also buying you." He said it reasonably, not hinting at what it truly might mean. "I like to keep my investments close."

Lycia offered Sharperson a shrewd gaze, then she nodded. His veiled demand didn't faze her. She had been bought and sold before. Besides, she could likely make use of his requirement when the time was right.

"What would I have to do in exchange?"

"Protect me. Fight for me."

"No more combats?"

"No more combats. Except for those that I authorize. Those that ensure we both make a tidy sum." He leaned his bulk atop the table once again, the wood groaning, his eyes flashing brightly. Although not from lust. Rather from greed. "If you spill your blood, it's for me now."

"Nothing else?"

"Nothing else ... for now. But who can say where things will lead in the future?"

12

A NEW DYNAMIC

"Kendric, please listen to me." Ursina spoke as calmly as she could, all the while her irritation threatening to get the better of her. She had been having the same conversation with her husband for the last several minutes. Kendric had been picking at the issue from a different direction each time, unwilling to let the matter go. "I don't know where Aislinn and her Protector have gone. I only know that they are no longer in the Shadow Keep or in the city itself."

"Aislinn would not have left without telling me where she is going," Kendric countered, just as he had several times before. "She wouldn't. I was there when she was born. I know her. She wouldn't leave without telling me." Sighing, he shook his head. Worried. "Something has happened to her. I can feel it in my bones."

"The Aislinn you knew when you were in the Southern Marches might not be the Aislinn you know now," Ursina replied with as much composure as she could manage. She had said much the same thing several times before. As a result, what little patience she had left for her husband was waning quickly. "You have not seen her for years. People change with time."

"She has changed, yes," Kendric admitted, "but that's only natural. She's grown up. Even so, Aislinn has not changed so much ..."

Ursina shut her eyes and blocked out her husband's words. There was no point in listening. He wasn't saying anything she hadn't heard before. And she doubted that he would buttress his argument with anything new.

Feeling the pressure behind her eyes beginning to build, she worked to maintain control over her temper. To find the calm that she needed so that she could end this dialogue and they could move on to more important matters.

Even though Kendric didn't entertain the same perspective as she did, Ursina thought Aislinn Winborne disappearing was the best thing that could have happened to them. She had told her husband that several times already, but it had yet to sink in. His stubbornness getting in the way.

Of course, in truth, Aislinn and her Protector hadn't disappeared. Although Kendric didn't need to know that. That would only muddy the waters of their current conversation all the more.

"Kendric, please," Ursina broke in, gripping his arm gently when he walked past. The ruler of the Shadow Keep had been pacing in his office ever since Ursina walked through the hidden doorway and given him the news. "I don't know where she and her Protector have gone. I don't know why they have gone. But we must move on. There is business we need to attend to. Matters critical to our welfare and the welfare of the city."

"I know, Ursina, I know," Kendric replied. Concerns regarding the Wraiths and the Murk were never far from his mind. "It's just that ..."

"You worry for her," Ursina replied, looking up and

catching her husband's eyes with her own. "I would expect nothing less from you." She patted his forearm gently with her free hand, earning a smile from him. "You are a good man and a good uncle. But you must remember, my love, that Aislinn is not a child. She is a young woman. I have found nothing to suggest that she didn't leave the city of her own free will. You said she had an adventurous spirit. Perhaps she simply decided to go off on her own for a time. And if she did with that Protector of hers I'm sure that she's in good hands."

"That may be, Ursina," Kendric replied with a nod, "and I value all that you've done to locate her. But we need to find her. We need to get her back safely. We need ..."

Ursina looked down and shut her eyes, shaking her head ever so slightly as she sought the calm that continued to elude her.

She loved her husband. She did. But she couldn't do this anymore. She couldn't.

No matter how hard she tried, she couldn't do it. It needed to stop.

"No," Ursina interrupted her husband with more force than she intended.

Kendric stopped talking midsentence, shocked to have been brought up short. He looked down at his wife, his brow furrowed, eyes drawing closer together.

Ursina wasn't looking up at him with that small smile of hers that he enjoyed so much. Her expression was hard, matching her eyes, her mouth a thin line. And there was a twist of anger in the slight curl of her lips.

He had never seen this side of his wife before, and he didn't know what to make of it.

"No? What do you mean no?" demanded Kendric, although he didn't raise his voice. He kept himself under control, not wanting to antagonize Ursina, because the spiky essence that she was radiating was making him nervous. Even so, he was struggling to stay calm, a range of emotions rushing through him. Most dominant of all his instinct to protect his niece rather than protect himself. "Aislinn is like a daughter to me, Ursina. I must ..."

Kendric's words caught in his throat when Ursina's eyes flashed, the violet he was so enamored with replaced by a black that covered her entire sclera.

He tried to pull back from her, startled, terrified, but he couldn't move. Ursina's iron grip tightened on his forearm, her fingers digging into his flesh, a cold energy surging into him.

His wife's eyes locked onto his, and what he saw there chilled him. Those orbs of black flashed and swirled. Almost making him think that he was seeing his wife for the very first time, and he didn't like what he was seeing.

More frightening, he was losing himself. He could feel it. His mind, enjoying a clarity that was becoming more and more rare for him, beginning to cloud.

Kendric was having a difficult time thinking.

He couldn't hold on to a thought no matter how hard he tried.

His memories of his niece were slipping away.

Memories of his brother.

Of his time growing up in the Southern Marches.

All replaced by a fog that was more insidious than the Murk that brought with it the Wraiths.

"Ursina, please, you need to help me. I can't ..."

Ursina's eyes sparked with a black fire, sending an uncontrollable surge of fear down his spine and then out into his extremities. He tried to resist the darkness that was building within him. He tried to push it back. To maintain control over himself.

But he couldn't. No matter what he did, he couldn't.

Still he fought.

He couldn't let this happen.

Not now.

Not with his niece ...

"Ursina, please! You must ..."

Ursina gripped his arm with even greater strength, her nails digging into his flesh and drawing blood.

The cloud of black became an overwhelming tidal wave against which he was powerless. And through it all, as his mind slipped away, as his consciousness shriveled, locked away into the very back of his brain, his eyes remained on his wife's, those orbs of flashing pitch having taken hold and refusing to let go.

"I must do nothing, Kendric, other than what must be done to protect our interests."

The intensity of her gaze finally lessened when she sensed that her husband was back under her control. Only then did she slowly begin to pull the threads of the Curse back into herself.

The tainted energy released its hold on Kendric, although the corrupt residue of her power remained, continuing to burrow its way into him. Taking him. Making him its own. Just at a more measured pace.

As the Curse dissipated within her, Ursina's eyes slowly changed. The stormy black retreated to her pupils, then disappeared entirely, the violet back in place.

She was about to say something to Kendric, to apologize for what she had made him do. She waited instead.

Her husband wasn't there yet. He was still locked away within himself. It would take a few heartbeats more before he returned to her.

She hated doing this to him. She understood the cost. To her. Even more so to him. But she had no choice.

His memory, bad to begin with, was only getting worse, and that slide would only accelerate after this latest conflict between them. After what he made her do for the benefit of them both.

Having some sympathy for him, she relaxed her grip on his arm. With a thin stream of the Talent, she healed the cuts caused by her fingernails. Then she sent a burst of energy into him, hoping that it would help to slow even more the effects of the Curse, knowing and hating that she could not stop the transformation occurring within him in its entirety.

She closed her eyes for a breath and sighed heavily. A feeling of powerlessness rushed through her.

Her efforts weren't working as they used to. The Curse was conducting its conquest within her husband at a much more rapid rate.

And what she had just done to him, fogging his mind, pushing him away from his current train of thought, hadn't helped him.

When she opened her eyes again and looked up, she saw that Kendric finally had returned to her.

At least as much of him as could be expected.

The man she loved. The man she was slowly …

Ursina refused to continue with that line of thought as he offered her a tired smile. When he did, it never failed to warm her heart.

Yet she couldn't get past her dark thoughts. When the time came that she could no longer arrest the progression of the Curse within him, she would need to make a decision.

But until that day …

She had other matters to worry about.

"Ursina, what are we …" He stopped himself, his face flushing red. What had just happened came back to him. Not what his wife had done. Not realizing his wife had wiped that from his memory. Rather, he recalled that the illness plaguing him had reared its ugly head again. He was embarrassed. Scared. Impotent in the face of the disease that afflicted him. "How long?"

Ursina looked away from her husband, not answering him, as tears formed in her eyes.

"How long?" he repeated more forcefully though still gently.

"I don't know, my love. I'm sorry, but I don't know."

Kendric pulled his eyes away from his wife, then closed them. He nodded slowly.

"She's my niece, Ursina."

Ursina didn't reply right away. She was surprised that he could remember that much after what the Curse had done to him.

She should have been worried.

But she wasn't.

Instead, she was proud of him, even though his strength of character made what she needed to do that much more difficult.

He was still fighting. He was showing a fortitude against the Curse that she had seen lacking in so many others.

"I know, my love."

"My niece," he repeated more forcefully.

"Yes, my love, I know." Ursina reached out again, this time grasping his hand, squeezing his fingers warmly. "But she's more than just that. She's a threat."

Kendric stared at Ursina for quite a long time, the shadows in the room lengthening, playing around the edges of his office, seeming to take shape behind him.

Then he nodded. Reluctantly. Acknowledging the truth of what she said.

"It was a mistake, Ursina. What we did. The decision that we made." He sighed heavily, all of what little energy he had left draining out of him. "We should never have taken such a risk as we did."

"I'm sorry, my love. In the end, it will be worth it. I promise you."

He nodded again, then took a deep breath. When he looked at her, his eyes were clear. The cloud that had been plaguing him just minutes before dissipating, drifting into the background.

"Tell me the truth," Kendric demanded quietly.

"It's too late, my love. We are both too far gone. To try to leave the path that we have taken ... it's not possible. Better to face what stands in front of us rather than worry about what is waiting at our backs."

She wished that she could have offered Kendric something more positive. Even lied to him after seeing how his hope died upon hearing her words.

But she couldn't do that to him. She wouldn't. She loved him too much.

It was too late. For him. For her.

She had done many things in her life that she regretted. But this ...

What she had done to Kendric, what she had done for Kendric, was the greatest regret of them all.

She had chosen this path.

She had thought that she could navigate the challenges, the perils, the demands that others had failed to maneuver around.

She had discovered much to her everlasting regret that she was no different than any of those other Magii.

The Curse had proven too strong.

Too seductive.

Too jealous.

She had sought to tame the Curse.

And she had learned too late that in actuality the Curse had tamed her.

She was what she was. She could not change that now.

That left her with only one path.

A path that could lead to even more power than she already

wielded ... or complete and utter ruin for her and the man she loved.

13

TIMELY MEETING

"Have you done this before?"

Rafia kept her eyes on the long column emerging from the tangle of heart trees to their south that was snaking its way down the trail. A few hundred all told. Maybe a third soldiers. The rest forced laborers. Or so it appeared.

"More times than I can count," Declan replied. "I started as a scout in the Royal Guard."

Declan nodded to himself as he swept his eyes across the landscape around them. Sharperson's Guard had picked a good location. Easy access only from the east and even that limited by a series of crags and crevices that rose up to the north and south.

A natural chokepoint.

Declan and Rafia lay atop a tall ridge, hidden within the long grass and shrubs that grew rampant along the crest. Behind the ridge towered a taller crag. And behind that an even taller one. And another. And another. Until the series of crags ran smack into one of the tallest peaks in the Highlands.

From where he and Rafia were situated, they looked down upon a rough trail that was only a hundred yards to their front but several hundred yards below them. On each side of the track grew purple and white heather mixed in with a few patches of wildflowers that had won their place in the gorse.

At the far end of the dale, just a quarter mile away to the north, right at the edge of the wood, a large fort was under construction. One of many, in fact, in this region of the snow-capped peaks.

The Highlanders had their brochs. It seemed that Sharperson was seeking to challenge them with his wooden keeps. They were of a simple square design to ensure fast construction. Timbers twenty feet in height formed the walls, which were anchored by a tower on each corner.

A demonstration of his power, Sharperson likely believed. He probably dreamed of extending his sway back into the Highlands from this line of fortifications that had sprung up in just the last month.

But Declan knew what dreams were made of.

Torstan Sharperson was not in a position to push back against Jakob Kestrel.

Not yet.

Not ever if the Highlanders had their way.

The Governor was sending out companies of soldiers and conscripted laborers to build outposts that marked the border of the territory patrolled by his Guard. That was true.

However, until Sharperson figured out how to eliminate the leader of the rebels, he was doing no more than seeking to consolidate control over the small southwestern section of the Highlands that he still governed. And even then, his hold over what was now no more than ten to twelve leagues of terrain was tenuous at best.

Declan was willing to give Sharperson some credit. The forts weren't a bad idea. They could prove useful if employed in the right manner.

He had done much the same when serving in the Caledonian Royal Guard near the Trench. He and his comrades had used their fortifications to range into the Shattered Peaks and hunt the Ghoules who had forced their way through the Weir.

There was only one problem with Sharperson's strategy, however. He had come up with it too late.

The fort that Declan was studying, just like all the others he had observed while he made his way along the edge of Sharperson's territory, was not yet complete. And until those redoubts were, they were vulnerable.

"Are we going to try for a closer look at our target?" asked Rafia, referencing the column that was now traipsing right below them, the soldiers and prisoners all out from between the trees. "Or was this all just because you wanted to get close to me?" She lay shoulder to shoulder with Declan, giving him a slight nudge to prove her point, although not enough to reveal their position. "Because there are easier ways to get close to me. You should know that by now."

"I'm doing this to stay in practice." Declan ignored at what the Magus hinted as best as he could, a faint touch of heat rising in him. "It's not a skill that I want to lose."

"You do realize I could use the Talent to hide us," Rafia prodded.

"I'm well aware," Declan admitted, returning his eyes to the long column below them, "but you may not always be with me. So I can't rely on your unique skills all the time."

"What do you mean I won't be with you?" she demanded in a whisper.

Even with her irritation, she remembered that a loud voice would carry a great distance on the wind that was blowing off the top of the mountain and down into the small valley below. She didn't want to give them away.

Declan shifted to his right, giving Rafia a warm smile. He understood why she was acting this way. Their relationship was new. They both were still settling into it.

"There's no need to be so sensitive," he said once he caught her eyes. He returned her nudge. "You might be working on another task while I'm doing this. That's all I meant."

Rafia didn't reply right away, realizing that she had jumped to a foolish conclusion.

"So I'll be stuck with you?" she asked, needing some way to hide her brief feeling of embarrassment that was confirmed by her flushed cheeks.

"You will." Declan turned his attention back to the column. "Whether you like it or not."

Rafia smiled at that last comment. Declan wasn't like Sirius. She shook her head when she pulled her eyes away from him and returned her gaze to the men and women walking by, once again focused on the matter at hand. "What do you see?"

"Bait."

"What do you mean?"

Declan started pointing out several prisoners who were linked to the long chain that Sharperson's soldiers were using -- the same chain likely employed previously to bring unfortunate souls to work and die in the mines until Jakob Kestrel and his Highlanders had put a stop to that -- although his movements were careful and slow so that he didn't disturb the grass and shrubs hiding them from detection. "They don't look right. They don't look like the rest of the prisoners."

"They're plants," Rafia exclaimed softly. A clever play if you were expecting, or seeking to entice, trouble to come your way.

"That's my guess. They want us to attack."

"They do. They think they can take us."

"So the stronghold they're building ..."

"Is just as much a lure as a fortification," Rafia concluded. "Sharperson doesn't think we can let pass such juicy bait. He's trying to play us."

"He doesn't know what's happening in the rest of the Highlands."

"He doesn't," Rafia agreed. That conclusion twisted her lips into a devious smile.

"None of his Guard will go beyond the boundary they've established. They don't want to take the risk."

"And Duff's work to eliminate or misinform the Governor's spies ...," began Rafia.

"Seems to be working," Declan finished. "Would you mind searching around us with the Talent? My guess is that there are two companies of Sharperson's Guard somewhere close by just waiting for us to spring the trap."

Rafia did as Declan asked, reaching for the Talent and then extending her senses in all directions for five leagues around. "You're wrong."

"By how much?"

"Three companies of soldiers instead of two. All hidden away in the many dales surrounding the fort."

"All on higher ground, I assume?"

"Indeed they are," Rafia confirmed. "As soon as we go after that fort, they'll know."

"And then they'll come at us from behind and twist the screws of the vise."

"Not a bad plan."

"No, not bad at all," Declan grunted, "but not good enough."

"You still want to go after this group?" asked Rafia, already knowing the answer before she asked the question.

"I do."

"Even while knowing that we're walking into a trap?"

"I do. Most of those people are being forced to do Sharperson's work for him. They don't deserve that."

"The jaws of the trap will close quickly," Rafia remarked.

He turned to her again, giving her a mischievous smile. "Then we just need to be quicker. Besides, if we know it's a trap, is it really a trap?"

Rafia's smile only grew bigger, caught up in Declan's good humor and confidence. She already could see the wheels turning. "What do you have in mind?"

"I DON'T UNDERSTAND why we're taking this risk. Do you think they will be there?"

"They will be," Jakob replied.

His voice contained a confidence that was lacking in Saraa. It also revealed that he was tired.

Not because of their journey of several days. Rather because of the conversation. Although Saraa either wasn't paying attention to that hint or she didn't care.

When she felt the need to discuss a topic, she never let go. Not until she was done.

"How can you be so certain?" Saraa asked, her doubt floating above her like a cloud. "We've only just started working with them."

"I have faith that they'll be there, Saraa. There's no need to worry."

Jakob didn't tell the Highlander that he had been tracking their allies' progress for the last few days, just to make sure that all was moving forward as it should. If he did, she'd likely keep pushing him on the matter. Taking it as a sign that he agreed with her. That he didn't trust their new friends.

Which wasn't true. He did trust them.

He was tracking them because plans changed as soon as you put them into play, a fact that his father had drilled into him time and again, and he wanted to be ready for when that happened.

But so far, surprisingly, they had yet to face a single variable that required adapting their tactics. His Highlanders were almost in position. Assuming nothing went wrong, by the end of the day they would be within a league of the Stone and flooding into the territory that Sharperson still claimed as his own.

Just as important, the several other bands of Highlanders Jakob had set to work would be in position as well before the sun set.

Coordination was the key. If their timing was off and Sharperson's Guard figured out what was going on, there was a good chance that the rebellion he and Duff had set into motion would come to an ignominious end.

However, if they succeeded, then the Highlanders would have a clear run at the Stone. With that would come the chance to remove Sharperson from power with a minimum of bloodshed.

Wisely, Saraa decided not to push any further. At least not on that topic. Nevertheless, unable to help herself, she shifted to an issue that had kept her mercurial temper at a slow boil ever since Lycia joined them.

"And you have faith in the gladiator as well?"

Jakob didn't reply immediately, his grimace slowly turning into a knowing smile. He had expected this from Saraa. Duff had warned him. He just didn't want to deal with it now. Again.

"I do. I wouldn't have agreed to the plan otherwise."

"Why?" demanded Saraa. Her voice was louder than she intended, drawing Duff's gaze, the Highlander carrying his oversized blacksmith's hammer over a shoulder as they climbed the trail that was taking them between two peaks that towered above them on both sides.

Jakob took his time before replying, needing to be careful as they traversed a rockslide that covered a large section of the trail. Also wanting to give Saraa a few seconds to calm herself. Or at least to try to calm herself.

She had disliked Lycia from the very start. That much was plain. And it had only worsened as Lycia proved herself to

Jakob and the other Highlanders. He was willing to admit as well that he and Lycia spending a good bit of time together likely didn't help.

He understood Saraa's motivation in that regard. Yet with all that was at stake now wasn't the time for that conversation. Although he knew that he couldn't let her continue to stew.

"Why not?" Jakob replied.

His response stopped Saraa in her tracks. Her face a mask of confusion. "Why not?" Her tone became slightly incredulous. "Why not? That's why you're willing to work with her?" She began walking again now that they were clear of the rocks, catching up to him. "With all that's at risk, you're willing to put everything we're trying to build into the hands of a gladiator who only knows killing?"

Jakob sighed. Clearly, Saraa missed the point of what he said. So much for trying to be clever. So much for actually trying to make her think about his question.

Although it was understandable. It would take her in a direction that she didn't want to contemplate.

"Saraa, what I meant was that I have no good reason to distrust her. I understand the risk we're taking, and I believe it's a risk worth taking."

"How could you *not* distrust her?" Saraa hissed quietly. "She shows up to help us at the perfect time. She ingratiates herself with you and Duff and everyone else. Always there when you need her. Making herself more important to our efforts. Biding her time until she finds the perfect moment to stab you in the back."

"I don't take Lycia as someone who stabs a person in the back. If she's going to stab you, she's going to do it with her looking you in the eyes."

"Jakob!" Saraa growled, not appreciating what she took to be an unnecessary moment of flippancy.

"Saraa, she's put her life at risk countless times." Jakob

spoke as calmly as he could manage. His desire to snap at his friend because of her obstinacy was growing, and he was finding it more and more difficult to avoid that. "She's doing so right now, in fact. Remember, if something goes wrong, then she's on her own. There's no way we get to her in time to help her. Not like when I and Lycia got to you in time at the mine."

Saraa ignored Jakob's argument, caring little for what the gladiator may or may not have done for them. "Have you ever considered that perhaps she did all this to get where she is now? So that she could do what she really needs to do?"

Jakob studied Saraa for quite a long while, the trail becoming a series of switchbacks that would take them to the plateau above. A distance of a few hundred feet as the crow flies but almost a quarter mile as they worked their way along the face of the crag. "Do you really believe that?"

"That the gladiator is working against us? That she's a spy?" Saraa snorted in derision. Shaking her head in disappointment, she strode ahead of him, seeking the vanguard of the column that was already past the first turn and now above them. "What I can't believe is that you don't believe that."

Jakob stopped then, stepping off the trail and up against the rock, allowing the Highlanders behind him to pass by. He watched as Saraa worked her way farther up the trail and then disappeared around a bend along the mountainside. She'd be visible again in a few seconds.

Lost in thought as he waited for her to appear above him, it took him a moment to realize that Duff had stopped next to him. His friend hadn't said a word. He was simply waiting. Understanding what was going through Jakob's mind.

"You heard what Saraa said?" Jakob finally asked.

"I did," Duff confirmed. He shifted his hammer from one shoulder to the other. "You're in a tough spot, lad, and Saraa just made it that much more difficult."

Jakob nodded, thinking about what Duff had just said. And

what he hadn't. "Do you think there's any truth to her concerns?"

Jakob didn't believe there were, and he had talked with Duff about this before. Still, he needed to hear it again from him.

"I don't, no. The Crimson Devil was with us as soon as she joined us. I have no doubt about her or her intentions."

"But you do have concerns," prompted Jakob.

"I do," Duff confirmed with a nod. "But not with respect to the gladiator."

Jakob nodded, then looked at Duff. His friend, who was usually smiling, wasn't. Instead, his expression was grim. There was a sadness in the very back of his eyes that likely mimicked what Jakob was feeling then as well.

"We'll need to deal with this," Jakob finally said. "We can't wait much longer."

"Agreed."

"After we take the next step," Jakob decided. "You think it can wait until then?"

"I think it can, yes," Duff agreed. He gave Jakob a companionable pat on the back and began to walk up the trail, finding a break in the column of Highlanders working its way higher within the peaks.

Jakob caught up to him a few seconds later. "But not beyond that?"

"No," Duff replied with a disappointed shake of his head. "We can't wait any longer. We've gained all we can from leaving things as they are."

Jakob nodded sadly. "You already know how this is going to play out."

Duff sighed. "No, I don't know. I simply suspect."

"Your suspicions are rarely misplaced."

"And in this case, I hope they are," Duff replied. "Although you're correct. I'm usually right." He said it without a hint of conceit or humor in his voice, although his eyes sparked with a melancholy humor.

"I didn't ask for this, Duff," Jakob grumbled.

"I know, lad. The blame lies with me in part." Duff gripped Jakob's shoulder again, giving him a friendly squeeze. "But in truth, that's why you are who you are now."

"Because I didn't ask for this?"

"Exactly. If you had wanted what you are now, then this would never have worked."

"That doesn't make it any easier."

"I know, lad. It doesn't. The burdens of leadership and all that." Duff offered Jakob a grin, hoping to pull him from the dark path his thoughts had taken him. "For what it's worth, I'm sorry, lad."

Jakob turned his sharp gaze on the Highlander, his green eyes flashing. "No you're not."

Duff tried not to reveal the truth of his perspective, but it was too hard not to. "I'm not, you're right."

Only a heartbeat passed before both Jakob and Duff started laughing.

"You must do what you must do," Jakob murmured quietly once the moment had passed.

"Exactly so, lad. Your father had the right of it."

"Faster, you curs!" yelled Maxen. The Sergeant, thumbs tucked into his belt, walked along the eastern-facing wall of the fort. "This needs to be completed by the end of the week! If it's not ... well, you don't want to know what's going to happen to you lot if it's not."

Maxen laughed softly to himself when he heard the sound of a handful of whips cracking behind him. Inevitably, that was followed by several shrieks of pain that gradually ended in groans.

His men were doing their best to emphasize the point he was trying to make. Good. At least they could manage that.

He needed the workers working. Not moaning and groaning and lying in the mud.

Nevertheless, he had learned at a very young age that words never mattered as much as deeds. So Maxen had made that maxim a regular part of his practice as he rose through the ranks as a soldier.

A few whippings here and there would do wonders for the few hundred people he and his men had scooped up from the Stone and the surrounding farmsteads and then brought here to build another of Sharperson's forts. His approach would help his workers focus less on their fate and more on what they were tasked with doing.

A necessary lesson, because his workers weren't doing enough.

Thinking about his dilemma, he probably should have grabbed a couple dozen more before making his way here.

The construction was progressing at a slower pace than he would have liked, although they were farther along than he expected what with the fact that none of the people he had snatched were skilled laborers.

In fact, he really should feel good about their progress. Much of the bastion was complete. The four corner towers were already in use, his men standing a lazy guard, as were the handful of barracks, one for his soldiers and the others for the workers. All visible through the gaps in the walls.

And that was the problem right there. That's why he was on edge.

The walls.

Those facing to the west and the north were complete. The

southern wall should be done by the end of the day. Only a few more logs needed to be cut and set into place.

His primary concern was the eastern wall. The timbers were buried in the ground next to each tower and ran for a dozen feet in each direction. The main gate also was set in place, the balustrade on that section of the wall already complete.

It was just a matter of eliminating the wide breaches on each side, the logs needed to close those gaps and connect the walls to the gate stacked neatly off to his right.

Until that was done, he and his men were vulnerable.

He didn't like being vulnerable. He would have preferred to be back in the Stone and staying clear of all the trouble the Highlanders were causing.

But he wasn't.

He was here instead.

And there was the rub, wasn't it?

The Highlanders.

Ever since they had named the lad the Lord Kestrel, the world that Maxen and his men had helped the Governor create had fallen in on itself. And, with the rebels continuing to push, that world was in danger of collapsing entirely.

Although not just yet, the Kestrel's attacks dropping off in the last week. Probably preparing for a larger assault, Maxen mused.

He had received word that there were several Highlander patrols moving through the surrounding countryside.

He didn't know why. He could guess, however.

Testing in all likelihood. Wanting to determine how strong the Governor's last set of defenses were.

That didn't really bother him. The Highlanders taking such risks would help to make his other task easier, because he and his men weren't there just to build the fort.

He had hoped that the chain gang that had arrived just a

few hours before would catch the interest of the Highlanders. Draw them closer. Then he and his soldiers could snap closed the jaws of their trap.

No such luck unfortunately.

The journey from the Stone had been uneventful, his soldiers unmolested. That might be why some of his men were demonstrating a rambunctiousness in their current work that was uncommon when compared to their other assignments. Under other circumstances that wouldn't have bothered him. Now, however, it could delay the completion of the fort.

The snap of the whip sounded just to his front. Then again. A third time.

Maxen hurried down the trench faster than he would have preferred, every few feet a laborer digging into dirt, rock, and roots with the goal of deepening the foundation for the timbers to be fixed into place.

Maxen understood that making a point was necessary at times, but he couldn't afford to lose any more workers until the bastion was complete.

He reached Ennis before the soldier could give the unlucky woman another strap of leather, grabbing his arm and holding it in place.

"They can't work if you kill them," Maxen explained in a tight voice, "and we need them to work. Otherwise we'll be doing it ourselves, and no one's going to like that. Least of all me."

He wondered for a moment if he would need to deal with Ennis much as Ennis was dealing with the woman. The man's eyes didn't look right.

That didn't surprise Maxen. Ennis had demonstrated several times before that he enjoyed this type of work more than he should. It allowed him to connect to a darker side of himself that he could indulge only rarely.

Maxen's hand drifted down to the dagger on his belt. Ready. He breathed easier when Ennis' eyes lost their crazed look.

"My apologies, Sergeant," Ennis panted out, flushed, still excited. "Just trying to make sure the woman understands what is required of her."

Maxen released Ennis' arm and then looked down at the worker. She lay in the mud, her back, stripped of flesh, exposed for all to see except for a few threads of what had been her shirt.

"A little less zeal, Ennis," Maxen ordered, though in a calm voice, not wanting to send the soldier back to the grisly place where he had been. He knew that Ennis could fly off the handle in a flash, and he had no desire to kill him. At least not right then. "One stripe will do for now. Just to keep them on task. Yes?"

Ennis finally breathing easier, he stepped back then, nodding and looping his whip into a circle before latching it onto his belt. "Of course, Sergeant." He looked down at the woman, who continued to whimper, one cheek pressed into the mud. "I believe she understands what I was trying to tell her. I'm sure she's learned her lesson."

All the while, the workers around the moaning woman continued to expand the ditch that would serve as the foundation for the gate. None of them wanted to experience what the unfortunate woman had, knowing how quickly they could capture the interest of Ennis and the other soldiers who were more than willing to instruct with pain.

Maxen didn't bother to reply, simply nodding to the man who had been kicked out of three Duchy Guards for various offenses.

Yes, he was right about Ennis. He enjoyed this type of work -- hurting people, making them do what they didn't want to do -- much too much.

Several of the men with him had served in one of the Caledonian Guards. And just like Ennis a good number of them had been drummed out for various reasons.

What Maxen viewed as a key weakness of the Sharperson Guard was compounded by the fact that many of the men he now led hadn't served in one of the Duchy Guards. In large part because the Guards wouldn't take them. These men, dubiously identified as soldiers, were little more than the dregs of society who relished their work because they got the chance to take out their grievances and all the slights that they had suffered in life on those who could not defend themselves.

It was a sad state of affairs. Maxen couldn't dispute that. Although not entirely unexpected.

Governor Sharperson needed soldiers, as many as he could afford. Therefore, he wasn't too picky about his recruits so long as they did as he required when he required it and how he required it.

Maxen would readily admit that made his job harder. There was nothing he could do about it, however.

He had no choice other than to work with what he had. Because he had yet to figure out how he was going to get himself out of the Highlands.

With this Lord Kestrel riling up the Highlanders, and the very assignment he was engaged in right then confirming that Sharperson's control over these rugged peaks was waning rapidly and likely on its last legs, Maxen wasn't a fool. He knew which way the wind was blowing.

He had no desire to be here when that wind became a gale. Even so, he couldn't desert. At least not here. Not yet.

He needed to get back to the Stone first and grab the golds he had hidden away. With his stash, he could take a ship from Ballinasloe and sail to the west.

Locking away those distracting thoughts, he watched as Ennis walked farther down the line. The man already was caressing the grip of his whip with his left hand, his other on the hilt of his sword. It wouldn't be long before Ennis was back at it. Scarring another worker ... or worse.

Shaking his head in annoyance, Maxen concluded that he didn't have a choice. He was going to have to kill Ennis. He would do it tonight when the man was out on watch. Tell the others the Highlanders must have gotten him. That would give him a few days of better discipline and focus before it faded just as it always did.

How he had gotten to this place in his life ...

Maxen would have liked to have said that he didn't know. But he couldn't because he knew exactly how he had ended up here.

He had served in the Roo's Nest Guard for more than a decade, until he had been kicked out for being drunk on duty. A small offense in his opinion, although his Captain at the time didn't agree with him.

He thought upon his arrival in the Territories that he could start fresh. Instead, he had learned much to his chagrin that he had little self-control when it came to a mug of ale or a glass of wine -- he wasn't particular really -- and he could never stop after a single drink.

If Sharperson was hiring the dregs of society, then Maxen was one of them. He could admit that to himself. Although he refused to go so far and say that he was as bad as Ennis.

Maxen only hurt people if he had to. Not because it was fun.

Wanting to convince himself of that, Maxen was about to reach down and see if he could help the woman regain her feet. A loud voice at his back stopped him.

"The brave men of Sharperson's Guard. How disappointing. Nothing but misfits and fools trying to play at soldier."

Although Maxen couldn't ignore the truth in those words, still he bristled. He turned around slowly, scarcely noticing how quiet it had become.

His soldiers stood stock still, their eyes drawn toward the stentorian voice that had insulted them so casually. Even the forced laborers stopped working, pickaxes and shovels resting in the dirt, their expressions demonstrating more than just curiosity. There was hope there as well.

Maxen's brow furrowed, trying to make sense of the two people standing fifty yards away at the edge of the wood. An obviously fit older man with short grey hair, the hilt of a sword sticking above his right shoulder. He wore a leather armor that had gone out of style decades ago. And right next to him a woman with dark, curly hair streaked with grey. Her multicolored cloak matched the sparks in her eyes.

Rather than allow his annoyance to fester, Maxen studied the pair, trying to determine who they might be and why they would so brazenly challenge several companies of Sharperson's Guard.

For the life of him, he couldn't figure them out. Who in their right minds would so easily make themselves targets for a chain gang?

"Who in the blazes are you?" the Sergeant demanded.

"I'm Declan," the older man replied as if he wasn't concerned in the least to be facing off against two hundred soldiers who stared at him as if he were a piece of fresh meat. "And this is Rafia." He offered the woman a nod of respect when he introduced her.

Maxen's brow furrowed even more. He was beginning to think that something wasn't quite right with these two. That they might not be all there.

"Are those names supposed to mean something to me?"

"I don't know why they would, unless you want them to." Declan shrugged. "You asked. I answered."

Maxen was about to ask another question. Then he closed his mouth. He couldn't quite understand what was happening here. Worse, he couldn't quite understand why this man and woman were making him so nervous even when he had so many soldiers at his back.

To hide his growing apprehension, he gave the two interlopers a short laugh. He didn't know how to handle the pair, but he did know what he could do with them. "I take it that you're here to help with our construction project? I'm sure the good Governor Sharperson will appreciate your efforts."

Several of Maxen's soldiers, including Ennis, who now had his whip back in his hand, took a few steps toward the intruders, laughing ominously at Maxen's insinuation. They were stopped in their tracks by the woman's snort of derisive laughter.

"Far from it, Sergeant," Rafia replied. "We are here to help these people return to their lives."

"I'm sorry, what did you say?" Maxen wasn't quite sure that he had heard correctly.

"You have no right to force these people to work for you," Rafia stated, the hard edge to her voice making Maxen's teeth ache.

Another silence descended, this one interrupted by the laughter, hesitant at first, then slowly gaining in strength, that worked its way through the soldiers watching the encounter playing out before them. Although the laughter seemed more forced than anything else, a defense mechanism, which only made Maxen more nervous. Because it was a clear sign that his men were anxious as well.

"Funny," Maxen said after joining in with his men for a time, if only in an attempt to ease the tension that tightened his chest. "But we have work to do. And you do as well. You'll be joining the people you want to help. The more the merrier, of course."

Ennis and the soldiers with him didn't need to be told what to do next. They began to walk toward the man and woman again. Yet once more they were stopped cold.

"Blood Company!" Declan ordered in a booming voice.

Ennis and his squad stumbled back quickly as a line of soldiers, scuta to their front, spears over their shoulders, advanced out from between the trees. Forming up behind he older couple, they locked their shields together.

The tenor of the engagement changed in an instant. What Maxen and his men first believed was nothing more than two old fools demonstrating their stupidity by challenging them had become a much deadlier encounter.

"The Blood Company?" Maxen murmured more to himself than anyone else.

He had heard of just such a troop, picking up bits and pieces of news in the Ballinasloe taverns. He had been in the Territories for almost five years, so he had left Caledonia well before the Ghoule invasion.

Whether it was true or not, he couldn't say, although he assumed more true than not since the tidbits he heard tended to fit together.

Anyone could name themselves the Blood Company ...

Still, there was a flintiness to the man's gaze and a serious-ness that radiated off of him that told Maxen that he was speaking the truth. And if the one named Declan was speaking truthfully, and the stories that Maxen had heard ...

He surveyed the cold-eyed man and woman staring at him and his soldiers, a flash of fear shooting through him.

"I don't understand ..." Maxen began, not sure what to do next, playing for time so that he could wrap his mind around the uniquely perilous situation in which he found himself.

"There's really nothing for you to understand," Rafia cut in. "Except, of course, that you and your men's services are no longer required in the Highlands. Best that you leave while you still have the chance."

Maxen stared at the woman, then took a half-step back when her eyes flashed dangerously, suggesting a power that he didn't comprehend. The rational part of his mind telling him that she was offering him excellent advice.

Nevertheless, he was in charge of these three companies of soldiers. And Blood Company or no, he held the advantage in numbers.

"My men and I serve the …"

"Yes, yes," Rafia interrupted again. "Torstan Sharperson. We're well aware. But you must face a hard truth, young man." She smiled then, the menace in her expression sending a rumble of disquiet through the soldiers standing at Maxen's back. "Torstan Sharperson won't be with us for much longer. Once he's gone, the Highlands belong to the Lord Kestrel. You and your men really don't want to be here when that happens."

Maxen's eyes widened as he struggled for a solution to the problem he faced now. A problem he had never anticipated.

He had assumed that at some point he would take on a few squads of Highlanders. That's why he and his men were there after all.

To draw the rebels out.

It seemed, however, that their efforts had attracted the attention of a different adversary altogether. One that could be just as dangerous as if not more so than the Highlanders.

Not being a very creative individual, he fell back on what he had learned while serving in the Roo's Nest Guard.

Despite the reputation of the Blood Company, assuming that these fighters actually were the gladiators of the Blood Company, he still enjoyed a distinct advantage in swords. Best to play off that. Best to demonstrate some bravado and hope that his men were ready for what he was going to require of them.

"You two can dream all you want, but that's all it is," Maxen said with as much swagger as he could muster, which really wasn't all that much because he found it almost impossible to pull his eyes away from some of the larger fighters standing behind the two interlopers. "No more than a dream. And it doesn't matter who you claim to be. We outnumber you by at least four to one. More like five to one."

It was only three to one, but he was throwing out numbers as much to put the shield bearers off balance as to bolster his soldiers' backbones. "So you can stand there all you want trying to intimidate us. It's not going to work. When we're done with you, those of you who are still alive will be put to work. Simple as that."

"Is that so?" asked Declan.

"It is," Maxen confirmed. The Sergeant fought hard to ensure that his voice didn't crack. The men and women facing off against him made him distinctly uncomfortable. So much so that he was beginning to wonder why he had waited to desert. Too late now. He had started down this path. He had no choice now but to keep on it. "So better for you all to drop your weapons and make this easy for all of us."

"You believe that you can stand against us because you have more fighters than we do?" Declan snorted.

"I do," Maxen replied, again working hard to ensure that his fear didn't come out in his voice.

"Did you hear that, Rafia?"

"I did, Declan. This Sergeant seems to be fixated on numbers. Perhaps I could do something to make him understand just how precarious his position is."

With a flick of her wrist, white sparks shot from her fingers. Those sparks avoided the astounded soldiers, maneuvering around them and settling on the manacles locked around the wrists of the men and women forced into servitude.

In just a heartbeat, those sparks burned through the steel without harming the workers. A clatter of steel followed, the manacles dropping to the ground.

There was a moment of stunned silence. The freed workers, holding shovels and pickaxes, stared at their wrists in wonder.

Then they picked their heads up and glanced around. They didn't know what to do, still not quite comprehending what had just happened.

The guards didn't know what to do either, never having seen the like. Never believing that such a thing was possible.

Declan's gravelly voice breaking the silence made many of the workers and soldiers jump. "This is your chance, lads and lasses. I'd make the most of it."

None of the laborers moved, looking at the soldiers standing around them, still not quite sure of themselves. Then they looked at one another, a silent decision being made as one. Their hands flexing around the handles of their tools, they shifted their hard gazes back toward the soldiers.

A collective scream of rage burst forth from several hundred throats, the enslaved men and women charging the soldiers, shovels and pickaxes proving to be just as deadly as the swords and whips the soldiers carried.

Worse for Maxen and his men, the workers didn't fight on their own for very long.

"Blood Company," roared Declan, "advance!"

The battle didn't last very long. The workers falling upon Maxen and his men with a rabid intensity while the gladiators employed a cold precision to the mix that ensured that the soldiers' resistance, barely there to begin with, faded that much faster.

Those not cut down in the first few seconds shifted their focus almost immediately to escape.

Yet achieving that objective proved to be exceedingly difficult. Not because of the Blood Company, although the cold viciousness of the gladiators frightened them.

Rather it was the men and women under their thrall only just a few minutes before who terrified the soldiers even more.

The laborers, having been brutalized both mentally and physically for weeks, vented their rage in a bloody release. And the gladiators, who were quite familiar with the barbarity inflicted upon the people unfortunate enough to be caught in the Governor's snare and had little love for those who enslaved others, had little desire to intervene.

Declan and Rafia didn't even bother to join the fight. They didn't see the need.

When all was said and done, in just a quarter hour most of the soldiers were dead, a few were wounded with little chance of surviving, and a handful had managed to escape to the west.

Instead of sending a few gladiators after the fugitives, Declan let the men go. Their rampant fear would aid the Blood Company in their next task.

They had eliminated a good number of Sharperson's Guard, but there were still three more companies of soldiers nearby. As soon as the men who had fled found their comrades, those companies designated to close the trap would come in this direction.

Exactly as Declan wanted them to.

And these soldiers would be nervous.

Worried.

Prone to mistakes.

Their friends' frightening stories and dire predictions stinging their ears.

"Just so you know, there's another column of soldiers working its way to the west from the Stone," Rafia said, having searched around them with the Talent as soon as the skirmish concluded.

"Distinct from the groups hiding in the vales?"

"Yes."

"How many?"

Rafia spent a few seconds more using the Talent to study the companies that she had located. "Five hundred in all. Probably a few more."

"And all of them making their way here," Declan said,

nodding his head as if that thought pleased him. And it did, because despite being outnumbered, he'd rather that his targets come to him rather than him having to fight five distinct clashes.

"If they're not already, they will be soon," Rafia confirmed.

"Then let's get started." Declan strode toward the incomplete fort, his eyes burning with purpose. "Blood Company, we have nowhere to go and we have enemies coming our way. What are we going to do?"

"Stand! Fight! Die!" the gladiators all shouted, their words echoing off the surrounding mountains.

"Stand and fight, yes," Declan corrected. "We'll leave the dying to Sharperson's soldiers." He pointed toward several of the bodies that littered the ground around the incomplete bastion. "Leave the dead where they lay. Now's the time to make this fort our own."

"HOLD! HOLD!" Declan kept repeating.

He could understand why the gladiators of the Blood Company, less than a hundred fighters in all, were anxious to build on their success.

The additional companies loyal to Torstan Sharperson that had converged on the fort had learned of their opponents from the few soldiers who escaped the initial clash, and they didn't know if they should believe what they were told.

A force a third of the size that had been stationed there had decimated Maxen's companies?

And some old woman had removed the workers' chains with magic?

Impossible.

Clearly, those who fled the fight were terrified, no longer able to see reality. Cowards one and all.

But then the doubt burrowed in.

What if the soldiers who fled were speaking the truth?

Just in case, the five additional companies coordinated their efforts, entering the battle at the same time so that they could press the defenders of the fort and put them under so much pressure that they buckled within minutes of the attack.

A good strategy.

Nevertheless, it didn't go as planned.

The soldiers who attacked the fort and the Blood Company had proven only one truth since they emerged from the heart trees.

They were very good at dying.

The ground between the wood and the fort had become a killing field, the bloody and torn bodies of the soldiers making it difficult to advance on a straight line. That and the timbers the Blood Company had rolled into place.

Doing much as he had done when defending the isle of Haven, Declan had his gladiators position the logs for the fort's walls in a unique design that funneled Sharperson's soldiers where he wanted them to go and not where they wanted to go. His approach bottled up the attackers, reducing the number that could push forward at the same time.

Declan understood that his tactic wouldn't work for long. He assumed that whoever was leading these troops would employ a new strategy that would allow the bulk of Sharperson's forces to engage with the Blood Company rather than just a few squads.

But that was all right with Declan. After all, he was only playing for time. He wasn't playing to win. Yet.

"You're taking all the fun out of this," Majdi grumbled.

He stood in the center of the shield wall, anchoring the line. Jenus was on one side of him, Dorlan on the other. There was a great deal of blood splattered across their scuta. None of it theirs. Thanks in large part to Tehana, Asaia, Kollea, and the other fighters standing behind them who were more than willing to teach the attacking soldiers a lesson with whip, spear, and sword.

"He's right, Declan," Jenus said, supporting his friend. "One good charge and they break."

"If they break then they scatter, and I have no desire to chase them through the Highlands," Declan replied in the hard voice the gladiators knew all too well. One which told them that there was no point in trying to continue the conversation. "You'll have your fun soon enough."

"You're a spoilsport," Rafia murmured to him so low that no one else could hear.

Declan didn't bother to respond. He could tell that she was bored. She had stayed out of the fight so far, but she'd have her chance to become involved soon.

Silence fell across the ranks of the Blood Company then. None of them wanting to test Declan's patience.

Sharperson's soldiers had pulled back to where the wood bordered the churned-up mud. An undercurrent within their ranks suggested not only unease but also fear.

The soldiers had lost a fifth of their number, dead or wounded, in the last attack alone. Another advance like that and Stevan, who led these combined companies, would need to consider making a strategic retreat.

But not yet. If Stevan pulled back now word would get back to the Governor, and Sharperson wasn't known for handling failure well. No, better to adjust his approach and get more of his men into the fight.

Then, if they failed to break the line, he could think about falling back, arguing that he didn't have enough men to do the job. The Governor couldn't challenge him then.

First, though, Stevan needed to buy some time so that his troops could reorganize and the squads tasked with clearing the battlefield of the logs could begin their work.

Leaving that latter task to his corporals, the Sergeant walked out from his soldiers' ragged line. He stepped carefully around the bodies of the dead, not wanting to slip in the mud, not wanting to come face to face with the men who had fared so poorly against the small group of fighters standing against them.

Once he was halfway across the field, Stevan climbed up several logs until he stood on a pile of timber that lay fifty yards from the fort.

"You've done well," Stevan began, his voice carrying easily across the distance. "Even so, the numbers favor us. We'll be merciful, but only if you surrender now."

Silence met his words, the shield wall waiting to his front standing strong, the scuta not moving a knuckle. That worried him, although he was pleased to see several of his squads make their way out onto the muddy field and begin to move the logs.

"You have my word," Stevan tried again.

The silence continued for almost a minute more before a strong voice called out, "Your word is worth little."

Stevan searched for the voice, settling on the man who stood atop the eastern wall of the bastion, just above where the gates should have been, a woman standing next to him.

"It's a fair offer," Stevan continued, ignoring the insult though it chafed to do so. "You took the fortress, but now you have nowhere to go."

"You're wrong about that."

"Am I?" Stevan replied with a forced chuckle, trying to infuse his voice with a confidence that he wasn't feeling. "Who are you to tell me I'm wrong?"

"The man who's probably going to kill you."

Stevan fought not to take a step back upon hearing that, knowing that if he did he was going to fall off the log on which he was standing and end up in the mud. His anxiety came from the fact that a small part of him, actually a rather large part, believed the man.

"Say what you want," Stevan finally answered, gaining some confidence as his men made good progress on several of the obstacles that had turned the battlefield into a maze. Knowing that he needed to keep the man talking, hoping that doing so would keep the shield wall in place and give his men more time to clear the field, he tried again. "And where is it that you're going to go?"

"To the Stone of course."

Stevan found it hard not to snort out a laugh. Admittedly, this small troop had done well to take the fort and then hold it against two attacks. But the Stone? That was a ridiculous thought.

"You're sure about that?"

"Quite sure," the man with the booming voice atop the balustrade replied.

"And why is that?"

"Because I know the young man who seeks the Stone. And he's not someone who will stop until he's achieved his objective."

Just then, another figure stepped onto the parapet above the unfinished main gate. He looked familiar.

Stevan's eyes widened, his bowels loosening, when he saw the young man and the woman standing next to him turn their palms upward, spheres of energy dancing across their fingers.

Then, with an almost casual flick, those spheres shot from their hands, streaking through the air with an ear-splitting hiss, crashing into the logs scattered about the battlefield.

The timber disintegrated into thousands upon thousands of splinters and shards, many of which found a home in the unsuspecting soldiers working in the mud.

Stevan watched it all in disbelief. His horror threatening to paralyze him.

He knew now who the young man on the balustrade was. He had heard stories about what he could do. Although he never expected to find him here.

His eyes widened even more and he choked on his spit when more spheres of energy shot down from the battlements. Several of them speeding directly toward him, the shriek of the energy burning through the air deafening him.

"Our Lord Kestrel certainly is thorough," said Rafia.

"Jakob."

"Jakob?"

"Yes, Jakob. The Highlanders call him the Lord Kestrel, but he prefers Jakob. He hasn't gotten used to the title even though he manages the responsibility quite well."

"You learned this how?"

"It was quite obvious the first time I spoke with him."

"He reminds me of someone I know," murmured Rafia.

"Yes, he does," Declan agreed, thinking of Bryen, "and for more reasons than just that."

Declan watched as Jakob made his way toward them, although it was taking him a good bit of time to do so. There was something very familiar about the young man who stopped to speak with every Highlander he came across as he wound his way around the heart trees behind the fort.

Declan could understand why the men and women of these rugged peaks had taken to Jakob so quickly. He cared about them. He had proven that right from the start, before the rebellion even had begun. Perhaps most important, he didn't ask them to do anything that he wouldn't do himself.

And he was clever. Declan had liked the plan that Jakob suggested to him.

The Blood Legion would attack several of the forts along

Sharperson's defensive perimeter from behind. If they didn't take the bastions outright, they would hold the Governor's soldiers in place so that the Highlanders could come at them from the east.

A rock and a hard place.

If executed properly, Sharperson's soldiers stood little chance.

From what Rafia reported after using the Talent to check on the progress of that strategy, just as had happened here had happened everywhere else.

The Highlanders had shown little mercy.

They had little cause to do so.

Sharperson's defensive line was a shambles, and now the path to the Stone was open. They would be heading in that direction as soon as the sun fell, masking their approach under the cover of darkness.

"All seems to be going according to plan," Rafia said, Jakob finally having reached them.

Jakob smiled. "Yes, but we know what plans are worth."

"Very little," Declan answered with a grin. The more time he spent with Jakob, the more familiar he seemed. For the life of him, though, he couldn't quite understand why that was the case.

Rafia's eyes narrowed as she studied Jakob, then she shifted her gaze to Declan. She saw it then. "Jakob, I don't mean to pry …"

"She does mean to pry," Declan said just under his breath, although loud enough for both Jakob and Rafia to hear.

Jakob smiled.

Rafia scowled before she continued. "But you seem quite familiar to me."

Jakob shrugged. "I don't know why that would be the case, Magus Rafia."

Rafia didn't bother to correct him, Jakob having been told that he didn't need to use her honorific, yet still he did.

"Who was your father, Jakob? Perhaps that will help me to figure it out."

"The man who raised me was Dougal."

Declan stood a little straighter upon hearing that. "Dougal?"

Jakob shifted his focus to the former Master of the Gladiators, surprised by how uneasy the hardened fighter appeared. "Yes. Dougal."

Declan stared a bit harder at Jakob. "Dougal's last name, lad?"

"We weren't supposed to use our last name," Jakob mused, thoughts of his father making him smile even as his usually flashing green eyes dimmed a bit with sadness.

Declan nodded approvingly at Jakob's caution, understanding its cause. He couldn't quite believe that this could be happening. And after all this time. Because he could see it now. His rising emotion threatening to release a flood of memories Declan had locked away long ago. "Tell me anyway."

Jakob studied Declan for a few heartbeats more. Measuring him. His hand drifted to his chest, his fingers brushing the Blood Ruby hidden beneath. A habit that he had not broken himself of. And just as quickly he pulled his hand away.

The stone was warm. If it hadn't been, he would have been worried. Because of that heat, he decided that it was all right for him to answer.

"Blackgard. Dougal Blackgard."

Jakob's response hit Declan like a brick. The last of his doubts gone. He tried to hide his reaction, but he doubted that Jakob missed it, because Rafia certainly didn't. In fact, the Magus was giving them both a knowing smile, as if she had solved a puzzle that had been bothering her for quite some time.

"Your father has gone to the other side?" Declan asked softly, a deep sorrow working its way into his voice.

"He has."

"If I may ask, how did he die?"

Jakob didn't answer right away. This wasn't something that he liked to talk about. Furthermore, the look in Declan's eyes, his desperate need to know, made him uncomfortable. "Saving my life."

Declan nodded upon hearing that, clearing his throat. He would have expected nothing less. "Why didn't you say that Dougal Blackgard was your father? You said he raised you."

"He did. He was my father. But ..."

"But what?"

"Nothing," Jakob replied, a mysterious smile curling his lips. "Just thinking back on some of what my father did and said before he died. That's all."

"What is it?" asked Rafia. She was intensely curious about what was passing through Jakob's mind.

"Just wondering if I should trust what my instincts are telling me?"

"Do you always trust your instincts, lad?"

"I do," Jakob replied without a second thought. "My father taught to me to do that."

"Your father was a smart man. A brave one too." Declan wanted to say more, he believed that he should say more, and glancing quickly at Rafia, he could tell that she agreed with him.

Instead, he held back. For the first time in years he was afraid. Worried about what might happen if he took the next step.

"There's more to discuss," Jakob said before Declan could decide whether he was ready to travel down a road from which there was no return. "But that will have to wait. We have other matters that we need to deal with first."

Declan nodded, more in thanks than anything else, grateful that Jakob had let him off the hook. Clearing his throat, he motioned toward Saraa, who was waiting for them deeper within the wood.

"You sure you want to do this?" Declan asked. He and Duff had spoken in depth once the Highlanders eliminated Sharperson's soldiers.

Jakob glanced toward Saraa, a deep sadness welling up within him. "I don't have a choice. You must do what you must do."

Jakob's words pulled Declan's gaze. He was about to say something. Instead, he closed his mouth abruptly. "More words of wisdom from your father?"

"Just so."

"As I said, a smart man."

14

MORE THAN JUST DINNER

"The Crimson Devil deigning to grace my doorstep," Torstan Sharperson mused between bites of food. "I didn't think that you were going to come this evening. You declined my last two invitations."

The way he was looking at her made Lycia think that he viewed her as just another piece of meat, no different than the strips of pork that he was chewing on. "You gave me no choice, Governor Sharperson," Lycia replied lightly, though with a hint of pique in the residue of her voice. "Your men were quite clear that I would be joining you tonight."

She spoke the truth. He hadn't given her a choice. The soldiers informing her that her attendance was required.

She wanted to make that point to him. She needed him to know that she wasn't someone who would accede to his wishes without pushing back, though not in a way that might upset him.

Sharperson liked a challenge. He viewed her as a challenge, which was to her advantage. But if she pushed back too hard, he might view her as something more than a challenge.

He wanted to break her. Lycia understood that. She had

known that the instant she met him outside the gates to the Little Pit.

However, she knew as well that he wanted to break her in his own way. He wanted to take his time. And she would give him that opportunity, because doing that coincided with her interests as well.

Sharperson stared at her as he bit into a chicken leg, grease dripping down his hand, a piece of meat falling off the bone.

She was feeling slightly sick to her stomach because of his display. Nevertheless, she added the necessary amount of obsequiousness to her voice, not wanting to anger him. Simply wanting to make him work for what he desired. Certain that he liked it that way.

"My apologies, Lord Sharperson. As I said, I follow a specific methodology while preparing for my combats. Otherwise I would have been here as you wished."

Sharperson nodded, continuing to stare at her. Chewing. Loudly.

Gauging her.

Testing her.

She couldn't tell if he was upset with her or just in one of his moods. Perhaps he was trying to figure out what to do next.

She had not been at the Stone for long. Though it had been long enough to learn that Sharperson was not impulsive. Everything he did, he did only after careful consideration.

She believed that was one of the reasons why Jakob and his Highlanders had enjoyed so much success against Sharperson and his Guard.

Jakob moved with a blinding speed. Attacking. Adjusting. Attacking again. Adapting. Shifting his focus to another part of the Highlands. Then attacking once more. A pattern that couldn't be deciphered. The only constant his aggressiveness.

Jakob refusing to give Sharperson the time to think. Forcing him to react. Not allowing him to plan.

Her eyes never leaving his, Lycia offered Sharperson a smile mixed with a raised eyebrow. He leaned back again, her action having the desired effect. Turning his thoughts in a certain direction.

He was intrigued with her. Just as she wanted him to be.

Lycia finished her meal at a measured pace, eating a few slices of chicken and a mix of roasted vegetables, while Sharperson shoveled more food into his large body than she thought possible or wise.

Although she wasn't as disgusted as the first few times she had to spend time with him at the dinner table, his capacity to gorge himself still disturbed her. The setting, the opulence, the unnecessary extravagance didn't affect her any longer.

Nor did the eight soldiers positioned around the table, two standing no more than a step behind her, hands always on the hilts of their daggers.

Lycia didn't think the pair at her back stood much of a chance against her if it came to a fight. They probably thought the same. Which was why they were smart enough to know that a quick thrust of a dagger in her back was all that was needed to ensure that they never had to engage in a combat and test their theory.

Of course, the two soldiers at her back didn't concern her. Nor did the other soldiers positioned around the dining room.

Except for one.

She doubted that she would ever relax in the presence of the largest of the eight.

With all the scars marring his visage, she was certain that he was a skilled fighter. And she was quite curious about how he came to lose such a large part of his ear. How he had acquired his limp as well.

Yet none of that concerned her so much as the other aspect to Sharperson's shadow that made her feel as if ants were crawling over her skin every time their eyes met. His lack of empathy perhaps. The sense that the only pleasure he took from life was when he was taking a life.

Reeki was his name. Sharperson's confidante and friend. Guardian as well.

Always there. Always ready. Always willing.

No matter what might be required of him.

During the past week she had learned quite a bit about him from the men and women risking their lives in the Little Pit.

He was always at his master's back. Protecting him. Ensuring that Sharperson was treated as he deemed he should be.

An ever-present caretaker. A threat to anyone who displeased the Governor.

And if Reeki wasn't at Sharperson's back, then you needed to worry. Because whenever Sharperson sent Reeki out on a job, it was for one reason and one reason only.

The other combatants had seen Reeki fight in the Little Pit. Watching the man had terrified them.

He was devilishly fast. He was relentless. He was incredibly skilled.

He also enjoyed it, the other fighters explained, several of them giving her wild-eyed stares while they offered bits and pieces of what they had observed from his combats.

Reeki liked to play with his adversaries before he slid his steel into their flesh.

Sharperson's bodyguard savored the killing. The blood. Even more that last look of fear in his opponent's eyes right before he snuffed out the light for good.

Thinking of all that, Lycia glanced at the hulking presence.

Reeki was staring at her. Although not as Sharperson had been staring at her throughout dinner.

Sharperson's interest had been quite distinct from his guardian's.

Lycia had dealt with everything thrown at her in the Colosseum. The stares. The taunts. The screams. The curses. The tears.

None of it really affected her. None of it unsettled her.

She ignored it all, focusing on what she needed to do to ensure that she wasn't dragged across the sand.

Yet it was different with Reeki.

He didn't seem to be worried about whether he could kill her. From what she could decipher from that brief glance, he believed that he could kill her. In fact, he believed that he would kill her if ever the two stood across from one another.

She'd like to think that she could defeat him after surviving in the Colosseum for more than five years. Still, she got the sense that the man would give her quite the battle.

She snorted softly. She had spent so much time on the white sand that she couldn't wait to escape the Colosseum. Yet that experience had become so ingrained within her that now she missed it.

Not the fear. The blood. The gore. The mayhem.

Rather she missed the challenge.

Lycia had fought every day since she reached her agreement with the Governor. She had yet to face any real danger, however.

Sharperson had been true to his word. He had given her the golds to pay her debts, and she had made a show of doing just that while spending an afternoon visiting various merchants with businesses in the Stone, using men and women trusted by Duff. Assuming that Sharperson would check up on her to ensure that she wasn't trying to play him.

As a part of their deal, Sharperson had manipulated who she was going to fight to guarantee that she won. A foregone conclusion regardless of who he put up against her. Still, he needed to demonstrate his power whenever he could. She wasn't going to complain about it, though it irked her to a certain extent. If only because it went against her ingrained principles.

Sharperson also had asked her to join him for dinner after every one of her combats. That hadn't been part of the bargain.

Nevertheless, it had proven to be a valuable tool that she used to keep his focus on her rather than on what was occurring just beyond the perimeter his soldiers had established slightly more than a league from the Stone.

When she ate with him that evening, knowing that her gentle rejection of his last few requests would only stoke his infatuation with her, she entranced him further by describing the process that she used to evaluate each of her contests.

He spent several hours peppering her with questions as a result.

He wanted to know why she made a certain decision at a specific point in the combat. Why a backhanded slash instead of a stab? Shouldn't she have come back around rather than pivoting and dragging her blade across her opponent's belly? Why step in rather than step away and give herself more room to maneuver? Why pivot and risk a blade slicing across her ribs instead of stepping back and turning?

She answered each of his questions succinctly and dispassionately. Maintaining the aloofness that so appealed to him.

Because she knew that there was more to her presence at his dinner table than just his interest in her skill with a blade.

He wanted more from her.

He wanted her.

All of her.

It was just a matter of when he would demand it.

Having tired of asking her questions, his eyes back on his food rather than on her, Sharperson spent the next few hours regaling her with stories about his time growing up in Roo's Nest. Several of the stories, which she only listened to with half an ear, had to do with his brother Talus. Whether because he looked up to his older brother or was more than happy to be free of him, she couldn't determine.

Of course, thanks to Bryen, Talus Sharperson was dead. His younger brother either wasn't aware or didn't care, and she wasn't about to ask him which one it was.

After that, Sharperson made it a point to note how Reeki had always been there for him. At his back. Ready to do whatever he required. No matter who was involved. No matter what was needed.

She wasn't really paying attention, instead thinking about what Jakob might be doing at exactly that moment. Although she was slightly distracted by those thoughts, she still heard the warning that Sharperson gave her in his roundabout way.

She directed her focus toward Sharperson every once in a while as she picked at what was left of her meal, nodding every so often to suggest that she was listening, however poorly.

She tried not to shake her head in disbelief every time she looked at him. He was draped in robes that were a deep red, the flickering light making them appear almost black. He also wore some kind of crown made of silver atop his bald scalp.

She knew that he was conceited. In fact, she was doing her best to use his arrogance against him. Yet she had not expected this. Such an obvious display.

Despite losing most of the Highlands to Jakob, Sharperson was doing all that he could to make himself look like a king. It seemed that if his current reality wasn't to his liking, he created one that was.

Good for him ... until that reality shattered.

"It seems unnecessary based on what I've seen from you in the Pit," Sharperson said, picking for a third time at her excuse for not eating with him the last few days, "and my ensuring that you not face an adversary who can actually make you sweat."

"Perhaps, my Lord, but it's a habit that's hard to break. Just as it's hard to not review each combat in depth, searching for weaknesses and ways to improve my own efforts. You're skilled with a blade. I'm sure you understand the need."

Sharperson nodded at that, his eyes, blazing with an unseemly fire, fixed on her. More of a glare, actually.

Though not one of anger. A different emotion. She ignored it as best as she could, staring right back at him.

"Yes, I can understand that," he finally said. He leaned forward, shoving the dishes and platters out of the way and settling his meaty arms on the table. "Have you never thought to be more than just a gladiator, my lovely?"

"Why, my Lord?" Lycia replied with a shrug of her shoulders. "I can remember nothing else. I can do nothing else. As you surmised, that's why I'm here. The gladiatorial games have ended in Caledonia. Here, in your Territory, I can be who I am. Who I am meant to be."

Sharperson nodded again, her response pleasing him. Then he offered her a lascivious grin. Pushing himself up, he removed his bulk from his overwide chair and walked slowly around the table toward her.

The guards behind Lycia stepped back against the wall, Sharperson wide enough to take both their places.

Lycia didn't turn her head even though she desperately wanted to. She didn't like having Sharperson where she couldn't see him.

Yet there was nothing that she could do. Instead, she concentrated on restraining the shudder that wanted to race through her because he crowded her so. Finding this to be the hardest thing she had done since leaving the Pit.

Sharperson couldn't contain himself for long, his patience limited with his quarry within his grasp. He leaned down and put his hands on her shoulders, squeezing gently. Then he brought his lips close to her cheek and whispered into her ear.

"You're a beautiful woman, Lycia. A smart woman. I'm sure you've figured out that with me, you can be so much more than just the Crimson Devil."

"You mean a soldier in your Guard, my Lord?"

She knew exactly what he meant. However, she didn't feel the need to aid him in his quest. He had liked the fact that she had been playing hard to get ever since they had made their pact. There was no reason not to continue along that track until it no longer became tenable.

"That, yes, of course," Sharperson murmured softly, his lips still up against her ear. His meaty hands began to knead her shoulders with greater intensity, mirroring the urges that were welling up within him. "Perhaps something more than that, my lovely."

"Why would I want to be more than I already am?" Lycia replied, continuing to play the fool, leading him down a path of her own making. "As I said, I am just a gladiator. Why would I dare to hope to be any more than that?"

"You should know, Lycia, that here in the Territories, what you were doesn't matter," Sharperson explained. He stood back up, although his hands remained on her shoulders, his thick fingers pressing down gently. "All that matters is what you can be. And with me, you can be whatever you want." He leaned back down quickly, faster than she thought possible for someone of his size, and put his lips right up against her ear. "Whatever I want you to be."

She fought hard not to move, her survival instincts urging her from her seat, her desire to get away from him almost too strong to resist.

Lycia could kill Sharperson whenever she liked. Reeki and the other soldiers wouldn't have the chance to stop her. Although they might have the chance to kill her after she was done.

True, she didn't have a weapon, the guards searching her

just as they did each time she visited Sharperson's private quarters. But she could do quite a lot with the fork that she had slipped up her sleeve without anyone noticing.

A stab to his eye right over her shoulder would do the job so long as she drove the utensil all the way into his brain. Not too difficult a task for her. She had done much the same on the white sand, although that time with a dagger.

Even so, she didn't follow through on her inclination. She wasn't certain that if Sharperson fell on her she could get free of the table fast enough to evade Reeki. And before she fought that one, she wanted to make sure that she had the space to maneuver.

That thought turning her gaze in his direction for just a heartbeat, she caught Reeki staring at her. Emotionless. An almost inhuman gaze. To him she was just another kill.

If it came to it -- when it did, she corrected, understanding that eventually they would be crossing blades -- she promised herself that she would prove him wrong.

But now wasn't the time to think about that.

And now wasn't the right time to make her play.

She was close to achieving her objective, and that meant she needed to do more than kill the Governor. She needed to put on a performance that pulled all the eyes of the Stone inward, toward her, when the time was right.

Then and only then could she give up the charade and give in to her instincts.

Sharperson's hands began to massage Lycia's shoulders again, although this time with a surprising delicacy. He kept his lips right by her ear.

"Think of what you could gain, my lovely," he whispered. "Think of what we could do together. You need only agree." He pushed himself up then, his eyes burning with a fiery lust that he had no desire to hide. In fact, his robes couldn't hide it either. "You see yourself as a gladiator. I see you as so much more. With me, you can go far."

"I will think on what you've said, my Lord."

"Do more than think, my lovely. You need to decide. If we are to be partners, we need to be tied at the hip. There can be nothing between us. Nothing at all."

Lycia fought hard not to twist around and stab her fork into what Sharperson was pushing into her back. Clearly, he was thinking with more than just his brain.

Finally, after taking several deep breaths to ensure her anger remained at a simmer, she offered what she hoped Sharperson would perceive as a temporary delay. "The night before a combat I need to be alone, my Lord."

"To get your head straight," he said, pressing harder into her back before finally stepping away.

"Exactly, my Lord."

"And you won't make an exception for me?" Sharperson teased, his tone hopeful while also resigned.

"There's a lot of money riding on tomorrow's combat. I'd hate to put that at risk for a single moment of carnal bliss when there could be so many such moments in the future."

Sharperson's smile turned devious as he studied her for a few heartbeats. "I knew there was a reason that I was attracted to you. We will *talk* more after your victory tomorrow."

He walked away from her, moving back to the head of the table, Reeki once again at his back. Sharperson nodded toward the foyer, dismissing her. Having failed to get from her what he truly wanted, it seemed that he had tired of her company.

Unwilling to ignore the opportunity that he had given her, Lycia exited Sharperson's private quarters, the soldiers following her to the door. She turned back briefly when she stepped into the corridor.

Sharperson was staring at her, although at this distance she couldn't quite interpret his expression, Reeki's shadow draping itself over his ward.

When the guards finally shut the door, and Lycia stood alone in the hallway, for the first time since she sat down to dinner she breathed easier.

Although not for long.

A larger problem staring her right in the face.

How was she supposed to stay away from Sharperson after tomorrow's combat?

The sick feeling in her stomach deepened. She realized that she wouldn't be able to.

No matter what excuse she might give him, he wouldn't accept it.

As Sharperson had said during their first meeting, he had bought her.

And he was right.

He owned her.

He would do with her what he wanted no matter her skill with a blade.

And clearly, he wanted her. Badly. That much was obvious. Much too obvious.

Lycia shook her head. Her anger rising. She refused to give Sharperson what he desired.

Yet even with that terrible possibility taking up residence in the back of her brain, another aspect to their latest encounter nagged at her.

Things had been progressing well here at the Stone for her. But now, after tonight's dinner, for some unknown reason, the foundation she had constructed felt as if it were tilting. Threatening to crumble.

She needed to determine why that was the case, yet she couldn't focus on that now.

During dinner Sharperson had given up some critical information. She had been listening intently to that part of his monologue. About how he was going to eliminate his rival and then reclaim the Highlands.

The Governor let slip that he knew where Jakob Kestrel was. That could mean only one thing.

There was a traitor in Jakob's ranks.

Worse, she had no good way to get this critical information to him.

Unless ...

She thought about what would be required of her. It didn't take her long to make her decision.

This couldn't wait. It was too important.

Not seeing a soul, she walked down the hallway to the main tower. Peeking through the entrance, she confirmed that no one was about.

On silent feet, she made her way down the staircase curling along the wall. Instead of stopping at the ground floor where Sharperson had put her in an apartment, she slipped behind several soldiers visible in the frame of the doorway and continued deeper beneath the citadel.

She stopped every few seconds just to make sure that she was alone.

And she believed that she was.

It was quiet. Not a sound to be heard. Nothing to be seen. Nothing but shadow created by the torches set here and there in the wall.

Every few flights a doorway appeared. Sometimes soldiers were stationed there. More often they weren't.

Getting by the guards, more interested in their conversations or their dice games, wasn't much of a challenge.

That failing allowed her to move a bit faster.

It wasn't long before she reached the deepest basement in the Stone.

She stopped before stepping out into the long hallway that stretched out in front of her. She couldn't see the end of the corridor, the gloom winning against the few intermittent torches still burning, most of them having died out long before.

Still not a sound. Still no sign of movement.

Jakob had told her about what was down here. How he and Duff had barely escaped.

So though the urge to complete her task intensified, not enjoying the feel of the space that she had just entered, she took her time before silently walking out of the tower and making her way down the corridor.

All the while looking for the tell-tale sign of what might be lurking down here with her.

Blood-red eyes.

Every few feet, she stopped. Just to make sure. And each time she did, she sensed nothing that gave her any cause for concern.

Reaching the junction exactly where she thought it would be, she turned to the right and began to make her way along the hallway.

There were even fewer torches here. More darkness than light until after just a few more yards there was nothing but darkness.

Lycia wasn't worried. She had anticipated this. It meant that she was moving in the right direction.

She was almost where she needed to be when she halted abruptly.

Back around the corner, closer to the base of the tower, she thought that she had heard a noise.

A scratch maybe.

It could have been a rat.

Then again, perhaps it was something else entirely.

Worried, she stood there. Waiting. The fork that she had pilfered now out of her sleeve and gripped tightly in her hand.

The minutes passed slowly.

She didn't hear another sound.

She didn't see anything move in the darkness.

Nevertheless, she remained in place.

She didn't trust the silence.

It didn't feel right.

She expected to hear a knock. A scrape. Some kind of noise.

But nothing.

Feeling foolish if she remained in place any longer, despite her anxiety she decided to continue farther down the tunnel until she reached the point that she had been looking for.

The place along the wall at the very end where the dark was darker than the dark.

The tunnel that Duff and Jakob had used to escape when they reconnoitered the Stone.

She tripped after only having taken a few steps into the gap, reaching out a hand and finding the almost invisible wall before she fell face first to the ground.

A decaying body.

She didn't need to see it to know what it was.

The smell was enough.

One of the Stalkers that Jakob had killed.

Trailing her hand along the rough-cut wall, she stepped over the dead monster and made her way through the tunnel and out from beneath the Stone.

Lycia took a deep breath, enjoying the freshness of the air compared to the fetid odor of the pair of monsters rotting behind her.

With the night settling around her, she couldn't help but smile as she took in the peaks to her front, watching for a few minutes as they disappeared into the background.

Listening as well.

She was still thinking about that noise.

She didn't hear anything that should worry her. Nevertheless, her intuition was telling her to remain wary.

She was taking a huge risk by doing what she was doing.

The combats in the Little Pit that so worried Jakob didn't bother her. She doubted that there was anyone who might step out onto the sand who could vanquish her even if Sharperson didn't control the flow.

The real threat was Sharperson himself. Smart. Prideful. Always working a scheme, which meant that he was always on the lookout for schemes being played against him.

So far, she had succeeded. For how much longer she could do that ... well, she didn't know. Hopefully she wouldn't need to for much longer. Because she had no desire to deal with him tomorrow night.

Lycia could walk away now. She could head straight down the slope and disappear among the heart trees below.

She would no longer have to worry about the attention Sharperson was lavishing upon her. She wouldn't have to deal with what he would demand of her after her next combat.

Jakob certainly wouldn't blame her for getting out while she could. She had achieved a good part of her objective.

But not her entire objective, she reminded herself. And she had yet to break a promise to someone she cared about.

She wouldn't do that now.

She would finish the job that she had started.

Jakob and his Highlanders were counting on her.

Besides, this was her plan. She would see it through.

So far, it had worked exactly as she wanted. And if her time in the Stone came to an end as she hoped and believed it would, Sharperson would no longer be a problem for anyone. It just meant speeding up the process.

Pushing her worries to the side, she smiled, feeling the connection. They had agreed that he would search for her outside the Stone every night at a particular time. If she wasn't there, he would leave her be to focus on her task and avoid the threat of discovery.

"Should I be worried?" asked Jakob, his words sounding in her mind.

"Are you worried about me?" Lycia asked, her lips quirking into a small smile.

"I've been worried about you ever since you set foot in the Stone."

Lycia didn't respond right away. She hadn't expected such honesty from him and it appealed to her in a way that she never imagined possible. *"Thank you for that."*

Jakob waited a second before continuing, Lycia interpreting the delay as a touch of discomfort on his part. They had spent a great deal of time together since she had joined his band. They had discussed a great deal. But they had steered clear of certain matters that they both knew they would need to talk about eventually.

"I didn't think that we would be speaking now."

"Neither did I," Lycia replied, *"but we need to."*

"What are you concerned about?"

"Sharperson knows where you are," Lycia explained, not expecting the reply she received in response to her revelation.

"I know."

"You know? How could you possibly ..." Lycia nodded her head in understanding. *"You know there's a spy."*

"I do."

"How did you figure it out?"

"Does it matter?"

Lycia thought about that for a few seconds. *"No, it doesn't. What matters is that you know who it is."*

"I know." Lycia heard Jakob's sigh of resignation despite the distance between them. *"I'll deal with it. You needn't worry about anything other than what you need to do to ensure that you don't get swept up before time."*

"I can handle myself, Lord Kestrel," Lycia stated with a sharpness she hadn't intended. She sensed his concern, and it made her uncomfortable.

"I know you can, Lycia," Jakob replied in a gentle tone. *"As I said, I worry about you. That's all."*

Lycia nodded, although Jakob wasn't aware that she had. *"Thank you for that. I'm sorry. I'm just not used to ..."* Her words trailed off. She wasn't ready to reveal more than she already had.

"I know," Jakob replied, filling the silence. *"I understand. We're both sailing in the same boat."*

Lycia appreciated his understanding. Even more so, what he had revealed to her.

She looked back over her shoulder. She thought that she might have heard a scrape at the very far end of the tunnel. It could have just been a rat. Then again ...

Feeling the press of time, she offered Jakob one more piece of information that she believed he needed.

"Don't trust the tunnel that you and Duff used."

"Why do you say that?"

She shrugged, even though she knew that Jakob couldn't see the movement. *"Just a feeling."*

Jakob took a moment before replying. *"Don't worry. We have more than one stratagem in play."*

He didn't offer her any more than that. She wanted to impress upon him the importance of what she was telling him, but she knew that it was a waste of time to push him. Jakob's stubbornness was both impressive and irritating. Yet even knowing that, she felt the need to try.

"Jakob, I'm serious. I get the feeling that Sharperson might know more than just where you are."

"Don't worry about me, Lycia." Jakob's response contained a hint of warmth that tugged at her heart. *"I'll see you soon. Now move. There's someone coming up behind you."*

She didn't hesitate, trusting in Jakob's ability to use the Talent to search around her, particularly since it coincided with the skin on the back of her neck prickling.

Without making a sound, Lycia slid into a small crevice along the wall, disappearing into the darkness and becoming no more than a part of the rock that served as the foundation of the Stone.

Just in time. A large shadow with an obvious limp emerged from the tunnel.

Reeki.

She should have assumed as much.

Had he followed her after she left Sharperson's quarters?

That was the key question.

If he had, she might need to give more consideration to leaving the Stone now.

Thinking more about it, though, she didn't believe that he had. There was no way that he could have known that she had come this way.

He might be suspicious, but without any real evidence, he wouldn't go to Sharperson with his concerns. Not after Sharperson's display after dinner.

Lycia's first thought was to kill the hulking figure.

If she had a dagger, she would have.

Attacking with a fork wasn't a recipe for success, so she kept her back against the stone and stayed in the shadows.

Reeki stopped just a few yards in front of her. Not moving. Listening. Just as she had been doing.

He remained there for several minutes.

Through it all, Lycia kept her eyes focused on Reeki's back. If he turned toward her, she would sweep his bad leg. Once she got him to the ground, she would find a vulnerable spot for her fork before she made her escape.

She realized that she wouldn't have to take such a risk when, without turning, Reeki headed down the slope to the forest below.

Either looking for her or heading toward Miser's Way. She wasn't sure which.

Lycia waited several minutes more, keeping her eyes peeled for Reeki in case it was a ruse and he chose to come back up the slope. Seeing no sign of him, she slipped back into the tunnel and headed for her room.

She needed to be even more careful now. The final act of the play would be upon her in no time.

15

CHANGE IN COMMAND

"Any sign of her?"

"None yet," Isana replied. She kept pace with her daughter, she and Talia walking along the western wall of the Rock. "We're continuing to search the lower levels, and I've got squads scouring the docks and the city in case she made it across the harbor in one of the few longboats that wasn't destroyed during the battle."

Talia nodded. That wasn't the news that she wanted to hear. There was little that she could do about it, however. "The Blood Company didn't have any luck?"

"They didn't get the chance to search beneath the Rock," Davin replied. He walked just a few feet behind the two women. Limped, actually. And he was losing ground as he fell farther back, his badly wounded right leg hindering him. "As soon as they cleared the citadel, Declan took the Company back to the city to help deal with the few hot spots where the last of Roosarian's soldiers was putting up a fight."

"I heard they had holed up in a few warehouses."

"They did," Davin affirmed, giving Isana a nod.

"I hope none of your friends were hurt dealing with the dregs of Roosarian's Guard."

"Thank you for your concern, Isana, but there's no need," Davin replied. "Declan didn't waste any time or effort on an attack. From what I understand, they refused to surrender. Multiple times in fact. They wanted a fight. Declan wasn't in the mood. So he burned them out instead."

"That is quite ... effective," Isana replied, not sure if she should be horrified or impressed. Truthfully, she was a little of both.

"That's Declan," Davin confirmed.

"I like how he thinks," Talia growled. "When there's a problem, he finds the simplest solution."

"That's one way to describe his approach," Davin muttered under his breath, not feeling the need to recall some of his more difficult training sessions on the white sand.

Reaching the tower that anchored the southwestern corner, they began to work their way down the circular staircase. Ignoring the doors that led to each floor, they continued deep into the rock that formed the foundation of the citadel.

Davin tried to keep up with the two women. Despite his best efforts, he found himself falling a few more steps behind with every rotation they completed around the staircase.

His many injuries were slowing him down. The stripes across his back and shoulders and the cuts across his chest were nothing compared to the deep slash in his right thigh that had chipped the bone.

Rafia had healed the worst of his injuries with the Talent, but not all. She needed to save her strength for those truly in need of what help she could provide.

As a result, he was still alive thanks to Rafia's efforts, but he still felt as if he had served as a punching bag for Jenus, Majdi, and Dorlan.

Davin cursed under his breath. He hated being in this position. There was still more that he needed to do to help Talia solidify her hold on Ballinasloe and the Territory.

Yet there was little that he could do. Because of that he felt like an impediment.

The abuse that he had suffered while a prisoner of Hakea Roosarian had taken a toll on him. And although he tried to ignore it, Talia and Isana didn't.

They waited for him at the very bottom of the tower. When he reached them, they strode down the corridor, slowing their pace to match his.

"All is going well with the Council?" asked Talia.

"Quite well," confirmed Isana. "The meeting is this evening, but it's already been decided."

"What's been decided?" Talia wondered.

Ever since the fall of the Rock, Talia had been inundated with new responsibilities. Having no choice, she had given the task of finding Hakea Roosarian to Sirena and repairing the damage to the Carlomin wharfs to Hari Hoohannen and his wife so that she could concentrate on the larger issues affecting Ballinasloe. Once those were addressed, she would take up the challenges associated with administering the entire Territory and not just the capital city.

Isana chuckled. "You really don't know?"

"Know what?"

"The Council has declared you the ruler of Fal Carrach," huffed Davin, short of breath, the effort to stay with Isana and Talia despite the slower pace still a drain upon him.

"The decision was unanimous. They just don't know what title they want to give you when you assume formal command this evening," her mother added.

"You can't be serious?" demanded Talia, who continued down the hallway, not stopping until they entered the circular chamber in which Roosarian and the cowled woman created the Stalkers.

She looked at her mother, who gave her a cunning smile. It was her doing. Talia was sure of it.

Isana had been the one meeting with the Council. She had likely been the one to suggest that Talia assume Roosarian's place in the Territory without delay.

"It was their idea, not mine," Isana explained. "Are you all right, Davin Noname? Should you not be in bed?" The gladiator's face was pale, transitioning slowly to a deathly white, beads of perspiration on his forehead.

Davin waved her off as he came to a stop, ignoring the cold sweat trickling down his back. Isana was probably right. He probably should be in bed. But he refused to leave Talia alone until they found Hakea Roosarian. Preferably her dead body.

"I'm fine." Leaning on the haft of his spear, he caught Talia's eyes. "Your mother is right. The Council wanted you."

"I just wanted to remove Roosarian and then focus on growing our business," she protested.

"You can still grow the business," her mother said gently. "You'll just have some additional responsibilities to deal with." Isana shrugged then and gave her daughter a warm smile, nodding briefly toward Davin. "If you find the right person to help you, I'm sure you can manage all that you want and need to do with little trouble."

Talia wanted to offer another protest. Before she could, Davin's words stopped her.

"You had to have assumed that this would happen."

"Why do you say that?" she demanded, struggling to come to grips with what was going to be required of her later that evening.

Davin chuckled. Although only very softly. Laughing too hard would have sent a bolt of pain from his throbbing leg out into his body, and he didn't want to experience that again.

"You're probably the smartest woman I know. You thrive on strategy. You were always a step or two ahead of Hakea Roosarian. That's in large part why you proved so successful sweeping clean the Sea of Mist and then taking her on here in the city. You can't tell me that you didn't think about the most logical result of all that you put into motion?"

Talia's less than pleasant response to Davin's statement was on the tip of her tongue. Rather than letting it loose, she held back. She closed her eyes, shaking her head. There was too much truth in his words for her to deny it now.

She knew what would happen if she succeeded in her various endeavors that were meant to weaken Hakea Roosarian. But she hadn't really thought about that inevitable conclusion, choosing to focus instead on getting the job done first. And now that it was ...

Why had she decided to come down here?

She hated being in this chamber, nothing but bad memories playing through her mind.

Well, not all bad.

Her relationship with Davin had become something more here. She had seen who he truly was in the tunnels that extended out from this same chamber. The lengths that he was willing to go in order to protect her.

Also, the black liquid was gone. Rafia had made sure of that. Scouring the chamber and every inch of the Rock with the Talent to ensure that none of that vile substance remained.

Maybe it was because she had come full circle and she felt the need for some closure. To put the past behind her so that she could focus on the future.

Maybe she felt the need to center herself. To regain her balance. To prepare herself for what was going to be required of her next.

A massive change that she had orchestrated had taken hold in just the last day, and the momentum that she had begun was only gaining speed.

The shadows that had filled the space were gone, replaced

by the torches that encircled the room. The cells were empty. The gloom above them on the balcony that wrapped around the chamber a dim grey rather than a pitch black.

"You are who you are, Talia," Davin grimaced, the pain in his leg beginning to throb even more. "You can't get away from that no matter how hard you might try."

"Just as it was for you, Davin Noname?" she teased.

"Just as it was for me," he admitted. Despite the pain that he was experiencing, he gave Talia the smile that always made her smile as well. "You need to decide what you want to be called. Governor? That doesn't really have a positive connotation anymore." Davin nodded as he gave this new dilemma more thought. "Queen? The traditional choice, although that might not appeal to the powers that be in Caledonia."

"Do we really care about the powers that be in Caledonia?" asked Isana. "The Burnt Ocean is quite a large barrier."

Davin's lips scrunched together as he considered Isana's perspective. "Probably not, but still something to think about. Appearances and all that." He placed more weight on the spear he gripped in his hand, the pulsing pain in his right leg becoming more intense. "We could always go with a more creative choice. Empress? Her High and Mighty?"

"That last certainly brings back memories of Talia as a child," Isana mused.

Davin snorted out a laugh, unable to help himself. Then he grimaced, bending at the waist as a fiery surge raced through him that didn't fade for several seconds.

"Enough," Talia ordered, although her smile remained. "We can deal with that later. And you, Davin, will return to your bed. Do I make myself clear?"

"As you command, your High and Mighty."

Despite Talia's scowl, Davin gave her a wink, enjoying one last poke before they got down to business.

"Although I understand why Davin is teasing you, this

remains a serious matter," Isana interjected, having enjoyed the give and take between her daughter and her gladiator. "A decision needs to be made, and better that we make that decision rather than the Council."

"We will deal with it tonight," Talia promised. "What other matters do I need to be aware of?"

Talia had not yet gained the title, but for all intents and purposes she already was ruling Ballinasloe and by extension Fal Carrach.

"The Stalkers that were kept here on the Rock are dead," Isana stated, her hard voice revealing her pleasure at being able to make that statement. "The city is clear of those monsters as well, but we believe that a few may have escaped into the countryside. Sirena has sent several companies out to hunt them."

"They understand the danger of doing that?"

"They do," Isana confirmed with a nod. "They know what to do. Sirena was very careful with who she assigned to that task."

"Good. And the damage in the neighborhood fronting our gate?"

From what she had seen from the Rock's battlements, several blocks had been set ablaze, many of the buildings and homes charred husks or piles of rubble as a result of the battle between Talia's soldiers and Roosarian's Guard.

"Much of the debris should be cleared by the end of the day, and our carpenters and stonemasons have already gotten to work where they can," Isana replied. "If all goes as planned, they should be done in a week. Maybe less."

"And what of Roosarian's Guard?"

"There is no longer a Roosarian Guard," Isana explained. "More than half of her troops were killed during the fight along the waterfront. The rest have taken one of two roads. A good number have already fled Ballinasloe, understanding what would happen if we caught them."

"But not all?"

"No, not all. Several companies refused to fight when Roosarian called upon them. These were all longtime veterans from other Guards. They did not believe that Roosarian was worthy of their loyalty."

"And they believe that I am?"

"They do," Isana replied with a hint of pride.

"And I assume that you've set up a vetting process?"

"Sirena will take the lead on that."

"Good," Talia replied, pleased that so much progress had been made in such a short period of time. "And what are we to do with the Rock?"

"It seems that we're stuck with it," Isana replied with a shrug. "Too much work has gone into it to tear it down and start again."

"A few ideas if I may?" asked Davin.

Talia and Isana both turned to him with raised eyebrows. Rarely was he so respectful. Usually he offered his thoughts without hesitating.

"What did you have in mind, Davin?" Talia asked.

"Several adjustments to the walls so that we can actually defend against an attack from the sea. A few redesigns of the Rock itself that I'm sure Master Hoohannen would be able to manage with little trouble. Perhaps most important, construction of a bridge that links the Rock to the mainland."

Silence permeated the chamber for almost a full minute. Talia and Isana stared at the wounded gladiator, who shifted his weight a few times. Because of his injuries, trying and failing to find a more comfortable position, and also because of the intensity of the stares that added to his discomfort.

"You would be willing to lead that project?" asked Talia.

"I would."

"Good. Talk with Hari and get started as soon as you can."

Davin didn't have time to smile at the gift that Talia had

given him, a shadow detaching itself from the gloom above and leaping down from the balcony.

Thanks to his injury, he stumbled more than stalked forward, knocking both Talia and Isana out of the way. And even with his struggles, he got the haft of his spear up just in time.

The clang of sword meeting spear echoed throughout the chamber. Before the shadow could pull back and swing again, Davin lowered his shoulder, knocking the cowled attacker back a few yards. At the same time, he stomped onto the hem of the assailant's cloak.

"The rat reveals herself," murmured Isana, Talia helping her mother back to her feet.

Hakea Roosarian.

Talia pulled the dagger from the sheath on her belt. She wasn't surprised to find the deposed Governor of Fal Carrach down here rather than trying to escape the port city.

"Can't get enough of me, can you, Crimson Giant?" Hakea taunted.

Her hair disheveled. Her clothes torn. Her face streaked with dirt and blood. Clearly she had worked hard to conceal herself within the Rock. Davin had to give her credit for that.

What disturbed him was the manic almost deranged look in her eyes. Hakea had not taken well her many defeats.

Davin set the butt of his spear onto the stone floor, leaning against the haft. The slash in his thigh had reopened because of his exertions, a stream of blood staining the bandage and his breeches. Beginning to feel faint, he was having a difficult time staying on his feet.

"Actually, I've had quite enough of you."

Davin was about to stalk toward her, probably more fall toward her, he realized, but he never took that first step.

Talia's strong but gentle grip on his forearm held him back and helped to keep him erect.

"She's mine." Talia's quiet voice was calm and cold.

She sheathed her dagger and then pulled her sword from the scabbard on her back. Placing herself in front of Davin, she squared up to Roosarian.

"You sure you want to take this risk, girl?" Hakea warned. "You've taken everything from me. I have nothing left to lose."

Talia stepped closer to Roosarian, narrowing the distance between them by half.

"I do," Talia replied, one foot in front of the other, staying on her toes, ensuring that she was well balanced. "I really do."

She was trying to achieve the coolheadedness that Davin had taught her in the practice ring. Yet she was finding it diffi-cult because of all the emotions that were welling up within her. Much of it driven by memories of her father, murdered at the command of the woman standing before her.

"Good," Roosarian hissed, "because you have a great deal to answer for."

Talia pivoted to her left, faster than the snap of a whip, avoiding Roosarian's sword slicing through the space she had been occupying just a heartbeat before. Then again. And once more.

Each time she moved, Talia pulled Roosarian farther away from Davin and her mother. She knew that Davin was hurting and that he wasn't at his best. With him down to a single leg, she didn't want to put on his shoulders the burden of having to defend himself and her mother.

"That's the best that you can do, *Governor*," Talia chided, gliding to the left to avoid another of Roosarian's slashes, Hakea's form based more on rage than technique.

Talia's taunt struck home. Growling in indignation, Roosarian intensified her efforts. Slashing and slicing. Doing everything that she could possibly do to break through her hated nemesis' defenses.

She met with little success, however. Talia was too quick. Too measured in her approach.

Rarely did their blades meet. More often than not, Talia need only skip to the side or take a few steps back to escape her.

That reality angering her all the more, Roosarian screamed in rage, giving in to her desires and rushing toward Talia.

This time, Talia didn't have a choice. She couldn't get out of the way in time. Raising her sword, she parried Roosarian's swing and then shouldered into her.

Knocking Roosarian off balance, Talia continued to advance. Her sword a blur, she kept herself under control, refusing to overextend herself as Roosarian had done.

Instead, she cut at the former Governor's edges, all the while staying in front of Davin and her mother, nicking Roosarian here and there as she moved her despised foe where she wanted.

Davin watched Talia take command over the combat, a touch of pride swelling his chest. She knew exactly what she was doing. And he knew why.

He had spent so much time trying to protect her, and now she was returning the favor.

Yet he was having a difficult time controlling his desire to join the combat. The need to aid Talia was instinctual. It had become a part of him.

Nevertheless, he realized that he couldn't. That he shouldn't. And not just because he'd be more of a liability than a help.

It wasn't his place to do so. It wasn't his fight despite all that Roosarian had done to him. Even though she had come within a heartbeat of turning him into a Stalker.

Although he didn't like it, Davin acknowledged that Talia needed to do this on her own.

This was her fight.

So he settled in to watch, though doing so pained him more than his injuries.

With a lightning-fast attack, her sword a blur, Talia maneuvered Roosarian back against the wall of the chamber, the shelf that had once stored the black liquid used to create Stalkers right behind her.

Roosarian tried to push away from the stone, seeking more space to maneuver. She only succeeded in leaving herself open to a quick slash.

Talia cut with her blade. If she had hit the mark, she would have ripped Roosarian open from chest to gut.

Roosarian raised her sword just in time; however, she underestimated the strength of the blow. With a loud clatter, her blade fell to the stone floor.

For just a second, Roosarian stood there. Defenseless. Not quite believing that her death was just a heartbeat away.

Then she watched in amazement as Talia dropped her sword as well and pulled a dagger from the sheath on her belt.

Roosarian stared at Talia, not quite understanding why she was taking such a risk. "You think so little of me?"

"I do," Talia replied in a deadly quiet voice.

Roosarian didn't say another word. Her expression said it for all to see.

Her rage all consuming, no longer thinking clearly and not caring, she screamed in fury and pulled free her dagger, slashing at Talia.

Davin was impressed. He knew that Talia had a calculating mind. That she had the capacity to think several steps ahead of her opponents.

Watching her do that now almost took his breath away.

Roosarian believed that Talia had given her an opportunity. She didn't realize that it was actually a trap. That Talia was better with a dagger than a sword. That Talia wasn't trying to kill her, but rather she was trying to teach her a lesson first. And she was doing an excellent job of that.

As the dagger fight played out over the next few seconds, Davin recognized that the end was coming before Roosarian did.

Allowing Roosarian's dagger to slide across hers with a quick flick of her wrist Talia sent the former Governor's blade pinwheeling through the air.

In the blink of an eye, Roosarian felt the touch of cold steel against her throat.

Hakea gulped. She never anticipated that this could be how she lost her life. Dying at the hand of her most hated enemy.

"Do you recognize this?" Talia asked in a rock-solid voice, even as she struggled with a great many emotions. Pride. Regret. Anger. Grief. She had pulled the steel needle from her boot, tilting it up so that Roosarian could see it. "Your assassin tried to kill me with this. She failed."

Roosarian didn't reply, instead peeking down at the thread-like dagger at her throat. Thanks to Talia's pressure, the steel tip cut through a few layers of skin, a thin trickle of blood running down her neck.

Her eyes were wide. Her fear obvious. Yet Roosarian still hoped to find some avenue for escape even as her brain could think of nothing else except how she had failed so badly to create the world that she wanted.

With Roosarian frozen in place, Talia glanced briefly at Davin. When the combat had begun, her only thought was to kill the woman who had taken so much from her. Had almost taken so much more. But now, under her blade ...

Talia was hoping for some guidance.

Davin didn't give her what she wanted. His pride in her for what she had accomplished obvious. The other emotions that she really wanted to explore visible in the back of his eyes.

He simply gave her a sharp nod. He would support what-ever decision that she made.

"You're not worth it," Talia said, returning her gaze to Roosarian, a soft whimper erupting from the back of the former Governor's throat. "You're nothing now."

Talia was about to step away when she sensed a movement behind her. The needle ripped from her hand, the next time Talia saw the thin piece of steel it was sticking out of Roosarian's right eye. Driven deep into her brain, the dead woman's spasms confirmed her demise.

Isana pulled the needle free, then turned her hard gaze toward her daughter.

"You are a credit to your father, Talia. But I needed to do this. For Abram. For what this woman took from me."

Talia didn't say a word for quite some time, her eyes locked onto her mother's. Not even seeing Roosarian's body slide down the stone wall and slump to the ground. Finally, she nodded, her mother not stepping back until she did.

"Hakea Roosarian?" Declan asked in his deep voice. He stepped silently from the darkened hallway, coming to stand next to Davin.

Davin nodded.

"About time."

"What do you need, Declan?" Davin asked, knowing he wouldn't be there otherwise. "I thought that you were still taking care of matters in the city."

"We've addressed all the issues that remained," he replied with a hint of satisfaction. "The Blood Legion is in need of transport to the north."

"The north?" wondered Davin. It didn't take him very long to understand Declan's motivation. "You're going to help Bryen."

"We are."

"I'll have as many ships as you require ready to go on the tide," Talia replied. "We owe you a great debt."

"I'm simply glad that we could offer you some small assistance here," Declan answered, offering Talia a nod of respect. "Thank you for your generosity."

"I'm going with you," Davin said.

Declan's eyes remained on Talia for just a second longer. He recognized the emotions playing across her face even though she was trying to hide them.

The most dominant was fear. For what could happen if Davin took such a risk in his condition. He could tell as well that she wouldn't try to stop him. That left it to Declan.

"No."

Davin turned on Declan quickly. Faster than he should have, his wounded leg giving out beneath him. He would have fallen to the ground if not for Declan grabbing him around the waist.

"No," Declan repeated, this time using the voice that had been so familiar to the gladiators in the Colosseum.

"But Declan ..."

"Don't waste my time, lad," Declan grumbled, although he did so in a gentler tone, understanding how hard this was going to be for him. "You're in no condition to do this. Besides, you have responsibilities here to manage now."

"Yes, but we won. I can ..."

"Your place is here now, lad. You need to heal before you can do anything else. Besides, Talia needs you now."

Davin was about to offer another protest. Going against character, he held his tongue. Hearing the truth in Declan's words, he nodded reluctantly.

Davin finding his feet again, Declan removed his arm from around his waist. "You can have him for good if you want him."

Talia studied Davin, nodding slowly. It was almost the exact same countenance as she had used when measuring the gladiator the first time they met.

"There's a part of me that's pleased to hear that. But there's another part that's worried."

"Good," Declan chuckled, turning to go. "It's best that you know what you're getting yourself into."

"Declan, are you sure ..."

Declan's hard gaze cut off Davin, although there was a hint of amusement in the back of his eyes. "I've taught you a great deal, lad. Although apparently I haven't taught you all that you need to know."

"What do you mean?" Davin's expression revealed his confusion.

"Your conversation with the Lady of Fal Carrach is not yet complete."

Declan gave the two another smile, then turned and walked back into the darkness of the corridor.

"I'll go as well," Isana murmured, "and make sure the ships are ready." She looked down at Roosarian's body a final time before following Declan, calling over her shoulder, "I'll have some of the soldiers dispose of this."

"What do you think Declan meant by that?" Davin asked when they were alone.

Talia gave him a look then that Davin didn't know how to interpret. "So smart yet so oblivious. Clearly, there is a great deal more that I must teach you."

16

THE BITE OF LOVE

Standing on the crest, a fall of several hundred feet just past the tip of his toes, Jakob found the darkness surrounding him comforting. Although that wouldn't last for much longer. He saw to the east the first very faint glimmer of the sun rising, the clouds behind the peaks afire in a pink that he knew would quickly darken to red and orange.

He and his Highlanders had made good time. Very good time, in fact, getting past Sharperson's defensive perimeter and leaving behind seven forts conquered in less than a day.

Yet they couldn't rest on their success.

Speed remained the key to their victory.

And he believed that they needed to move faster.

Jakob's gaze shifted away from the stars to the faint spark of torches that marked the walls of the Stone. And just a little farther to the west, pyres blazed brightly atop the Little Pit, the stadium connected to the citadel by a long stone bridge that ran across several freestanding stacks.

Sharperson was getting an early start there today. With what Jakob had discovered, that worried him.

As the crow flies, he was less than a mile away from

Sharperson's gift to himself, what was supposed to be a reminder of his greatness for those who entered or lived in his Territory. Four or five miles depending on the trails that he and Duff selected to make their approach.

His nerves were on fire, the urge to get moving acute as he considered the path to take. The end to what had been a months-long struggle was in sight. Before he could do that, however, Jakob needed to deal with a situation that he had left for far too long.

He had hoped that it wouldn't come to this. That time would provide a better perspective.

It hadn't, and now he couldn't avoid the distressing and painful matter.

He couldn't make for the Stone until this was done.

Jakob reached for the Talent, extending his senses all around him. At least the plan that he had developed with Duff was working. The other companies of Highlanders were all exactly where they should be, waiting for his signal to advance.

That made him distinctly nervous. Because nothing ever went according to plan within these peaks.

He extended his search.

Jakob shook his head, disappointed and resigned, although not surprised. He had just confirmed his worst fears.

Before releasing his hold on the Talent, he sent a quick message to Duff, allowing him to view what he had just seen with his natural magic.

"What did you do, Saraa?"

Jakob had sensed her approach as she stepped carefully around the roots of the heart trees that blocked the rocky shelf. He fought to control the emotions roiling through him, and not knowing how long he could contain them, he preferred to get right to the heart of the matter between them.

"What are you talking about?"

Saraa stopped a few feet away from him, her smile fading, a

flush of uncertainty racing through her. Even with his back turned, she sensed that he had closed himself off to her. That hurt more than she could have possibly imagined.

Jakob bowed his head for just a heartbeat, steeling himself for what was to come.

"What did you do, Saraa?" he asked again, his voice hard, demanding.

"Jakob, I don't know ..."

"Saraa."

The coldness in his voice shocked her. It felt like a slap across the face. She sought to overcome that by slipping a touch of anger into her voice. "I came here to tell you I love ..."

"Saraa, what did you do?" Jakob turned then, cutting her off. His blazing green eyes flashed in the waning darkness.

He didn't care what argument she might offer. He just wanted the truth from her.

For just a second, Saraa stood stock still, even as her body began to shiver. A mixture of remorse and shame. How could he have found out?

"I did what was necessary," she replied softly. There was no point in denying it. The look that Jakob was giving her confirmed that for her.

"You betrayed us," Jakob said very quietly, his words barely audible.

"I betrayed no one," Saraa replied hotly, hoping her anger would temper his own. "I protected us from her. I protected you from her."

"Who was it?" Jakob asked, not having any desire to listen to whatever defense she chose to offer.

"What?"

"Who came to you?" Jakob said. "Who put all this in front of you?"

He saw the flash of pain in the back of Saraa's eyes. For just a heartbeat, he felt for her, the anguish she was experiencing, and he hated himself for it.

He had wanted to help her out of the trap that had ensnared her, but he realized before this encounter began that he couldn't. No one could.

What's done was done. Now, only the consequences remained.

Saraa didn't know what to say. She had hoped that the conversation she had initiated with Jakob would go in a much different direction. She never expected him to challenge her in this way. She never anticipated that he might discover what she had done. There was nothing for it now, however.

"A woman," Saraa sighed.

"Wearing a cowl?"

"Yes."

"A sense of power radiating from her?"

"Yes," Saraa replied, her voice becoming even softer. Her shame taking hold.

"A quiet voice? Almost melodic?"

Saraa stared at Jakob. She didn't know what to give him other than the truth. How could he have known all this? "Yes."

"You never saw her face?"

"No."

Jakob nodded. He had suspected as much. The same woman he had spied briefly beneath the Stone when he and Duff barely escaped the Stalkers. The same woman who likely had a hand in many if not all of the hazards threatening the Highlands.

"What did she promise you?" Jakob asked quietly though forcefully.

Saraa tried to respond several times, struggling to utter a single word. The hopeful expression that she wore when she first approached Jakob turning to misery. "You."

"Me?"

"She promised me that you would be mine. That nothing would happen to you. That the gladiator would no longer be a problem and that you would be mine."

Jakob didn't know what to say. He was too shocked. He couldn't quite understand how Saraa could have deluded herself so badly.

She had sold him out because of her love for him and in the process had put all that Duff and the other Highlanders had worked for at risk. That was bad enough.

What was worse, however, was that thanks to Saraa and her hatred for Lycia, the gladiator had walked into a trap. Jakob had to assume that Sharperson knew Lycia's real purpose for being in the Stone.

If not at the start, certainly now.

Lycia had been alive just a few hours ago when he spoke to her.

Had anything happened to her since then?

Jakob didn't have time to check on her. He sensed what was coming toward them and needed to focus on that.

"They want me dead, Saraa. Dead!"

"She promised me, Jakob ..."

"They want anyone who disobeys them dead, Saraa."

Jakob shook his head in frustration. He had thought that he might be able to get through to her. To break down the walls that she had built around her psyche that had allowed her to commit this terrible act against her friends.

He was wrong. Saraa believed in what she had done. She thought that she was right to do it, no matter the cost to so many others.

"No, that's not true. She promised me that I would get ..."

"Think, Saraa," Jakob pleaded.

"Jakob, you know me," Saraa began. She took a step toward him, reaching out with her hand, which she dropped to her side when Jakob made no move toward her. She tried again.

"You know I care about you. You know why I'm by your side now."

Jakob closed his eyes, needing to take a second, his emotions threatening to overwhelm him. "Saraa, you ..."

"I did it for you, Jakob," Saraa pleaded, tears forming in her eyes. She had thought that he would understand. That he would see what she could see for them. "I did it for us!"

"Saraa!"

He should have been paying closer attention, but he had misjudged the pace while speaking with his friend turned traitor.

Jakob had thought that they would come at him directly, ignoring Saraa since he was the primary target.

He was wrong.

Catching the movement behind her, even as he reached for Saraa, trying to grasp her hand and pull her toward him, seeing the hope in her eyes that his perspective was her own, he knew that it was too late.

"Jak ..."

Saraa's words died in her throat, the razor-sharp claws of a Stalker punching through her back and out her chest.

The monster ripping its claw free just as quickly as it appeared, Saraa collapsed to the ground.

Blood-red eyes burned in the darkness almost as brightly as Jakob's green. The Stalker opened its fang-toothed maw to roar its pleasure at its kill. It never got the chance.

Jakob shot forward in a blur, whipping free the daggers sheathed on his back and attacking with a controlled ferocity.

Jakob could have used the Talent to destroy the Stalker. He didn't.

He feared that if he did, he would give away his location to the woman responsible for creating the Stalkers. The woman who had corrupted Saraa. He didn't know if she was close, and he didn't want to take the risk.

The Stalker growled. Raising its forearm to block Jakob's slash, the monster succeeded, though it earned a nasty slice down to the bone for its efforts.

The Stalker was fast.

Jakob was faster.

His next slash a feint, Jakob used that split-second of distraction to drive the blade gripped tightly in his other hand into the Stalker's groin.

The monster groaned, then sagged, trying to figure out what mistake it had made, not understanding why its strength and focus faded so swiftly.

Jakob pulled the dagger free after giving the steel a nasty twist, then sliced with the blade in his left hand.

The Stalker bending at the waist, its claws dropping down to the devastating wound below its midsection, it never felt Jakob slice across its throat. The blade cutting all the way to its spine, the monster's hunch turned into a sagging fall.

Jakob stepped out of the way of the dying monster, knowing exactly what was going to be there to greet him.

Three more Stalkers.

Spaced out in front of him.

All of them eyeing him hungrily.

Jakob glanced down at Saraa. He wanted to go to her. To help her. She was still breathing, though barely.

But he couldn't. Not yet.

Jakob moved away from the dead Stalker at his feet, not wanting to have to worry about tripping over the body in the combat to come.

He gestured with one of his bloody daggers, motioning for the Stalkers to come toward him.

The one in the center took the bait.

Gliding out in front of its brethren, the anxious Stalker created the angles that Jakob preferred.

An instant later, a series of sharp whistles pierced the

silence, arrow after arrow streaking through the air and slamming into each Stalker. Three shafts. Six. Nine.

The onslaught continued for several more seconds, Jakob watching with a pleased disgust.

The Stalkers thrashed around the ledge, more and more arrows slamming into them. Thinking only about getting away from the fiery spikes that plunged into their bodies. Forgetting the reason that they were there to begin with.

One Stalker lost track of where it was on the overhang, falling over the edge, its cries dying when it crashed onto the rocks at the bottom of the ridge. Another Stalker dropped dead the instant an arrow slammed through its left eye and into its brain.

That had to be Tommie's work, Jakob believed. He walked over to the third Stalker, which more resembled a pincushion as it lay on the rocky ground, twenty shafts buried in its body.

The monster was gasping for breath and in obvious pain.

Jakob believed that the Stalker deserved to die. But not in this way.

Jakob leaned down and with a quick swipe slit the monster's throat, putting the creature out of its misery.

Leaving the dead beast in his wake, he hustled over to Saraa. Kneeling down next to her, he grasped her hand.

"I'm here, Saraa. I'm here." His eyes watering as he watched her gasp for breath, all his anger, all his disappointment, all his resentment, drained away.

"Jakob, I'm sorr ..." Saraa choked in pain, struggling to get the words out.

He studied her wounds quickly, understanding in an instant that there was little that he could do other than stay with her until the end, which wasn't very far off.

"I know, Saraa. I know."

Jakob gave her a sad smile, then leaned down. He gave her a soft kiss on her forehead. Her skin was already cold.

"Jakob, I only wanted to be with you. I only wanted ..."

She wheezed, her body arching, a debilitating cold shooting through her.

"I know, Saraa."

"You'll remember me, Jakob? In a good light?" Saraa gasped out the words. "I was a fool. I know I was a fool. I'm so sorry. I'm so ..."

"I will always remember you, Saraa. How could I not? You were there when we started all this. When we decided to claim the Highlands for our own."

Saraa smiled then, the light in her eyes beginning to grow dim. "Good," she finally managed to whisper, the last of her strength flowing out of her. "Thank you, Jakob. Thank ..."

Jakob remained where he was for several minutes, holding Saraa's hand long after she had passed to the other side.

He understood what had driven her to do as she had done. And though she had committed what could have been the ultimate betrayal, he felt as if he had betrayed her as well for not reciprocating the feelings that she had for him.

His guilt threatening to crush him, he locked it away. He would deal with it. Just not now.

Now, he needed to finish what he had started.

Pushing himself up, he locked eyes with the men and women who had stepped out from between the heart trees. With a nod, Tommie and the other archers trotted over, seeking to salvage the arrows that they could, knowing that they would be needed in the battle to come.

"Sharperson knows about Lycia," Jakob said.

Duff nodded. He would mourn Saraa later. She had been a good friend. He just never thought that her love for Jakob would come to this. "Then we better go kill him before he kills her."

17

FIRST THINGS FIRST

The Blademaster didn't blink an eye when the Lady of the Southern Marches and her Protector stalked out of a portal constructed of a spinning white mist. He caught a glimpse of the Murk at their backs before the gateway snapped closed.

"By those expressions of yours, I assume that events didn't transpire as you would have liked in the north." The Blademaster appeared grim, determined, just as he always did.

"We're still alive," Aislinn replied. "Beyond that, we've got a few more challenges that we need to address." She shook her head in annoyance. "As if the one in Shadow's Reach wasn't difficult enough."

Having received Aislinn's communication through her use of the Talent, the Blademaster had reached the summit of the peak a few leagues to the north of Shadow's Reach just an hour before. Benin and a few other soldiers were with him, all of them sneaking out of the city so that the Governor and his wife would be none the wiser.

Klines doubted that either of the Winbornes were paying

much attention to what was going on in the capital of the Northern Territory. The growing unrest. The increasing fear.

Their eyes and those of the Northern Guard were turned toward the north, watching for the Murk. And for good reason.

They probably sensed what he had.

The Wraiths had tested the city more times than was necessary. It wouldn't be long before the monsters in the mist came with the Murk ... and stayed for good.

When that happened, their concerns regarding Ursina and her schemes would mean nothing.

The Wraiths would slaughter the city's inhabitants and claim Shadow's Reach as their own.

"How much time do we have?" the Blademaster asked.

"Enough to at least deal with Ursina and the poison she's been feeding my uncle."

The Blademaster gave Aislinn a questioning look. "Do you believe that your uncle is blameless in all this? That only Ursina is the cause?"

Aislinn closed her eyes, taking a deep breath, needing a moment to push back the anger threatening to color her decisions. "No, I don't. My uncle must carry some of the blame. How much?" She shrugged. "I don't know."

"And you understand the possible consequences of what we're about to do?"

Aislinn nodded. "I do." She scrunched up her face, revealing her displeasure. Her determination as well. "It's necessary." Her eyes shifted to Bryen, catching his. "You must do what you must do."

"You must do what you must do," he repeated.

"You're certain about the cause of what's going on in Shadow's Reach? With your uncle?"

"We're certain," Aislinn hissed through gritted teeth. "We face more than just the Curse."

She explained briefly what Rafia had learned upon her

examination of the vial of black liquid given to her by Talia Carlomin. That, combined with what she and Bryen discovered in the chamber beneath the Shadow Keep removed all doubt.

"The Ancient One?" the Blademaster mused. "You two certainly do have a habit of bringing stories best left as stories back to life."

Benin and the soldiers with him, listening intently to the conversation, barely made a sound at the mention of a primordial evil long thought trapped in the Spirit World seeking to break free from his prison. There wasn't a hint of fear. Just concern. An acknowledgment of the scope of the challenge they faced. Their discipline a credit to the Blademaster's training.

"We do what we can," Bryen replied, tongue in cheek.

"Perhaps you should try a little less hard." The Blademaster snorted softly at the Protector's lack of emotion. For the gladiator, it seemed that the Ancient One was simply another combatant to defeat, Bryen's decade on the white sand having eliminated the fear that would have paralyzed most anyone else at the thought of challenging such a monster.

And all credit to Aislinn as well. She had explained what occurred beneath the Shadow Keep as if she was doing nothing more than reporting on the weather. Apparently, several of her Protector's characteristics had rubbed off on her.

"As if the Wraiths weren't problem enough," grumbled Benin.

"Exactly," groused Aislinn, her pique plain in her voice. "There always seems to be another threat that we must deal with beyond the obvious."

They were all thinking much the same thing. They had come to New Caledonia hoping to leave behind the challenges they faced there with respect to the Curse. They should have known that it was a vain hope right from the start.

For Bryen, that conclusion brought his grandfather to mind.

The Magus had believed that the Curse was prevalent everywhere in the world. It was just a matter of how deeply it had snaked its way into a particular Realm and in what form.

Here, in the Territories, it seemed that the Curse was just beginning to expand its hold. Perhaps with what they planned to do they could hamper that growth before it became unmanageable.

A worthy goal, he believed. But not an easy one.

The Ancient One …

Bryen had never shirked from a fight when a fight was necessary. But this …

He shook his head, deep in thought. He would do what was required of him because the threat presented by the Ancient One could not be underestimated.

It was said that the Ancient One could gain dominion over the Natural World if the being escaped the Spirit World. Then nothing could stand against him or the monsters he would bring with him from his domain. Some of these monsters ones that he and Aislinn had fought already.

"Yes, but where's the fun in life without a real challenge," Bryen said, his words serious, his expression more carefree.

"Not very helpful, Protector," grumbled Aislinn.

"No, but the Protector is correct," the Blademaster replied, smiling at Bryen's dark humor. "Where is the fun in life without a challenge."

"The Wraiths will require our attention, but not yet." Bryen's expression now matched his serious tone. "The Ancient One is not yet fully in the Natural World. We know that for a fact. However, we know as well that he is in league with the Dark Magus who used the power he gifted to her to create the Stalkers. Through her, and likely in other ways, he is already touching the Natural World, if only peripherally."

"So rather than worry about him …" prompted the Blademaster.

"We deal with his servant first," Bryen concluded, bringing them right back to where their conversation began. "Ursina first. That's our focus. Once done, we move on to the next challenge."

"You make it seem like it's going to be a walk in the park," said the Blademaster, giving Bryen a cunning smile.

"Far from it," Bryen replied, returning the Blademaster's grin with one of his own. "But it can't be any worse than taking on the Ghoule Overlord or the Kraken and their King."

"Exactly so," the Blademaster agreed.

"I'm beginning to rethink my decision to come to the Territories," Benin grumbled under his breath, although not softly enough.

For a moment, there was silence. Then a round of laugher broke out within the small group.

"Stalkers, Wraiths, and the Ancient One with whatever monsters he can send through the Rip in the Veil," said the Blademaster after everyone released the tension building within them. "Not to mention a Dark Magus. It seems that your list of enemies only grows longer."

"Such is our fate," Bryen confirmed. "Even so, we do have a little time before the Wraiths invade with their Horde."

Aislinn nodded in agreement. "Nothing has changed. We must deal with Ursina first. Once done, we move on to the next threat."

"Do we have the resources to do that?" asked the Blademaster. "I have no doubt that you and the Protector can manage her use of the Curse. Nevertheless, there is more to this situation than just that. An angry husband and possibly the Northern Guard standing in our way."

"Not yet, but we will," Bryen replied.

The Blademaster nodded. "They'll get here in time?"

"They will. Have no fear of that."

"Good, because our next battle is about to begin," Aislinn

said. She had been searching around them with the Talent, not surprised that they were a target once more.

"She found us?" Bryen asked. He could sense it now, the threat streaking toward them. Reaching for the Talent, it didn't take him long to identify this new peril.

"If not her, then her master."

"What are we dealing with now?" asked the Blademaster.

"Look above us," warned Bryen.

The eyes of everyone on the narrow plateau shifted toward the thick clouds. For a few seconds, there was nothing to see. Then, in a flash, three black streaks broke free from the grey overcast and shot down toward them.

"What are they?" Benin asked, his long beard braided into the shape of an axe, the design he preferred before going into battle.

The Blademaster believed that it was a fortuitous choice. "I don't know. They're there but not."

"Shadow Dragons," said Aislinn.

"Shadow Dragons?" asked Benin.

She shrugged. "It seems the appropriate term."

"The work of the Ancient One?"

"Most likely. Probably at the request of his servant."

"He knows we're here, which means that Ursina does as well," Bryen said.

"That would be my guess," Aislinn confirmed.

"Form square!" ordered the Blademaster.

His men responded instantly to his command, although it was a very small square, only one row deep with barely enough room for Bryen and Aislinn to stand in the center with the Blademaster.

"These look to be similar to the creatures we fought in the Shadow Keep," Aislinn murmured.

Bryen nodded. From what he could discern as the monsters shot toward them, the Shadow Dragons were much the same as the Fiends that had attacked them -- half substance, half spirit, which stood to reason since these monsters were only partially in the Natural World. Even so, despite that limitation, the long spiky fangs and sharp claws of the creatures that were half the size of the black dragons roaming the Trench certainly looked real enough.

"Steel won't be enough against these creatures." In a flash, Bryen infused the weapons of the soldiers standing around him with the Talent, their blades glowing brightly.

That would help, Aislinn knew. But it wouldn't be enough.

They stood little chance if the monsters crashed into them, as appeared to be their intent. That meant eliminating the primary advantage the monsters enjoyed.

Right before the Shadow Dragons ripped them to shreds, Aislinn crafted a thin shield of the Talent, fixing it in place above them in just a heartbeat.

Her quick thinking had an immediate impact.

Unable to stop in time, the Shadow Dragons slammed into the shimmering barrier with a smack that echoed off the surrounding peaks. Stunned by the bone-crunching collision, two of the beasts slid to the rocky ground. The third, not as badly hurt as the other two, got its claws beneath it and tried to launch itself back into the sky.

Bryen refused to allow an easy escape. With a lightning-fast thrust, he drove the Spear of the Magii right through the shield and into the belly of the Shadow Dragon seeking to take flight.

The monster shrieked in agony, its wispy black substance flaking away as the Talent burned through it. Before the Shadow Dragon could escape him, Bryen ripped the blade free and punched through Aislinn's shield once again, this time digging deeply into one of the creature's wings.

The Shadow Dragon's ear-splitting shriek intensified, the creature desperate to end the fiery pain burning through it.

Unable to launch itself into the air, the Shadow Dragon threw itself off the barrier, Bryen's blazing steel finally coming free.

"That's what we can expect?" asked the Blademaster, who had watched Bryen's maneuver with interest.

"That's the best that we'll be able to do," Aislinn said. "Spirit and substance mixed together. Only the Talent has any effect upon them. And what's contained in your weapons will help but likely won't be enough."

"Wonderful to hear," the Blademaster grumbled, his sharp mind already turning over this new dilemma, seeking some solution to what looked to be a losing battle for them.

The injured Shadow Dragon fell heavily to the ground. Then, pushing itself painfully back up, it dug its sharp claws into the dirt and rock and dragged itself away from the shimmering white and the one who had wounded it so badly.

Having reached what it judged to be a safe distance, the Shadow Dragon swung its maw back around, the monster hissing angrily, snapping its jaws a few times to emphasize its point, even as its tenebrous flesh continued to burn.

The other two Shadow Dragons glided around them, advancing from different directions. Wanting to avoid an injury similar to what their brethren suffered, they feinted an attack and then a few more.

They did little more than that, however. Failing to find a weakness to exploit, they scrambled back time and again. Wary of the shining steel.

Bryen didn't believe that their caution would last much longer. He doubted that their master exercised much in the way of compassion. The Ancient One had sent the Shadow Dragons to kill them. These monsters would complete the task, no matter the cost to themselves.

That created a risk that Bryen wanted to avoid. The Blademaster and his men would stand strong against any attack. But there was little chance of surviving an all-out onslaught. They didn't have the ability to manipulate the Talent themselves, and he doubted that he and Aislinn could protect against the Shadow Dragons while at the same time trying to drive the monsters from the field.

"It seems that we've reached an impasse," said the Blademaster.

"Maybe not," Bryen replied.

His eyes a cold, flinty grey, he stepped out from the ranks of soldiers, spinning the Spear of the Magii from one hand to the other.

The three Shadow Dragons stood their ground. Though not for long. Much like a moth being drawn to the light, they stalked closer to the Protector. Drawn perhaps by his perceived vulnerability.

Every so often they snapped at Bryen, who danced away with ease. Each time he did so, he pulled the three dragons farther away from the Blademaster and his soldiers.

Having judged that he had gained enough distance, Bryen stopped, driving the tip of his spear into the rocky ground.

The wounded monster kept its distance, wary, uncertain, despite the opportunity that Bryen was presenting to it. The other two Shadow Dragons seemed to have forgotten the injury he had inflicted upon their brethren, digging their claws into the ground, preparing to leap at him.

"What's he going to do?" the Blademaster asked. "He can't expect to kill all three of them."

Aislinn's eyes widened when she felt Bryen open himself not only to the Talent, taking in as much of that power as he could without fear of burning himself out, but also to the Seventh Stone, the artifact within him buttressing his efforts by gifting him even more energy for his use.

"He's not going to kill them," Aislinn said, realizing what her Protector had in mind. "He's going to destroy them."

At that very instant, Bryen disappeared, a nimbus of bright

white light forming around him. The intense glow forced Aislinn and the soldiers with her to shield their eyes. They turned away instinctively when three separate pulses of blinding energy blasted out from the circle of light, each one streaking toward a Shadow Dragon.

When Aislinn swept back around, glowing sword at the ready just in case, Bryen stood there calmly on the ledge, leaning on the Spear of the Magii.

Where the trio of Shadow Dragons once stood, there were now three permanent scorches burned into the stone, each a perfect representation of one of the Shadow Dragons.

"How did you learn to do that?"

Bryen shifted his gaze to Aislinn. He smiled, clearly happy with the results of his efforts. That he had succeeded, yes, but even more that he had found a solution that didn't require the Blademaster and his soldiers to engage in what likely would have been a bloody fight.

"Viktor offered a suggestion when I connected to the Seventh Stone. I decided to take him up on it."

"Good advice."

"Yes, he's quite pleased with himself," Bryen replied. He pushed off the ground with his spear and strode toward Aislinn, his expression matching that of the Blademaster. Grim determination.

"I'm tired of surprises. It's time to deal with your aunt."

"She's not my aunt," Aislinn protested, although she certainly wasn't going to argue with him about the rest of his statement.

18

SO IT BEGINS

"Anything to worry about?"

Duff crouched next to Jakob. He and the hundreds of Highlanders at his back hid among the heart trees that grew just beneath the Stone, a grassy knoll that led to the citadel's foundation stretching out before them.

"We have a lot to worry about," Jakob replied, his gaze never leaving the crag upon which Sharperson had built his fortress.

Duff waited several seconds for Jakob to expand on his comment. He didn't.

"Would you care to offer more in the way of detail?" Duff grumbled.

Jakob remained quiet for several seconds more before finally turning his focus toward Duff. "Do you trust Kerala?"

"I do," Duff replied, "about as far as I can throw him."

"That's not the affirmation that I was seeking."

"Don't worry about Kerala," Duff explained. "Jemaal and a few other lads are sitting on him now. He's a slippery little man, Sharperson's chamberlain, but he won't lie to us. He wants Sharperson gone just as we do. He won't take a risk with our friends keeping him company."

"I'll take your word for it," Jakob replied. "It's as we thought."

"The passageway we used to escape the Stone?"

"Full of them," Jakob replied with a calm few others could manage despite his discovery.

"Not surprising."

"No, not surprising," Jakob agreed. "Everyone ready?"

Duff looked back over his shoulder. Bertie, Martin, Tommie, Benyen, and so many more Highlanders stared back at him. Steely. Forbidding. Also excited. That spark obvious in their shining eyes. They had been waiting for this opportunity for quite a long time.

"We're ready."

"Then we place our trust in Kerala," Jakob replied. "Give me a second."

It had taken them longer to reach their position than Jakob would have liked. He had hoped that they could approach the Stone under the cover of darkness. But it wasn't to be.

It was a few hours past dawn, the sun already beginning to brighten the sky to the east as it inched above the peaks. The only benefit of their timing was the fact that a good number of the soldiers that they thought would be stationed on the Stone's parapet were instead over at the stadium that morning.

Jakob knew why. He had searched with the Talent, locating Lycia.

She could handle herself. He was certain of that. She was a better fighter than he was, after all.

Nevertheless, she was alone. With no chance of immediate assistance if she required it.

That reality ate at him. He wanted to help her. Hopefully get to her before it was too late. But he couldn't put his own desires above the Highlanders' larger goal.

Lycia had achieved the distraction that they sought. The lack of guards on the Stone's walls proved it.

Reaching for the Talent, he did as he had done when he first escaped the Wraiths in the Murk. Using his natural magic, he hid the Highlanders in plain sight, blending all of them into their surroundings.

When the guards atop the battlements looked down, they would see nothing more than heart trees and the long grass blowing in the wind and not the several hundred armed invaders advancing toward them at a measured pace.

"Good?" Duff asked. He could see all the Highlanders, so he wasn't certain that Jakob had done as he had promised.

"Good," Jakob replied. "Remember, any movement that's too swift or ..."

"We know," Duff replied. His impatience getting the better of him, he pushed himself up. "Slow and steady. No unnecessary motions. No noise. Just a casual stroll up the slope to the base of the wall." He shook his head in amusement. "What will likely be the strangest attack ever to take place in the Realms."

Jakob smiled at that. "Just think of the story that will be written about us."

"Actually, I've already written the first few pages," Duff replied. He trusted Jakob. He trusted what he could do with the Talent.

"Why am I not surprised." Jakob's green eyes flashed brightly in the shadows, his tone hard. "As my father liked to say, kill or be killed. And it's past time that someone killed Sharperson."

"As you say, Lord Kestrel," Duff nodded, smiling at the intensity of Jakob's comment.

He had never doubted his decision to push Jakob down the road that had led them all to this point. He had just never thought that they would get here so quickly. That rather than years it would take only months.

What he saw now on the young man's face, his flinty expression, the purpose that radiated from him, told him why they had been able to push forward with their plan so swiftly.

Jakob was a force unto himself, and his skill with the Talent only boosted that characteristic.

For the better when it came to the Highlanders.

For the worse with respect to Sharperson and anyone else daring to get in his way.

Jakob nodded in return, then walked out from the wood. Duff right at his side, the other Highlanders streamed out behind them.

None of them appeared to be nervous, although almost all of them were.

Many of them had assaulted fortifications before. They understood just how difficult it was to seize a barricade or a citadel. Because the defenders always enjoyed a distinct advantage.

As the Highlanders maintained their slow approach, many of them recalled previous assaults. The mad dash followed by bouts of terror mixed in with exhilaration, pain, joy, doubt ...

The list went on.

It was hard to think during such an attack. The primary concern avoiding arrows and other projectiles. The rocks and boulders dropped from the walls. The burning oil and pitch poured through funnels that extended out from the parapet.

Yet here, now, they were taking part in an attack that went completely against their previous experiences. Seemingly without a care or concern in the world, they were walking up a hill with the surrounding gloom quickly shifting to a muted brightness.

"Can they see us?" murmured Bertie. He walked next to Martin. Between them, the two Highlanders had several decades of experience as soldiers. In consequence, they were having a very hard time viewing their paced walk up the hill as an attack on the Stone.

"No," Martin replied. "I don't think so."

"Shut it," Tommie ordered quietly. "No noise. If the soldiers on the walls could see us, they'd be peppering us with arrows by now. Keep moving and keep quiet. I have no desire to run this morning just because you two feel the need to prattle on like two old men with nothing better to do."

Duff heard the brief conversation behind him. He didn't feel the need to add anything. They were halfway up the hill already and closing quickly on their objective.

With every step they took, the handful of soldiers walking the parapet above them gained greater clarity. Yet none of the soldiers who glanced down at them shouted out an alarm. Jakob's deception holding.

Just a few minutes more, and the Highlanders stood within the shadows of the wall. Invisible to the soldiers above unless they leaned over the parapet.

"This is it," Duff said.

He led Jakob and the Highlanders farther to the east along the base of the crag until he reached a narrow crevice that was only visible when he stood within a few feet of it.

"You're certain?"

Duff nodded. He pointed to the three scrapes of chalk along the edge. "Jemaal's work."

Jakob examined the natural gap in the stone. Then he extended his senses.

For the first few yards, most of the Highlanders would have to scoot through, turning sideways. After that, however, the path became a large tunnel that would allow them to move with a great deal more speed.

Most importantly, the tunnel was empty.

"Then let's get to it," Jakob ordered, turning sideways and slipping through the crevice before Duff could stop him.

Grumbling under his breath, Duff followed. Jakob was too important to their cause to take unnecessary risks. The lad should have known by now that he didn't always have to be the first person into the breach.

Yet still he was, Duff failing to remove that characteristic from Jakob's personality. In fact, he doubted that he ever would.

It wasn't long before all the Highlanders slipped through the gap and into the tunnel. When they did, Jakob released his hold on the illusion that had protected them from the eyes on the parapet.

Still, he wanted to keep his Highlanders' presence beneath the Stone a secret for as long as possible. To that end, rather than flinging several balls of blazing white up toward the ceiling so that they didn't have to navigate the pitch black blind, he connected to each Highlander with the Talent, giving them the ability to see in the dark.

That done, searching through the base of the citadel with the Talent one more time to ensure that nothing had changed, he issued a quick command. "Archers to the front."

Tommie and several dozen men and women responded in an instant, arrows already nocked to their bows.

"How far?"

"Just a hundred yards. To the east." Jakob began walking down the tunnel, Duff staying at his side, the archers spreading out in front of them.

When they came to a fork in the path, Jakob selected the one that led to the right. He stopped inside a large cavern that was fifty yards wide and a hundred or more yards long.

The perfect place for a fight.

Even more so, an ambush.

There they waited.

Jakob extending his senses beneath the citadel, all of the Highlanders seeing what he could see because of the link between them.

"They know we're here?" asked Duff.

"That would be my guess," Jakob confirmed. Several dozen

Stalkers were gliding toward them through the handful of tunnels that led to the cavern.

"Wonderful."

"But they probably don't know that we know they know we're here. So at least we have that."

"You enjoyed saying that, didn't you?" Duff asked, slightly amused, even more irritated by Jakob's lack of anxiety over the approaching monsters.

"I did." Jakob shifted his focus to Tommie and the other archers. "You have your targets?"

Tommie nodded. "We do." She and all the Highlanders could see where the Stalkers were, a handful of the creatures already moving into the cavern from the far end, their blood-red eyes just becoming visible in the darkness.

"One flight then squads move forward to finish what's left."

Many of the Highlanders nodded, although they didn't need to.

It was a force of habit.

They had all fought in the Murk thanks to Jakob's application of the Talent. Doing the same now in the pitch black would be little different. They could see just as well as if hundreds of torches had been set in the walls to light the cavern.

"Yes, Lord Kestrel," Tommie replied.

"On my command." Jakob waited just a few seconds more, wanting to ensure that all the Stalkers entered the chamber and that those at the front were only a few dozen yards away before the skirmish began. "Fire!"

Dozens of steel-tipped shafts whispered through the black, each one streaking toward a monster that thought it was safe in the dark.

~

Lycia strode out onto the brown sand of the Little Pit.

Her name capturing the interest of the people living at the Stone and the surrounding environs, there was barely an open inch to be found on the benches that extended up to the very top of the stadium. Adding to the size of the massive crowd, a large number of spectators created places for themselves among the wreckage of the collapsed western stand.

The low murmur of conversation shifted when the Crimson Devil appeared, transforming into a crescendo of cheers – and not a single jeer -- that echoed around the circular stadium.

The experience seemed no different than all the other times she had walked out through the ramshackle gates.

Except for one key characteristic.

She entered the Little Pit on her own.

She had yet to see who her opponent would be.

That fact planting a seed of worry within her, she kept her gaze hard, focused, when she stopped near the center of the ring, waiting patiently as the screams and shouts slowly died away and then disappeared altogether when Governor Sharperson pushed himself up from his overlarge, ornate chair and leaned on the stone railing of his private box.

"You thought you would get away with it?" Sharperson called down to her.

Lycia's eyes narrowed, not expecting Sharperson to begin this way. Realizing that this was not to be just another combat for her.

The handful of worries that had plagued her since the night before – what had happened in Sharperson's suite, her decision to exit the Stone and speak with Jakob, her fear that Reeki might have followed her through the tunnel -- quickly blossomed into a tangible alarm.

Still, she managed her concern. Understanding that she needed to play her role until the very end. And if all went well, that end was coming soon.

Staring up at Sharperson, catching the manic, prideful glint in his eyes, she confirmed her fear.

He knew.

Somehow, he had figured it out.

Or, more likely, someone had betrayed her.

Lycia shook her head ever so slightly in a mix of amusement, resignation, and rising anger.

She should have assumed as much.

She had thought that she was playing Sharperson.

And perhaps she had been.

For a time.

Not anymore.

Now Sharperson was playing her.

Coming to grips with that, there seemed to be little point in trying to lie to him.

There was only one way that this confrontation was going to conclude. Nevertheless, she might as well make the Governor work for it. The more time that she earned, the better her chances. Assuming, of course, that the rest of the plan she had worked out with Jakob was moving forward as she hoped it was.

"Get away with what?" Lycia gave Sharperson a bemused expression, one that earned a few quiet chuckles from the crowd.

Sharperson had tried to throw Lycia off right from the start. He hadn't.

That annoyed Sharperson, though he refused to show it. He stared down at her for several seconds more, finally breaking out into a harsh laugh that was designed to hide his irritation and disappointment. "I've known for quite some time, my lovely. There's no point in trying to deny it."

"Deny what?" If nothing else, Lycia knew how to be difficult. Bryen and Davin could certainly attest to that.

Her smile turned to a smirk when she saw how the Governor's expression soured because of her obstinance.

"This is how it's going to be, my lovely? After all that I've done for you? After how well I treated you?"

Lycia snorted in disbelief. "After how you tried to get me into your bed, you mean?"

Sharperson leaned back at that, never expecting that the gladiator would challenge him in this way. He had thought that she would simply want to get to the part where she could match steel with steel.

Yet it seemed that he had underestimated her. Again.

She knew exactly what she was doing. He knew as well. And he realized that he needed to be careful as he ran his gaze over the crowd, his expression becoming shrewd.

The spectators had come here for a combat, not to listen to a spat. And it was quite clear that because of her success, the crowd loved the Crimson Devil a great deal more than they loved their benefactor.

He had seen it before, having been a connoisseur of the gladiatorial games in Tintagel when he was younger. The spectators, fickle at best, could turn on him in a flash.

Sharperson expanded his smile, pretending to nod to some of the people in the crowd, his efforts more often than not returned by hard gazes and glares.

He wasn't a fool. He knew that he was not well loved.

How could he be with the rebellion brewing in the Highlands?

Yet for all his wits, he had failed to consider this possible outcome from the game he had set in motion. Rather than getting right to the combat and killing the woman who sought to undermine him, he had wanted to dangle her over a cliff for a time and poke at her before dropping her. He understood now that giving in to that desire was a mistake.

A bolt of concern shot through him when he realized that he had put himself in a precarious position.

Sharperson had a good number of soldiers here in the Little Pit and along the causeway that led to the Stone, but certainly not enough to match the number of people watching the current spectacle.

If the crowd was sympathetic to the gladiator's plight, what would they do?

Even after only a week of combats on the brown sand, the crowd loved and respected the Crimson Devil. The many sour expressions now directed his way confirmed that truth.

Swallowing a few times and then licking his lips, he concluded that he needed to move this exhibition along faster than he had planned. He didn't want to give the gladiator the chance to turn the crowd against him.

"That you are in league with the rebel, my lovely. That you came here seeking my removal. Do you deny it?"

"The rebel?" Lycia repeated with a hint of confusion in her voice, her nose crinkling as if she were deep in thought.

Sharperson closed his eyes and took a deep breath. Rather than lashing out as he wanted to, he fought to remain calm. He needed to present himself as a beneficent ruler. A façade, nothing more, that was true, and one that the bulk of the crowd likely would not believe.

Still, he couldn't afford to antagonize the thousands of people who with the appropriate spark could become an angry mob. A possibility that he had failed to consider while orchestrating that morning's primary event.

"Please, my lovely, there is no reason to draw this out. I have incontrovertible proof that you are in league with the rebel who seeks to claim the Highlands for his own and then enslave these good people."

Sharperson motioned with both hands, attempting to

include the crowd in his pronouncement. From what he could see after just a cursory glimpse, his words fell flat.

Instead of expanding on his argument, knowing that he had little chance of swaying the crowd to his side with rhetoric, he chose expediency instead. It was time to bring this episode to a close so that he could return to the safety of the Stone. The murmurs running through the crowd now, faint to begin with though growing in strength, were making him nervous.

"Your fate is sealed, my lovely, no matter what you might have to say," Sharperson said in a patronizing tone. "You are a traitor to the good people of the Highlands. Admit it so that we can move on."

It was Lycia's turn to give the Governor a shrewd look. She knew what Sharperson was trying to do. He had thought to make an example of her. And he had become so enamored with his own cunning that he had missed the most obvious consequence of his decision.

Sensing the change within the crowd, the rumbles of disapproval cascading down into the Little Pit gaining strength, she decided to see how much farther she could push the spectators.

"The rebel, you say," Lycia challenged, pursing her lips, furrowing her brow, as if she needed to think about to whom Sharperson might be referring. "Jakob Kestrel, you mean?"

"Yes, the rebel. Are you admitting your guilt, my lovely?" Sharperson's eyes had taken on a rapacious glow.

"The Jakob Kestrel who has been building brochs throughout the Highlands to protect against the Stalkers, slavers, and Wraiths? The Jakob Kestrel who has sought to serve and defend the people of the Highlands against any and all threats? That Jakob Kestrel?"

"The Jakob Kestrel who ..." Sharperson began to hiss, his face turning red with rage.

Lycia cut him off before he could get going. "The Jakob Kestrel who will take on any challenge facing the Highlanders, doing all that he can to help them achieve the new lives they dream of?"

Several loud murmurs of approval started to work their way through the crowd, some of the spectators even stomping their boots on the benches to emphasize the truth of her words.

Recognizing her opportunity, Lycia tried to make the most of it. "The Jakob Kestrel who enters the Murk without fear to battle the Wraiths? The Jakob Kestrel who does nothing for himself and all for others?"

Emboldened as the murmurs within the crowd became more strident, many of the men and women now shouting their agreement despite the soldiers stationed around the Little Pit placing a hand on the hilts of their swords, a few even brandishing their weapons, Lycia pushed harder.

"The Jakob Kestrel who has given his blood, who has risked his life, more times than I can count, all so that the people living within these mountains can be free?"

Lycia smiled, cheers ringing out from the crowd. She locked eyes with Sharperson then. "Jakob Kestrel might be a rebel in your eyes. But in mine, he is a hero." She stepped closer to Sharperson, who stood twenty feet above her and glared down with hate in his eyes. "Jakob Kestrel has done what you haven't for the people living within these peaks. It is for that reason that Jakob Kestrel is the rightful Lord of the Highlands."

Rather than a raucous cheer, much to Lycia's surprise, her declaration led to a shocking silence.

The crowd had not expected such brazenness from her. They had not expected to reach this point so quickly. One in which the tiniest shift on the scale could push them all in a direction that they had mused about but not yet contemplated in any great detail.

Although by the looks and nods that the men and women in the stadium were giving her, Lycia believed that they were doing that now, because they agreed with her.

Could she push the crowd over the edge? Help them take that final step?

She didn't get the chance to find out, Sharperson seeking to reclaim what authority that he could.

"Jakob Kestrel is a traitor," Sharperson hissed through gritted teeth. "I am the Lord of the Highlands. *Me.* The charter was given to me." Sharperson bit off his last few words to emphasize his point. "I will always be the Lord of the Highlands."

"You are not the Lord of the Highlands. You are using your power for your own gain. The real Lord of the Highlands is using his power to help those in need."

"I am the Lord of the Highlands!" Sharperson roared, no longer able to control his temper.

"You are in name, perhaps," Lycia replied. "At least for a little while longer. Enjoy what time you have left."

"Is that a threat, my lovely?"

"No, *Governor* Sharperson, that's a promise."

Sharperson forced himself to stare into the gladiator's implacable glare. He wanted to look away, beads of sweat forming on his bald head, a shiver of fear working its way through his body. But he couldn't.

He was engaged in a combat right then with the gladiator, one that was more important than the clash of steel that was about to follow. If he didn't demonstrate the power that he sought to exercise, then he lost.

Because he could feel the eyes of every single person in the stadium fixed on him. Waiting to see how he was going to respond.

Perhaps even wondering if they should demonstrate their displeasure with him and their agreement with the Crimson Devil's claims. The people living in and around the Stone coming to believe that it was time to take action rather than just stew and complain.

"I knew that I was going to enjoy this," Sharperson said, seeking to imbue his voice with as much strength as he could muster, knowing that he needed to exercise some control over the situation that he had created before he lost it for good. "But after this, what will be our last exchange, I simply can't wait. Just like this uppity Lord Kestrel, you are a traitor. And there is only one penalty for traitors."

Sharperson nodded over his shoulder. Within seconds, the gate beneath his private box began to open.

Usually, the dead were dragged across the sand and through that gate.

But not today.

Not for the spectacle that Sharperson had planned.

Lycia couldn't say that she was surprised to see who her next opponent was to be. In a way, it was inevitable. And fitting, perhaps.

Because she doubted that there was anyone else truly loyal to Sharperson other than the hulking figure who strode out into the Little Pit who stood any chance of serving as her executioner.

"You have fought the best, Crimson Devil. And you have survived every contest. But you have never fought Reeki."

19

THE IMPREGNABLE STONE

A sphere of flaring power shot through the darkness, revealing the cavern for an instant before it winked out.

Blasting into the last Stalker still standing in the underground chamber, the energy burned the monster to ash in a flash, not even giving the creature time to scream, before slamming against the stone wall and fading away as if it had never existed to begin with.

What the orb revealed was a gut-churning although necessary display.

Two dozen Stalkers lay dead or dying. Pierced by arrows. Slashed and cut with swords. Stabbed with spears.

His Highlanders had been efficient in their work. Nevertheless, Jakob felt the need to engage the last Stalker. The monster close to the tunnel on the far side.

An easy path for escape if Jakob allowed it.

He didn't.

The Stalkers' wild attacks did them little good. They found themselves to be no match for the disciplined Highlanders who fought with a precision and teamwork that ensured that not a single man or woman suffered anything more than a few shallow scratches and gashes, requiring only a binding before they continued their advance beneath the Stone.

"It seems like you're in a bad mood, lad," Duff said as he approached the pile of cinders that just seconds before had been a beast crafted from the Curse.

This was the tunnel that he and Jakob were planning on taking. A few squads would go with them. The rest of the Highlanders had other assignments to complete. If all went to plan, they would take the Stone with a minimum of bloodshed.

Duff snorted quietly at the thought. Nothing went to plan. Success depended on what you did when the plan fell apart. Although it certainly helped to have someone who could employ the Talent by your side when that happened.

"It's that obvious?" Jakob asked.

"It is," Duff replied, "but the lads and lasses feel more at ease when you are. They like it when you're angry."

"Why is that?"

"Because it makes their lives easier. As you just demonstrated."

Jakob smiled at that. Although not with any real purpose. Rather with a barely contained rage.

"I am angry, you're right. I'm tired of dealing with people who believe they can do anything they like for their own benefit."

"Good. That's how we need you right now."

"The vengeful Lord of the Highlands?" mused Jakob.

"Exactly."

Jakob nodded once more. "Easily done."

Without another word, Jakob and Duff stepped over the pile of ash and into the tunnel. At the same time, Martin, Bertie, and Tommie led their companies into the other tunnels.

The Stone was under attack, and Torstan Sharperson wasn't even yet aware of that potentially fatal fact.

"Run while you can, little girl. It will do you no good. You only delay the inevitable."

Lycia ignored Reeki's taunt. Sharperson's shadow rushed her as soon as the combat began. She assumed that he thought that he could take her by surprise. Perhaps even kill her with a single stab.

Lycia disabused him of that notion with a deft grace. Pivoting out of the way, she allowed him to pass her by like a charging bull.

Rather than kick out with her leg and send him sprawling into the sand as she had done so many times before while fighting in the Colosseum, instead she jumped into the air, then used her momentum to flip backward before landing on her feet.

Her remarkable maneuver, which excited and enthralled the roaring crowd, saved her life.

Reeki halted his progress faster than anyone watching believed possible. Turning with a deceptive agility, he slashed with a dagger that he kept hidden against his hip.

If he had struck true, Lycia would have been lying on her back in the Little Pit, struggling to breathe, her throat slit and her blood turning the brown sand black.

Much to Reeki's surprise, however, he didn't.

Lycia escaped him, giving him a frown of disappointment. The game between them just getting started.

Lycia gliding around the Little Pit with an unmatched adroitness.

Reeki stalking after her.

When their blades met the cacophony created by the spectators increased to a deafening level, the clash of steel striking steel lost.

After their blades met, their engagement fast, fierce, and

furious, their motions so swift that their weapons appeared to be no more than grey blurs, they pulled back from one another to reassess and decide what to try next. Seeking to overcome the challenge of getting past the other's defenses. The challenge they anticipated.

Neither gained anything more than a few streaks of red on the other's arms, shoulders, chests for their efforts. Neither was able to achieve the desired killing blow.

They were evenly matched.

They were exceedingly competent.

And they were patient.

Through it all, Torstan Sharperson leaned over the railing of his private box, cheering on his bodyguard and friend. Desperate for the Crimson Devil's death. Reveling in the bloody experience that he had crafted for the watching thousands. Thankful that the combat and the expectation of a bloody end had pulled their thoughts away from him. Using this spectacle to paper over the cracks in his rule.

"Perhaps you should take your own advice, earless," Lycia shot right back at him.

Reeki's expression remained just as it had been when the combat began. Dispassionate. Cold. Not giving away what he was thinking or feeling or planning.

Nevertheless, she saw in his eyes how her words stung. Almost as if he wasn't used to being teased, which, as Lycia thought about it, probably was the case.

Who in their right mind other than a gladiator who had survived the Pit would seek to antagonize a man more dangerous than a Stalker?

"Run from me now or I'll drag you across the sand myself."

Reeki stopped then, staring at her. Then, unexpectedly, he gave Lycia a broad grin that more resembled a sneer. "You play the game well, girl. But you won't be playing it for much longer."

With a speed remarkable for such a large man, and one with a now permanent limp, Reeki took three steps that were more lunges then launched himself into the air. Sword beginning above his shoulder, he swung with his blade as he came back down to earth.

Lycia didn't bother to parry the strike. She was strong. But she wasn't as strong as her adversary. If she remained where she was and attempted to block Reeki's blade, she ran the risk of a broken blade and his steel burying itself in her flesh.

Instead she avoided the attack altogether with a swift step to the right. Wary of Reeki's dagger, she brought her sword up vertical to the ground. At the same time he drove the tip of his sword into the sand rather than her chest she caught Reeki's smaller blade aimed for her lower back.

The scrape of his dagger against her sword was music to her ears. Yet she didn't savor it for long. Kneeling quickly, with her free hand Lycia pulled her dagger free from the sheath on her belt and plunged the blade into the back of Reeki's already damaged knee.

If it had been anyone else she had wounded in such a way, she would have continued her assault. Prepared to finish her adversary. Writhing on the ground. Screaming in agony.

She knew better with Reeki.

He acknowledged the pain of his wound with a hiss that he pushed through clenched teeth. And that was it.

Lycia had hoped for more though she expected less, not doubting that Reeki would remain a dangerous foe until she stole the light from his eyes.

Her belief was confirmed when Reeki spun on his knees, a cloud of sand swirling around him, and swung his sword viciously through the air.

Anticipating just such a maneuver, Lycia already was well beyond the arc of the slash that targeted her waist, having launched herself backward as soon as she punched her dagger through the flesh and bones of Reeki's knee.

Reveling in her success, the roars and wild jubilation of the crowd -- screaming for blood, screaming for victory, screaming for her -- intensified to a level that set the stadium shaking and quivering.

Lycia didn't hear any of it.

She didn't see any of it.

She focused solely on the hulking figure who pushed himself up from the sand and turned slowly to face her.

The mask that Reeki used to hide his emotions slipped away, replaced by a rictus of pain and a snarl of hate and disgust. The last two sentiments were for both his opponent and himself.

He had never faced a situation such as the one he was dealing with now. One in which his adversary was just as skilled as he was. Just as intent on the primary task of killing before being killed.

That realization changed the dynamics of the combat for him.

Reeki looked up to his right, catching Sharperson's eyes. The Governor nodded, understanding what was being asked of him and releasing him from the restriction that he had placed on Reeki before he walked out onto the sand.

Sharperson had wanted Reeki to draw out the fight. To make the gladiator suffer. To teach her a lesson and in doing so teach the crowd a lesson as well.

That's why Reeki had rushed her at the start, hoping to wound her so that he could play with her for a while before finishing her. Just as he did with all his other opponents.

Yet the gladiator failed to follow Sharperson's script, and Reeki had suffered for it.

Now, however, with Sharperson's permission, Reeki could

fight as he wished. He could fight to survive. Because that's what the combat had become for him.

No matter what he might say to rattle the gladiator, he knew the truth. She was an accomplished fighter. If he was to have any chance against her, he needed to kill her quickly. His damaged and dragging leg would only make it easier for her to kill him the longer she stayed in the fight.

"You die now, girl. No more games."

"So you say, earless," Lycia taunted. Sheathing her dagger, she pulled her second sword, a mirror to her first, from the scabbard across her back. This time she didn't wait for Reeki to attack. Slicing both blades through the air with murderous intent, she strode confidently toward him. "Let's see if you can back up your words. Let's see how you enjoy what you so enjoy doing to others."

"What would that be, little girl?" Reeki asked, already moving to his side, more stumbling than walking now as he put the stone wall at his back. His screaming knee a hindrance and limiting his maneuverability, he knew that no matter how much he might not like it, he had to cede the momentum to the gladiator.

"Inflicting pain and suffering," Lycia replied.

The sword in her right hand sliced through the air for Reeki's throat. The sword in her left hand arced right behind it.

"First squad into the tower!" Martin ordered. "Second squad clear the parapet to the next staircase!"

The Highlanders swept down the battlements like a swarm of bees, the men and women breaking off as ordered.

Martin assumed they would face more of a fight atop the walls of the Stone, but it wasn't to be. And he was glad for that.

Sharperson had left no more than a depleted company to

maintain the watch, clearly not believing that he had much to worry about thanks to the forts he had constructed a league to the east, west, and north that were supposed to keep Highlanders like him away from his center of power.

That mistake didn't bother Martin as he trotted down the walkway, his Highlanders flowing around him. Grim. Expectant. Focused on their assignments.

Because of Sharperson's overconfidence, they had needed to kill only a few of the men standing watch, and those really just to make a point. Most of Sharperson's Guard had been more than willing to surrender upon seeing the Highlanders streaming toward them. Steel at the ready. Expressions murderous.

"Jaki, take your squads through the tower here and across to the other side. Set up a shield wall in the tower. If anyone comes up from that direction, kill them. No questions asked."

"With pleasure," she murmured, cutting to the left and leading twenty Highlanders in that direction.

Jaki understood why Martin had given her the task. The tower that rose in the center of the Stone gave access to the walls from four different directions. If a counterattack came, it would start there. Better to strangle it before it even got started.

Martin didn't bother to watch Jaki go. He was confident that she would do exactly as he required, just as he was confident that every other Highlander with him would do the same.

If his attack continued to progress as it was, he would have the Stone's battlements under his sway in less than an hour.

"This isn't much fun at all," Tenny grumbled.

"Maybe not, my friend," Bertie replied. "But better boring than fun when you're conquering a fortress."

Tenny couldn't argue with Bertie's logic. "They're hiding in the storage room most likely. Just like in the other barracks we've cleared out."

"I don't doubt it. Why don't you take a squad and flush them out."

"And if they resist?" Tenny asked.

"We already have plenty of prisoners. If they want to fight, teach them the error of their ways."

Tenny grinned then hustled down to the far end of the barracks, his squad right at his back, their eyes focused on the door just past the washroom that led into the storage area.

Bertie followed at a more leisurely pace. He doubted that there were more than four or five soldiers seeking refuge at the back of the barracks, most likely matching the number of beds with rumpled blankets that he passed. The several hundred other bunks empty. Those soldiers ordered to man Sharperson's forts and serve as his primary line of defense against men like him. Those soldiers now dead or captured.

Sharperson pulling so many of his companies away from the Stone had proven to be a major mistake. A gift to the Highlanders as well. And Bertie was more than willing to reap the benefits of the Governor's miscalculation.

He had expected a bloody fight as soon as he and his Highlanders began their attack on the barracks that were situated in the very center of the Stone. And he had worried for no reason.

They had caught most of the soldiers asleep, and their low numbers confirmed that Sharperson had only a cursory guard here with him in the citadel. No more than a handful of companies at best.

Sharperson had assumed that with the nasties he had hidden below the Stone he had nothing to fear from the Highlanders while he was behind his walls.

Arrogance at its best, Bertie tsked. With such conceit, you got what you deserved.

"Any problems?" asked Bertie when he reached the storage room, the door opened wide.

"Unfortunately not," Tenny grumbled. The soldiers hiding there had surrendered without a fight. Weapons on the ground, hands raised, before Tenny said a word.

This being the last of the barracks that Bertie needed to clear, he smiled. Pleased. He was ahead of schedule, which meant that he could move forward with the next part of the plan.

"Take two squads and make sure the northern gatehouse is ours."

"And the other one?" Tenny asked as he stalked back the way that he had come, his squads at his back, all of them hoping for more of a fight as they took up their next assignment. Hoping for more of a reason to kill the men who had inflicted so much misery on them for so long.

"Donel!" Bertie shouted. The merchant turned rebel strode toward him, his squad standing guard at the door on the far side of the barracks. Searching for stragglers or hideaways and finding none. "Clear the southern gatehouse!"

"We're all set, Tommie."

The archer, seeing the world through her spectacles, nodded. She had anticipated more of a ruckus by now. A larger fight breaking out. But barely a whimper from the soldiers charged with guarding the Stone.

It seemed that Martin and Bertie were doing their work better than any of them could have hoped for.

"Good. Stay sharp. Stay ready. We move soon."

Alara nodded and stepped back into the shadows. Her eyes swept all around, looking for any possible threats and finding none other than the peril that she and the hundred other archers presented to anyone foolish enough to challenge the Highlanders.

Tommie, standing at the very edge of the archway and hidden within the gloom, kept her eyes on the causeway that extended out in front of her. She ignored the screams and roars erupting from the stadium that was three hundred yards distant at the far end of the stone footbridge that was built across the tops of several tors.

Instead, she kept her focus on the soldiers positioned every twenty yards along the arched bridge. None of the men had a clue as to what was going on in the citadel. Nor did the several squads of soldiers milling about at the gatehouse that served as the main entrance to the Little Pit.

Good. It would make what the Highlanders needed to do next somewhat easier.

Because they now faced the obstacle of a natural chokepoint.

If they were to remove the Governor, they needed to navigate the elevated causeway and get into the stadium before the soldiers could lower the portcullis built into the gatehouse.

Not an easy task, admittedly. But she didn't like easy tasks. She preferred challenges.

And this one appealed to her.

She had always wanted to meet Torstan Sharperson. Preferably at the end of one of her arrows.

"Any trouble?" asked Duff.

He and Jakob stopped right next to Tommie, staying in the darkness, pleased to see that the soldiers positioned along the bridge had no idea as to what was coming their way.

They had left the Highlanders to their assignments, knowing that so long as Martin, Bertie, and the others followed their instructions the Stone would fall with barely a fight.

A disappointment for some of the Highlanders.

A positive result in their opinion.

And now one task remained.

Killing Torstan Sharperson.

In that respect, the thought of more blood didn't bother Jakob and Duff in the least.

"None at all," Tommie replied. She reached up, removed her spectacles, and placed them carefully in the leather pouch hanging around her neck. Then she pulled an arrow from the quiver on her back and nocked the shaft to the taut string of her bow. "We eliminated a few of the Governor's soldiers on the way here, quietly of course, but there weren't many to begin with. Whatever Guard he has left is over at the stadium."

"We played him for a fool," Duff confirmed. "And now he's going to pay a heavy price for that."

"That he will," Tommie agreed. "You ready, Lord Kestrel?"

Jakob turned toward Tommie, lost for a moment, using the Talent to observe what was going on in the Little Pit. "Are you calling me that just to irritate me?"

Tommie snorted out a quiet laugh, Duff smiling as well. "Of course. But that's not the only reason."

"You need to get used to it, lad, even though you don't like it. You are who you are now. You decided that at the Grove. You can't escape what you've become. Best to just go with it."

"More words of advice from the man who put me in this position." Jakob tried to incorporate a tinge of blame into his voice, but he failed. Since he had lost his father, in many respects Duff had assumed that role. Giving him advice even when he didn't want to hear it.

"You put yourself in this position," Duff replied with an enigmatic smile and a wink. "I just put the road you needed to take to get here in front of you."

"I hate it when you're right."

"I know, lad," Duff replied. "I can understand. Now shall we finish this? Are you ready?"

"I am," Jakob replied without hesitation.

"Are we going to do this quietly like we did on the way here?" Tommie asked.

Jakob gave her a menacing smile. "No, we're going to make some noise."

"That's what I wanted to hear," Tommie said. She issued several quick commands with hand signals that were transferred down the line of archers.

Just an instant later, Jakob strode out onto the elevated causeway, Duff at his right shoulder.

Sharperson's soldiers standing watch closest to him barely had the chance to turn in his direction before a swarm of arrows descended upon them.

They stood little chance. Taken by surprise. Having no time at all to comprehend what was happening. Dying at their posts. Feathered by three or four arrows each.

Their initial attack completed, Tommie and several squads of archers raced after Jakob and Duff, both of whom appeared to be completely unconcerned by the fact that while they stalked across the bridge the soldiers at the far end were scrambling into a loose formation to stand against them.

The soldiers' thoughts of attack quickly shifted to saving themselves as wave after wave of arrows flew through the sky. There was nowhere to run on the causeway unless they retreated to the gatehouse. The archers quite pleased by that fact and more than willing to make the most of it.

Jakob and Duff, Tommie and her archers forming a protective shield around them, advanced steadily toward the Little Pit. They ignored the soldiers who were dead or dying, all of them pinned by a fist of arrows if not more.

They were more than halfway across the bridge when the surviving soldiers finally pulled back and the portcullis slammed down, blocking the Highlanders' way.

The soldiers seemed to think that they had gained the protection that they needed from the Highlanders, having seen more rebels emerging from the Stone, a steady stream racing across the footbridge toward the stadium.

"Jakob, if we're caught out here for too long, we could ..."

"Have no fear," Jakob said, cutting off Duff. He recognized the risk of a counterattack just as the Highlander did.

Jakob had no intention of allowing that to happen. Particularly since he knew that Lycia was engaged in a fight to the death.

Reaching for the Talent, he held his hands out to his sides, spheres of glowing white energy forming just above his palms.

Lycia dove to the ground and rolled, kicking up a spray of sand behind her.

Enough grainy particles got into Reeki's eyes that she earned the brief respite that she desired, her adversary having to stop and wipe the stinging grit from his face.

He had almost tricked her. He had placed himself against the wall of the Little Pit as if he feared that he couldn't move fast enough to defend himself. Playing off the wound to his knee that she had given him. Making it appear as if he was on his last leg ... literally.

And she had almost fallen for it.

She had believed that he was no more than a wounded animal that needed to be put down.

He was far from it, however.

He was still an animal, but now Reeki had stolen the initiative from her. After feigning exhaustion, even leaning his back against the stone to suggest that he couldn't use his leg at all, he had pushed off the wall and exploded toward her.

His sword, no more than a streak of grey, sang through the air. Before she could recover, he sliced across her ribs, opening up a long gash, thin but deep, blood cascading out of the wound, a steady drip continuing down her leg and marking her movement through the sand.

The momentum shifting in a heartbeat, the shouts and screams of joy from the thousands of spectators died. Even Sharperson had gone quiet.

No one in the crowd expected Reeki to demonstrate such cunning. To have conned the Crimson Devil so effectively.

Lycia growled in anger upon thinking that. Because it was true. She was so intent on killing him that she failed to notice the almost imperceptible signs that all was not really as the bastard fighting her made it seem.

Having wounded Reeki, she had grown too overconfident, and she was paying for that now.

Even with her own exhaustion growing thanks to her blood loss, she refused to retreat. Standing in the center of the Little Pit, she crossed both blades above her head, halting Reeki's powerful blow just a hair from splitting open her skull.

She was grateful for what little luck stayed with her. But she was stuck now.

She had no way to extricate herself from Reeki's blade. The hulk using his greater size to his advantage, pushing down with his sword, refusing to allow her to slip away.

Reeki's steel close to cutting into her nose, Lycia did the only thing that she could.

She snapped at Reeki with her teeth. His brief moment of surprise and then hesitation allowed her to roll to her right. As she did, she kicked out with her left leg.

Reeki had taken control of the combat, yet even with the manic fury that was driving him, he was slower than he normally would be.

Lycia was grateful for that debility, her boot connecting with Reeki's damaged knee.

Screaming in pain, stumbling, he was too slow when he

slashed at Lycia during her escape, swinging for her neck and missing.

Yet when she came back to her knees, despite the pain of his wound, despite the fact that his leg could no longer bear his weight, Reeki was there.

Cutting down with his sword, employing all the power that he could call upon, he tried to cleave Lycia in two. Savoring the prospect. Ultimately disappointed.

Lycia got her swords up in time. Once again crossing her steel and catching Reeki's blade before he could bury it where her neck met her shoulder.

Gritting her teeth from the effort of keeping his blade away from her, Lycia stared up at the man who was about to kill her.

She knew it.

She could feel it in her bones.

She was on her knees and she couldn't move. Locked in place. Needing to focus her full attention on the grey steel that was slowly, inexorably, reaching for her.

Her strength fading.

Her muscles turning to jelly.

The blade only inches away now.

Coming closer and closer.

She glanced up briefly, catching the manic look in Reeki's eyes.

The growling soldier appeared to be more possessed demon than man now.

The true predator revealed.

Intent on only one thing.

Killing her.

Lycia tried to fight him.

She tried to push his sword away.

She willed herself not to give up.

But she couldn't do it.

She had used up whatever reserve of energy she had left.

Reeki was stronger than she was, and the wound he had given her along her ribs was affecting her badly now.

Her arms were shaking.

Her strength almost gone as her blood colored the sand beneath her.

Reeki's steel no more than a knuckle from her eyes now.

Lycia knew it.

So did Reeki.

A thin string of spittle hanging from his lips, his eyes widened in delight as he prepared for one final fatal push.

Then the combat would be done.

And so would the Crimson Devil.

His muscles bulging, his snarl shifting into a terrible smile, he grunted with the effort of forcing down Lycia's crossed blades, his steel getting closer and closer to its intended target.

Lycia was out of ideas.

She was almost done.

She had never anticipated that her end would come in this way.

Yet she had no choice but to accept her fate.

All she could hope for was that she had done enough to allow Jakob to take the Stone.

Despite her fading strength, despite her quivering muscles, Lycia growled softly. She refused to go to the other side easily. She sought and found the last ounce of willpower that she could call upon, delaying the inevitable.

Reeki's blade just about to cut into her neck, a deafening explosion rumbled through the stadium, a massive cloud of stone and dust blasting through the main entrance.

The power of the shock wave was so great that it set the entire stadium shaking, the ground itself rolling like an earthquake had struck.

Even Reeki, so intent on killing Lycia, couldn't stand against the energy roiling beneath his unsteady feet. Only able to use one leg effectively, the towering hulk slid to the left.

Reaching out a hand to catch himself, he had no choice but to pull his sword away from his victim.

Falling to his knees, one hand digging into the sand, he turned back around as soon as the ground stopped shaking, ready to finish what he had started.

He was too slow.

Lycia was badly wounded.

She was tired.

She was weak.

But she was ready.

And she refused to give up.

Before Reeki could shift in her direction, Lycia stood in front of him, plunging the tip of her sword right through his mouth and out the back of his head. She held her steel there for a few seconds, watching the light leave Reeki's eyes, making sure that he was dead, watching his body go through the last of its shudders, before pulling her weapon free.

Too tired to move, Lycia dropped to the sand. Kneeling. Bloody swords held loosely in each hand.

The commotion and terror caused by the explosion died away slowly. The stadium still stood, although there were now several large cracks and gaps in the walls, and the western stand that had collapsed once before had shifted dangerously, the people brave enough to perch there hastening to get off the scaffolding before another tragedy occurred.

Nervous, afraid, but still curious, the spectators watched the drama conclude before them. Silent. Never anticipating such a result though they had hoped for it.

Even Torstan Sharperson was stunned, unable to speak, unable to move as he gripped tight to the stone railing. Never believing that the Crimson Devil could kill Reeki. His friend.

His guardian. The person to whom he had entrusted his life since he was a child.

Refusing to accept his loss, Sharperson's disbelief quickly turned to anger and then to the desire for revenge.

Uttering a primal scream, Sharperson pulled a dagger hidden beneath the sleeve of his robes. Holding the tip between thumb and forefinger, bringing the weapon back toward his ear, his eyes burning through Lycia's back, he never had the chance to make the throw.

He looked down in shock when he heard the thump and felt the punch of the arrow as it slammed into his chest, knocking him away from the balustrade and back into his chair.

Crumpled against the backrest, Sharperson tried to push himself up.

But he couldn't.

He couldn't do anything at all.

He couldn't see.

He couldn't hear.

He couldn't feel anything other than the cold that swiftly spread out from his chest and consumed him.

"Not bad," Tommie said.

She stood next to Jakob on the far side of the Little Pit as Highlanders streamed into the stadium through the shattered portcullis, disarming the last of Sharperson's Guard, none of whom had any desire to engage with these savage folk now that their paymaster was dead, an arrow through his heart.

"I've been practicing since our last contest." Jakob had pulled the bow from the quiver strapped across his back and nocked an arrow as soon as he sprinted into the stadium, having only one desire.

Getting to Lycia before she died.

He had failed to save Senna.

He would not fail Lycia.

Jakob's eyes remained on the gladiator. Fearful. He didn't know how badly she was hurt.

Bow still in hand, he leaped over the balustrade and raced across the sand, catching Lycia before she collapsed.

"About time," she murmured when she felt Jakob's arms around her.

Jakob smiled at that. Using the Talent, he evaluated her many wounds, focusing particularly on the one along her side. He sighed with relief. She was hurt badly, but not so badly that he couldn't aid her.

"Let me help you up," he said.

His hand around her waist, he lifted her back to her feet, Lycia leaning into him. He turned her slowly, her steps more a shuffle, as they made for the gate beneath Sharperson's private box.

They had gone no more than a few feet when they stopped, struck by the silence.

Jakob looked up, uncomfortable, every eye upon him. Duff standing at the railing just above him, the Highlanders, Jakob's Highlanders, having flooded into the stadium.

Their expressions said it all.

Proud.

Grateful.

Free.

"Long live the Lord Kestrel!" Duff shouted, his words echoing off the stone of the arena. "Long live the Lord of the Highlands!"

The silence disintegrated into a deafening roar that threatened to bring the unstable stadium down for good.

"Would you please stop being so difficult."

After Duff's acclamation of Jakob's position within the

Highlands, Jakob had ignored the screams and shouts, waving a hand half-heartedly, as he carried more than walked Lycia into a small chamber beneath what had been Sharperson's private box.

Setting her on a bench, he used the Talent to heal her wounds. She would be tired for several days and would need time to regain her strength, but that was much better than the alternative.

Jakob started with the wound across her ribs before moving to the many cuts and slices on her forearms, thighs, and chest.

Lycia sat there quietly at the start. As she began to feel better, however, she also began to fidget.

She found the whole experience somewhat surreal, bringing back memories of spending time in the training room beneath the Colosseum with Bryen, her brother, and so many of her other friends after surviving another combat on the white sand.

"You're good at this," Lycia murmured. She was leaning down, her lips almost touching Jakob's ear as he placed his hand over a slice across the top of her shoulder. A stream of natural magic flowed out from his fingers, cleansing and then closing the wound, nothing more than a thin scar left when he was done.

"It's one of my more useful skills," he replied in a quiet voice. Feeling slightly uncomfortable. Her breath on his face sending a pleasant shiver through him. Still, he tried to stay focused on his task.

"Blowing apart a portcullis to get to me in time seems like a useful skill as well."

"Duff told you about that?"

"He did. He was quite proud of you. He'll be able to craft a great story based on your emphatic entrance into the Little Pit."

"He likely will. You're right about that."

"I didn't need the help," Lycia said softly.

Jakob looked up then, done with the last of her wounds. Their gazes locked together, neither willing to let go, their noses almost touching.

He didn't say anything, although his eyes blazed with a green fire. Not with anger as she had seen before. But rather with a different emotion.

She smiled then, almost reluctantly. "All right, maybe I needed a little help, just at the end."

Jakob chuckled at that, understanding how hard it was for Lycia to admit that. "It's only fair."

"Why do you say that?"

"The Stone fell because of you, Lycia. We had very little to do thanks to your efforts."

Lycia nodded at that, her eyes turning mischievous. "Then I guess you owe me."

"That I do," Jakob admitted. "How would you like me to repay the debt?"

For several seconds there was nothing but silence between them. At the same time, they leaned in, their lips touching, holding, for several heartbeats.

Then slowly, reluctantly, they pulled back, even as they continued to stare into one another's eyes.

"Why did you do that?" Lycia finally asked, a slight blush coloring her cheeks, although she didn't care.

Jakob smiled. Even now, Lycia felt the need to be difficult. "I wanted to do it. It seemed like the right thing to do."

"Do you always do the right thing?"

"Only when it has something to do with you."

Lycia nodded, evaluating his response. Her smile broadened not long after, that mischievous look still in her eyes. "Why did you stop?"

Jakob smiled.

Then they moved toward one another again.

20

PAINFUL DECISION

"Are you certain, Ursina?"

"I am, my love. More certain than I ever have been before. I'm sorry." She saw how her pronouncement affected her husband, his face falling, a hint of devastation appearing, slowly replaced by a forced acceptance.

"How is it even possible?" asked Kendric, finding it hard to understand how Aislinn and her Protector could have survived the Murk. Emerging from that confounding fog unscathed despite the Wraiths that hunted them.

He didn't bother to question how his wife knew this. He had learned long ago that it was better not to ask a question if you didn't want to know the answer.

"Your niece and her Protector exercise powers that we did not imagine possible," she explained. "The fault is mine. I worried about those two for so long, yet never considered what they might truly be capable of."

Ursina hoped that her Master's action, forcing Aislinn and her Protector into the Murk, would eliminate the pair as threats. But it wasn't to be.

It seemed that even the Ancient One was fallible at times, a thought that she would certainly keep to herself knowing his proclivity for ending quite painfully the existences of those of his servants who displeased him, turning them into the monsters that he so liked to send into the Natural World when it suited his purposes.

Yet though the Ancient One's plan had not worked out as hoped that didn't mean that Ursina could not take action herself.

She knew where the two were at that exact moment.

Her first instinct was to attack them. To prevent them from returning to Shadow's Reach.

But with what tool?

The Wraiths couldn't kill them. Nor could her Master's Shadow Dragons. And she had sent the last of her Stalkers out to hunt for other quarry.

She could make more, but she worried about the risk involved.

She had used her husband's blood and spirit just the other day. He was still recovering from that effort. She could sense it. See it.

He appeared drawn. Haggard. Weaker than he should have been.

That worried her. He was usually pale after she used him to revitalize the roiling black that was the physical manifestation of the Curse. But he always regained his strength quickly.

Not now, however.

His color wasn't good. Pale still, almost grey. More concerning, the black spark in the back of his eyes was larger and more prominent than it ever had been before.

Initially, just a flash every so often. Now a consistent pulse that was unmistakable.

She could create more Stalkers. Yet if she did, would she lose Kendric for good?

That was a risk that she was unwilling to take. They would need to employ a different approach. There was no other way.

"Call them, my love. Call what we have left to us. They must be brought back."

"Ursina, do you really believe that this is necessary? She's my niece. I was there when she was born."

Ursina reached out and grasped Kendric's arm with an iron grip. Threads of black shot from her palm, surging into his body.

She leaned away from him, shocked, although she didn't let go.

Kendric was fighting her.

He was resisting her efforts, his eyes locked onto hers, his body shivering as an invisible battle occurred within.

She was impressed and disappointed both at the same time. Impressed with her husband. Disappointed in herself for seeking to break through the barrier he had constructed within himself.

If she had played her hand more effectively when Aislinn first appeared, then she wouldn't be in this situation now. But she hadn't.

She had underestimated the young woman and her Protector, never thinking that they would get to the bottom of the mystery so swiftly.

That was water under the bridge, however. She could not afford to focus on the past. She needed to concentrate on the present and the threat that was coming their way.

She tried to reason with him as sweat began to pour off his forehead, Kendric's efforts to stand against the Curse draining him, every muscle in his body quivering from the struggle.

"Your niece and her Protector have discovered what we are doing below the Shadow Keep. Do you think that they will understand? Do you think that your *brother's daughter* will understand why we are doing what we are doing?"

Kendric's gaze, fixed onto hers, wavered then.

Seeing that, she continued with her argument. "They will not understand, Kendric. They will accuse. They will threaten. They will seek to destroy us."

Kendric held his wife's gaze for a few heartbeats more, then ripped his eyes away from hers. Her words tore at his heart. Nevertheless, he couldn't deny the truth in them.

His defenses against the insidious black seeking to consume him began to waver. That was all the opening that the Curse needed, the tainted power punching through his hastily constructed barrier. Coursing through him.

Kendric felt himself drifting away. Losing himself to the power that Ursina had introduced to him.

The power that she believed would give them all that they wanted in the world.

The power that Kendric feared would take from them all that they had achieved.

But he couldn't voice that concern any longer. With his strength, his lucidity faded. He became more amenable. No more than a vessel for his wife.

Ursina watched the change happen within her husband. How he lost himself to the Curse. As he became lesser than what he had been.

It tore her apart on the inside. It was because of her that this was happening to him.

Yet despite her knowledge, despite her own power, there was nothing that she could do to help him.

Even her efforts to slow the progression were proving less effective. She didn't know when, but sooner than she would like she would lose her husband to the Curse.

Even her real Master couldn't help her in that regard.

"I understand your love for your niece, Kendric. But we have no choice now. It is either us or them. And we must think of our future together. We must think of our family."

Kendric closed his eyes. When he opened them again, they were a solid black, sclera as well. He nodded reluctantly. "You are right, Ursina. You are always right, even when I don't want you to be."

"Call them, Kendric. Bring them back home. They are our only hope now. We can't stop your niece and her Protector from returning here. But we can be ready for when they arrive."

21

WORK NOT YET DONE

"You've been hiding from me."

Jakob turned slowly, smiling as he watched Lycia approach. He stood atop the central tower of the Stone, the perch soaring three hundred feet into the sky and giving him an excellent view of the Highlands. The snowcapped peaks extended far to the north. The gentle hills that led to Ballinasloe rolled away to the south.

"Duff has kept me busy," Jakob replied.

He saw the glint of amusement in her eyes. She was teasing him. One of her favorite things to do.

"That he has," she agreed. Stepping past him, she leaned against the parapet that circled the tower. Jakob joined her.

Lycia gazed to the north, refusing to look to the west, having no desire to glimpse the Little Pit. She was done with the gladiatorial games and the stadiums in which they were held.

"How does it feel?"

"How does what feel?" Jakob asked. Standing close to the woman who had ...

He was grateful when Lycia clarified before his thoughts got the better of him.

"How does it feel to be responsible for all this?" She nodded toward the mountains that dominated their view.

Jakob snorted softly. "I didn't want this."

"You've made that abundantly clear," Lycia said, giving him a nudge with her shoulder. "No one believes you."

"No one believes ..." Jakob sputtered.

"I'm just kidding," Lycia laughed, cutting him off. "Everyone knows that you didn't want the responsibility of ruling the Highlands. That's one of the reasons why everyone wants you to have the responsibility of ruling the Highlands."

"I have to admit there's a strange kind of logic to all that," Jakob grumbled reluctantly.

"There is indeed. Now answer my question."

Jakob smiled. Lycia never let anything go. "Overwhelming."

"Duff and the others will help, you know."

"I know," Jakob admitted. "They already are."

"But ..."

Jakob started and stopped several times before finally revealing what he was feeling. "But I don't want to let anyone down."

Lycia nodded, looking at Jakob from the side. His green eyes flashed brightly when they caught the sun.

Another reason why everyone wanted Jakob Kestrel to rule the Highlands. He cared about them.

"I think so long as you're worried about that, you'll do just fine as the Lord of the Highlands."

"I appreciate your confidence in me."

"I do what I can," Lycia replied with a broad grin.

"That you do."

"Is that why you're up here?" Lycia asked. "Trying to escape your new duties?"

Duff had conducted what was supposed to be a small ceremony declaring Jakob the Lord of the Highlands. The Highlander deciding that the acclamation in the Little Pit wasn't enough to mark the occasion.

Thousands of Highlanders who had gotten wind of the proceeding agreed, flooding into the Stone. What was supposed to have been a governance function had instead turned into a larger celebration.

Then, the next day, Jakob and Duff had gotten down to business. Assuming control of the Stone. Removing any vestiges and symbols of Sharperson's authority. Giving those few scoundrels still alive who had served in Sharperson's Guard an ultimatum. Leave the Territory then and there or the Highlanders would go hunting.

And those were the easy tasks.

Sharperson was dead. His slavers and soldiers no longer threats. Yet the Stalkers remained. And it wouldn't be long before the Wraiths came with the Murk once again.

"I needed a break," Jakob admitted.

"I can understand that." She leaned against his shoulder. Neither of them minded the touch. "There's more to it than that, however."

Jakob shook his head in amusement. He should have known. "You think you know me so well."

Lycia gave him another nudge, apparently her favorite way of communicating that morning. "I do. I know you better than you know yourself."

"Then tell me what I'm thinking."

"That your work isn't yet done. You've claimed the Highlands, but there's still more you have to do."

Jakob shifted his gaze to Lycia. He didn't bother to protest. She was right. And he really shouldn't have been surprised that she was, because she was right as well that there were times when she seemed to know him better than he knew himself.

"What gave it away?"

"That look in your eyes. You get the same look right before you're about to start a fight."

"I'll have to keep that in mind so I don't give away so easily what I'm thinking," Jakob nodded. "That's quite a skill that you have."

Lycia smiled, then turned and leaned back against the balustrade, her eyes finding Jakob's once again. "It's one of the ways I survived in the Pit."

"That makes sense."

"Now are you going to tell me?"

"Tell you what?"

"Do you always have to be so difficult, Lord Kestrel?"

"It's one of my unique skills," he replied with a straight face.

"Which I've learned much to my regret." Lycia's gaze hardened. "Tell me."

"We should talk about that kiss," Jakob suggested, seeking to change the subject, if only for a time. He knew that he needed to tell Lycia, he just wasn't sure how best to do that.

"Why do we need to talk about it?"

"Why are you so unwilling to talk about something like that?" Jakob asked. "It's almost as if you're afraid to reveal what you're really feeling."

Jakob realized that he might have pushed too hard with his comment. He was glad when Lycia answered honestly and didn't take his question as a challenge.

"Because life hasn't turned out as I wanted."

"Fair enough," Jakob replied. "Life doesn't turn out the way most people want."

"Words of wisdom from the Lord of the Highlands. Your new position is already going to your head."

Jakob ignored Lycia's sarcasm, understanding her goal. "It's just something that I've learned. If life had turned out how I wanted, at least initially, I would still be living in Roo's Nest."

"What do you mean initially?"

"Life is change. You either flow with it and adjust or fight it. The trick is finding that balance. When to fight what's happening and when to adapt to what life is willing to give you. It's hard because you want to push back. It's natural. But as my father liked to say, best to not be fixed on what you want and more on what you can do."

"Now you're beginning to sound like Declan."

Jakob smiled at that. He could understand why. Like father like …

He pushed that thought to the side, not having time for it now. This discussion with Lycia was too important.

"I'll take that as a compliment."

"I didn't necessarily mean it that way."

"Now who's being difficult?"

"It's one of my unique skills," Lycia replied in a soft chuckle.

They looked at one another with complete seriousness for several seconds, then broke out laughing.

"Focus on what you have, not on what you want. That's all I'm saying."

"How do you know what I want?"

"I don't know," Jakob admitted. "I'd like you to tell me."

Lycia stared at Jakob for quite some time, never expecting the conversation to head in this direction. Could she take the risk? Should she? It had only been a few kisses. No more than that. Yet those kisses had seemed like so much more. A confirmation of sorts. An acknowledgement of what had grown between them.

Was she wrong?

There was only one way to find out.

Steeling herself as she did when she walked out onto the white sand of the Pit, she offered a response that was almost a whisper.

"You want to know what I want?" she mused, closing her eyes, head bowed. "I want someone who loves me. For me."

Jakob nodded. Then he leaned in close, their foreheads almost touching. He was taking a risk now, but he'd never forgive himself if he didn't.

"Open your eyes, Lycia. You have that."

She looked up, eyes sparkling with delight, the realization striking her.

"I have you."

"You have me," Jakob confirmed.

Reaching for one another, slowly at first, then with more haste, when their lips touched, there was a spark between them that neither had ever experienced before. They leaned back for just a second, startled, then smiled before leaning back in. Their lips touching once again.

For the next several minutes, there was nothing in the world for either of them but the other.

Until they sensed a presence at their backs.

"Aloysius! What are you doing here?" Jakob couldn't believe that the old Magus had journeyed across the Burnt Ocean and found him here, now of all times.

He took a few steps toward his former instructor and got no further, Lycia's hand gripping his arm tightly. He didn't understand why she was holding him back until he looked into her eyes.

She shook her head slightly, just enough for him to see.

Jakob's eyes narrowed, then he nodded.

Lycia was right. He could sense it just as she could, his shock and happiness dampening the warning.

There was something about Aloysius that seemed off. Jakob felt now much the way he did before he engaged with a Wraith in the Murk. The hint of menace. Of evil approaching.

Thankfully, Lycia sensed it first, not burdened by his relationship with the old Magus.

"I needed to get away," Aloysius replied. He took a few steps toward Jakob, arms wide as if he planned to hug him, then stopped. He watched the girl standing behind Jakob pull him back toward her. His eyes narrowed, his smile fading to a frown. "I thought it best to come after you. To offer what help I could."

Jakob's brow furrowed. He had been surprised by Aloysius' warm smile.

In all the time that Jakob had spent with the old Magus, Aloysius never smiled. He grouched. He grumped. He complained. He never, ever smiled.

And a hug? That was unheard of.

Jakob squared up to Aloysius, standing on his toes, one foot slightly in front of the other, taking comfort in the fact that his daggers were within easy reach.

Watching how he positioned himself, Lycia released his arm and took a few steps away from him and to the side, hands hanging loosely by her sides.

"How did you find me, Aloysius?" Jakob asked. "The Territories are a big place. You must have started in Ballinasloe."

"Of course I started my search in Ballinasloe," Aloysius replied, chuckling softly, his smile back in place. "How could I not? It's the only major port on the eastern coast of New Caledonia." He took another step toward Jakob, then stopped when both Jakob and Lycia took a step back, keeping the distance between them. "What are you worried about, lad? As I said, I'm here to help you."

Jakob nodded, not responding. Instead, he studied the old Magus. The sense that something was off was getting stronger the closer the old Magus came. Jakob's skin was prickling, just as it always did when he was under threat from the Curse.

And with the Stone in Highlander hands, the Stalkers gone, there was only one potential source.

Aloysius himself.

Jakob reached for the Talent, the natural magic of the world surging through him. He kept his gaze fixed on Aloysius the entire time.

Jakob's eyes narrowed as he began to understand. Aloysius had taught him a great deal in the year they had spent together before Jakob and his father fled Caledonia.

A key lesson had involved a Magus' ability to sense when another Magus was employing the Talent. That skill was based on proximity. The closer the two Magii were, the easier it was to detect the application of natural magic.

Jakob standing just ten feet away from Aloysius when he pulled on the Talent should have drawn some reaction from the old Magus. But it hadn't.

"When you were in Ballinasloe, did you talk to Sorscha? Was she the one who told you where we went?"

Aloysius shifted his focus toward Lycia. The Magus' warm eyes turned cold, flinty. Almost inhuman. Only for a flash, however. His good humor and affability swiftly returning.

Both Jakob and Lycia watched it happen, confirming their beliefs. Those beliefs shifting to fears.

Even so, they stood their ground, knowing that the scene had yet to reach its climax.

Besides, they had nowhere to go, the tower's stone balustrade at their backs.

"Yes, Sorscha pointed me in this direction. How else could I have found you?"

Lycia reached over both shoulders, pulling her swords free. "You are not who you say you are."

Aloysius appeared to be confused for a few seconds, then smiled again, moving his now dead eyes from Lycia to Jakob. "What is she talking about, lad? You know me."

Jakob took another step back, standing even with Lycia, when Aloysius took another step toward him.

Then he stopped, his countenance calculating. "I know it's been a while, but I don't understand why you're afraid of me? Is it because of this girl, lad?" Aloysius snorted out a laugh that didn't sound right. "Has she gotten her claws into you already."

Aloysius shook his head, seemingly unsurprised. "I'm here to help you, lad, just as I helped you before. I'm here to continue your education in the Talent among other things."

"In the Talent?" Jakob asked. "I can certainly use the instruction. But what of the Blood Ruby? Will you be able to teach me how to use the Blood Ruby as well?"

Lycia's head whipped toward Jakob, not understanding the reference. Even so, she didn't miss how Aloysius' eyes widened when Jakob mentioned what she assumed was a jewel. Nor how the old man's visage changed from a smile to a rictus of greed before quickly returning to a smile.

"Of course, lad. Why else would I be here? You have the Blood Ruby in your possession, do you not?"

Aloysius extended his hand. This time Jakob didn't step back. He had nowhere to go. Instead, a sphere of blazing white light danced across the top of his right palm.

"What are you doing, lad?" the old Magus demanded. His voice had changed. Becoming scratchy, as if it really wasn't his. While his blue orbs slowly turned black.

"You are not Aloysius," Jakob said in a deadly quiet voice.

"What are you talking about lad?" Aloysius protested. He was about to take another step forward. He stopped when he heard what Jakob said next.

"Did you really believe that I wouldn't know, Skath? After our last encounter?"

A dozen questions rushed through Lycia's mind. First and foremost, what was a Skath?

She ignored them all. She was too experienced not to know that a fight was about to begin.

Silence descended atop the tower then. Aloysius stared at Jakob. Jakob locked eyes with the old Magus. Or rather what appeared to be the old Magus.

As the standoff continued, despite the peril of their circumstances, one question continued to plague Jakob.

How did the Skath find him?

Aloysius had told him that he had nothing to fear in that regard.

It struck him like a bolt of lightning. The Blood Ruby. The Skath hadn't tracked him, the monster had tracked the artifact.

Aloysius had used the Talent to shield the Blood Ruby from the Skath. That protection must have vanished when the Skath killed Aloysius and took his form.

Slowly, the Skath began to smile. That smile quickly became a snarl.

The old Magus' kindly voice changed for good then, becoming harsher, a rasp, like a claw scraping across a stone.

"Your knowledge will do you little good, boy. I will take what you kept from me when you helped the Magus. Then I will take its partner. That done, my Master will finally walk in this world again."

"Why did you kill Aloysius?" Jakob demanded, his hate and anger plain in his voice. "He didn't even have the Blood Ruby."

"No, he didn't," hissed the creature. "I killed him because I needed his skin." The figure of the old Magus shrugged, although not in a natural way, the movement both striking Jakob and Lycia as wrong. "He put up a fight, but it was little use. He was weak. He died screaming. Begging."

"He died fighting," Jakob cut in. "That was Aloysius."

The monster that had become Aloysius smiled then. "Tell yourself what you need to hear, boy. Your teacher is dead. And I will have what I came for."

"No you won't," Jakob replied with a calm that he didn't know that he could attain while facing off against a creature that he didn't think that he could defeat.

Aloysius had told him that only with the Blood Ruby linked to the Blood Dagger would he have the strength to challenge a Skath or any other creature from the Spirit World.

Jakob had a sense of where the Blood Dagger was, but it

would do him little good now. To have any real chance against a Disciple of the Ancient One, he needed to have the Blood Dagger in hand along with the jewel.

"So a battle it's to be," chuckled the Skath, the sound chilling. Inhuman. Grating on Lycia's and Jakob's ears. "You couldn't stand against me before. What makes you think you can do so now?"

Jakob didn't bother to reply. He was already moving. Flicking the sphere of energy with his hand, forcing the Skath to glide back several steps to avoid the sizzling power, Jakob followed, using the momentary distraction to lunge and slash with the Talent-infused haladie he now held in each hand.

The Skath drifted back as if he wasn't even stepping across the stone, twisting and turning as he went, contorting himself to avoid the blazing steel in ways that no human possibly could.

That only made sense to Jakob as he continued his assault. The Skath wasn't human. The creature wasn't a part of the Natural World. It shouldn't even be in the Natural World.

Jakob halted his attack when he reached the center of the tower having achieved his goal. Driving the Skath away from Lycia.

The Skath cackled then, Aloysius' face cracking, the flesh tearing apart, a black mist beginning to seep through.

"You fought me once, boy. And you knew then just as you know now that you couldn't defeat me. Yet that doesn't seem to bother you in the least. Impressive. Very impressive. Foolish as well. Better for you and your friend if you just give me what I want."

A noise much like paper ripping sounded across the top of the tower. As it did, Aloysius' image began to change, more cracks appearing, widening, ripping entirely, the black mist surging through the mask with greater speed and force. The figure hidden beneath growing, enlarging, stretching, expanding.

"Jakob, how do we fight this thing?" Lycia asked. She stood next to him now, swords held at the ready, taking in the creature that had emerged from what had been the old Magus.

The Skath stood more than eight feet tall, covered by a wispy black robe that was tattered and torn and seemed more ephemeral than real. Long, sharp claws extended from beneath the sleeves. The creature's burning black eyes stared out from beneath its cowl with an unending hatred for anything that was living.

"*We* aren't going to fight it," Jakob said, his eyes never leaving the Disciple of the Ancient One.

"*We are* going to fight it," Lycia countered in a very measured tone. She would not yield to him on this. "It is as it was, Jakob. It is as it will be. If we are to be together, we are equals. In all things. No matter what."

Jakob growled in frustration even though her words warmed his heart.

He tore his eyes away from the Skath for just a few seconds, catching Lycia's determined gaze, wanting to make sure that she understood.

"Steel does not work against a Skath or any other creature from the Spirit World."

"Then make my steel more than steel," Lycia ordered.

He shook his head in frustration. He should have assumed as much. Although he couldn't say that he was disappointed.

"*It is as it was. It is as it will be.*" Lycia's words rang true to him. In all things they would be together. No matter what. Life and death.

In a flash, Lycia's blades glowed brightly, Jakob infusing them with the Talent.

"Cut at the edges and don't get too close," he said. "I will try to keep the Skath busy. The creature's power is much like the Curse, though more potent, so be careful."

Lycia grinned maliciously, then moved away from him,

taking up a position a few yards to his right. Ready to take advantage of any opportunities that might come her way.

Turning back toward the Skath, Jakob noted how the figure floated a few inches off the ground, staring down at him hungrily.

"I will have the Blood Ruby, boy," rasped the Skath. "Give it to me now, and I will kill you and the girl quickly."

"We don't die easy," Jakob countered, rushing toward the Skath as he spit out the words.

His daggers sliced through the air, appearing to be no more than flashes of white as he cut and slashed.

The Skath glided back and away from him, streaking around the top of the tower to avoid Jakob's attack.

Several times Jakob succeeded in slicing off the edge of the Skath's cloak, the wispy black swirling away and disintegrating entirely before it touched the stone floor.

Lycia did as well, seeking to come at the monster from behind or the side, the Skath only allowing her a few brief cuts.

They could do little more than that.

The Skath too fast. Too nimble. Too clever.

It wasn't long before a raspy rumble of laughter escaped the monster's cowl, the creature coming to a stop along the parapet.

Jakob and Lycia had penned in the Skath.

But they knew better.

They were where they were because the monster permitted it.

The Skath was playing with them.

"You believe that you can stand against me?" hissed the Skath, more amused than angry, its voice rising to a shriek. "I stand second only to my Master, and you believe that you can stand against me?"

The Skath extended its right claw, pointing toward Lycia, a black mist shooting out from its razor-sharp fingertips.

Lycia's eyes widened in alarm when those threads of black

wrapped themselves around her, twisting and turning with a blinding speed. In less than a second, her arms were tight to her sides. Her blades useless.

She couldn't even scream, although she refused to display such weakness as the bonds of black covered her mouth.

She was trussed like a pig.

Worse, she felt herself moving. Looking down, she realized that she was.

Toward the parapet and the drop of several hundred feet.

The Skath was going to throw her over the edge!

And she could do nothing to stop the creature, struggling vainly to break free from the constricting bonds of mist.

Jakob stared in horror as Lycia drifted slowly across the stone, the battlements now only a few feet away.

What was he to do?

His use of the Talent had done little for them during the brief combat.

Cursing himself for acting the fool, he realized what was required of him if he was to have any chance against the Skath. He needed to give the Ancient One's Disciple what the monster wanted. Just not in the way that the creature desired.

Sheathing his daggers and pulling free the Blood Ruby from beneath his shirt, he gripped the artifact tightly with his right hand.

"Stop!" roared Jakob, his rage knowing no bounds.

The Skath turned toward him then, Lycia's progress halted. For a time.

"Give the jewel to me boy, and I will put you both out of your misery."

Jakob ignored the yearning that was so plain in the Skath's hissed words. Instead, he opened himself to the power of the artifact, allowing the incredible energy contained within to mix with that of the Talent that already filled him to bursting.

His green eyes flashed then. Blindingly bright.

He felt like he was going to explode, the power surging through him threatening to rip him apart from the inside out.

Remembering one of Dougal's many lessons, he took a deep breath and sought to clear his mind.

To focus on what he needed to do and nothing else.

Somehow, he succeeded.

In an instant, he gained the calm upon which his life and that of Lycia depended.

He saw the world with greater clarity now. His mind calculated with greater speed. He moved faster and with greater precision.

Because it appeared as if the world around him had slowed.

Most important, he had mastered the power of the Blood Ruby that he had mixed with the Talent, and that power wanted to be released.

Demanded to be released.

Jakob was more than happy to accommodate.

"You will never gain the Blood Ruby, Skath," Jakob said in a voice that didn't sound like his own. "I promise you that."

Before the monster could respond, Jakob struck. Pointing the hand that contained the Blood Ruby toward the Ancient One's Disciple, a torrent of energy, white streaked with red, blasted into the monster.

Lycia dropped down to her feet as soon as the energy struck, free from her bonds.

She sprinted over to Jakob, ready to help if there was need.

But she didn't think that there would be.

Jakob stood as if he were rooted into the stone. Implacable. Unyielding. And very, very angry.

The energy laced with red appeared to be never-ending, biting into the Skath, slicing into the creature made more of spirit than substance, shreds of black flaking away, then larger pieces. Splinters followed by squares then entire folds.

The Skath tried to fight back. Screaming in rage. Attempting to call on the power gifted to it by its Master.

But the monster couldn't do as it wished.

Jakob was too strong. Too determined.

In a flash and with a rumble of thunder that shook the very foundation of the tower, the Skath vanished.

Seemingly burned away, although Jakob knew better.

Jakob released his hold on the Talent and the power of the Blood Ruby as soon as the Skath disappeared.

He looked down at the jewel, which flashed brightly in the sunlight. Then he studied his palm.

When he first touched the artifact in Aloysius' cottage, it had left a faint imprint on his hand, an exact replication of the jewel. That imprint was no longer faint.

It had been seared into his skin, the mark clear for all to see. Yet his flesh had healed instantly, and the process had occurred without a hint of pain.

"Did you destroy the Skath?" asked Lycia.

She looked down at what Jakob was holding in his hand, transfixed by the jewel for just a second before she reached out and grasped Jakob's free hand with hers. That brought Jakob back from wherever he had gone.

Jakob sighed, disappointed. "No, I didn't. I just drove it away like the last time I faced it."

"You came up against a Skath before?" Lycia was incredulous.

"Not by choice."

Jakob quickly filled her in on what had happened in Aloysius' cottage. The battle that had darkbeen fought. And how that clash had been the final push that had sent him and his father across the Burnt Ocean.

"So you can't destroy this Skath with just the Blood Ruby."

"No," Jakob confirmed, placing the jewel back beneath his shirt and against his chest, a comfortable warmth spreading through him as a result. "I need to combine the Blood Ruby with the Blood Dagger. Only by doing that will I have the ability to destroy the Skath and send it back to the Spirit World."

"The Spirit World?" mused Lycia. "A Skath serves the Ancient One?"

Jakob looked at Lycia in a new light. "You certainly know your history and myths."

Lycia smiled shyly at that. "Declan was very thorough in his instruction. And after all that I've had to deal with since the battle began against the Ghoule Overlord, I have little cause to disbelieve what others might view as no more than a fairy tale. Particularly after seeing this Skath face to face." She gripped his arm with greater strength. "I'm sorry. About Aloysius. I take it he was important to you."

"He was," Jakob confirmed. "He taught me how to use the Talent. He was irascible. Demanding. Never satisfied." He sighed. "And a good friend."

"I know the type." Lycia smiled. "Do you know where the Blood Dagger is? I assume that the Skath will come at us again."

"You're right. The Skath will not stop until it has what it wants." Jakob's expression, hard to begin with, somehow became even harder. "I do know where the Blood Dagger is. It's to the north. It's in Shadow's Reach."

"You're certain?" Lycia gave him a look that told him that he needed to provide her with more of an explanation.

"The Blood Ruby and the Blood Dagger are connected. Because I bear the Blood Ruby, I can sense the Blood Dagger."

He took a deep breath, then turned toward the north. The rugged peaks of the Highlands greeted him. They had a long way to go and not much time.

He assumed that the Skath would make a play for the Blood Dagger before coming back for the Blood Ruby. He assumed as well that there was likely no one in the Northern Territory who could stop the creature from obtaining the weapon.

"You delayed your search for the Blood Dagger," murmured Lycia, understanding what Jakob had done. The danger in which he had been willing to place himself for the sake of so many others.

"I did. I probably shouldn't have. My father told me what I needed to do before he died. But I couldn't leave the Highlanders to their fate." Jakob shrugged, as if his decision was of little consequence. "Now that the Highlanders are free, I need to finish the task that my father and Aloysius gave me."

"You risked all that for the Highlanders? If the Skath found you before now then ..."

"The Skath didn't," Jakob interjected. "We were lucky, I know, and I'll take it. We need to go north and finish this. We can't let the Skath obtain the Blood Dagger."

Lycia smiled knowingly then. "Well, it's a good thing that we need to make for Shadow's Reach anyway."

"What do you mean?" Jakob asked, believing that the requirement to retrieve the Blood Dagger before the Skath did was reason enough.

"I spoke with Bryen before I found you here atop the tower. He needs you."

"Me? Why?"

"You're the Wraith who is not a Wraith."

Jakob shrugged. "I've earned the name, yes, but what does that have to do with us going to the north?"

"Bryen said that he needed the Wraith who is not a Wraith."

"He's found the source of the Curse in the Territories?"

"He has," Lycia replied, "but that's peripheral to why he needs you. He can deal with that peril. However ..."

"The Murk is coming." Jakob finished Lycia's thought for her. "For good if the Wraiths can manage it."

"Correct. That's what Bryen told me. Yet there's more to it than that."

"What do you mean?"

"Bryen and Aislinn clashed with several Wraiths in the Murk. Once they escaped the fog, they searched to the north. The monsters in the mist are coming. Not just a few scouts. Thousands of them."

"That does change things," Jakob admitted, having only dealt with a few dozen Wraiths at a time when the Murk came before. And that had been more than enough for his tastes.

"And coming with the monsters in the mist is the Wraith Lord."

Jakob stood there quietly, taking in what Lycia had just told him.

The same Skath that attacked Aloysius in his cottage. Killing the old Magus once Jakob had left and stealing his form.

And now the Wraith Lord.

He couldn't quite wrap his mind around these two challenges that had been thrust upon him in quick succession. But it really didn't matter.

As his father liked to say, you must do what you must do.

Duff wasn't going to like the risk that he was about to take, but his friend didn't have any choice in the matter.

"The Skath has a head start on us. Even with horses, I have no doubt that the Ancient One's Disciple will make it to Shadow's Reach before us."

"You're certain that the Blood Dagger is there?"

"I am. I can sense it." He patted the Blood Ruby beneath his shirt to emphasize his conviction.

"Are you keeping any more secrets from me?" she asked with an arched eyebrow. "No other ancient weapons or monsters that I need to know about? If we're going to join our futures together, then there can be no secrets."

"No, nothing," Jakob replied. "Now we need to get moving.

We might not be able to, but we at least need to try to get to Shadow's Reach before the Skath does."

"Don't worry about that," Lycia said, unconcerned by this new challenge. "Bryen has sent a friend to help us out."

Before Lycia could explain, a shriek shattered the quiet of the tower, a large shape soaring right over them.

Jakob lifted his eyes upward, shielding them from the sun. "A Griffon." He gave Lycia a knowing look. "Now who's keeping secrets?"

22

AN UNANTICIPATED REUNION

"This will all be over soon, my love. Have no fear."

"I never fear when you are by my side, Ursina," Kendric replied in a gentle voice. He hid the sadness that was creeping through him as much as he could. He had never wanted any of this to happen. Yet what he wanted didn't matter now. "You know that."

Ursina reached out with her hand, grasping his arm tightly, squeezing a few times, sending a stream of the Talent into her husband before letting go. Not a lot, needing to conserve her strength. Just enough to give him that slight boost that he clearly required.

Ever since their brief confrontation and what he forced her to do, Kendric had been flagging. More rapidly than before.

It was becoming more obvious. And unavoidable. Unstoppable.

She had not wanted to use the power gifted to her by the Ancient One in such a way.

Kendric had given her no choice.

She had needed him to be stronger then. But he ...

She clamped her lips together, seeking to control the irritation, disappointment, and regret rising within her.

Now was not the time to question decisions they had made years before.

They had talked about this. They had decided. They were committed.

Now was not the time to pull back.

Now was the time to push forward.

They had risked so much already. There was no point in not risking all.

Ursina sensed that they were balancing on the edge of a scale. Which way that scale would lean would depend on how the events of the next few hours played out.

She had been in this position before.

A reckoning was coming.

And when it did, she needed her husband by her side.

Ready to do what was required, no matter what that might be.

In the past, she never would have doubted him.

But now?

Ursina worried about him.

Kendric had fought for so long and so hard.

A valiant effort. Still, a doomed one.

The Curse was proving stronger.

Just as it always did.

She knew that from personal experience, so she certainly couldn't fault him.

He had not complained. He had not wavered. He had done all that he could. All to no avail.

She had watched the change occurring within him. She could only hope that when the confrontation to come was over, once she had eliminated those who threatened them, she could find some way to remove the taint that was consuming him.

More hope than reality she knew.

The signs of what was happening to Kendric were all too clear. The hint of black in the back of his eyes was gone, his scleras and irises now the color of pitch.

But that was only one of the visible reminders of the changes taking place within the Lord of the Northern Territory.

His grey skin had gone even greyer. In a certain light Ursina perceived the threads of black just beneath the surface. Spreading. Writhing. Multiplying. Consuming. Taking control.

She already had experienced what he was being forced to go through. The key difference was that she had been trained as a Magus. She could work with the power that took her. Ease the transition. Reduce the pain. Ensure that a large part of who she was remained.

Kendric couldn't. He had no skill in natural magic. He could only suffer through the change.

And, assuming he survived it, what the result would be when the transformation was complete ...

Ursina did not know.

She promised herself that he would survive it.

She would make sure of that.

No matter what, she would ensure that her husband survived.

She needed him.

She couldn't imagine a future without him.

It was just a matter of mitigating the transition that he was undergoing, using the lessons that she learned for his benefit, then teaching him how to manage what he became.

She had battled the tainted power that she craved so desperately just as he was. She had learned that it was better to give in. To acknowledge the strength of the Curse, and then work with the tainted power. Mold it. Reach an agreement of sorts.

Acknowledging the true master but in so doing creating

boundaries that allowed the individual to remain the individual ... and not just a tool.

She would show Kendric how to do that once they were done here in the chamber beneath the Shadow Keep, the cauldron of boiling black at their backs.

Kendric had saved her. She would save him. By any means necessary.

"Do as I taught you, my love," Ursina instructed. "They are almost here."

Kendric nodded, closing his eyes. When he opened them again a few seconds later, Aislinn stood at the far side of the cavern, the green luminescence from the moss growing on the walls and ceiling illuminating her and her Protector.

"What have you done, uncle?" Aislinn's voice was strong. Disappointed as well. "I never thought that you, of all people, would follow such a path."

Before he could reply, Ursina did. "We are in a new world. We all must do what we must if we hope to survive."

"That's an excuse that can be used for most anything you decide to do," Bryen countered.

He took a few steps forward and away from Aislinn, slowly spinning the Spear of the Magii from one hand to the next. He knew that Ursina's willingness to talk was because of her desire to delay. He sensed what was coming toward them.

"And who are you to challenge us, Protector?" demanded Ursina. "You are no more than a slave."

"A slave I have been," he replied calmly, quietly. "But I am a slave no longer. What I am now is someone who understands what happens when you succumb to the Curse. When you demonstrate a weakness from which you can never recover."

Ursina laughed then. "You believe that we are weak, Protector?"

"We know that you are weak, Ursina," Aislinn confirmed. "That is why we are here now. Because of your weakness."

Ursina's eyes settled on the young woman standing before her. The resemblance to her husband was strong. As was the certainty and confidence that she exuded.

Kendric had been much the same when she first met him. Before the change began.

"What you see as weakness I see as courage," Ursina argued. "Few have had the courage to take the road that I have. To take the road that we have." She chuckled then, a deep sound, unsettling coming from such a petite person. "So you are mistaken, Lady of the Southern Marches. But that's not surprising. You are young. Inexperienced. You do not really understand what it is to make decisions in the real world. You do not understand what it means to exercise real power."

As Ursina defended their actions, Aislinn's gaze stayed on her uncle. She shook her head sadly when she saw it, a lump of grief sitting in her stomach. His eyes. It was undeniable. Still, she needed to try. One more time.

"Please, uncle," Aislinn pleaded. "You are better than this. You are not the person you have become."

Kendric shifted his focus toward her, seemingly lost in his own world until then. He smiled as if he was seeing her for the first time.

"I am sorry, Aislinn. But it's too late."

The blades on Bryen's spear flared, Aislinn pulling her sword from the scabbard across her back, infusing the steel with the Talent as well.

They moved back-to-back, watching as the blood-red eyes sparked in the depths of the several tunnels that met in this chamber that wept the essence of pain and death.

The blood-red eyes focused solely on them.

FOR WHAT SEEMED like an eternity yet was only a few minutes, there was nothing but movement. A natural flow. Decisions made based on instinct rather than thought.

Bryen and Aislinn keeping their backs to one another.

Their blazing blades slicing through the air with a lethal efficiency.

Holding at bay the dozens of Stalkers seeking to rip them apart.

Aislinn brought her sword back around in a tight arc. She cut down with her shining steel, biting through flesh and bone, severing a Stalker's claw before it could rip into her ribs.

The wounded monster reared back in agony, knocked from the mix of attackers. Just as quickly, however, another Stalker was there.

She had anticipated just such a result, her steel slicing neatly across the throat of the Stalker that took the wounded creature's place and lunged for her.

Caught mid-motion, unable to halt its progress, the Stalker skidded on the slick, bloody stones, reaching up uselessly toward its damaged flesh, its blood pouring past its clawed digits. The beast dropped to its knees, sagging, the light in its eyes slowly fading.

Having little compassion for the beast, she kicked out. Catching the Stalker in the shoulder, the creature tumbled to her left and collapsed right into the path of two of its ilk racing toward her from that direction.

The Stalker closest to her tripped over its dying brethren. It never got back to its clawed feet, Bryen taking advantage of his just having killed a Stalker himself to slash down with the Spear of the Magii, removing the beast's head from its neck in a single swipe.

The other Stalker only stumbled, one clawed foot digging into the stone, the other sliding to the side.

That was all that Aislinn needed. With a lightning-fast slash and impressive precision, she cut across the beast's throat before it could right itself.

Their left side now blocked with bodies, Bryen and Aislinn turned to face the other Stalkers that cared little about how fast or how easily so many of their number had fallen to the two Magii.

Bryen slashed from hip to chest, slicing across one Stalker's waxy black flesh, the creature's guts spilling out, tangling its feet.

As soon as that monster crumpled, another was there to take its place.

Aislinn stabbed through the side of the Stalker's knee. Its claws reaching for the stone to lighten the impact of its fall, Bryen finished the beast before it even hit the ground, punching his blade through the Stalker's armpit and into its heart.

Bryen pulled his spear free with a sharp twist and jabbed, his steel piercing another Stalker's gut. The smell of charred meat wafting up as the blazing blade of the Spear of the Magii burned through the beast's core, Bryen kicked out. Catching the dying beast in the chest, the Stalker flew backward and took with it a handful of beasts hungry to join the fight.

"This isn't working," Bryen murmured, waiting for the fallen monsters to regain their clawed feet.

Eliminating so many of the Stalkers so quickly had earned them a brief reprieve. The others pulling back and studying their prey.

Bryen and Aislinn made use of that time to climb over the pile of Stalker dead and place their backs against the lichen-covered stone wall, thereby reducing the possible avenues of attack against which they needed to defend.

"Any ideas?" asked Aislinn.

She kept a wary eye on the Stalkers spreading out around

them, preparing for their next attack. For just a heartbeat, she glanced at Ursina and Kendric.

Ursina was grinning at her maliciously. Despite her and Bryen's initial success, clearly she was pleased, likely believing that their end was near. That eventually the Stalkers would prove too much for them.

Strangely, her uncle didn't appear to be paying attention to them at all. His eyes were closed, a look of deep concentration on his face. Could he be the one?

"Can you sense it?" Bryen asked.

He was spinning the Spear of the Magii slowly from one hand to the other. One of his habits that he had acquired while fighting in the Pit. Clearly, despite several dozen Stalkers milling about in front of them, he was far from intimidated.

Bryen's question got Aislinn thinking, her mind leading her down a specific path when she also took into account her uncle's expression and the Stalkers' behavior.

"No, I can't. But you do." She nodded toward her uncle. "Is Kendric controlling them?"

Bryen nodded. "He is. That's why they attacked in a coordinated fashion. That's the only reason. He's guiding them."

"Then why are they holding back now?"

Bryen shrugged. "I don't know. Maybe he doesn't like what he's doing and he's trying to fight it. Maybe it's because more than a dozen Stalkers will be joining those already standing against us within the minute and he wants to improve his odds. Either way, this isn't time to be wasted."

Aislinn hoped that Bryen was right. That her uncle was fighting against the pull of the Curse. They couldn't rely on that, however, if they were to have any chance of leaving this chamber alive.

"Can you do something about my uncle controlling the Stalkers?"

Bryen nodded after thinking about the challenge Aislinn gave him. "With the Seventh Stone, yes."

"What do you need?"

"A few minutes alone with your uncle."

"Done!" Aislinn said with a sharp nod.

Calling on the Talent surging within her, from her left hand she sent a blinding stream of energy blasting into the Stalkers to their front.

The monsters too slow to move out of the way were incinerated in a flash, the others scrambling to both sides to avoid a terrible death.

Bryen was gone before the Talent even struck. Swinging his spear from left to right and back again to ensure that none of the beasts made a play for him, he raced through the gap Aislinn created and charged toward Kendric and Ursina.

Ursina and Kendric each dove to a different side, dodging out of the way of the white-hot energy that set the moss at their backs afire and scarred the stone beneath.

Before Ursina pushed herself up from the ground, strands of black danced across her fingertips. Filled with an almost uncontrollable hate, she sent shards of the Curse streaking toward the Protector, who had veered toward Kendric, his spear already sweeping down through the air in a streaky blur of white.

Regaining his feet, stumbling only briefly from the shock of the blast, Kendric reached for the sword on his hip, turning to stand against the Protector.

Desperate to protect her husband, Ursina howled in rage.

She was too late!

The same time that the Protector swung down with this spear, Kendric gripping the hilt of his sword with two hands to parry the blow, a shield of shimmering white mixed with red formed around them. When the shards of tainted power struck, they fizzled ineffectually against the barrier for several seconds before slowly dying away, consumed by the power that the Protector used to defend against her attack. A power that Ursina could sense but not quite understand.

Back on her feet, Ursina's face twisted into a bitter mask. She screamed in fury, watching helplessly as the Protector continued his attack, forcing Kendric in whichever direction he chose.

Her husband fought valiantly, but he could do little more than evade the rapid-fire slashes and slices. The Protector's blows so strong and his steel so hot that to do anything else ensured nothing more than a melted blade and an agonizing end.

Refusing to give up, Ursina sent bolt after bolt of black at the shield that moved with the Protector. None of her attacks succeeded, the Curse playing across and then slowly dissolving into the barrier.

Understanding the cause of her failure did her little good. She had no idea how to deal with the power that thwarted her, which meant that there was nothing that she could do to shatter the shield and save her husband.

Maybe that was her mistake. She was searching frantically for some solution to what appeared to be an unsolvable problem. Instead, maybe she should focus less on the Protector and more on the one the Protector protected.

Ursina turned her attention away from her husband and toward his niece.

Kendric's control over the Stalkers had weakened severely because of the Protector's attack, her husband unable to concentrate on anything other than keeping himself alive.

The beasts had reverted to their innate nature as a result. Not fighting in a coordinated fashion. Instead, fighting each other just as much as they fought Aislinn, who was happy to employ that weakness to her benefit.

She kept her back against the wall, making the best use of the confined space. The bodies of the Stalkers piling up around her. Her fiery blade cutting through flesh and bone with a lethal ease.

Ursina had little faith that the Stalkers, dying much too quickly for her taste, would succeed without her husband's guidance. Still, they were doing enough to give Ursina the opportunity to salvage what had become a dire situation.

Calling on as much of the Curse as she could manage without fear of destroying herself, she flicked her wrist, sending a fiery sphere of swirling black surging toward her husband's niece.

Ursina grinned with delight. Aislinn had turned to challenge a Stalker coming at her right side. She had no chance to defend against Ursina's attack from her left.

"No!" Ursina shouted at the top of her lungs. Shocked. Dismayed. Not understanding how Kendric's niece avoided the surprise she sent her way.

Until she saw the woman in multicolored robes, hair astray, strands of energy dancing around one hand. With the other, she snuffed out the magical barrier she had constructed at the very last second that prevented Ursina from killing Aislinn.

"Anisru." Rafia stared at the Dark Magus. Sadness and regret were plain on her face. "I can't say that I'm surprised. I just hoped that it wasn't you. That you hadn't fallen so far. Unfortunately, as Sirius so liked to say, hoping doesn't make it real."

Ursina didn't know what to say. She could barely breathe. She had not heard her real name for so long that it had become nothing more than a memory to her.

How could Rafia have found her? After all this time? After all she had done to cover her tracks?

She thought that she had escaped the Magus at Roo's Nest. Yet there Rafia stood.

Ten yards away.

That smug, disapproving look that had so irritated her when she was growing up there to torture her once again.

"Mother," Anisru hissed through clenched teeth.

Without another word and a quick flick of her wrist, she shot a stream of tainted energy streaking toward Rafia.

"WHAT SHALL we do about the Protector?" asked the Blademaster.

He stood at the end of the tunnel, still in the gloom, Benin and the rest of his soldiers right behind him.

Just a few yards to his front the green moss illuminated the chamber and the bloody clash taking place beneath the Shadow Keep. They would never have gotten there in time if not for Rafia's ability to detect and destroy the magical illusion put in place to mask this tunnel.

"Leave him be," Declan grumbled. The gladiators of the Blood Company stood at his back. Quiet. Calm. Just as they always were. But he could sense it. They were eager. Anxious. They wanted to get into the fight. They wanted to aid the Protector. "He knows what he's doing. And we leave Rafia to her task as well."

"That makes things much easier," the Blademaster acknowledged. "Benin."

"Yes, Blademaster," the grizzled soldier replied, stepping forward to stand at Klines' shoulder. His long beard was woven into the shape of the battle axe that he carried in his right hand.

"I would like to speak with the Lady of the Southern Marches."

"Of course, Blademaster," the former sergeant replied, his

eyes sparkling with anticipation, his lips curling with amusement. They had acted out much this same scene before while fighting Ghoule Legions in Caledonia. "Soldiers of the Royal Guard! We advance in wedge formation."

The soldiers moved into position with barely a thought.

"We make for the Lady of the Southern Marches!" Benin ordered.

The Blademaster marched right behind the point of the wedge, the soldiers he had trained and fought with in Caledonia emerging from the tunnel. The Stalkers completely unaware of the threat advancing toward their backs.

Declan watched with delight as Klines and his troops bit deeply into the Stalkers milling about Aislinn. With their disciplined ferocity, it wouldn't be long before they relieved the pressure that the Lady of the Southern Marches pushed back against.

Yet by attacking in such a way, the soldiers with the Blademaster were vulnerable at the sides and the rear. That was why Declan waited.

It took longer for the Stalkers to identify the weakness than he anticipated. Once they did, however, the monsters moved rapidly to take advantage of it.

A large number of the beasts halted their frantic efforts to get at Aislinn, instead moving to the left and right, seeking to crush the soldiers' flanks together.

Exactly what Declan wanted.

"Majdi. Jenus." The two gladiators stepped up next to Declan. "You know what to do."

"With pleasure," Majdi rumbled.

Without another word the gladiators sprinted out from the tunnel, Majdi moving to one side, Jenus to the other, the men and women of the Blood Company right behind.

Declan stepped out into the chamber at a more leisurely pace. Ready to fight. Not expecting that he would have to. Not with the two columns of gladiators crashing into the shocked Stalkers like an avalanche of stone sliding down a mountain.

THE SOUND of steel striking steel echoed loudly within the barrier Bryen had crafted around him and Kendric. A small price to pay to ensure that Ursina could not intervene in the combat.

"You don't need to do this, Kendric," Bryen stated bluntly, keeping the Lord of Shadow's Reach pinned against the wall, never allowing him to get his back more than a foot off the stone. The double blades of his spear flashed so frequently and so furiously that they seemed to be more streaks of light than steel.

"I do need to do this," Kendric grunted. He raised his sword just in time, catching one of Bryen's sharp edges before it cut across his shoulder, earning another nasty nick in his blade. "I have no choice."

"You do have a choice," Bryen countered, the blade on the other end of his spear whipping around blazingly fast as he swung the weapon with one hand. "You always have a choice. You should know that better than most."

Kendric gripped his sword tightly with both hands. He wasn't strong enough to block the Protector's strike outright. The best that he could do was deflect each shockingly swift blow.

Despite all the skill and tenacity he put into his defense, he didn't doubt that the Protector could have killed him a handful of times already. Yet he hadn't. And Kendric didn't understand why.

"I didn't have a choice," Kendric grunted. He was barely able to parry the Protector's next attack, which flowed right from the last, a tight curve of steel that would have taken Kendric's head from his shoulders if it had connected.

"If you believe that, Kendric, then you're a fool."

Bryen knew firsthand what it took to battle the Curse when it sought to make you its own. He had survived that challenge in large part because he refused to accept defeat. And he had learned that's what it largely came down to.

The Curse was a corruption that would only grow once it bit into you. But it couldn't take that first bite unless you allowed it. Unless you accepted the ancient evil while comprehending what it would do to you in the end.

"And I don't take you for a fool."

Such a comment normally would have filled Kendric with rage. It didn't. Rather, guilt flooded into him instead. Because the Protector was correct no matter how much he didn't want to admit it to himself.

He did have a choice. Before all this had started. And he had chosen the path that his wife had wanted him to take in spite of his many reservations.

He had convinced himself that doing as she wanted him to came from his love for her. And it did. He desired nothing more than to make her happy. To bring her joy in this world.

However, he had done it for a darker reason as well.

Kendric allowed himself to be seduced by what she offered him. He wanted that power. He needed that power. Believing that even with the cost attached to that power, it was worth it, because that power allowed him to achieve the objectives he and his wife had set for themselves.

It wasn't until he trod the path he selected and gotten a real taste of the tainted power that Ursina had gifted him that he realized his mistake.

"It's too late, Protector," Kendric grimaced, hissing in pain as Bryen sliced across his forearm with a shining blade. Barely a cut, yet more painful than any wound Kendric had ever received before, his flesh sizzling, the burn intensifying.

"It's never too late, Kendric," Bryen countered. "Everyone makes mistakes. What matters is what you do once you realize that you've made a mistake."

Kendric chuckled softly. The Protector was trying to get him to think about more than just their combat. Wanting to clear his head, he tried to step back and gain some breathing room.

Bryen wouldn't let him, following right after Kendric, fiery steel singing through the air.

For the next few seconds, Kendric could do nothing more than dance, dodging more than defending the Protector's strikes, resigning himself to the fact that this was a combat that he could not win.

The Protector was stringing him along. How much longer that would continue, Kendric had no idea.

"There is no redemption that can be earned from the mistake that I have made. From what I have done to achieve my own ends."

"There is always a way, Kendric," Bryen challenged. "You just might not like the choice you need to make."

Growling in anger, more at himself than at his opponent, Kendric shifted to a one-handed grip and lunged.

Bryen pivoted, allowing Kendric's blade to pass by him. Before Kendric could pull back, Bryen cut down with his spear, slicing through Kendric's sword with an ear-splitting shriek and a flash, leaving jagged and partially melted metal halfway down the blade.

At the same time, Bryen kicked with his left foot, sweeping Kendric's legs out from under him.

Grunting in shock, his back and head slamming against the stone, Kendric gasped for the air that wouldn't come. When the black spots finally cleared from his vision and he could breathe again, he realized that he couldn't move.

The Protector had knocked his broken sword from his hand and placed his own blade against Kendric's throat, his free hand on Kendric's forehead and pushing the back of his bloody scalp against the stone. If Kendric moved just a hair, he was dead, the Protector's steel slitting his throat.

"Why haven't you finished this?" Kendric demanded in a whisper. Angry. Embarrassed. Not understanding how all his and Ursina's plans could have fallen apart so quickly.

Bryen shook his head in disappointment, as if Kendric should have already known the answer to his own question. "Because you're Aislinn's uncle."

Kendric's pure black eyes flashed upon hearing that. "There is nothing that you can do for me. But you can do something for her. Take Aislinn away from here. Take her somewhere safe."

"An admirable request."

"I don't want anything to happen to Aislinn. I never did. You have to believe me. Take her away to somewhere safe. Please!"

"She wouldn't go if I tried to drag her," Bryen replied, "and I'm certainly not going to do that. She'd gut me."

"Please, Protector! I am lost. There is nothing to be done but kill me. Get her away from here." If he was to lose his life on this day, so be it. But he couldn't bear the thought that his niece was in the same dreadful position as he was, death on her doorstep as she fought a pack of Stalkers eager to chew on her bones.

Stalkers that he had called here at Ursina's instigation.

For just a moment, he found that he couldn't breathe, and not because of anything that the Protector was doing to him.

What had he become?

This was not who he was.

This was not who he wanted to be.

"You're wrong, Kendric."

Kendric's brow furrowed, the Protector's voice drawing him

back from the pit of despair into which he had almost fallen. "What are you talking about?"

"I'm not going to kill you, but there is something that I can do for you."

Bryen strengthened his grip on Kendric's forehead, threads of white sparking off his fingertips. He understood the risk of doing too quickly what he had in mind, but he couldn't afford to delay. And he couldn't take his time.

He couldn't leave Aislinn to fight so many Stalkers on her own for much longer. It was asking too much of her.

He'd rather risk killing Kendric than place the woman he loved in even greater danger.

Before he released the power that he controlled, already linked to the reservoir of energy contained within the Seventh Stone, he breathed a sigh of relief.

Out of the corner of his eye he glimpsed the men and women rushing into the chamber and joining the fight. The Blademaster and his soldiers, which meant that Declan was close at hand as well. Likely waiting for the right moment.

Less concerned now about Aislinn, Bryen sent several threads of energy surging into Kendric. The effect was immediate.

Kendric's body stiffened. Seconds later, he began to shiver then shake uncontrollably.

Bryen pulled back the steel that he held at Kendric's throat just to be safe as he sent more of the Talent into Aislinn's uncle, scouring him clean of the Curse, the power of the Seventh Stone proving to be too much for the tainted energy that was a finger's breadth away from claiming Kendric as its own.

Bryen didn't rush now, having more time to work thanks to the arrival of his friends. Understanding that he needed to be thorough. Knowing that if he left even a speck of the Curse within Kendric, then it would simply grow once more and consume Aislinn's uncle as it had done before.

He ignored the sounds of the battle surging around him, lost in what he was doing, time having no meaning.

Almost done, the Seventh Stone burning away the last of the corrupted power, Bryen leaned back in surprise.

He had not expected to come upon this challenge, but he probably should have.

It was much as it was when he healed Noorsin Stelekel after her confrontation with Tetric. To find what ailed her, he had needed to search for the Curse hiding within her, the evil taint trying to mask its presence and prevent its discovery.

And just as had happened then, as he searched for any remnants of the tainted energy within Kendric, he felt that tiny prick at the very edge of his consciousness.

There but gone an instant later.

Looking down at Kendric's eyes, the man still shaking as if he suffered from a high fever, Bryen confirmed it. The orbs were no longer pure black. However, every other second he saw that tiny spark of the Curse in the very back.

Bryen knew from experience that brute force would do him little good in a situation such as this. Delicacy was required.

With that guiding his thinking, he allowed his mind to drift. Focusing on nothing and on everything both at the same time.

There!

That same prick.

But gone just as fast.

Fleeing.

Attempting to escape him.

He tried again.

There!

Before he could grasp it, the Curse slipped through his fingers.

He lost his concentration for a few heartbeats, hearing the sounds of the fight growing in intensity despite the shield that protected him and Kendric. Sensing the Talent and the Curse being flung about the chamber. Understanding what that meant.

If he was going to save Kendric, he needed to do it now.

Once again, he allowed his consciousness to drift.

This time he was ready.

As soon as he felt the prick of the Curse, he pinched it with the Talent. The Seventh Stone did the rest, latching onto and then destroying the last of the tainted power within Kendric.

Or so he hoped.

Bryen checked Kendric's eyes just to make sure. Not a speck to be seen.

Satisfied, Bryen pulled Kendric to his feet. Holding him in place as he regained his bearings.

Drenched with sweat, his breathing ragged, Kendric felt as if he had fought on the battlements against the Wraiths for the better part of a day.

"Why did you do that? Why not just kill me?" Kendric croaked. "It would have been easier for you."

"I almost did," Bryen admitted, not wanting to tell Kendric just how close he had come to sending a bolt of the Talent right into his brain. "Thankfully, I didn't have to."

"But the risk you ..."

"Aislinn never gave up on you," Bryen replied simply. "I didn't do it for you. I did it for her."

Kendric stared at Bryen, not quite believing the generosity and belief that Aislinn and her Protector displayed. Understanding now why Aislinn and her Protector had chosen one another.

"Thank you," was all that Kendric could whisper.

Bryen nodded. "Thank Aislinn. If I had it my way, I would have just killed you. Less trouble for me."

Kendric smiled weakly at that, hearing the truth in the Protector's words and valuing it. His response proved to

Kendric that Bryen would do whatever was required to ensure that Aislinn was kept safe.

His expression changed swiftly. Now crestfallen. The full ramifications of what he had almost done hitting Kendric like a hammer blow across his jaw. He could barely stay on his feet, the Protector reaching out just in time to ensure that he didn't fall to the ground.

He had been about to sacrifice his niece for a power that offered nothing more than pain, fear, and subjugation.

How had he fallen so far so fast?

How could he have ...

Kendric's disparaging thoughts disappeared in a flash.

Shrugging out of Bryen's grip, he staggered more than sprinted across the chamber.

Aislinn fought with a deadly precision, having just killed one Stalker by gutting the beast with her sword. But another monster that he had called to this chamber beneath the Shadow Keep was rushing toward her from her blind side.

Only twenty long paces away, the Stalker would be on her before she could turn to face the beast.

Kendric had to get to her in time.

He had to!

He could not rectify the mistake he had made, but he could do whatever was necessary to ensure that Aislinn didn't pay the price for his own weakness.

THE SHARD of black streaking toward Rafia promised her an excruciating death.

If the tainted power struck.

It didn't.

Bringing her hands together and then spreading them apart just as quickly, the Magus formed a shield of gleaming white that she tilted to a right angle. Rather than having to bear the full brunt of the potent strike, she deflected the Curse, the corrupted energy glancing off the shield and slamming into the stone ceiling above her, the green moss withering and dying at its touch as a web of black spread across the rock.

Rafia shook her head, disappointment and anger plain on her face. Not because of her opponent. Rather because she hadn't figured out who the real threat was before she and Declan brought the Blood Company to Shadow's Reach.

She should have known. The truth had been staring her in the face the entire time.

Yet she hadn't seen it.

Whether because she had missed some key piece of evidence or she simply didn't want to …

That was a failing she could consider later. Not in the middle of a combat such as this one.

"This is what you've sunk to, Ani?" Releasing her shield, Rafia took a step toward her daughter. "I knew you were stubborn. I knew that you always thought that you could do what others couldn't without having to fear the consequences. I just never knew how far you had fallen. The lengths to which you were willing to go to gain …"

Rafia sighed. Eyes filled with sorrow. "Was it worth it, Ani? All the misery you've caused to achieve your own ends?"

"I'm no different than you are, mother, no matter what you might tell yourself." It was Anisru's turn to shake her head, this time in amused disdain. Her initial disbelief at Rafia confronting her disappearing in an instant. She should have expected as much from the woman who had raised her. "You deluded yourself ever since you began teaching me how to use the Talent. You never recognized my true potential. You never trusted me."

"That's what you believe?" Rafia scoffed. "We are similar in many ways, Ani. You're right about that. But we are different in others. Which is why I had little reason to help you when you decided to take a path that I told you could only lead to ruin." Rafia took another step toward Anisru, now no more than a dozen yards separating them. "I didn't see what I wanted to see, Ani. I saw what you could become. What you have become because of your arrogance and pride."

"You sound jealous, mother," growled Anisru.

"Jealous? No. Disappointed? Yes," Rafia replied forcefully. "You had a choice, Ani. You were on your way to becoming one of the strongest Magii to ever walk the face of the earth. But that wasn't enough for you, was it? You needed more. You always needed more."

"I blame you for that failing. Like mother, like daughter."

"Me?" Rafia's brow furrowed. "How could you possibly blame me? I did all that I could to ensure you stayed on the right path."

"Tell yourself what you need to, mother. As I said, we are very much alike. The primary difference being the fact that I had the courage to follow a path that you didn't."

"I told you many times, but you didn't listen," Rafia responded with a heavy sadness. "Taking that path has nothing to do with courage, Ani. That path has everything to do with desire. With weakness. You were not satisfied with what you were. What you had. You decided that you needed to be something more. You believed that the path you chose would give that to you." Rafia tilted her head to the side, studying her daughter as she used to do when Ani was younger. "Tell me, Ani, was it worth it? Was turning to the Curse all that you imagined? Did it give you what you sought? Or did it take more from you than you ever thought possible?"

Anisru glared at her mother with a mix of indecision and indignation in her eyes. How could Rafia possibly have the temerity to challenge the decision that she made? How could she look at her right then as if she was better than she was?

Her mother was not better than she was. She never had been. Anisru just hadn't realized it until she was older.

Rafia's own failings. Her mother's weaknesses. All of which Rafia attempted to foist upon her.

Anisru growled, clenching her hands into white-knuckled fists. She thought she had gotten past all that. Yet she had not seen her mother for more than five years and it seemed like nothing had changed.

A ceaseless conflict between them. She seeking to expand her knowledge and her power. Her mother seeking to hold her back and prevent her from seeing the world for what it really was.

It could have been so different if her mother had listened to her. If her mother had been willing to work with her rather than fight her every step of the way.

Anisru had pursued knowledge of the Curse with the goal of finding a way to tame it.

She hadn't. She would be the first to admit that.

The Curse had proven too strong. Too persistent. Too seductive.

Anisru hadn't stood a chance when she began walking the path that few other Magii had the courage to travel.

But she might have proven more successful in her efforts if her mother had chosen to help her rather than treat her like a child.

"There's no point to engaging in this conversation, mother," Anisru sighed. "Just as there was no point to engaging in this conversation before you forced me to flee from Caledonia."

"I didn't force you to do anything, Ani," Rafia replied, shaking her head with a deep regret. "The decisions that you made put you here. You must accept responsibility for what you have become."

"I made those decisions because you weren't there to help me," Anisru spat. "I didn't have a choice!"

"You always had a choice, Ani! Always!" Rafia's eyes blazed with anger. It was as if they had reverted to their roles when Ani was first learning to use the Talent. Rafia trying to teach her. Ani challenging her at every turn. Both believing that they were right and the other wrong. A struggle rather than a lesson. "As I told you then, I would not help you become what you have become. I would not help you become a slave to the Curse. But I see that my unwillingness to do that did you little good. You serve the Curse. You don't even serve yourself anymore."

"Actually, your unwillingness to aid me did a great deal of good, mother," Anisru countered, a sphere of black mist beginning to spin atop her right palm. "It showed me that I couldn't count on you or anyone else. I could only count on myself."

Rafia closed her eyes for a brief moment, guilt cascading through her. For failing Ani. For not having the courage to do what was required when she had the chance.

She had hoped that if she ever found her daughter again that circumstances might be different. A false hope, she knew, but still she had held onto it.

She and Ani were much alike. Her daughter was correct in that regard.

Stubborn to the point of obstinance. Believing that they could do what others couldn't.

Yet in Ani there was something more. A craving for power that Rafia had identified at an early age. She had tried to help her daughter manage it. To ensure that Ani never fell into the trap that so many other Magii had.

She had been a fool then and now.

Rafia lost her daughter, what she had been, the moment Ani touched the Curse. There was no reason to believe that she could ever have her back. That Ani would ever want to come back.

"I'm sorry to hear that, Ani," Rafia sighed, feeling somewhat lost upon concluding that nothing had changed between them. Knowing as well what was demanded of her.

She was the Master of the Magii after all, and there was only one penalty for a Magus who turned to the Curse.

A small part of Rafia always had been grateful that she and Sirius failed to catch Ani when she made her escape from Roo's Nest. Now, she recognized that she had allowed a useless emotion to rule her.

Better to have done the deed then. If she had, then she wouldn't be back where she started.

Needing to kill her own daughter.

"You have nothing to be sorry for, mother. You taught me an important lesson."

"What was that?"

"To do what needs to be done no matter the cost."

Rafia nodded, struck by the irony and immediate application of Ani's comment. "The unofficial family motto, unfortunately."

With a quick flick of her wrist, Rafia sent sparks of energy shooting toward her daughter. Because of the wide arc of the attack, Anisru had to stand her ground, unable to dodge out of the way.

To defend herself, Anisru wove the mist into a spinning black, the sparks of white crackling as they struck the dynamic barrier.

"Is that the best that you can do, mother? Is this why I am free today? Not because of some sense of motherly love but rather because I am indeed stronger than you? More skilled? More determined?"

Rafia had heard much worse from some of her previous opponents, yet the words coming from her daughter bit particularly deep. Even so, she blocked away the pain that they caused.

Ani was her daughter. More important, however, she

was also a Dark Magus. She needed to be treated just like any other Magus weak enough to be tempted by the Curse.

"I'm just getting started, Ani."

Rafia and Ani attacked at the same time, streams of white and black meeting in the space between them. The deafening collision of the two competing energies caused the chamber to shake dangerously, small pieces of moss-covered stone crumbling down from the ceiling.

For the next several minutes, both mother and daughter wore expressions of grim determination. Neither moved an inch, seemingly rooted in place. Attacking and defending with the Talent and the Curse, neither able to get the better of the other as shards and spikes screamed through the air, failing to strike home, the energy in play more and more putting at risk the structural integrity of the chamber as larger chunks of rock fell to the floor.

Getting nowhere, at the same time they both stepped back. Not needing a break, but rather acknowledging the challenge that they faced.

Mother and daughter were too evenly matched. Or so Anisru believed.

"I don't want to do this, Ani."

Anisru snorted in disbelief. "Of course you do, mother. This is who you are. I'm just another person to be hunted down because I did what you didn't want me to do."

Rafia opened her mouth to reply, then bit back the words. She had never really believed that she would see Ani again. Nevertheless, she had hoped that if she did, she could talk some sense into the girl.

With Bryen's ability to use the Seventh Stone to fight the Curse, she had actually begun to believe that maybe, just maybe, he could help Ani as he had Noorsin and Aislinn's father.

Yet what was the point of trying to help someone who didn't want to be helped?

The Curse had become too much a part of Ani. It defined who she was now even though she couldn't see that. Or she didn't want to see that. Or she didn't care.

Even if Bryen succeeded in drawing the poison from her body, when next Ani got the chance to reclaim what was lost, she would allow the Curse to take her once more.

It was a foregone conclusion.

Once touched by the Curse, you were no longer who you were before. You were only what the Curse wanted you to be.

Resigning herself to that hard reality, Rafia reached for the Talent. She had been holding back. Hoping beyond hope that she wouldn't have to do this.

Knowing then that she did have to do this.

Ani was too far gone.

The Ani who had been her daughter was no more.

How she hated when Sirius was right. That there was no point in trying to save someone who refused to be saved.

Preparing to send a blast of energy toward her daughter that she doubted Ani could defend against, Rafia hesitated for just a heartbeat.

She saw the change that came over Ani. Arrogance replaced by desperation. And then the realization that it was too late, her daughter's face falling then twisting into a rictus of pain.

Rafia followed Ani's gaze. She shook her head in sadness, watching what was playing out before her.

Much of what made her daughter who she was no longer was real.

Her love for her husband was real, however, that much was plain.

Anisru had turned away from Rafia when out of the corner of her eye she glimpsed a figure sprint past her. All concerns over her mother fading in a flash.

Rather than allowing the Stalker to drive its claws into Aislinn's back, Kendric pulled a dagger from the sheath on his hip and leapt through the air.

"No!" Anisru screamed, yet the Dark Magus knew that it was too late before she gave voice to her heartache.

Kendric succeeded. He landed on the Stalker's back and drove the dagger deep into the muscle, distracting the monster and halting its attack.

He could do little more than that, however, the powerful creature flinging him from its back, the steel stuck in its shoulder of little concern to the beast.

Kendric hit the wall heavily, smacking the back of his head against the stone. Woozy, seeing double, still he managed to regain his unsteady feet.

His hands went to his boot, seeking the thin dagger he kept there. Having no other weapon with which to defend himself.

He was too slow. The Stalker already upon him, before he could grip the soft leather wrapped around the hilt, the Stalker punched. A terrible pain ripped through him as he was lifted off the ground.

Anisru screamed in horror as Kendric stared into the blood-red eyes of the monster before dipping his chin, not quite believing that the Stalker's claw was lodged in his chest.

Then he was falling, his feet hitting the stone and giving out beneath him.

Bryen couldn't save Kendric. He did kill the Stalker, taking the beast's head with a quick swipe of the Spear of the Magii just a second after Kendric dropped to the ground.

Then he moved toward Aislinn, defending her back as she took on another Stalker.

Anisru's fear became despondency, the crumpled form of her husband lying on the stone floor taking her breath away.

She couldn't understand why Kendric had done that. Why

he had risked himself for his niece when they had their future waiting for them.

She couldn't believe it.

Her greatest love.

Her only love.

Gone.

Anisru's hand went to her belly. She took a step toward Kendric, stumbling instead.

Rafia, forgetting that they had been fighting just seconds before, reached out to help her daughter stay on her feet.

Anisru refused her mother's offer with a snarl, her eyes blazing ferociously, her reason gone.

Before she fell, Anisru made use of the power gifted to her by her Master, blasting a shard of the Curse into the stone floor right between her and her mother.

Rafia's natural reaction was to turn away from the destructive energy and construct a shield with the Talent to protect herself from the blast.

Exactly as Anisru wanted.

When Rafia spun back around just a heartbeat later, Ani was gone, the spinning portal of black mist closing behind her.

"I'm sorry, Aislinn," Kendric gasped, a thin line of blood trickling out of the corner of his mouth and down his lips. "Truly."

"You saved me, uncle." Aislinn knelt by Kendric's side, gripping his rapidly cooling hands with her own. "There is nothing to be sorry for."

Bryen stood just behind her. Spear held loosely in his hand. Ready if necessary. Yet knowing that the fighting was done. For the moment at least.

Now it was just a matter of ensuring that all the dead were truly dead.

The Blademaster had taken on that grisly task, working his way through the chamber, Benin and several other soldiers making certain that the Stalkers littering the stone floor would not rise again.

Declan had sent the Blood Company into the passageways that led away from the chamber. Despite Bryen telling him that there were no more Stalkers to kill, he wanted to check for himself, or rather give the gladiators a task, their blood still up.

That done, Declan walked over and stood next to Bryen, standing silent vigil with him as the Lord of the Northern Territory breathed his last.

Bryen had examined Kendric after killing the Stalker. He was skilled at healing with the Talent. Yet there was nothing that he could do for Aislinn's uncle. The damage was too severe, even for him.

"I have so much to be sorry for, Aislinn," Kendric whispered. "So much."

"Let it go, uncle."

"I can't, Aislinn. I can't." Kendric gripped his niece's hands in a tighter grip, using what little strength was left to him. "Where is Ursina?"

Aislinn tried to answer several times, tears beginning to run down her cheeks.

"She's gone, uncle."

Kendric took that knowledge as a physical blow, gasping silently as a wave of pain rushed through him.

"She's alive?" he asked when he caught his breath again, almost pleading.

"She's alive," Rafia replied. She knelt down next to Aislinn, gripping her shoulder warmly before pushing herself back to her feet. "You have nothing to fear."

Kendric nodded, a small smile playing across his lips as the light in his eyes slowly faded. "Good. That's good. I was worried about her." He shifted his head to the right, although he had lost his ability to see, his body beginning to shut down. "Protector?"

"I'm here, Kendric," Bryen replied in a soft, solemn voice.

"Bryen," Kendric corrected, his voice growing weaker. "Thank you. For what you did. For allowing me a clean death."

"You saved the woman I love, Kendric. I could do nothing less for you."

"Thank you. Thank you." A series of coughs wracked his body then, the trickle of blood leaving his mouth becoming a stream. "Aislinn?"

"Yes, uncle." Aislinn's tears were flowing freely now. Striking Kendric's cheek in rapid succession. Yet he couldn't feel them.

"Leave her be." His breath slowed, the words harder to find. "She didn't know what she was doing. Leave her ... be."

Aislinn closed her eyes, bowing her head, as Kendric passed. Releasing his hands, she placed them gently on the stone, then leapt up and into Bryen's arms, needing a moment to allow her grief to pass through her.

Kendric was far from perfect. But she wasn't thinking about the role the Lord of Shadow's Reach had played in helping to create the Stalkers. She was thinking about the man who had given her a wooden sword as a birthday present, setting her on the road that had taken her here.

"Anisru?" asked Declan. "I thought Kendric's wife was called Ursina."

"She's both," Rafia replied. "Ursina here in the Territories. In Caledonia ..."

"Anisru."

"You know her," Declan said gently, the pain flashing in the back of Rafia's eyes unmistakable. "And not just because she used to be a Magus."

"No, not just because of that," Rafia admitted. "Anisru …
Ani … is my daughter."

"Your daughter?" Declan exclaimed. The Master of the
Gladiators' stoicism was legendary. But this bit of unexpected
knowledge broke the mask he usually wore, his shock evident.

"My daughter," Rafia repeated. "Actually, my and Sirius'
daughter."

"She's a Keldragan?"

Rafia turned toward Bryen, Aislinn lifting her head from his
shoulder, both of them staring at the Magus with shocked
expressions.

"She was," Rafia affirmed. "Your …" Rafia held up her
hands. "Honestly, I don't know what she is specifically in rela-
tion to you. But what she is now isn't what she was. She was
born a Keldragan and a Riverstone. As soon as she gave herself
to the Curse, she became something else."

"This is a revelation that I wasn't anticipating," Declan
admitted.

Rafia gave Declan an anxious look. "I hope you don't think
less of me."

"Why would I do that?"

"I kept this secret to myself."

Declan offered Rafia a stern look, but he could only do it for
so long, a warm and understanding smile breaking his countenance. "We all have our secrets, Rafia. We don't always get to
choose when they're revealed."

Rafia nodded her thanks to Declan, greatly relieved that he
understood. She reached out and grasped his hand with
her own.

"Do you think that she loved my uncle? Or was she just
using him?"

At first, Rafia didn't know what to say, not wanting to add to
Aislinn's pain. She had learned during her long lifetime,
however, that it was better to be honest rather than evasive.

"Using him, yes. To create the Stalkers. To manage those beasts. She was the Dark Magus creating havoc in the Territories. She anchored the Curse within your uncle, giving him the ability to control them, at least to a certain extent. He fought it until the very end. Protecting you more important to him."

Aislinn attempted to process what Rafia was telling her. She was devastated. Then, quickly, she became angry.

Kendric had made some terrible mistakes, yet she believed that he hadn't made them without Ursina's – or rather Anisru's – helping hand.

"I'm certain as well that she loved him. In her own way. As best as she could."

Aislinn nodded at that last. Her expression hardening. She had made a decision. "We need to find her. She has much to answer for."

"We will try," Rafia promised. Her daughter had escaped her before. After seeing the damage that she had caused here in the Territories, Rafia knew that she couldn't allow her to escape again. "It will not be an easy hunt.

"That will have to wait," Bryen said. "The Wraiths are coming. No more than a few hours away. We need to deal with the monsters in the Murk before anything else."

23

HOLDING THE LINE

"We had to do this?" grumped Lycia.

Jakob smiled. She wouldn't have observed his reaction if not for his linking to her with the Talent, which allowed her to see in the Murk that enveloped Shadow's Reach and the surrounding countryside. Nor would the several squads of soldiers from the Northern Guard who had joined them deep within the grey.

"I thought it best that we prove that we can fight in the Murk. It will give the men and women behind us greater confidence to watch and learn before the larger battle begins."

Jakob had taught Bryen, Rafia, and Aislinn how to employ the Talent so that the soldiers could see all that was around them despite the wispy grey threads that blinded them. Doing so ensured the first fair fight against the Wraiths. A reality that the defenders of Shadow's Reach could only dream about until Jakob and the other Magii appeared.

Lycia couldn't dispute his logic. And, admittedly, she wanted to be right by his side in the smothering fog as several thousand Wraiths glided toward them. In fact, she couldn't imagine being anywhere else but there.

"Everyone ready?" Jakob asked with the Talent, communicating in the minds of the soldiers who had advanced several hundred yards out in front of the main line.

He received in his own mind a series of excited replies and not a single worry. The soldiers not voicing their responses, understanding the danger of making even the slightest sound.

Better that his skirmishers were excited, not afraid. So long as they didn't allow themselves to become arrogant they stood a good chance of dealing a hard and bloody first blow to the oncoming Wraiths.

"Stick to the plan. Twenty-four Wraith Scouts are coming our way." Jakob knew that the soldiers, who were spread out along both his sides in a loose arc, saw all that he saw as he extended his senses into the gloom. Still, he felt the need to repeat what they had discussed. They couldn't afford to make any mistakes now. Not if they wanted to survive the engagement. *"They won't know we're here until we reveal ourselves. Brief, sharp attacks. Then we retreat. If we leave a few of them standing, so be it."*

"We can't finish them?" asked one of the soldiers at the far end of the line.

"No, if you don't kill them in the first few seconds, we'll get them later. Not now. We want to make the Wraiths wonder about how we're doing this to them. A little indecision will help us during the larger battle." Jakob's bright green eyes sharpened. The Wraith Scouts were less than fifty yards away and closing fast. Still unaware of what waited for them in the Murk. *"Be ready. Strike then go."*

Jakob and Lycia shifted their focus toward the creatures working their way through the mist. The Wraiths approached in a long, jagged line. They likely knew that most of their adversaries were only a few hundred yards farther to the south.

That many soldiers could not stay silent. And Jakob didn't want them to. He wanted them to make enough noise to draw the attention of the Scouts. The scrapes of whetstones across steel and the frequent murmur of quiet conversations enough to do the trick.

Jakob and Lycia waited a few seconds more. Barely breathing. Not moving. One leg slightly in front of the other. Standing on their toes. Ready. Quiet as mice, though having a deadlier bite.

Three Wraiths approached, now within twenty yards of them.

The monsters in the mist were taking their time. Not feeling the need to rush. Likely not expecting to meet any resistance until they ran into the large force of soldiers arrayed closer to the walls of Shadow's Reach.

Exactly what Jakob wanted, because he meant to make use of that false belief.

Ten yards.

He and Lycia still didn't move. They didn't make a sound.

They would be able to see the Wraiths when the Wraiths saw them. As a result, they still had time. And they didn't want to give themselves away. Not yet.

Five yards.

Their hands flexed on the hilts of their weapons.

The Wraiths stopped abruptly.

Did the monsters know where he and Lycia were?

That fear played through Jakob's mind for several seconds.

But no, it wasn't that.

It was just the Wraiths moving as they usually did through the fog.

Slowly. Stopping and starting. Testing. Seeing if they could rouse any prey that might be hiding from them. Not realizing that in this instance, the hunted had become the hunters.

Jakob and Lycia held their positions. Calm. Collected. Knowing what was going to happen, they just needed to be patient for a short while longer.

The seconds dragged on into a minute. Then several minutes.

The Wraiths didn't move. They didn't make a noise.

Neither did Jakob and Lycia. Hoping the soldiers with them could demonstrate the same patience.

Then the Wraiths stepped forward again.

Four yards.

Three yards.

Two.

Before the Wraiths could pick them out in the Murk, Jakob and Lycia struck.

Lycia slashed with the sword she held by her side, ducking down as she did so. Rather than cutting across the Wraith's chest, she sliced deeply into both shins.

The monster hissed in pain. His natural response was to bend over, his claws reaching for his wounds.

The Wraith kept dropping toward the ground, crumpling, Lycia already behind the monster and driving her sword through the small of his back with a two-handed grip.

Jakob attacked with the haladies that felt so right in his hands.

He stabbed with one double-bladed dagger, taking a Wraith in the knee right between the bones. Before the monster could even acknowledge the terrible wound with a shriek of pain, Jakob silenced him, slicing across his throat.

He didn't bother to admire his handiwork, concentrating on the third Wraith who had been walking a few steps behind the other two.

This Wraith had heard and then seen what happened to his brethren. He had his haladies in his clawed hands.

It did him little good.

Lycia attacked from his right, stabbing with her sword.

The Wraith dodged out of the way so that the steel scraped across his ribs rather than punching between them.

A good maneuver that saved his life, though not good enough.

Because Jakob was waiting for just such an opportunity, slicing across the back of the Wraith's left leg and severing the hamstring.

The Wraith dropped to one knee, howling in pain.

That's all that the monster could do, Lycia already waiting to silence him. Stabbing through the back of the creature's neck with her blade.

Before the dead Wraith collapsed to the ground, Jakob and Lycia were away. Sprinting through the fog. Following their skirmishers. Making for the small host tasked with defending Shadow's Reach from the Wraith invasion.

JAKOB AND LYCIA emerged right in front of Bryen, Aislinn, and Rafia. They would never have known that the Highlander and the gladiator were there if not for their use of the Talent.

"They're coming," Jakob said simply.

He and Lycia then took their places next to the three Magii. Ready for the next act in the fight to begin, Jakob confirming that every one of his skirmishers made it back to the line, killing eighteen Wraiths, wounding six, and they only receiving a few flesh wounds for their efforts.

A good beginning.

But only the beginning.

As all that mattered with this drama was the conclusion.

"We're ready," Bryen replied. He spun his double-bladed spear from one hand to the next, just as he always did before a combat.

With the Talent, he communicated Jakob's information to Declan, who anchored the right flank with the Blood Company, and then to the Blademaster, who commanded the left flank with the bulk of the Northern Guard, only a few companies charged with guarding the walls of Shadow's Reach. Of course, the soldiers' efforts on the parapet would mean little if the Wraiths won the battlefield.

Bryen had not expected Jakob and Lycia to appear out of the blue on Arabella's back, reaching them just a few hours before. If not for Jakob's timely arrival and his quick lesson on how to fight in the Murk, Bryen could only imagine just how terrible a fight it would have been against the Wraiths. Likely a defeat before the battle even began.

But now he felt a great deal more confident. And for those who had never experienced the touch of the Talent in this specific way, it had been a revelation, particularly for the soldiers of the Northern Guard, who had fought so many times against the Wraiths with so little to show for their bravery.

They could see in the Murk.

They could fight in the Murk.

And they would.

With a vengeance.

"WHERE ARE THEY?" demanded the Wraith Lord.

He stood with several thousand of his Wraiths at his back. All of them expectant. All of them eager. All of them ready to begin the conquest that they hungered for.

With the Wraith Lord's skill in moving the Murk, the Wraiths could move with the nurturing grey. They could conquer the lands to their south. They could conquer any land in the Realms. Because no one stood a chance against the Wraiths while in the Murk.

Yet all was not going according to plan. The first line of Scouts had yet to report.

"They are dead, Lord, or as good as," the Wraith Hunter replied.

He had been worried about his Scouts delayed return, so he had gone in search of them. He had not expected to find what he did.

Only a handful of his Scouts still alive, and those too badly wounded to drag themselves across the ground.

He had put them out of their misery himself.

Such was the Wraith way.

If you couldn't fight, you were useless to the Horde.

"What do you mean?" demanded the Wraith Lord.

"Slaughtered, Lord," he replied simply.

"How is that even ..."

The Wraith Lord stopped himself, his expression tightening. He should have expected as much.

In fact, he had. The Wraith Lord believed that this combat was unavoidable, and that appealed to him. He just never anticipated that it would happen this far north. He had assumed that based on all the reports that he received it would occur in the Highlands instead.

"Is it his work?" asked the Wraith Lord, his raspy voice hopeful.

"I believe it is, Lord."

The Wraith Lord nodded. Pleased.

"Take the city," the Wraith Lord ordered, "and bring me the head of the Wraith who is not a Wraith."

"Hold the line!" roared Benin.

The former Sergeant in the Royal Guard fought right next to the Blademaster, covering his right side. Argenta Rensom, commander of the Northern Guard, wove a web of steel to the Blademaster's left.

Klines had fought a Wraith before in the streets of Shadow's Reach, the monster in the mist scouting the city.

The Blademaster had sent the Wraith back the way he had come. He had drawn blood as well.

It had been a hard combat, however. Fighting based almost entirely on instinct, the grey gloom impeding his vision and dulling his ability to hear. Making him question his decisions.

But not here. Not now.

He could see in the Murk as if it wasn't even there, and because of that the soldiers he fought with were more than holding their own.

The Wraiths had yet to break through their shield wall, and if all went to plan, if the men and women of the Northern Territory maintained their discipline, they wouldn't.

He was grateful that Argenta had listened to him when he walked into her office rather than putting him in a cell. That was probably because they knew each other. They trusted one another.

Argenta had served in the Royal Guard before she sought to make her way in the Territories. Klines had trained her for several years.

Rather than offering him disbelief and scorn for the claims that he made, she had asked him to take her to the chamber beneath the Shadow Keep.

That visit was all that was required for her to believe. All the whispers that she had heard and ignored finally made sense.

She was devastated and disappointed.

Devastated because she had trusted Kendric Winborne. She thought that he was a good Governor, or at least he wanted to be, trying to do his best for the people living in the Territory. Disappointed because she didn't recognize what his wife had done to him.

Her eyes widened with concern. She had allowed her mind

to wander to her mistakes at the worst possible moment, a Wraith leaping over the shield wall, the soldier in the second line missing the monster with a sweep of her sword.

Argenta raised her blade just in time, catching the dagger that came slicing in a tight arc toward her throat though realizing it wouldn't be enough. She could never turn in time to parry the Wraith's other dagger that was about to punch into her gut.

Cringing at the pain that she expected was about to consume her, she gave a start instead, the Wraith's dagger knocked to the side by a careful swipe of the Blademaster's steel.

"To the shield wall, Argenta," the Blademaster ordered in his quiet and commanding voice. "Get the spears in place to defend against any more of these monsters seeking to leap over the line. This one is mine."

Argenta struggled against her natural urge to continue the combat, then nodded and accepted the Blademaster's order. Stepping back to the shield wall, she issued a quick series of commands, every other soldier in the second line sheathing their swords and picking up the spears that lay on the ground right behind them.

"You think you can do better human," hissed the Wraith. The monster in the mist stood calmly in a comfortable crouch, haladies held at the ready.

"There's only one way to find out, Wraith," the Blademaster replied. "Shall we dance?"

The Wraith stared at his opponent for several seconds, then grinned. In a flash, the Wraith's bone-white daggers sliced through the air, barely visible in the grey wisps that flowed between them.

The Wraith growled in anger. The human who had the gall to stand against him wasn't there. He had pivoted to the side and then slid a few feet to the left, easily avoiding his attack.

"You think this is a game, human," the Wraith rasped. "You seek to play with me?"

Klines snorted softly. "No, Wraith, I seek to kill you."

The Blademaster dodged to the right side this time, the Wraith stabbing with his dagger in a wickedly fast motion, the blade missing Klines' hip by no more than a whisker.

But the Wraith wasn't done, the blade in his other clawed hand following the first in a broad arc from hip to shoulder that would have sliced Klines open and spilled his guts onto the ground if it connected.

It didn't.

The Blademaster had moved again, bringing his sword around in an arc of his own.

Ignoring the dagger aimed for his chest, Klines instead focused on the blade in the Wraith's other hand, which was just then coming up as a jab, the creature seeking to drive it right between his ribs.

The Blademaster barely had to move his steel, simply placing his blade in the right position. The Wraith's momentum did the rest.

The Wraith jumped back, staring in horror at the stub where his clawed hand had once been. His adversary slicing cleanly through his wrist.

Eyes widening in shock, the Wraith howled as his blood spurted from the terrible wound.

The creature never had a chance to revel in its agony, the Blademaster stepping in close and driving his sword straight through the Wraith's gut, giving it a twist before he pulled the blade free.

Klines left the dying Wraith at his feet, turning back to the shield wall, a small smile breaking his grim countenance.

The Northern Guard was more than holding.

They were winning.

"I THOUGHT this would be harder, Declan," rumbled Jenus. "I was looking forward to more of a challenge."

The Wraiths attacked the Blood Company time and time again. They had yet to do anything more than scrape their steel across the scuta the gladiators used to keep the monsters at bay.

"It would be a different story entirely if we couldn't see them in this confounding grey."

Jenus nodded. Before he could respond, he punched down with the rim of his shield, driving the sharpened steel completely through most of a Wraith's boot.

The monster reared back, hissing in pain, his mind needing several seconds to catch up to what had befallen him.

Better if he had stayed focused on the fight despite the severity of his wound.

Because as soon as the Wraith hobbled back a few feet, Asaia struck. The sharpened spike at the tip of her whip shot over Jenus' shoulder, piercing the Wraith's right eye. When she pulled the tip free with a vicious tug, the dead Wraith collapsed to the ground to join the dozens of others who had died in a useless, unimaginative attack.

As the many bodies demonstrated, these Wraiths were used to one type of fight. They excelled at it.

The hunt.

Stalking their prey.

Killing their prey before their prey was even aware that they were there.

They were not used to having to stand against their prey as equals.

"You're right about that, Declan," Jenus admitted. "Still, not much of a challenge."

Declan didn't argue with the gladiator. They had all fought in the Pit against all manner of monsters and men. They had all survived. And thanks to their discipline and training, they were demonstrating to the Wraiths that without the advantages the Murk provided them, these monsters in the mist were no better than any other opponent they had faced on the white sand.

Declan grinned proudly. All credit to Jakob for getting here in time and sharing the knowledge that allowed them to challenge the Wraiths in their own environment.

In addition to seeing in the Murk as if the grey wasn't even there, the Talent gave Declan a broad view of the battlefield, and he was pleased by what he observed.

The ferocity of the Wraith attack had died down where he stood on the right flank. With so many of their brethren lying dead and dying, the Wraiths were forced to confront a situation they had never experienced before, and they had yet to figure out what to do about it.

Sensing an opportunity, Declan issued a sharp command.

"Blood Company, advance ten yards!"

The gladiators responded immediately, glad to finally have the chance to attack.

As a single unit the shield wall pushed forward, stepping over the emaciated bodies at their feet, spears shooting over the shoulders of the shield bearers as they forced back the Wraiths who dared to stand against them.

The Wraiths fought with a desperate savagery. Even so, they were shocked that their adversaries were advancing, never anticipating the maneuver.

The monsters in the mist tried to hold their ground, but they couldn't.

The wall of steel was too strong. The Wraiths' will wavering.

Having reached the position that Declan ordered, the Blood Company halted its push forward and formed a new line.

For several seconds, the Wraiths forced to scramble back during the gladiators' advance didn't know what to do. Just as Declan hoped.

He issued another order, grinning as he did so, knowing that his gladiators were going to enjoy this next part. "Shield wall to teams! One minute!"

The defensive line broke apart in an instant. A spear or a sword partnered with a shield bearer, each team sprinting in silence toward the flat-footed Wraiths, intent on the kill and creating as much havoc as they could in the allotted time.

In the first few seconds of the attack, twenty Wraiths fell before the monsters in the mist realized that they needed to find a new way to defend themselves. But by then it was too late, the gladiators cutting through the Wraiths' ranks with ease.

All of the gladiators counting to sixty seconds in their heads, as soon as the minute was up they disengaged from the Wraiths, trotted back to their original position, and reformed their shield wall.

"Thank you, Declan," Jenus said, once again anchoring the center of the Blood Company's line. "I needed that."

"We all did," Declan replied. "Now be ready for the next chance."

~

"How much longer?" Aislinn asked. Spheres of white-hot energy shot from her hands, targeting a fist of Wraiths who were seeking to break through the Northern Guard's shield wall.

The orbs, no larger than a child's ball, burned to a crisp those Wraiths unable to skip out of the way, their greyish-white flesh charring and flaking away as they died.

Rafia lifted her arms so that they were parallel to the ground, sparks of energy dancing around her fingertips. When she whipped them toward the ground, lightning bolts blasted down through the fog, incinerating the Wraiths who were attacking the center of the line, behind which she, Aislinn, and Bryen stood, all three using the Talent to aid the soldiers wherever needed.

"Not long," she replied, pleased with the success of her latest work. The Wraith advance ground to a halt after her strike. "This is new to them. They likely have yet to meet a foe who has challenged them as we are."

"Then let's see if we can force them into making a faster decision," Bryen suggested.

The blades at each end of the Spear of the Magii glowing with a blinding intensity, he spun the weapon faster from one hand to the next, a glowing circle of white streaks appearing before him.

Rather than picking his targets as he would usually do, he had another goal in mind. Bryen sought to capture the attention of the Wraith Lord. To do that required a tactic that Declan had taught him just days upon setting foot in the Pit.

Shock and awe.

He did that now, using the Talent rather than steel.

Bursts of energy shot from each of the blades as he shifted his focus from the left flank to the center and then all the way to the right. Wherever the sizzling shards struck, a Wraith died.

Then, just to make sure that the Wraith Lord didn't miss the point that he was trying to make, Bryen sent streaks of power arcing through the sky, all of them targeting the leader of the Wraiths who stood several hundred yards behind the line of battle, a phalanx of guards surrounding him.

The energy hurtled down with a shriek, only seconds away from destroying the Wraith Lord, when a simmering shield of black appeared right above the small group.

The Talent struck the barrier with a resounding thunder, the ground shaking because of the force involved when the two competing energies met.

Bryen didn't expect his attack to destroy the Wraith Lord.

He used it as a test instead, judging his adversary's strength in the Curse.

The Wraith Lord could call upon a massive reservoir of that tainted energy. That only made sense since the monster was inextricably tied to the Murk.

Yet that also was a weakness, and one that Bryen meant to exploit at the right time. When the Wraith Lord wasn't in a position to defend himself and his Wraiths as he was doing now.

Bryen would have to wait a little while longer for that, however, and it seemed that they would need to put in play the strategy that he and Jakob had discussed just an hour before since the Wraith Lord had not yet come out to play.

That was all right. He would be ready.

He smiled ever so slightly as the Wraiths all along the line pulled back, giving the defenders of Shadow's Reach time to regroup and enjoy at least for a few minutes the fruits of their labor.

Until the Wraiths attacked again.

Although Bryen hoped that resolving this clash wouldn't come to that.

"You have failed," the Wraith Lord hissed.

His displeasure at having to defend against the attack from the Magus with the glowing spear was quite evident in his flashing black eyes and the fury that radiated out from him in waves, his closest target the creature standing next to him.

"Not yet, Lord," the Wraith Hunter replied. "A setback only. More luck than skill from the human."

He did not want to admit defeat. Not yet. If he did, he would have to pay the ultimate price. And he was not yet ready to do that.

Their prey demonstrated a skill and resilience within the Murk that he had never anticipated. He was certain it had to do with the Magii who stood with the defenders of Shadow's Reach. But there was nothing that he could do about them in that moment.

The Wraiths had attacked the humans multiple times and had gained no ground, failing to break through the steel barrier that stretched across the plain. Even when he sent his Scouts around the flanks, they achieved nothing.

If it wasn't the soldiers holding both sides with a ferocious intent, it was the cursed Magii using the Talent to prevent his Scouts from getting in behind the humans and causing chaos.

If his Scouts could do that, just once, the Wraiths would sweep through the humans from the rear, destroying their formation, hunting them down as was their wont and practice.

But they hadn't, and that goal seemed more and more unlikely.

Every Wraith attack failed.

And with every attack more Wraiths died.

The battle had ground to a halt as a result.

A stalemate.

And now one of the Magii actually had the audacity to attack the Wraith Lord. An insult of the highest order.

"The Wraith who is not a Wraith still lives," the Wraith Lord murmured. "I can sense him in the Murk. Many of our Scouts lie dead at his feet."

"You can sense him?" The Wraith Hunter hadn't known that was possible.

"I can. He is touched by the Talent. Thus his ability to move in the Murk like a Wraith."

The Wraith Hunter nodded, understanding quickly. "The boy has given the skill that he has in the Murk to those fighting with him. That is why we have not defeated them yet."

"Correct," the Wraith Lord replied. "He and the Magii are why these humans still breathe."

"He is the key, Lord," the Wraith Hunter agreed. "Kill him and the defense will crumble. The city will be ours."

"He is one human."

"He is the key, Lord," the Wraith Hunter repeated. "If I kill him, the humans will waver. They will be unsure of themselves. And then, while they struggle to understand what has happened …"

"I destroy the Three Magii and our Scouts hunt unimpeded in the Murk once more."

"Exactly, Lord," the Wraith Hunter confirmed with a respectful nod.

"Pull the Scouts back," the Wraith Lord ordered. "Let us see if we can give you the combat that you so desire. As soon as you kill the boy, I will kill the Magii aiding him."

24

STRONG STAND

The defenders of Shadow's Reach stood fifty yards from the Wraiths. Despite the distance and the swirling, blinding grey, they viewed their adversaries clearly.

They could only assume that the Wraiths could see them with the same clarity, Bryen reporting that the Wraith Lord was using the Curse in the same way they were the Talent in an effort to even the odds on the battlefield, hoping to give his Scouts a greater chance of success against a shield wall that had yet to bend much less buckle.

"Do you think this is a wise idea?" Bryen asked.

Jakob stood right next to him. "Probably not."

"And you still want to take this risk?"

Jakob didn't reply right away, Lycia, who stood only a few feet away from him, catching his eyes. Rather than giving him the look that he expected, one that told him that he was acting the fool, her expression was grim instead. She nodded.

"It's worth the risk," she murmured quietly.

Jakob smiled. Lycia trusted him. And if she trusted him, then he needed to trust in himself.

"I do," he replied. "Events are moving as we want. There's no reason to get in their way now."

Bryen nodded, expecting nothing less from the young man who had claimed the Highlands for the Highlanders. Fitting, he thought, two reluctant revolutionaries working together.

"Then get ready. Here they come."

Two Wraiths stepped out in front of the other monsters in the mist, gliding across the ground and stopping when they were no more than twenty yards away from the shield wall.

"You have fought well."

Bryen assumed that the creature who spoke was the Wraith Lord. He looked little different from the other Wraiths except for the cloak of grey and white hanging from his shoulders. Thanks to the Seventh Stone, however, he sensed the Curse surging through the Wraith.

"And we will continue to fight," Bryen replied. "Have no fear of that."

The Wraith stared at Bryen for several seconds, his words aggravating the leader of the Horde. Rather than reveal his annoyance, the Wraith Lord took in everything about the spear-wielding fighter, Bryen standing out in front of the shield wall, Lycia and Jakob with him. The Wraith Lord nodded upon observing the blades of the Spear of the Magii glowing softly with the Talent.

"You are one of the Magii."

"I am," Bryen replied.

"Know that you live only because I have not yet deigned to kill you. Enjoy what little time you have left."

Bryen smiled at that, feeling as if he was right back in the Pit, his opponent attempting to intimidate him. Distract him so that he could attack when Bryen least expected it.

Less than impressed by the Wraith Lord's games, Bryen kept the snort of laughter that wanted to escape from doing so. Before he did what he needed to do, Bryen wanted to give Jakob the chance to fix a memory into the Wraiths' minds that they would not soon forget.

"That's very kind of you."

"Do you mock me, Magus?" the Wraith Lord demanded.

"I take it that you are the Wraith Lord?"

"I am. The Horde answers to me."

"A much smaller Horde now than when this battle began."

Bryen offered the taunt with a straight face, although he smiled when he saw how the Wraith Lord scowled in response.

"You seek to challenge me, Magus. That is not very wise."

"I will challenge you when the time is right, Wraith." Bryen nodded toward the creature standing a few steps behind the Wraith Lord. "Why don't we move this along. You and I are not yet the main event."

"Perceptive," the Wraith Lord replied, nodding, pleased that his adversary was not a fool. "I will make you an offer."

"What would that be?" Bryen asked, already knowing with what the Wraith Lord sought to tempt him.

"Send out the Wraith who is not a Wraith. If he wins, we will return to the Wyld."

"And if he doesn't win?"

The Wraith Lord smiled at that. "Then you and the other Magii leave this fight and we will allow the humans with you to return to their city. We will give them three days to prepare their defenses before we come. You have my word."

"So that you regain the advantage you have in the Murk?"

The Wraith Lord shrugged, then grinned evilly. "A fair bargain."

"And if the Wraith who is not a Wraith fails, you believe that I and the other Magii will adhere to this bargain?"

"You will ... or you won't. Either way, the Wraith who is not a Wraith dies."

Bryen smiled again. It was quite obvious that the Wraith was lying. He had seen it many times before on the white sand.

Try as he might, the Wraith Lord could not hide the deception that he sought to employ, his pure black eyes sparking with anticipation giving him away.

"We accept your offer," Bryen replied, "so long as the Wraith who is not a Wraith wishes to take up the blade."

"I more than wish it," Jakob stated in a strong voice, his desire and confidence clear in his tone. "I welcome the chance to kill the Wraith Hunter."

Jakob gripped Lycia's shoulder warmly, taking strength from her nod of support and the message in her eyes that was only for him, then stepped past Bryen, moving toward the two Wraiths. His stride measured. His gaze strong.

"Bold words, Wraith who is not a Wraith."

The Wraith Hunter stepped past the Wraith Lord at a nod from his Master. Finally he could do what he had been waiting so long to do. He would kill his tormentor. Then his Master would unleash the Curse upon the Magii at the exact moment his steel sliced across the boy's throat. When those three died, so would the humans' ability to resist the Wraith Horde.

"Not bold if they prove true." Jakob stopped just a few yards away from the Wraith Lord's second in command.

He had come up against the Wraith Hunter before, escaping him in the Murk. Shaming him. Putting his position within the Horde at risk.

He hoped that the history between them would chip away at the clarity the combat between them would require. If the Wraith allowed his emotion to reign, Jakob could make use of the advantage gifted to him.

Growling in anger at the perceived slight, the Wraith Hunter lunged at Jakob. One dagger stabbed toward his gut. The other followed right after the first, the Wraith anticipating where Jakob would move so that when his initial attack failed he would cut across Jakob's throat with the second blade.

A quick, very immediate end for the Wraith who is not a Wraith.

But Jakob didn't act as the Wraith Hunter anticipated. Rather than dodging out of the way, he rushed toward the Wraith, closing the distance between them swiftly, the Wraith Hunter's surprise visible in his eyes.

Then, instead of standing tall, Jakob slid across the ground, his feet slamming into the Wraith's legs and flipping the monster in the air. At the same time, Jakob slashed with the dagger in his left hand, the tip of the blade cutting across the Wraith's thigh and leaving a long, thin streak of red in its wake.

Rather than continuing his attack, Jakob pushed himself back up and held his ground, watching as the Wraith Hunter scrambled to regain his feet.

The Wraith Hunter's anger was plain for all to see. Jakob had drawn first blood. No more than a narrow slice, but enough to remind the Wraith Hunter that this wasn't the first time that the Wraith who is not a Wraith had cut into his flesh.

"You believe that you can win the Dance of the Daggers, Wraith who is not a Wraith?"

Jakob gave the Wraith Hunter a grin designed to irritate him. How his adversary's eyes narrowed confirmed that he succeeded. "I already have. Many times. How else do you think I earned your weapons? How else did I become the Wraith who is not a Wraith? You have hunted me, but you have not killed me. While I have killed every Wraith you have sent against me."

Jakob had hoped to aggravate his adversary even more. Perhaps even stoke his fury and push him into a rash decision. It didn't happen.

The Wraith Hunter's expression became thoughtful instead, although the anger remained just beneath the surface. Then he nodded. "You should be proud, Wraith who is not a Wraith. No one has ever done as you have done. But as is the way of the world, your luck will come to an end."

"And what if it's not luck?" countered Jakob.

Before the Wraith Hunter could offer a response, Jakob was on him.

For the next several minutes, there was nothing but movement and silence except for the shriek of steel sliding against steel. Several times Jakob used the manacles on his wrists to deflect a strike so that he could bring his dagger around more quickly and not allow the Wraith Hunter to gain the momentum in what was proving to be a very even contest.

Jakob gained more than just a few wounds for his efforts, although nothing debilitating, as did the Wraith Hunter. Until finally, after a flurry of activity that was so fast that neither man nor Wraith could track it, they were chest to chest, the Wraith Hunter looking down with his pure black eyes at Jakob's green, their blades locked together. Neither willing to move because neither was yet ready to step back.

"Your end comes, Wraith who is not a Wraith. You thought that you could escape me, but you can't. I will bury my blade in your heart when we are done."

"Have no fear," Jakob grunted. The Wraith Hunter was tall and thin, yet he was also quite strong, and he was using his greater height to push down on Jakob and hold him in place. "I have no desire to escape you now."

"That is foolish of you, Wraith who is not a Wraith," the Wraith Hunter hissed, the strain of what he was doing revealed by the vein that pulsed on his forehead.

"Why?" Jakob dug his boots into the rough ground, understanding that he wouldn't be able to hold off the Wraith Hunter for much longer. Needing just a few more seconds.

"Because I'm going to kill you now. I will wipe away my shame. This hunt has continued for far too long."

"You're certain that you can kill me?"

"I am," the Wraith Hunter replied, his confidence growing as Jakob began to bend backward at the waist.

"Why do you believe that?"

"Because no one has escaped me," the Wraith Hunter grunted, pushing even harder with his blades, seeking to force the adversary who had haunted him for so long into a mistake. "Ever. And no one ever will."

"Except for me," Jakob replied. He gave the Wraith Hunter the grin that had so irritated him before, watching his expression work its magic once again, the Wraith's eyes flashing with anger.

"Except for you," the Wraith Hunter admitted.

"Then let's finish this, you and I," Jakob said. Before he finished speaking, he was falling backward.

Surprised by Jakob's action, the Wraith Hunter tried to stand tall, pulling his daggers back as he attempted to set his body in the dirt.

He couldn't. He was strong, but in what Jakob was doing now, the Wraith Hunter's tall and thin frame worked against him.

Jakob dropped one of his daggers and with his free hand grasped the Wraith's greyish white leather armor.

Because of his body's momentum as Jakob fell backward, and the fact that he got his legs beneath the Wraith Hunter, his boots kicking into the monster's gut and earning a loud oomph for his efforts, the Wraith flipped in the air.

Jakob stayed with him, refusing to let go. Crushing the breath from the Wraith when the creature landed heavily on his back.

Before the Wraith Hunter could gasp for air, Jakob punched his dagger through the bottom of the creature's jaw, the Wraith convulsing before falling still when the tip of Jakob's steel pierced his brain.

"THE COMBAT IS OVER." Bryen's strong voice carried easily in the silence that draped itself over the plateau upon the death of the Wraith Hunter. "You will return to the Wyld as you promised."

The Wraith Lord studied the Wraith who is not a Wraith. The young man standing over his former lieutenant. Bloody haladies in hand.

It seemed that he would have to be the one to kill this troublesome human who moved in the Murk like a Wraith.

But that would have to wait. His strategy remained in play despite the boy's surprising success.

"I think not."

Bryen shook his head in mock disappointment. "Why am I not surprised?"

"It is the way of the world, Magus. I will do and say whatever is necessary for my Wraiths to thrive. For our domain to grow."

"Even break your word?"

"My word means little when given to a human."

"I assumed as much," Bryen replied. "Let's be done with this. Do your worst."

"I will. You and those with you will pay the price for your recklessness. For not understanding the strength of the Wraiths and the power of the Murk."

With the Seventh Stone, Bryen sensed the tremendous amount of the Curse that flowed through the Wraith Lord. The leader of the Wraiths was pulling on the corrupted energy contained within the Murk itself to add to the power that he controlled on his own.

Just as Bryen wanted him to do.

Therefore, he didn't try to stop him. Instead, he waited for the moment that he knew would come.

The grey mist around the Wraith Lord began to spin. Slowly at first. Then faster and faster. Until a tornado made of the Curse twisted right above the Wraith Lord, growing larger and larger as the monster drained the Curse from the Murk.

Just a heartbeat later, the Wraith Lord pointed toward Bryen, sending the tornado that was now a hundred feet in height and spinning with a terrifying speed, directly at him.

As the whirlwind dipped down toward him, Bryen stood strong, feet rooted to the ground. He spun the Spear of the Magii slowly from one hand to the other, studying the Wraith Lord's creation.

The tremendous power contained within the tempest created a tumultuous wind that increased in intensity, whipping through the tall grass, sucking in the dirt, and tugging at the soldiers arrayed behind Bryen as the Wraith Lord forced his creation closer and closer to him.

Yet despite the funnel of corruption seeking to consume him, Bryen still didn't move. He was the bait for a few seconds more, the Wraith Lord so focused on him that he paid no attention to Rafia and Aislinn.

Calling on the Talent, they combined their strength, forming a barrier of gleaming white that shimmered into place right above Bryen and the other defenders of Shadow's Reach.

The tornado struck the shield with its full force. For a brief period of time, there was nothing but darkness, the swirling Curse spreading out across the barrier, seeking to break through, trying to swallow the energy that challenged it.

The shield held strong, however, Jakob adding his strength in the Talent to Aislinn's and Rafia's construction so that it blazed so blindingly bright that the Curse actually flinched, burning away at the fiery touch of the uncontaminated natural magic.

Feeling the pain of the power upon which he relied, his entire body prickling as if he was being jabbed by millions of needles again and again and again, the Wraith Lord realized his mistake.

Seeking to correct his error as quickly as possible, he attempted to pull back the Curse.

His eyes widened in disbelief, mouth dropping open in shock.

The Talent that formed the shield had latched onto the Curse, tendrils of white shooting out and stabbing into the corrupted energy, refusing to let go.

The Wraith Lord couldn't comprehend what was going on.

Giving in to his nature -- his need for dominance, his need to demonstrate nothing but strength -- he did the only thing that came to mind. He pulled in even more of the Curse from the Murk, siphoning it into the funnel cloud. Believing that he could overpower the Magii because nothing could stand against the energy contained within the smothering grey.

That's when Bryen struck, sensing what the Wraith Lord was doing, the grey of the Murk becoming whiter, more diluted, as the Curse was drained from it. Trusting that Aislinn, Rafia, and Jakob could keep the Wraith Lord busy for a few seconds more, he called on the power contained within the Seventh Stone.

Understanding the consequence of the Wraith Lord weakening the mist, rather than taking into the Seventh Stone the Curse that still remained within the Murk, Bryen attacked it instead. Raising the Spear of the Magii above his head, the weapon flashing brighter than the sun, he slammed one of the blades into the ground.

That action released the energy contained within the Giant-crafted weapon, a blinding flash of white light blasting out in all directions and burning through the weakened Murk. An ear-splitting shriek accompanied the destruction, the pulse of energy consuming the grey, an unstoppable surge of power racing to the east and west, destroying the substance that nourished and protected the Wraiths.

In a heartbeat, the Murk above the battlefield disappeared, the bright rays of the sun shining through.

The soldiers and the gladiators cheered, rejoicing in the victory. The walls of Shadow's Reach visible behind them.

The Wraiths suffered as the cleared channel expanded and lengthened for as far as the eye could see.

Shocked, trying to understand how he could have miscalculated so badly, the Wraith Lord covered himself with the Curse as quickly as he could, hissing at the brief touch of the sun. His flesh scalded, the skin flaking off from his arms and his legs, his leather armor sizzling. A reminder that beyond the Murk only pain and death waited for his Wraiths.

Forgetting his dignity, the Wraith Lord ran back to the safety and comfort of the Murk, the Curse protecting him.

The many Wraiths caught out in the light were not so lucky. Unable to protect themselves and not fast enough to return to the safety of the Murk, the creatures collapsed in the long grass, shrieking in agony, the harsh rays setting them ablaze, turning them into piles of ash.

Bryen ignored the devastation occurring in front of him, continuing his work with the Seventh Stone, doing much as he did when he rebuilt the Weir in Caledonia. In just a few minutes, he burned away the Murk, expanding the channel until it was a hundred yards wide.

Then, employing the advice given to him by Viktor Keldragan and Mikalya Benewyn – two of the Ten Magii whose essences were tied in perpetuity to the Seventh Stone, he ensured that what he crafted was less a barrier and more a magical wrinkle.

The Wraith Lord could not send the Murk back across the open ground.

Bryen creating a dead space.

He didn't release his hold on the Talent until he was certain, watching as the Murk at the instigation of the Wraith Lord attempted to reclaim the territory it had lost. No such luck for the Wraith Lord.

The instant the grey sought to pass through the channel, it flared then dissolved, the Talent Bryen infused into the ground doing the deed.

What he had done eliminated the Wraiths' ability to move southward.

Not convinced, the Wraith Lord tried again. Then again. And again. Pushing the grasping grey toward the open space.

Each time the Murk failing. The slightly charred Wraith Lord's efforts proving futile, the space now a killing field for the Wraiths' source of sustenance and protection. A trap. And a guarantee.

Bryen nodded in satisfaction, quite pleased with what he had done. The Talent laced into the ground would remain inactive unless the Curse contained within the Murk approached. As soon as the smothering grey attempted to cross, the natural magic would come to life, sparking through the tainted energy and keeping the space clear.

Destroying the Curse.

From one coast to the other.

Preventing the Wraiths from advancing any farther to the south.

"What you have done won't hold forever," the Wraith Lord snarled from the very edge of the Murk, refusing to step beyond the grey even with the aid of the Curse. "We will gain our revenge."

"You're right, but it will hold for now," Bryen replied, "and that's all we need to ensure that the Territories remain free."

"We will not stop coming," the Wraith Lord warned. "These will be our lands. They are meant to be ours."

Bryen smiled as he walked across the battlefield until he was no more than a few yards from the Murk, the Wraith Lord standing right in front of him. "So you say. But it will take centuries for what I have done to weaken to the point where you will be able to cross. By then I will have found a better solution. You will never have these lands. That I promise you."

"We are patient. We will never stop trying. We will have what is ours." Yet even as the Wraith Lord made his promises, he found it hard to believe his own words.

Bryen stared at the Wraith Lord, nodding, believing him, and reaching a decision at the very same time. "When you do finally breach this barrier, I will be here. Waiting for you. We can begin our combat again and see who lives and who dies."

The Wraith Lord did not respond, his eyes blazing with a black fire. His growling deepening. His anger knowing almost no bounds.

Rather than offer a useless threat, the Wraith Lord turned and disappeared within the Murk, his Scouts following him.

Disappointed.

Embarrassed.

Defeated.

For just a heartbeat, Bryen considered entering the Murk himself and continuing the fight. Seeking to weaken the Wraith Horde even more so that it would offer little threat to anyone for centuries to come.

He chose not to. Better to savor today's victory and then prepare for the next battle to come.

Just as Declan had taught him.

25

AN END THAT'S MORE BEGINNING

"Y ou heard?" asked Lycia.

Upon arriving in Shadow's Reach on Arabella's back, despite the urgency pressing down upon them after their clash with the Skath atop the Stone, she and Jakob put aside their search for the artifact that could be joined to the Blood Ruby. Instead, heading out into the Murk. Giving precedence to the more immediate threat presented by the Wraith Lord and his Horde.

That victory complete, they returned to the Shadow Keep with all speed.

A major challenge remained.

To address it, Jakob needed the Blood Dagger.

And even though Jakob had never been in the Shadow Keep, he led Lycia unerringly through the maze of passageways. He could sense the Blood Dagger, the intensity of his connection increasing with every step he took, the jewel hanging around his neck growing warmer as they drew closer.

"Heard what?" Jakob asked. He was distracted. His thoughts on the weapon that he was seeking.

"Bryen and Aislinn will be staying in the Territories. The Isle of Mist specifically."

"Why there?" He turned right where two corridors met. They were almost there.

"They assume the people who took refuge there will be moving back to the Highlands or one of the other Territories. They're hoping for some solitude."

"I would enjoy much the same," he admitted, turning left at the next junction. Not much farther now. "But I don't think Duff will allow it."

Lycia laughed softly. "That he won't. I'm sure that he's got months of work already lined up for you once we get back."

"More like years." Jakob gave her a knowing grin before shifting his focus back to the trail he was following, turning right before stopping in front of a large door that reached almost all the way to the ceiling.

Lycia noticed his reaction, not understanding. "What?"

"We," Jakob mused softly.

Lycia smiled as well, then punched him softly in the arm. "Focus. We already lost a good bit of time because of the Wraiths." She nodded toward the door. "This is it?"

Jakob answered with his own nod. He turned the knob and pushed, the door opening on silent hinges.

They waited a few seconds before entering. Giving in to a habit. Not having any desire to rush into a space with which they were unfamiliar.

Kendric's office, they assumed. Flickering candles set along the wall illuminated the large, comfortable chamber with a warm glow. The seal of the Northern Territory was carved into the headrest of the chair set behind a long table covered by various papers and just as many daggers.

In fact, taking a quick glance at the walls, except for the couches and chairs set near the cold fireplace, there seemed to be little else but daggers.

"Is it here?" Lycia asked as she ran her eyes across all the sharpened steel. Impressive. Likely some very expensive and sought-after pieces in the collection, many of them appearing to be quite old.

"It is," Jakob confirmed. He felt it at the very edge of his consciousness. But where?

Allowing the Blood Ruby to guide him, Jakob approached the wall of daggers behind Kendric's desk. He ignored all of the other blades, his gaze fixed on only one.

Or rather where one of the daggers should have been, a gap in the center of the wall staring right back at him.

"It should be here. I can feel it. But ..."

"But what?" asked Lycia, who stepped up next to him.

Jakob didn't respond right away, a chill rushing through his body as the Blood Ruby went cold against his skin.

Not thinking, just doing, Jakob grabbed Lycia around the shoulders and pulled her away from the wall, taking them both tumbling over the desk, knocking clear daggers and sending pieces of paper fluttering into the air as they rolled off the edge and landed in a tumble on the other side.

They had hoped to claim the Blood Dagger before the Skath arrived. It wasn't to be. The battle against the Wraiths allowing the Ancient One's Disciple to claim the artifact first.

"You are too late." The Skath spat the words out from beneath its cowl, only his long, clawlike hands visible. And in one the monster held a uniquely designed dagger. Three foot-long blades crafted into a single weapon, an empty slot in the steel grip.

"And you missed," Jakob taunted, he and Lycia already back on their feet.

The Skath had leapt down out of the shadows that hid a small alcove built into the beams running above the chamber, missing them both with its razorlike digits by only a hair because of Jakob's quick reflexes.

"I will not miss again," promised the Skath. "I have one artifact. I will take the other now."

The Ancient One's servant glided more than leapt atop the desk, swiping with its free claw. Hoping for a lucky strike.

Jakob and Lycia darted back before the slash struck home, Lycia drawing her swords from the scabbard across her back, Jakob pulling free his haladie. Then they each took a few steps to a different side. Moving away from one another. Giving the Skath two targets rather than just one. Wanting to make the monster's task more difficult.

The Skath reached toward Jakob, but it was only a feint. Turning swiftly to face the gladiator, the Skath twisted his towering frame just in time, the steel sliding past rather than through his body.

Believing that the Skath would make a play for Jakob first, Lycia had lunged with a sword, seeking the creature's vulnerable back. Her eyes widened in shock at how easily the Skath evaded what should have been a debilitating blow.

Lycia tried to halt her progress, not wanting to leave herself open to a counterattack. She wasn't fast enough, but she did have the foresight to raise her other sword just enough so that the Skath's claw struck her steel rather than taking her head from her shoulders.

The blow was so vicious and so powerful that Lycia lost her weapon, the blade flying from her grasp.

She had never relinquished one of her swords. Ever.

Rather than reaching for the blade that clattered to the floor a few feet in front of her, which would bring her even closer to her attacker, she ducked dand then rolled to the right, avoiding another of the Skath's slashes.

She ducked and rolled again, this time in the opposite direction, avoiding the Skath a third time and ending up right next to her blade. She picked up her steel and began to turn, hoping that she could defend herself in time.

Twisting back around, Lycia realized her mistake. She should have left her blade where it lay and continued to move.

The Skath was too fast for her, the monster's claw about to rip into the flesh below her ribs.

Clenching her teeth to prepare for the excruciating agony that she believed was coming her way, instead she gave a start, watching with a mixture of pleasure and relief when the Skath reared back instead, hissing in pain.

Jakob had gotten there just in time. His Talent-infused haladie sliced across the Skath's claw, cutting off two of the creature's razor-sharp digits. Yet rather than blood, a wispy black drifted out from the wounds.

Not having the time to consider what that substance was – a physical manifestation of the Curse or something having to do with the Spirit World -- Jakob continued his attack, slicing and slashing with his double-bladed daggers.

He wasn't foolish enough to believe that he could kill the Skath even with the Talent radiating from his steel. He was simply trying to force the monster away from Lycia. And he succeeded, the Skath gliding back toward the desk.

"You cannot defeat me, boy," rasped the Skath. "You are wasting your time. Give me the artifact and I promise that I will kill you and the girl quickly."

Jakob ignored the Skath, refusing to cede the initiative, moving the creature this way and that with his fierce attack. Staying close to the monster. Not wanting to give his adversary the chance to make use of the power gifted to it by its Master. The power against which even Aloysius could not stand.

Jakob's confidence grew as he took the fight to the Skath, gaining several more strikes, wisps of black flaking away at the touch of the Talent, although nothing that slowed the Skath down.

That was until the Skath, tiring of the game, changed the tenor of the fight by leaping backward over a couch when Lycia made a play for the monster from the side. She had been biding her time, looking for the right opportunity to help Jakob. And she thought she had found it.

The Skath cackled shrilly, staring across the small divide that had opened up between them.

"You simply delay the inevitable," the Skath warned. "Better to give in. Better to accept the fate that you cannot escape."

"I will accept whatever fate has in store for me," Jakob said solemnly. "But I will not surrender to it."

"A poor decision on your part, boy. You will pay for your arrogance."

The Skath flicked its empty claw, sending a streak of black right toward Lycia.

She tried to dive to the side, but it felt like her feet were rooted to the ground. She couldn't get out of the way in time. No one could have gotten out of the way in time.

A heartbeat before the tainted energy struck, a shield of shimmering white formed right in front of the gladiator, the Curse sliding off the tilted shield and slamming into the wall at her back, dozens of daggers shaking free from their displays.

Jakob had saved her life again, and it was in that moment that she realized the truth. Steel had no effect on this creature from the Spirit World. Even steel infused with the Talent had a minimal impact.

A frustrating conclusion for her, but the right one. Not wanting to be a distraction for Jakob since only he had the power to fight the Skath, she pushed herself back to her feet and slid behind Jakob.

She would help if she could, perhaps she could serve as a distraction, but she admitted reluctantly that this was Jakob's combat to win or lose.

A realization that proved timely.

The Skath turning his full focus on Jakob, the monster sent

shard after shard of the Curse toward him. Seeking to over-whelm the Bearer of the Blood Ruby.

Jakob stood strong against the attack, joining the Talent with the energy contained within the jewel hanging around his neck, his natural magic taking on a reddish tinge along with an additional strength that he hoped would allow him to chal-lenge the Skath.

Bolts of black. Spikes as long as a lance. Snapping whips. A cloud of swirling black.

All constructs of the Skath.

All failing to get past Jakob's defenses.

Yet despite his success, Jakob understood that what he was doing could only delay the inevitable. He could not defeat the Skath with just the Talent and steel. He could not stand against the Skath even while employing the additional power granted by the Blood Ruby.

He needed to take a different approach, remembering what Aloysius had told him after fighting the Skath the first time.

But would he get the chance?

Just then, the Skath stepped back, hissing in irritation at his continuing failure. Locking onto his adversary with a glare that could freeze blood. Not certain about how to press forward.

"I'll distract him," Lycia said, sidling up next to Jakob, taking advantage of the momentary break.

"You want to be bait?" Jakob whispered angrily. "No, I won't allow it."

"Allow?" Lycia demanded quietly, her anger plain. "You don't allow. I decide."

Jakob clenched his teeth together, holding back the curses he wanted to let loose, growling in anger instead. "You know what I mean. I don't want you putting yourself at risk when there's no good reason to do so."

"It is for a good reason," Lycia replied, even as she began to move farther away from him a step at a time. "It gives you a better chance of killing the Skath."

Lycia didn't get far. Declan, who had slipped into the chamber unnoticed, grasped Lycia's arm tightly and pulled her back toward the far wall and closer to the door.

"You know it just as well as I do, Lycia," Declan said in a voice that brooked no disagreement. "We can't fight a Skath, and if we try, we'll only get in Jakob's way. Make his job harder. He'll fight for us. He won't fight the Skath." He shook his head, clearly just as frustrated as she was. "This is his fight. It has to be."

Lycia wanted to protest, desperate to help Jakob. She didn't. She heard the truth in Declan's words. Reluctantly, she allowed him to pull her back so that Jakob would have more space and only himself to worry about.

"You wish to challenge me again? And after I killed the Magus? You are a fool." The Skath chuckled softly, a raspy noise that made Jakob's teeth hurt. "You should have learned your lesson the first time. You should have run and enjoyed what little time you had left."

"I'm only a fool if I lose," Jakob countered.

"You have fought me twice and survived only because you don't know what you're doing," the Skath taunted. "You got lucky. Why would you believe that you can win now? I have the weapon that you seek. Give me the artifact and, as I said, I will make your death quick. Painless. I will not play with the girl. She will join you in the Spirit World soon after."

"A kind offer," Jakob said, his sarcasm plain for all to hear, "but I think not."

"You will die here and now, boy!" hissed the Skath, gliding across the space that separated them, his patience at an end.

"Prove it," Jakob challenged.

Reaching out with his claw, wisps of black spinning with greater speed across his palm as the Skath called on more of the Curse, Jakob did the unthinkable, yet knowing in his heart that this was the only way that he could defeat the Skath.

He couldn't kill the Skath with the Talent or steel. He couldn't vanquish the Ancient One's Disciple with just the Blood Ruby.

But there was another weapon that he could use ... if he could get it.

That desire guiding him, Jakob shot a bolt of the Talent laced with the power of the Blood Ruby from his palm. Rather than targeting the Skath, he aimed for a spot on the stone floor just a foot in front of the monster.

When the energy struck, the blast shook the chamber and rattled the entire citadel, the walls flexing before settling back into place.

Most important, Jakob's attack forced the Skath to turn away from the blinding energy.

Just for a heartbeat.

Nevertheless, that was all the time that Jakob needed.

Launching himself at the Skath, he threw the haladie in his left hand, the steel spinning through the air in a fiery white circle.

It wasn't a killing throw. But it wasn't meant to be. It was meant to distract.

And it did, the sizzling steel slicing across the Skath's claw that held the Blood Dagger, taking three of the monster's fingers, wispy threads of black drifting up. Its grip on the weapon weakened.

The Skath, focused on defending against the blast of power and then the thrown steel, grimaced in pain from the wound its prey shockingly inflicted upon it, realizing too late the real goal of the attack.

The instant Jakob placed his hand on the hilt of the Blood Dagger, a bolt of electricity erupted from the weapon.

It didn't harm Jakob. Actually, it took away his aches and his exhaustion, filling him with a welcome strength.

The shock affected the Skath much differently, however.

With a shriek of agony, the power released blew the Skath backward, the creature forced to release its hold on the Blood Dagger. Its injured claw charred and smoking, shifting slowly from substance to spirit.

The Skath struggled to push itself off the ground, hissing because of the fiery torment that began in its blackened claw and coursed through the rest of its body.

Jakob didn't hesitate, knowing that now might be the only chance he got.

Reaching beneath his shirt, he pulled out the Blood Ruby. Ripping it free from the leather strap around his neck, he slid the jewel into the notch carved out of the Blood Dagger's hilt.

It fit perfectly. And clearly it was meant to be there.

The instant the Blood Ruby locked into place, a surge of energy shot out from the grip to the tip of each blade, the steel glowing a deep red.

That energy rushed into Jakob as well, filling him with a vigor and a purpose that he had never experienced before. That he savored.

"No! Give me the artifacts! You cannot do this!"

Jakob ignored the Skath, studying the weapon in his hand.

Much like the haladie that he had taken from the Wraiths, the Blood Dagger felt right in his grip. As if it was meant to be there.

He tested the weapon's weight, relishing its light feel. He spun it around his fingers as if he had used the dagger for years, not worrying that he would slice his fingers on the three razor-sharp blades that extended out from the hilt.

Yes, this would do nicely for the task at hand.

Jakob took a second to read the words the Giants of the Rime inscribed around the notch for the Blood Ruby.

"When the darkness surrounds, the light will prevail."

Jakob wasn't sure that he understood the true meaning of the phrase, but he was fairly confident his initial assumption was correct.

Sensing the Skath back on his feet, Jakob turned. The creature hadn't moved toward him yet. Likely thinking about what to do now that it had lost both artifacts. Uncertain. Perhaps even worried.

"It will not serve you," hissed the Skath, the creature coming toward him again. The Curse already dancing across the digits of its unharmed claw. A hint of frenzy in its pitch-black eyes. "You do not understand how to use it. Give it to me, boy! Give it to me! Now!"

"As you wish," Jakob replied in a much-too-agreeable voice.

He had fought the Wraith Hunter and killed the monster.

A deserved death, Jakob believed. But he was tired of death.

That brought to mind his father. About how Jakob would have liked to have had Dougal at his side so that his father could see what he had achieved first in the Highlands and then on the plain against the monsters in the mist.

A naive wish. He understood that.

Yet though Dougal had been taken from him, Jakob had gained what his father wanted for him.

His freedom.

A chance to make his own way in this world.

And the only obstacle that could still prevent that was the Skath who had killed Aloysius. His friend and mentor.

Dougal had taught him how to close out all that was happening around him when it was time to engage in a fight.

To achieve the oneness, the quiet, the clarity of thought required to do what others couldn't do.

To move through a combat as if he wasn't even participating in it.

To see the world from the outside, even while he was on the inside.

Sharpening his movement.

Honing his instincts.

Jakob did that now.

Although he did allow one emotion to remain with him.

An emotion that was roaring through him.

That was empowering him.

His rage.

Channeling his cold anger into the Blood Dagger, he filled the weapon with the Talent, the natural magic merging with and enhancing the power contained within the two artifacts, the Blood Ruby in his grip flashing blindingly bright.

Satisfied that he had what he needed, Jakob pulled the weapon back to his shoulder and threw it at the Skath.

The Blood Dagger spun through the air, moving so swiftly that it appeared to be nothing more than a comet of red and white.

"No!" screamed the Skath, raising his claw in a futile effort to ward off the weapon. All to no avail.

The Blood Dagger burned right through the Skath's wrist and then through his entire body, the energy contained within the weapon devouring the monster's substance and spirit. When the Blood Dagger emerged from the Skath's back, the weapon continued on its path, curling around the chamber.

Jakob extended his free hand right in front of him, snagging the Blood Dagger out of the air.

Yet his eyes never left the Skath, watching in fascination and horror as the energy released by the ancient weapon ate through the Ancient One's Disciple, slowly but surely, the creature turning to ash right before his eyes.

"We are not done, Sentinel!" the Skath shrieked even as the monster burned away. "The Ancient One promised me. He promised that I could take you. I will come again for you. I will come again ..."

The Skath, once a creature more than eight feet in height, a menacing presence more ghostly than real, faded away to nothing before it could complete its threat, the last of its substance flaking away and then disappearing entirely before the falling ash made it to the stone floor.

A welcome silence settled in the chamber then.

Jakob noticed that with the Skath gone, the Blood Dagger no longer glowed red, the steel only shining because of the sunlight streaming through the window at his back.

"Do you think you killed it?" Lycia asked as she ran up to the Highlander and pulled him into her arms. He was careful to hold the Blood Dagger out to his side, not wanting one of the blades to slice into her by mistake.

"In the Natural World, yes," Declan replied. "Jakob destroyed the Skath."

He walked over to Jakob and clapped him warmly on the back, then gripped his shoulder, his expression one of relief.

Declan was familiar with the power contained within the Blood Dagger when it was linked to the Blood Ruby, the two artifacts reaching their combined true potential, becoming the weapon essential to keeping the Ancient One in his prison.

But he had never seen the artifacts used together before, never having cause while serving as a Sentinel. And there was no guarantee that the bearer of the Blood Dagger would succeed.

It was still a combat with the Skath that needed to be won, and as Declan well knew any combat could turn on a razor's edge.

So Declan had watched with bated breath. Fearful. Hopeful. Desperate for Jakob to survive. He didn't think that he could bear the pain of losing him after having just found him.

"Meaning?" Jakob asked, requiring precision. He hugged

Lycia tightly to him before finally letting her go. Although the gladiator linked her arm in his, refusing to release him completely.

"You sent the Skath back to the Spirit World," Declan explained. "You ended that monster's existence in the Natural World. The only way to destroy a Skath completely is in the Spirit World, because that's the world of its creation."

Jakob nodded, disappointed though not surprised. Nothing was ever easy, just as his father had liked to tell him time and time again. "The Skath will continue to be a threat?"

"Yes," Declan confirmed, "although I doubt we'll have to worry about that monster or any other servants of the Ancient One at least for a time. With what you just did, you weakened the Ancient One. He will not be able to send another Skath through the Rip in the Veil right away."

"Comforting," Jakob replied with a strong dose of sarcasm.

"I aim to please," Declan replied with a smile, giving it right back to him. "You've also sent him a warning."

"A warning?" Lycia asked, a hint of concern in her voice.

"Yes, the instant Jakob defeated the Skath, the Ancient One knew. He will also know how ... and who."

"So a victory, but at the same time a new challenge."

"Exactly so," Declan affirmed. "The Ancient One knows that in order to obtain the Blood Dagger along with the Blood Ruby, the two artifacts that would allow him to Rip the Veil entirely and leave the Spirit World so that he could return to ours, he must ..."

"Kill me," interjected Jakob, who was shaking his head in resignation. "I should have assumed as much."

"No good deed goes unpunished," Declan stated with a self-deprecating smile, understanding it provided little comfort.

"Not very helpful, Declan," Lycia warned.

"It wasn't meant to be." He caught Jakob's eyes. "I need you to understand that the Ancient One is a threat that puts to shame all the other perils that you've faced. The Stalkers. The Wraiths. They are nothing compared to the Lord of the Spirit World and the servants that will do whatever is required to achieve his aims."

"Again, not very helpful," Lycia said, her tone scarcely containing her anger.

"It's all right, Lycia," Jakob said, reaching across his body and gripping her arm. "Declan is speaking the truth and that's what I need to hear." He nodded toward where the Skath had been standing. "Right before the Skath disappeared, because of the connection created by the Blood Dagger, I caught a glimpse of the Spirit World. What is lurking there. What it wants."

Jakob didn't have any desire to offer more detail on the vision that had terrified him in a way that nothing else ever had before. So as Dougal had taught him, he focused less on his fear and more on what he needed to do next. "I'm assuming that you can help me with this challenge that I won't be able to escape?"

Declan nodded in gratitude, thankful that Jakob had been listening to him. Even more so that he was willing to give him the chance that he had hoped for but didn't have the courage to ask for. "I can, yes."

"Thank you," Jakob said, his flashing green eyes telling the former gladiator that his appreciation had to do with more than just Declan agreeing to assist him.

Declan nodded. Not wanting the emotions rising up within him to be revealed for all to see, he turned his attention to the weapon Jakob still held in his hand.

"I haven't seen the Blood Dagger for decades. Without it, the Skath would have killed us all. Then again, even with it, there was no guarantee that monster wouldn't have."

"You've seen the Blood Dagger before?" Lycia asked, shocked by Declan's revelation. "How could you have?" Her gaze became shrewd. "Before you were sentenced to the Pit."

Declan nodded. "Yes. When I was younger. Before I came to Caledonia."

"The Skath called me Sentinel." Jakob had been thinking about that ever since the combat concluded.

"It did."

"Dougal told me about the Sentinels."

"I'm not surprised," Declan admitted.

"You and Dougal were from Skaffa Falls."

"We were, yes."

"You and Dougal were Sentinels," Jakob continued, having known the truth for some time although not having the chance to really think about it with all the other challenges set in his way.

Declan nodded. "Yes, as Blackgards we were required to serve as Sentinels, guarding against the coming of the Ancient One."

"Then why did you leave Skaffa Falls?" Lycia asked. "I don't know much about Sentinels, only what you taught me, but I thought you were bonded to your task with the Talent."

"We are," Declan replied. "However, Dougal and I, our father as well, were given a separate charge that required that bond to be broken. Incredibly uncommon, though incredibly necessary at the time."

Jakob nodded, beginning to understand. "The Blood Ruby."

"Correct."

"Wait, you've lost me," Lycia said, waving her free hand to slow down the conversation. "You came to Caledonia because of the Blood Ruby?"

"Yes, we did," Declan confirmed. He then raised his hands to stop what he assumed were the several questions on the tips of both of their tongues. "Let me explain."

Tired from the battle against the Wraiths, he sat down on the couch behind him. Jakob and Lycia settled onto the couch across from him. Jakob still grasping the Blood Dagger. His other hand holding Lycia's.

Declan smiled. He was pleased for both of them. They deserved a chance at happiness.

"This all started because of a Magus who arrived in Skaffa Falls more than twenty years ago."

"Anisru," Jakob said with a great deal of certainty, quickly putting the pieces together, Declan already having filled him in on what had happened beneath the Shadow Keep before he and Lycia arrived.

"Yes, Anisru. She presented herself to my uncle, Henry Blackgard, claiming to be sent by the Order of the Magii because they worried that there was a traitor among the Sentinels. A traitor who sought to release the Ancient One from his prison."

"She was the traitor," Lycia offered.

"She was," Declan confirmed, "although we didn't know it then. Because we had no reason to distrust her. Her story made sense as there were a great many more stirrings in the Valley of the Dead than was usual. More and more skirmishes. The creatures of the Ancient One slipping through the Rip in the Veil and seeking to escape the island."

He shrugged. "We were fools. All of us. We thought she was there to help. She was there to ..."

"Steal the Blood Ruby and the Blood Dagger," Lycia finished for him.

Declan's eyes flashed, already tiring of the interruptions after what had been a very long day. "Would you care to tell the story then?"

Lycia smiled, slightly embarrassed, but also enjoying the hint of irritation in Declan's voice. Just like Bryen and Davin, she had specialized in getting under his skin while fighting in the Colosseum, and she was pleased that she could still do so with such ease. "No, sorry, I'll stay quiet."

"Thank you," Declan growled. Shaking his head in annoyance, he continued. "It wasn't long after Anisru appeared that the Blood Dagger disappeared. A search was conducted. The only thing that my uncle was able to conclude was that the Curse was used in the theft. Or rather Anisru helped to confirm it."

Declan pursed his lips as if he were sucking on a lemon. "Some of us had our suspicions then, but we couldn't prove them. And before we could, an attempt was made to steal the Blood Ruby. Only a quirk of luck foiled the theft. That's when my uncle called on my father."

"And my grandfather?" asked Jakob.

"Yes, just so. Dennys Blackgard. His brother, Henry, gave him an assignment that had to be carried out in the utmost secrecy, because there was no doubt that whoever had stolen the Blood Dagger continued to hunt for the Blood Ruby. With my father's, your grandfather's, help, Henry engineered a pretense that, when all was said and done, led to my father's expulsion from the ranks of the Sentinels. And, under the assumption that Dougal and I could still be threats even with our father banished, we were expelled from the Sentinels as well. The bond broken."

"You were sent away with the Blood Ruby," Jakob said. "You were charged with keeping it safe."

Declan smiled, appreciating Jakob's quick mind. "We were. My uncle thought that the best way to keep the Blood Ruby safe was to remove it from Skaffa Falls. After all, the Blood Dagger could only be used to rip the Veil and release the Ancient One back into the Natural World if the Blood Ruby was affixed to it. With the two artifacts separated, the Ancient One's plan wouldn't work. Neither artifact on its own could do what the Ancient One wanted."

"Then how did you end up in the Pit?" Lycia asked, her curiosity getting the better of her.

"Just couldn't wait, could you?" Declan grinned. "When we took ship from Skaffa Falls with the Blood Ruby in our possession, we hoped that we would be free of Anisru and whatever other servants the Ancient One had sent after the Blood Ruby. Hoping doesn't make it real, of course."

"Where did they find you?"

"Roo's Nest. Within a day of making land. We were attacked. My father, Dennys, died in the fight. Dougal and I would have gone to the other side with him if not for Aloysius."

"Another Blackgard," murmured Jakob.

"Yes, and also a Magus as you know. He knew we were coming, and he got there just in time. He saved us. He also took responsibility for the Blood Ruby. Hiding it away. But we couldn't trust in just that. Dougal and I continued to the east, hoping to lead the Ancient One's hunters away from the artifact."

"How did you escape them?"

Declan smiled then, warmly, his eyes softening. "Your mother. Kristiana."

"My mother?" For a few seconds, Jakob couldn't breathe. He couldn't quite believe what he was learning, emotions that he had locked away a long time before threatening to break free, his eyes watering just like Declan's were.

Lycia gripped his arm, seeking to support him, more than willing to share her strength.

"Your mother. One of Aloysius' former students. A young Magus. She helped us to escape and then start new lives in Tintagel."

"What happened?"

Declan's smile broadened, not responding right away, lost in his memories. "For a time, all was good. Dougal and I joined the Royal Guard, although we never revealed who we were, of course. And Kristiana continued to check in on us, making sure that we had nothing to fear from the Ancient One." Declan shrugged as if to say he couldn't really explain what occurred after that. "The more time I spent with Kristiana, the more I fell in love with her. And for some reason I still can't quite understand, she fell in love with me."

"Perhaps it was your warm and affable personality?" Lycia suggested, offering a joke and realizing as soon as the words left her mouth that she actually might have insulted Declan.

He didn't take it that way.

"Maybe so," he replied, laughing softly, still lost in his memories. "It wasn't long before we were married. We had a good life for a few years. Until we were found."

"A Skath?"

"Yes," Declan nodded, his grim visage returning in a flash. "As well as some lesser lords of Caledonia who had turned to the cause of the Ancient One." Declan caught Jakob's eyes then, wanting to make sure that the young man understood. "That's something that you need to keep in mind. Not all of the servants of the Ancient One are from the Spirit World. Just like Anisru, there will always be others willing to give themselves to the Ancient One in exchange for whatever he promises them."

"A lesson I won't forget," Jakob promised.

Declan nodded, then continued. "Thanks to Kristiana, we escaped the Skath, but not those lords. Dougal and I fought them off as best as we could, but they brought their retainers as well. Worse, Kristiana was injured during the fight against the Skath. Dougal was wounded as well, I wasn't. I told him to take her to safety while I held them off. I would catch up to them later. He did exactly as he was supposed to. But I didn't get away."

"That's why you were thrown into the Pit."

"Yes. I killed several of the lords and some of their men, but not all of them. I paid for that failure in more than just the time I spent in the Colosseum."

He leaned forward on the couch then, elbows on his knees,

kneading his hands together nervously, needing Jakob to understand. "Once I was thrown in the Pit, I had no contact with Dougal or Kristiana, and they couldn't come see me for fear that another of the Ancient One's servants would find them. Because those curs were still hunting just as their master required." Declan's voice broke for just a second. "I didn't know, Jakob. I'm sorry. I didn't know."

"Didn't know what?" asked Lycia, not understanding.

"Declan didn't know that my mother was pregnant. He didn't know that he had a son." Jakob spoke quietly, somehow adopting the calm Dougal had taught him despite his roiling emotions.

Declan nodded, thanking Jakob for his assistance, working hard to control his emotions, even as tears began to slowly run down his cheeks. "Dougal raised you as his own. And he left Tintagel not long after you were born."

"Why?"

"The Skath returned and killed Kristiana. There was nothing that Dougal could do for me. So he put all his effort into doing whatever he could for you."

Jakob closed his eyes for a few heartbeats. Not sure what he was supposed to feel. He had never known his mother. Yet still he felt her loss deeply. He smiled then, thinking about his father. Dougal did everything that was ever required of him in order to keep Jakob safe, including giving up his life.

"I'm sorry," Jakob said finally. "You lost your wife and your brother and there was nothing you could do about it."

Declan nodded, appreciating Jakob's empathy. "True, but you're here. You survived. For that, I'm thankful."

"You can tell me more about my mother?" Jakob asked.

"I can," Declan confirmed. "I'd be pleased to do so. The only woman I ever loved ... until just recently. And you can speak to Rafia as well. She knew Kristiana. She helped to train her as a Magus."

Jakob nodded. He knew very little of his mother, Dougal rarely speaking of her. "He never told me any of this."

A deep sadness swept across Declan's face before the countenance he usually wore returned. "I'm sure Dougal wanted to, but he couldn't. It was too risky. I owe my brother a debt that I can never repay." Declan caught Jakob's eyes. "The servants of the Ancient One never stopped hunting for the Blood Ruby. Now that they know you have the jewel and the blade, they'll continue to hunt you. With even more determination now that the Ancient One knows the two artifacts have become one."

"I gathered as much."

"I'm sure you did. But now you have some additional responsibilities. You are the Lord of the Highlands. You earned that title and the people living there need you. You can't escape it."

"I wasn't planning to."

"I didn't think you were," Declan said with a grin that slowly became a bit more ferocious. "However, you're also a Blackgard."

"Which means?" Jakob was almost afraid to ask, but he had to. He couldn't ignore that claim upon him.

"It means, Jakob, that you're a Sentinel in every way but ceremony. You are a Defender of Skaffa Falls. You are charged with standing against the Ancient One."

"You're asking quite a lot, Declan," growled Lycia. "Jakob Kestrel. Jakob Blackgard. How is he supposed to manage both?"

"He'll find a way," Declan said, confident in Jakob's abilities. "But I want to state unequivocally that I am not demanding anything from Jakob. The Blood Dagger joined with the Bloody Ruby are. They have bonded with you, Jakob. No one else can use them until you die. The power of those artifacts now belongs to you."

The weight of what Declan just told him felt like a boulder pressing down on his chest, and he almost needed to make a physical effort to shift the burden so that it wasn't so uncomfortable.

"I am the only one who can stand against the Ancient One. I am the only one who can ensure he remains in the Spirit World. And if he breaks free, I am the only one who stands any chance at all of defeating him."

"That's correct," Declan replied, a deep sadness filling his eyes. An energy as well, because he had a new objective.

"And how am I supposed to prepare for all that?"

"Rafia and I will teach you."

"And I'll be here with you as well," said Lycia, pulling Jakob close and giving him a soft, brief kiss on the lips. "Just to keep you humble. And to protect you. From those rash decisions you like to make. I don't want to lose you."

Jakob smiled when Lycia let him go. "You won't. I'll be at your side until the very end."

Declan smiled. "For now we have won. For now we can enjoy the days to come."

But for how long?

Because the Master of the Gladiators knew that when one story ended, another always began.

26

INTO THE WYLD

"The Wraith who is not a Wraith still lives," hissed the Wraith Lord.

He stood just beyond the border of the Wyld, the Murk moving with him. There was no human settlement for leagues. Only the small gatehouse he stood in front of. Abandoned for years. Until now.

"I never promised you that I would kill the Wraith who is not a Wraith," countered Anisru, a babe swaddled in blankets held tightly in her arms. "I promised you the chance to kill him. And I gave that to you. It's not my fault that you and your Wraiths failed."

"Do not test me, Magus. The Murk obeys me."

"That may be so," challenged Anisru, "but I obey my Master. If you wish to challenge his power, then feel free to take the risk. Feel free to see which of us is stronger."

The Wraith Lord glared at Anisru for several long seconds, noting the whispers of black that radiated out from her, curling around her. Joining with the Murk. Almost as if she could control the grey just as he could.

He could challenge her right now and be done with it. But

was it worth the risk knowing who she was? Knowing what she could do?

Probably not, the Wraith Lord decided.

"I will be watching you, Magus. Have no doubt of that."

Anisru laughed then. An unpleasant laugh. One filled with promise and pain. "And I will be watching you. Have no doubt of that."

Rather than accept her challenge, the Wraith Lord glided deeper into the Murk, beginning the short journey back to what had once been Frisia, his guard of Scouts going with him.

Anisru didn't move until she was certain that the Wraiths were well away from her new home.

She had won. She and her babies were safe. For now.

Her daughter tucked away, sleeping in the gatehouse. Her son, more difficult, held in her arms.

Not knowing where to go upon Kendric's death, she went where no one would expect her to. A place where she would be left alone. Where she could decide what she needed to do next. A place where she could raise her and Kendric's children.

How long they could remain would depend on the Wraith Lord. But she would worry about that later.

The babe began to coo.

Anisru looked down, smiled, then rubbed her nose against his. "So much to say, Sombra?" She walked back into the gatehouse, the fire blazing to ward of the chill. Her daughter sleeping soundly in her crib. "You are much like your father."

Sitting down in the chair only a few feet away from the flames, she began to rock back and forth.

"Your father was a good man, Sombra. Too good. That's why he ended as he did."

Anisru had been heartbroken when Kendric fell. For just an instant she had lost herself. She had wanted nothing more than revenge on those who had caused her so much pain.

But with Sombra's and his sister's birth only months away,

she needed to focus on them. And she promised that she would.

She would bide her time and gain her revenge. When she was ready.

"He wasn't as strong as you, but no one will ever be as strong as you."

Anisru smiled as Sombra's eyes closed, the babe finally falling asleep.

"My little one, I will teach you all that I know. You will be strong. Fearless. Like your father. But unlike him, you will understand the value of the Curse. Your father never did."

She settled back into the chair, her eyes sparking with black specks as her smile became menacing. "We live in a world of shadows, my little lord. But it is our world. The shadows are ours. They will help us. Guide us. Teach us. And we will do the will of the shadows. When the time is right, we will bring the shadows with us. We will take what belongs to us. And you will rule, Sombra, my little lord of the shadows. You will rule."

THE END

KEEP READING for two chapters from *Stealing the Light,* Book 1 in my series *Legend of the Dragon Lord.*

BONUS MATERIAL

If you really enjoyed this story, I need you to do me a HUGE favor – please follow me on Amazon and BookBub. And if you have a few minutes, consider writing a review.

Keep reading for two chapters from *Stealing the Light,* Book 1 in my series *Legend of the Dragon Lord*. Order Book 1 from my author website PeterWachtBooks.com. Also available on Amazon.

LEGEND
OF THE
DRAGON LORD
1
STEALING
THE
LIGHT
AN EPIC FANTASY FICTION SERIES
PETER WACHT

Stealing the Light
By Peter Wacht

Book 1 of Legend of the Dragon Lord

This book is a work of fiction. Names, characters, places, and incidents are the product of the author's imagination or are used fictitiously. Any resemblance to actual events, locales, or persons, living or dead, is coincidental.

Copyright 2025 © by Peter Wacht

Cover design by Ebooklaunch.com

All rights reserved. In accordance with the U.S. Copyright Act of 1976, the scanning, uploading, and electronic sharing of any part of this book without the permission of the publisher constitute unlawful piracy and theft of the author's intellectual property.

Published in the United States by Kestrel Media Group LLC.

ISBN: 978-1-950236-57-2

eBook ISBN: 978-1-950236-58-9

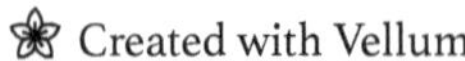 Created with Vellum

1. WORRISOME DISCOVERY

"This can't be right." Mikel frowned as he stared at the flakes of white that had hardened into ice and left several undeniable and undesired crusty shapes in their wake.

Lost in his own thoughts, he had almost missed them, never expecting to see prints such as these so far away from the jagged peaks that rose to the east.

Footprints twice the size of a man's. The same number of toes but pointed indentations that dug several inches down into the packed snow. Claws more than feet. Those talons able to rip open a man's gut with a single swipe.

"Not a good sign," he grumbled to himself. "Why would they come down from their burrows?"

Mikel snorted, shaking his head. Talking to himself again. A habit of his when he spent too much time by himself, which was a fairly regular occurrence these days thanks to his frequent trips into this frigidly cold often monochromatic landscape.

"No reason to ask," he murmured softly, answering his own question. "There's only one reason why a clan would come down from the mountains."

Adjusting the small pack that hung over his shoulder, he ignored the short sword scabbarded across his back, his hand instead drifting down to his hip. He took some comfort from the two-foot-long mace strapped there. Lightweight despite the hammer head on one end, a nasty curled spike on the other gave an experienced practitioner of the weapon a variety of options for defending himself ... or killing what required killing. Good for stabbing or slicing throats.

He knew that for a fact, having needed to do both more times than he cared to remember. Nightmares from several of those encounters ensuring that he didn't sleep for very long or very well during the cold winter nights.

Those troublesome memories had no place in the here and now, however. Better to stay in the present. Better to live with his own nightmares rather than become a victim of one of the nightmares that had decided to hunt well beyond their mountain territory.

He stood atop a small bluff hidden by snow and ice, a barely visible trail snaking its way down the side to the Barrows. For the next league, looking to the west and deeper into the Frozen Waste, he saw nothing else except for large, rectangular, snow-covered dunes that were a hundred yards wide and three times as long. Burial mounds Cadmus had explained, some containing the remains of creatures long dead and best forgotten.

There were broad paths between the mounds. Even so, when he entered the frosty ground set aside for the dead, he always stayed close to the side of a barrow and kept a wary eye.

Mikel was well aware of what to look for to avoid the death-traps hidden along those paths. Sinkholes dotted the space between the mounds. Covered only by a thin crust of snow and ice.

If you didn't die from the fall, you'd die in the pit if you didn't have the proper equipment for climbing out.

He did. Nevertheless, he had no desire to risk becoming trapped in a sinkhole, even if only for a few minutes.

Not when he was more worried about what was haunting the Barrows.

The tracks he identified, although wiped away to a large extent by the blustery wind, led in the direction he needed to go.

He shook his head in aggravation. More at himself than anything else.

Teodor had been right. His friend had argued against making the trip on his own, believing that Mikel should wait until he could join him.

It would only have been a delay of a few days. And there was other business he could have conducted on the Crux during that time.

That didn't matter, however. Despite his friend's wise counsel, he couldn't wait. Not with what he needed to do.

Mikel had made a promise.

And he always kept his promises.

No matter what those promises might cost him.

The trust placed in him too important.

It was hard earned ... and much too easily lost.

Mikel stayed where he was for a few minutes more. Wanting to get a better lay of the land. Seeking to identify anything out of the ordinary.

He didn't see anything from his perch that gave him any cause for concern. That meant very little, however. With the creature that made that imprint, he knew that he had virtually no chance of catching a glimpse of the monster before it buried a claw in him.

He needed to listen to have any chance of avoiding being caught by surprise, having little desire to be added to the cookpot.

He did that now.

Closing his eyes so that his vision didn't betray his hearing, he stood there for several minutes more. Not in a rush. Knowing exactly what he was listening for. And, thankfully, not hearing the rustle, sigh, or brief exhalation, that faint whisper or slight crunch, that meant his death approached.

Yet.

Because he had no doubt that it would only be a matter of time before he did.

Opening his eyes again, he studied the landscape of white that spread out before him. For as far as he could see, there was nothing but snow and ice. From where he stood, beyond the burial mounds that were closest to him, the environment appeared to be flat, the color and wind-swept nature of the ground hiding the rugged landscape, allowing it all to blend together.

A trick of the mind and the light.

A range of highlands extended toward the horizon to the west. In between, besides the Barrows, there were a host of perils in addition to sinkholes and monsters with razor-sharp claws that viewed human flesh as a delicacy.

That thought stuck in his mind, Mikel reached down, rubbing his right leg. It was bothering him. A soft ache that pulsed with greater intensity as he hiked down out of the mountains, his knee feeling as if it were filled with shards of broken glass.

An old injury. An aggravating injury. But not a debilitating one, and there was little else that he could do except deal with it.

Besides, there was a value to the pain.

A reminder of what could happen if he lost focus in the Frozen Waste for just a heartbeat.

Maybe he would get lucky.

Maybe the monsters had moved on, not finding any worthwhile game here.

Yes, and maybe a street rat like himself could live just below the Royal Ring on the Crux. A ridiculous notion.

He hiked a few hundred yards farther down the trail. All the while keeping a sharp ear. Just as much keeping a sharp eye out for any movement, even though he believed that if he did see something it would probably be too late.

He stopped again when he reached the bottom of the trail, standing in shadow, the first of the burial mounds greeting him.

Studying the churned-up snow at his feet, he rubbed absently at his leg and knee, seeking to reduce the pain to a more manageable level.

He realized then that his hope that the monsters already had moved off was no more than that. Just as he believed it would be.

He identified the tracks of several different beasts, their claws punching deeply into the packed snow.

Intermixed was another distinctive print that he hadn't expected to see here. Almost lost in the crush. A boot. A good bit smaller than his own.

Those tracks wound their way along the edge of the Barrows. The larger tracks followed.

Other than himself, what fool would take the risk of coming here on their own?

Everyone in the kingdoms to the south and east knew to stay clear of the Frozen Waste without the invitation of those who ruled this hard, unforgiving land.

And Mikel knew of only one human who currently had that invitation.

Even the bandits who roamed the mountains at his back stuck to the heights on the western side for the most part, having learned the hard way that the inhabitants of the Frozen Waste would be more than happy to make an example of them.

What to do about his unexpected discovery?

One person trespassing in the Frozen Waste.

The monsters of the mountains on their heels.

Mikel's own business calling to him. His discovery possibly an opportunity to avoid confronting these monstrous hunters himself.

Should he continue on his way and take a different path that led away from what would likely prove to be a bloody and gory mess?

Or should he follow the tracks and get a better sense of how many of these monsters had come down from the mountains?

Quite the dilemma.

He knew what he wanted to do.

But he rarely did what he wanted to do.

Usually he did what he thought he needed to do.

Even though that inevitably got him into trouble and made his life more difficult then he wanted it to be.

2. AN APPETIZER

Drin pushed herself up from where she crouched in the snow. Wary now. Scanning around her. Seeking any hint of movement. Any sound.

Blood.

At her feet.

A lot of it with a few pieces of tufted fur and long slices of flesh dotted with red that were already frozen still clinging to what was left of the skeleton.

When she picked one strand up between her gloves, it was so thin, so delicate, the flesh snapped in two when she applied barely any pressure.

"What could have done this?"

It had been a reindeer. She was sure of it despite the missing head. The few hoofprints she spotted in the snow confirming it for her.

"Not a polar bear," she mused. She swept her gaze once again around the sullied snow. There were no tracks suggesting one of the largest predators in the Frozen Waste was roaming close by. "So what then?"

Drin swiped her hair out of her eyes, realizing she was

doing it again. Talking to herself. A habit her father said she needed to break before she assumed her rightful place in the Kingdom.

Thankfully, with her father in excellent health, she had little cause to worry about that happening anytime soon.

Still, he was right. Talking to herself wasn't a good look when she was in line for the throne of the Crux. The First Families always looking for any hint of weakness. But she could work on that later.

Right now she needed to make a decision.

Head back the way she had come or continue on the route she had selected?

"It's a long way to go," she murmured to herself, Drin referring to the many hours and hard travel through the snow demanded of her to reach her current location.

The trail she sought that would take her back to the mountains and then home was less than an hour away from where she stood. It would save half the day. But it would lead her in the direction taken by whatever had killed the reindeer.

She decided on expediency in the place of caution. Drin took a few steps along the trail of blood that led away from the kill ground before she stopped abruptly.

She had been listening to nothing more than the whistle of the wind as it gusted through the spaces between the barrows.

Until just then.

A rustle that was different from any other noise she had heard since making her way down the trail to the maze of massive mounds teased her senses. It sounded like a snake sliding through the snow.

Without making a move, Drin searched around her, seeking any hint that might give away the cause of the noise that had set a bell of concern pounding in the back of her head. Seeing nothing but white. Hearing ... nothing except for the wind playing across the icy tundra.

Her search was made all the more difficult because she lost the sun when she left the trail, the shadows lengthening along the paths between the burial mounds. The wind growing louder in her ears.

She reconsidered her decision to come down here. To ignore her father's warnings and slip away from her responsibilities for a few days. Slip away from the person who she believed was asking more from her than she was ready or willing to give.

Drin shook her head. "Think before you do," she murmured to herself. Advice her father offered her more times than she could recall. Irritating because of its frequency. Now, useful.

The blood led off between the barrows.

That was the fastest route out.

What to do?

She needed to decide. Quickly.

This was her first time in the Frozen Waste. Admittedly, she was barely across the eastern border of the great white expanse, which began at the mountains towering behind her. Still, it was an entirely different world compared to the one she was used to. And her few hours of exploration excited her in a way that nothing else had in quite some time.

It was beautiful.

Just as she had been led to believe.

Perilous as well.

Just as the blood at her feet demonstrated.

After listening to all the stories while she was growing up, the desire to visit this strange land became an irresistible urge. In large part because she felt the need to do something that wasn't what she was supposed to do.

For as long as she could remember, she always did what she was supposed to do.

She didn't view that as a weakness.

She believed it a good thing that she took her responsibilities seriously.

Nevertheless, with all that was pushing down on her shoulders, at least for once in her life, she needed to feel ... free.

Drin really couldn't explain it in any other way.

She wasn't running away from her responsibilities. She knew what was required of her, and she accepted the burden. Gladly, in fact, understanding that the power and privilege her family enjoyed came as well with an accountability that she couldn't ignore. That she wouldn't ignore.

When she returned.

She just needed to slip away from Innsbruck for a few days and gain a brief respite from the constant pressures of her position.

She shouldn't be here. She acknowledged that now.

The Frozen Waste was forbidden unless you were invited to cross the border by the Giants of the Rime. And from what her uncle had said, the keepers of this frigid wasteland had not issued an invitation for decades. Perhaps even a century. No one could really recall the last time the Frost Lord allowed a visitor into his domain.

Which made it all the more curious to her how weapons, glass, and several other unique items were sold in Innsbruck. Items that were clearly of Giant making.

Though Drin had broken the bonds that formed the boundaries of her life if only for a few days, she hadn't broken the treaty between Innsbruck and the Giants of the Rime. She was just on the edge of the glacial, barren landscape. The border between the Frozen Waste and the Kingdom of the Crux never really decided. Neither Realm putting in the time and energy necessary to hammer out a resolution to the argument that had lasted since ... well, she really didn't know when.

Besides, her disobedience already had been rewarded. She

would need to deal with the Giants eventually. Best that she got a sense of their world before she did so.

Much of what she had seen after trekking along the edge of the Frozen Waste for only a few hours astounded her. Her lessons on what to expect not doing the captivating environment justice.

The massive barrows were only a part of it. Glaciers that reached for the sky. Frozen rivers, the ice thirty feet thick yet so clear that she could still see the water rushing below even though she couldn't hear the surge. Crevices hollowed out from the base of icy tors by the wind that polished the snow until it was blindingly bright when struck by the sun. Arches of strange and mesmerizing designs connecting the tors to create what looked like natural aqueducts. Dozens of pingos, the huge mounds of solid ice dotting the barren landscape seemingly without rhyme or reason.

She had not anticipated half of what she had seen. She had anticipated the cold and believed she was ready for it. Learning much to her detriment that she wasn't. The frosty temperature and even more frigid wind chilled her to the bone despite being bundled up in a thick, fur-lined jacket and leggings along with a hat that failed to cut the bite of the wind.

Even so, she was glad that she had taken her uncle's advice, surprising though it had been. Particularly since he was even more wedded to his duty than she was.

Having made her decision, Drin took a step down the bloody path. But no more than a step.

She didn't see anything around her. Nevertheless, she sensed that she wasn't alone.

How close her stalkers were, she couldn't say. But she was certain there were more than one.

"Think before you do," Drin repeated to herself.

Another whisper of movement to her front. Then one more at her back.

Her hunters had set the snare, and she had walked right into it.

She took a few steps to the right. There was another path there between the barrows that would lead her back toward the trail that she had taken down from the crag. The longer way home. Perhaps the only way home now.

Another dreaded whisper. This time from the west.

A shiver ran through her that wasn't caused by the cold.

Her hunters were herding her.

Either they wanted her to move in the only direction open to her or they hadn't closed the trap fast enough.

It was time to make another choice.

She heard the whisper again. Like a silk cloth being pulled across the ice.

Drin looked back over her shoulder. Maybe no more than twenty feet away based on the noise. Where could it be? She saw nothing more than the frosted side of a barrow.

No more time for thinking. There was only time for doing.

Hearing two more whispers of movement coming from both her front and back and only packed snow greeting her eyes, she selected the sole option open to her. She could only hope that there wasn't a fourth hunter waiting for her just up ahead.

She dashed off, pumping her legs as fast as she could, her boots crunching into the hardened snow as she ran between the short sides of two barrows.

The wind had returned. A blustery gale that she was running into, slowing her down. Forcing her back toward her pursuers.

She pushed even harder, hearing the movement at her back. She didn't need to look over her shoulder to know that her hunters were right behind her and closing the gap between them, the terrifying whisper of their movements replaced by a heavy crunch.

The end of the path coming up on her quickly, a deep howl that sounded much like a wolf's ripped between the barrows.

It faded quickly.

Sinkhole.

It had to be.

She probably ran right over it without disturbing the trap. But her hunters were bigger than she was, and they were heavier. That realization and the fact that they could stay with her despite the punch of the wind narrowed down what could be chasing her, none of what came to mind what she wanted to think about.

Drin picked up her pace as best as she could. The wind slacking. Allowing her to move with greater speed down the path. Unfortunately permitting her hunters to do the same.

She was less concerned about how many hunters remained. Now more concerned with finding a better spot to defend herself.

Although she had no doubt that she stood little chance of escaping, what she saw to her front gave her a very brief moment of hope.

Racing out from between the barrows, she found herself on a small plain, her hope dying quickly. A large bluff on the far side ensured that she had nowhere else to go.

Still, right in the center of the plain a fantastical ice sculpture rose several hundred feet into the sky. Her uncle had told her about these.

Marvelous creations crafted by the strange and powerful lightning strikes that often came with the blizzards that swept over this barren land. The energy blasted into the snow, throwing it into the air, the charge creating a design that froze in seconds because of the frigid temperature. What remained molded over time by the sun, cold, and wind.

Drin didn't stop to admire what waited before her. Instead, she sprinted right toward it, aiming for a spot where several of the razor-sharp branches carved of ice would offer her some protection.

She wasn't where she wanted to be, but it was the best that she could do.

She knew that she had to fight. There was no way to avoid it. At least here she could limit the number of hunters that could come at her at one time.

Skidding to a stop when she was between the razor-sharp branches, she spun back around, pulling the short sword strapped to her back in a smooth motion and ready to defend herself against whatever it was that hunted her.

Her heart froze when she identified the monsters that approached.

Peeling out of the white background behind them as they drew closer.

Their confident steps confirming that they didn't feel the need to rush. Certain that they could kill her whenever they desired.

Mikel couldn't understand why the woman was out here in the frigid wild on her own.

In a forbidden land.

Clearly having little real sense regarding the many dangers to be found in the Frozen Waste ... until some of those dangers found her.

Still, he was impressed.

The woman knew how to fight.

Short sword in hand, how she gripped the blade suggested that she had quite a bit of training.

That wasn't how she was defending herself, however.

Not yet.

Not until she had no other choice.

Instead she employed a unique skill rare in this part of the world.

Spikes of energy as well as other lethal creations made from the Talent shot from her palm. Keeping her attackers at bay for now, the position she selected ensured that she only had to worry about an assault from one direction.

A skilled fighter and a Magus.

Intelligent. Creative. Quick thinking. Headstrong as well to enter the Frozen Waste on her own without fully understanding the perils waiting for her, which suggested as well a worrisome obstinance.

A dangerous mix in his experience.

Mikel had to give the woman credit, though. She was doing well considering the challenge set before her.

She was facing off against Northern Trolls.

A fist all told, and there were more coming her way, drawn by the howls and barks of their brethren.

Mikel had fought Northern Trolls a few times before. He had never enjoyed the experience. And in each instance he had been grateful that he walked away.

Determined beasts. Cunning as well. And hungry. Always hungry.

The creatures were covered in a short but thick coat of white fur. It kept them warm in the below freezing temperatures of their homeland.

It also allowed them to blend in almost perfectly with their snow-covered environment. Quite an accomplishment since a Northern Troll was twice the size of a tall man in both height and breadth and exceedingly strong, muscles growing upon muscles.

Even their eyes were white. As were the tusks that curled up from their bottom jaw and the razor-sharp teeth that resembled fangs that were visible when they opened their short snouts to roar.

Each of the Trolls carried either a very large battle axe with a blade sharper than steel or a mace, both crafted from an ice that was harder than stone and found only in their mountain territory.

And, as the Trolls danced around her, seeking a way past her defenses, the Magus was learning that these gigantic creatures were terribly fast. Likely as well that they were strong enough to bear the brunt of her attack, knocking away with their oversized weapons the energy she sent their way.

Watching the engagement, Mikel also had to give the Northern Trolls some credit because they displayed a disconcerting cleverness. Rather than standing against the Magus' magical strikes, they used their speed to their advantage, evading her attacks more often than not. Ensuring that she did little more than tire herself out as they waited for more of their clan to arrive.

Based on how her expression had changed in just the last minute, it seemed that she had reached the same conclusion as he had.

Yet despite her difficulties and that blood-chilling realization, she demonstrated a tenacity that Mikel could only admire.

The Magus looked to be young. Maybe a few years younger than he was. And she clearly had not done her research before entering the Waste, because she had yet to figure out the best way to deal with Northern Trolls.

More than unfortunate for her. Likely a death sentence.

Once again, Mikel had a decision to make.

He could go about his business and leave the Magus to her fate. Some might even say a fate she deserved for so foolishly entering a forbidden land without the appropriate resources.

Or he could intervene.

Against a fist of Trolls.

More of the beasts coming this way.

If this was strictly a business matter, weighing the advantages and disadvantages, the decision was quite easy. Besides, he needed to get moving. He had somewhere to be.

But this wasn't just a business decision now.

There was more at stake here than money to be made or a favor to be earned.

Mikel uttered several choice curses as all the relevant variables ran through his mind and he calculated the odds of the several paths open to him as he lay atop a barrow only a few feet from the crest.

With barely a thought, relying on his instinct, he flipped himself over.

Just in time.

The massive mace crafted from ice smashed down right in the spot where he had been lying only a moment before, punching deep into the crusted snow and leaving a large hole rather than crushing his chest. The Troll who had snuck up on him from behind hissed in anger as he pulled his weapon free.

When the Troll lifted the mace above his head to continue his attack, Mikel was nowhere to be seen, having scrambled back behind the creature.

"Come on, ugly. Time for you to go to the other side."

The Troll spun around upon hearing Mikel's words. However, instead of rushing at him, the Troll held his ground. Grunting and huffing. Brandishing his weapon.

Mikel frowned. Not the usual behavior from a ravenous ...

He ducked and rolled, the huge axe crafted of ice sweeping through the space where his head had been just a second before, the blade taking a few locks of his hair rather than a large portion of his scalp.

He had just been thinking about the Northern Troll's cleverness, and his own attempt at cleverness had almost cost him his life.

And perhaps it still would, because now he stood against

two of the giant monsters, the second approaching just as quietly as the first.

He turned sideways to his opponents. They seemed more than willing to take a few seconds to study him. Not too concerned despite his discovering them before they could kill him.

He kept one eye on the Trolls while he searched the landscape at his back with a quick eye over each shoulder. Mikel hoped that there weren't any more of the creatures lying buried in the snow, waiting to take him from behind when the combat began.

He didn't think there were. All he saw were the tracks made by the two who had crept up on him and the perfectly smooth snow atop the barrow courtesy of the always blowing wind. No lumps that suggested he needed to worry about a third Troll joining the party.

That was a good thing.

Not so good was the movement to his front.

Mikel took a step back and pivoted, allowing the Troll to pass by him.

The beast missed with his axe again, the power of his swing pulling the creature off balance.

Mikel was more than happy to make use of that mistake. Trailing a leg behind him, he caught the Troll's back foot, which sent the creature sprawling when that errant back foot hit his other foot.

All the Troll was going to eat that afternoon was a face full of snow, Mikel attacking before he could push himself up.

Jumping onto the Troll's back with a knee and pushing his tusks back into the icy crust, Mikel brought the sharp blade of his mace down, piercing the back of the Troll's neck. He could have used the hammer on the other end of his weapon, but Northern Trolls had notoriously hard heads. If he didn't crush the creature's skull in a single blow, then he likely was a dead man, a result that he wanted to avoid.

The Troll flopped a few times like a fish out of water, then lay still.

Mikel pushed himself up from the creature's broad back and turned to face the other Troll. The creature hadn't moved, surprised by what he had just witnessed. Never anticipating such a result.

Wanting to take advantage of the Troll's indecision, Mikel sprinted across the top of the barrow, mace held above his shoulder as if he was planning to swing down toward the creature's hip.

Mikel's movement jolted the Troll into action. The creature raised his mace, prepared to catch the blow.

But it never came.

Instead, Mikel ducked and rolled past. In the same motion he sliced with his weapon's blade across the back of the Troll's legs.

Cut across both hamstrings, one severed completely, the other partially, the Troll dropped to his knees, bellowing in anger and pain.

The Troll was fast.

Mikel was faster, and he did much as he had to the first Troll. Slamming into the creature's back with his knees, he forced the beast's maw into the snow while also punching his blade through the back of the Troll's neck.

Two kills in two minutes. Probably less.

A good fight.

Nevertheless, Mikel wasn't happy.

Grumbling to himself, he pushed himself off the rapidly cooling corpse and turned away from the dead Trolls, the heat from the bodies drifting up into the frigid air. At this temperature, in just a few minutes they would be no more than icicles.

It seemed like his decision had been made for him.

Taking a quick look from the top of the burial mound to gauge what was happening below, he scrambled back from the lip. None of the Trolls were aware that he was above them.

Pulling free his snowshoes that were clipped to the back of his pack, he fitted them to his boots and locked them into place. He then pulled out two slim, fire-hardened boards that he fitted over the webbing on the underside of each snowshoe.

Knowing what would happen if he took a moment to think about what he was about to do, Mikel sprinted toward the lip of the barrow, mace in hand.

"You were a fool," Drin grumbled to herself as she carried on a constant commentary on her decision to enter the Frozen Waste. "Putting yourself at risk on a whim. Just because you ..."

She didn't get a chance to finish berating herself, twisting to her right side and blasting a series of short, sharp bursts of magical spikes toward the beasts inching toward her from that direction.

Against other opponents, she already would have won this combat. Few had the strength and ability to stand against a Magus.

But she was battling against Northern Trolls. And much to her consternation, they knew how to fight a Magus.

A fact that she wished she had known before she began her ill-fated journey. Because if she had known, she probably would have stayed in Innsbruck.

She had gained very little in her many attacks against the beasts other than a few superficial wounds that failed to slow down the dangerously swift giants. Learning quickly that the best that she could hope for was to buy a few more minutes to search for some avenue of escape as she struggled to keep the Trolls away from her.

Drin shook her head to clear it. There was no point in castigating herself now or reminding herself of the many mistakes she had made, in particular with respect to this clash.

She needed to focus on staying alive, and that meant ensuring the Trolls kept to her front. If one got on her flank, she was done for.

That was becoming a more difficult task as the cunning creatures patiently brought a more intense pressure to bear upon her.

She had picked a good place from which to defend herself. Three sides protected.

But she had trapped herself as well.

With the jagged spikes that guarded her, she had nowhere to go other than through the beasts who, based on the drool dripping down their tusks, viewed her as that night's meal.

What really got her goat was that her use of the Talent didn't bother her hunters in the least. The creatures not only demonstrated an admirable skill in defending against her attacks, but also feinted toward her regularly. Keeping her on her toes. Inching toward her. Tightening the noose. Soon to be in a position to strike a fatal blow.

It wouldn't be long before one of the beasts came in close and forced her to use her short sword. When that happened, the other Trolls would rush her and the fight would be over.

Both Talent and steel of little use.

And she had no doubt that moment was approaching swiftly. Several more Trolls had joined the hunt, drawn by the sounds of the combat and the calls of their brethren.

Savvy creatures indeed. The Trolls were allowing her to tire herself out.

At the same time, they made sure she had little chance of getting away from them. They were more than happy to bide their time, looking for just the right opportunity, clearly unconcerned that they hunted a Magus as they sought to push her into that single mistake that would lead to her death.

Drin was angry.

At herself for taking this risk.

For not realizing what strategy these Trolls were employing before it was too late to break free.

Even more so for not really understanding the threat these creatures presented before she entered the Frozen Waste.

Big. Fast. Dangerous. Clever.

Clearly displaying attributes she had not learned about during her training.

A lethal mix as she feared she was about to discover.

An instant later what she dreaded most occurred.

She made a mistake.

One of the Trolls on her left side had climbed the mesmerizing ice sculpture, ignoring the sharpness of the frosty limb that cut into his claws, more concerned with coming at her from the flank.

She defended herself with the Talent, targeting the branch rather than the Troll.

The blast of energy shattered the ice, sending the beast flying backward, his body riddled with bloody shards.

She wasn't done. Sensing the movement on her other side, when she swept back around to manage the Trolls pushing in on her right who sought to take advantage of the distraction provided by their badly wounded brethren, her foot slipped in the snow, taking her down to one knee.

Recognizing her peril, she could do nothing more than rely on her instincts, raising her sword to defend against the battle axe already sweeping toward her head.

Drin knew without a doubt that her efforts wouldn't be enough.

The Troll was too fast and too strong.

The beast's axe would shatter her blade then split her in two.

Right before the icy blade bit into her flesh and bone, a blur slid right by her, slamming into her attacker with a bone-crunching smack.

The collision left her rescuer just a few feet away from her while the Troll tumbled through the snow, coming to a stop when the beast slammed against the sculpture, a long shard of ice sticking out of his chest. The great weight of the Troll snapped off the branch, the creature sagging to the snow, only able to manage a soft gurgle as he died slowly, the icy lance having skewered his lungs.

Drin had less than a second to take in her unanticipated though much-appreciated champion.

He was big, almost hulking. Even so, he moved with a surprising nimbleness. Kicking off his snowshoes, he placed his back to hers.

"I'll take the right flank."

She didn't have the chance to argue, the Trolls on her side pushing toward her once again. The shock of seeing their brethren impaled wearing off quickly.

To hold them, Drin fired a continuous burst of energy at her attackers, forcing them back several steps. A few even growling in pain, unable to avoid the searing heat she blasted in their direction.

Those few seconds she earned allowed her to observe the big fellow on her other side. Despite his size, he was deceptively fast. Efficient as well. Economical and graceful in his movements and his decisions. Almost as if he'd come up against Northern Trolls before.

Forgoing the short sword scabbarded across his back, he feinted toward a Troll to his right who was trying to sneak around them.

The Troll took a deft half-step back. A natural reaction, but also one that cost him as a slice of ice from the jagged branches behind him pierced his broad back.

Mikel left his adversary gasping out a bubbly blood, the Troll dropping to his knee, struggling to breathe. Continuing his motion, Mikel spun around swiftly while bringing himself close to the snow-covered ground.

With all the strength that he could bring to bear, Mikel slammed his mace into the second Troll's knee, grinning devilishly when he heard the bone shatter followed just a breath later by a roar of agony.

Before the wounded Troll hit the ground, he was dead.

Mikel swiped with the other side of his weapon, his already bloodied blade slashing across the falling creature's throat.

One opponent eliminated, Mikel turned toward the beast with the bloody back.

The wounded Troll bellowed in rage. Ignoring the pain and the blood gushing down his back and between his fangs, the beast swung with his axe.

Mikel dodged out of the way. When the blade of ice swept past him, he kicked out with his boot, connecting with the beast's knee and bending it backward at a severe angle.

The Troll bellowed in anger again, though this time not only because of the pain of his second injury. Also because his wild swing threw him too far to the right, sending him stumbling into the icy branches on that side.

Mikel finished the Troll with a swift kick to his lower back, ensuring that the beast was fixed in place, caught on the frosty spikes that stuck out from his back in four different places, three of them fatal wounds all on their own.

Pivoting toward the Magus, Mikel ready for the next combat, the Trolls appeared to have lost interest in the fun of the hunt after losing so many of their brethren. They wanted only the kill now, and they were preparing to rush their quarry come what may.

"Target the ground in front of the Trolls!" he shouted.

Drin didn't hesitate even as she cursed herself for a fool. Sheathing her sword, she did as ordered, sending blazing bolts of energy blasting into the crust just twenty feet in front of her.

Right where the Trolls stood.

They were fast. They were strong. But they stood little chance against the power she exercised.

Particularly since the environment worked with her, the eruption of white blocking the sun.

When the gusts of wind buffeted away the snow and ice swirling in the air, several sinkholes were revealed that just needed a little nudge before giving way, taking three of the Trolls a hundred or more feet belowground.

She doubted that trio would be escaping their prison, assuming they survived the fall. Three more of the Trolls wouldn't be rising again either, their smoking and charred bodies confirming that fact.

That left only three of the beasts standing against her.

Feeling more confident after her first taste of success and with an ally covering her back, Drin decided on a different approach. Remembering what happened to the Troll who dared to climb the branches of ice, she made use of the sculpture that had offered her some much-desired protection. Using the Talent, she broke apart several of the branches above her then with a flick of her wrist sent the razor-sharp shards streaking toward the surviving Trolls.

Two died in seconds. Able to defend against a few of the icy lances though not all. The third escaped harm except for a slice across his side only because his companions bore the brunt of the attack for him.

Realizing that he was alone, wounded, and stood little chance against the Magus and the human who wielded his mace as if it was a part of his hand, the last Northern Troll turned and fled as swiftly as he could.

With the wound he had sustained, it wasn't as fast as he wanted. His gait more a staggering stumble than a sprint.

Mikel reacted with barely a thought, refusing to allow the beast to lead more of his brethren after them. Pulling a slim dagger from his belt, tip of the blade between thumb and forefinger, he flung the blade end over end through the air, the steel coming to rest in the back of the Troll's neck in much the same place where Mikel had dispatched several other Trolls at the beginning of the fight.

Nodding with satisfaction when the Troll crumpled in the snow, he kept his mace in hand as he walked across the battlefield. Checking each body to make sure they were dead. Examining the sinkholes with the same thoroughness to confirm that they had nothing to worry about from the beasts who fell through the ground. Then heading toward the Troll farthest away from them and pulling free his dagger, wiping the blade clean on the dead beast's fur before sheathing it and walking back completely at his ease, almost as if a clash against the most feared monsters of the mountains was just a normal day for him.

Stopping in front of Drin, Mikel gave the Magus an appreciative nod. For someone half his size, she certainly packed a punch. Sharp eyes matched her sharp features, and the lines around her mouth suggested that she liked to smile, although not now. Anger her primary emotion.

"This isn't a full clan," Mikel said, not put off by the Magus' close study of him. "I took down the last one so that he couldn't bring the rest this way. But I likely only bought you an hour. Best that you get moving now."

Drin heard what her unexpected ally said. She chose to ignore him. There was some aspect to the man that caught her eye, though she didn't know what exactly. And that bothered her. Usually she could read people with just a glance.

He was big. Not only tall, but also broad. Though it didn't look like he had an ounce of fat on him.

He wasn't particularly good looking. His nose broken several times and permanently crooked. His short beard failed to hide the several scars that crisscrossed his cheeks and neck. A deeper one across his brow.

Yet his smile put her at ease in an instant. Despite his very cold eyes. Colder than the gust of wind that blasted into her and turned the sweat covering her body to ice.

What was it about this fellow that made her feel like she was standing on the edge of a precipice and thinking about jumping in?

She wasn't attracted to him.

She was ...

She didn't know what she was.

Curious?

He wore clothes quite different from hers. A thin jacket unlike the bulky one that was doing very little to keep her warm. Thin pants as well, not lined with fur. Gloves. A knit cap.

All a mesh of grey, white, and blue that allowed him to blend into the environment almost as well as if not better than the Northern Trolls did.

Where did he get clothes like that?

And why was he there in the first place?

No one had permission from the Giants of the Rime to enter their homeland.

"Who are you?"

"You did hear what I said, right? You have an hour at most. You need to get moving."

"I did." Her voice took on a harder edge. "I ask again. Who are you?"

"No thank you?" He offered her a raised eyebrow. "I don't know that you would have made your way out of this mess without my assistance."

"I had everything well in hand," she replied, though her voice lacked the conviction to support her statement.

"Of course you did." His sarcasm dripped from his voice like molasses.

"Nevertheless, my thanks." She nodded as if she had completed a slightly unpleasant task and now it was time to move on to the next one. "Now answer me. Who are you?"

Mikel smiled in amusement. Just like every other Magus he had met. And he had met more than he cared to. Single-minded to a fault and dangerously hard-headed. "No one of consequence."

"Are you always this difficult?" Drin demanded. He had aided her. Saved her life most likely, though she refused to admit that to him. Still, her natural curiosity was getting the better of her manners. That didn't bother her, however, because she was not used to being treated this way.

"Usually, yes," Mikel replied without a hint of embarrassment. "Now you need to get out of here. The snow is moving through the glass."

"The snow? Isn't it supposed to be ..."

"I was just taking literary license is all," Mikel explained, finding it harder to keep the smile on his face as the young woman poked and prodded. "You need to get moving, Magus. The Northern Trolls aren't done with you."

That last comment seemed to break her train of thought. "Why would they be down from the mountains?"

"Hunting," Mikel replied with a shrug, as if it was the most obvious of explanations.

"For what?"

"You."

"Me?" How could they know who she was? Why would they care?

Then it came to her. Who she was didn't matter to them.

"They're hungry. You crossed their path instead of the reindeer or polar bear they were seeking. Easy prey they probably thought. Though you'd be no more than an appetizer for them."

"I don't know how to take a comment like that," Drin replied, almost laughing because she wanted to avoid thinking about what would have happened if her rescuer had not arrived when he did.

"However you like. Nevertheless, I suggest you take my advice. Head out of the Waste. Quickly. If you get into the lower peaks and one of the forts along the trail before dark, you should be fine."

Mikel turned then. Picking up his snowshoes, he strapped them to his pack and strode toward the trail that would take him deeper into the Barrows.

"Pleasure to meet you, Magus," he called over his shoulder, giving her a wave without looking at her. "Now you know the Giants of the Rime are only one of the threats to be wary of in the Frozen Waste."

In just seconds, he was gone. Fading into the snow and ice. Moving just as quietly as a Northern Troll.

Drin took a breath, the moisture she released frosting. She had been holding it until he disappeared. More than just curious about him now.

Who was he?

Why was he there?

Perhaps most important, why did he risk his life for hers?

The end of the chapter.

To keep reading *Stealing the Light*, visit my author website at PeterWachtBooks.com or Amazon.

MORE BY PETER WACHT

THE REALMS OF THE TALENT AND THE CURSE

THE LEGEND OF THE DRAGON LORD

The Painful Truth (short story)*

Stealing the Light (Forthcoming 2025)

Sacrificing the Queen (Forthcoming 2025)

Roar of the Broken Bear (Forthcoming 2025)

Rise of the Dragon Lord (Forthcoming 2026)

THE TALES OF CALEDONIA

(Complete 7-Book Series)

Blood on the White Sand (short story)*

The Diamond Thief (short story)*

The Protector

The Protector's Quest

The Protector's Vengeance

The Protector's Sacrifice

The Protector's Reckoning

The Protector's Resolve

The Protector's Victory

THE TALES OF THE TERRITORIES

(Complete 8-Book Series)

Stalking the Blood Ruby (short story)*

A Fate Worse Than Death (short story)*

Death on the Burnt Ocean

Monsters in the Mist

The Dance of the Daggers

Bloody Hunt for Freedom

A Spark of Rebellion

Shadows Made Real

Shadow's Reach

Storm in the Darkness

THE SYLVAN CHRONICLES

(Complete 9-Book Series)

The Legend of the Kestrel

The Call of the Sylvana

The Raptor of the Highlands

The Makings of a Warrior

The Lord of the Highlands

The Lost Kestrel Found

The Claiming of the Highlands

The Fight Against the Dark

The Defender of the Light

THE RISE OF THE SYLVAN WARRIORS

*Through the Knife's Edge (short story)**

THE FALLEN KNIGHT SERIES

*The Death of the Dragon (short story)**

The Dragon Awakens

Duel With a Dragon (Forthcoming 2025)

Beware the Dragon (Forthcoming 2025)

The Dragon Returns (Forthcoming 2025)

* Free stories can be downloaded from my author website at PeterWachtBooks.com. My books are also available on Amazon and other online retailers.